Ray Anthony was born in Kingston Jamaica in 1958 and lived with his grandparents until 1968, when he came to Britain to join his parents. Educated in south London, when he had the choice, he studied only maths and science - he found the arts crushingly boring. His first employment was in retail management, then he joined the Royal Air Force. After leaving the Royal Air Force he changed career to media sales management. It was during this time that he discovered he had a hidden creative bent. *'Less of my time was being spent on selling or managing, and more on shuffling pieces of paper. Writing strategic reports did my brain in, so I started 'jazzing them up'. The bosses were not amused. If I wanted to keep my job and my sanity, I had to find some release.'* In 1987 he started writing his first novel. He is now a media sales consultant and finds that training salespeople gives him ample scope to exercise his theatrical predisposition.

Also by Ray Anthony

Science Fiction
Interdictor
Armour
Captain
Empress

Contemporary Fiction
Interface
All Woman

Non Fiction Humour
Thinking Man's Guide To Pregnancy, Childbirth & Fatherhood

PILOT

Ray Anthony

ACE - London

ISBN 978 1 8382975 4 1

PO Box 10289
London SW17 9ZF

www.acebooksonline.com

Sapience, *s ´pi- n*s, n. discernment: wisdom: judgement

1

DOWNSIDE

The Sub Lieutenant sat strapped into his console and stared out at the starfield. Over the months this view had lost most of its excitement. At the Naval Academy he, like most Cadet Officers, had dreamed of graduation and a first tour on board a Battle Cruiser. When the postings were announced he, like most of the graduates, was disappointed. His posting was to an Earth orbit space station and there wasn't much glamour in that. He supposed that it had something to do with his qualifications in electronics, or the lack thereof. Still, it could have been worse, much worse. He could have been given a downside posting. If you got 'downside' on your first tour your naval career was over before it had even begun.

At first, he hadn't thought this posting too bad; space station tours were usually short, normally just a year. On these 'weightless' stations the tours were even shorter, usually four months. He was only seventeen; he had four months to show how bright he was. At the academy he hadn't really had a chance to shine and, anyway, at least he was in space, clocking up space hours, he felt confident that he would get a Battle Cruiser on his next tour.

He had been in space before of course, all cadets had space training. His first time as Officer Of The Watch, had been the first real opportunity he'd had to marvel at the beauty of the Milky Way. It was the first time he'd been in space without someone looking over his shoulder and assessing his every move. He used to enjoy staring out into the cosmos, dreaming about the time when he'd get out there amongst the stars in a Battle Cruiser. But he didn't do that anymore. He'd quickly discovered why the weightless tours were only four months long: boredom - crushing, unending boredom. In zero G recreational activities were limited; even movement around the station was regulated. When he'd asked why the station had to remain weightless, he was told that an artificial gravity, or one induced by spin, would affect the delicate sensory instruments.

It wasn't as if he had a lot to occupy him. There were often days, sometimes even weeks, when there was no traffic except one or two transit craft. Occasionally a flotilla or even a strike fleet would come in, then there would be round-the-clock activity. Unfortunately, that happened all too infrequently and, usually, all he did was count off the days until his posting ended. He no longer cared if he went to a Battle Cruiser; he wouldn't even mind a downside post. Anywhere, as long as it wasn't here or on another weightless.

The mass detector lights started flashing and an audible warning sounded; it had picked up non-random motion at maximum range, just inside Jupiter's orbit. The Sub Lieutenant lazily turned to the console and absentmindedly waved his hands over the console. 'Scanning' identified the mass as a small vessel, still too far away to identify its class, heading towards Earth at trans-light speed.

Pilot

Trans-light speed? Trans-light velocity inside the plain of the solar system was 'verboten', it caused massive gravitational disturbances. If a Navy Captain did that, he would step out of his ship to find the shore patrol waiting, and then he or she would step straight into a court martial. This could only be some Air Force jockey. The Sub Lieutenant dialled up the emergency frequency, he was going to give this Flyboy a statute warning...

"Hello Space Con Four. Space Con Four, this is X-Ray Tango One Five, squawking 200765. Request vector for entry Earth downside, over," a voice crackled over the super-light comm.

XT? That wasn't a standard call sign. It could be one of these 'irregular' flights; flights that no one was supposed to know anything about. However, the squawk code was correct; he'd keep the statute warning up his sleeve. "X-Ray Tango One Five, this is Space Control Four. You are identified. What is your destination downside? Over."

"One Five. Destination AFB Oymyakon, over."

AFB Oymyakon? So, it probably was an Air Force ship, but he wasn't yet 100 percent sure. "Space Control Four. Roger. Destination, Air Force Base Oymyakon. Wait." He checked his screens. "Wait." He checked his transit schedule. "One Five, zero space traffic for Oymyakon. You have priority over air traffic. You are clear for direct reentry. Decelerate and steer 0021/5628/1431. Oymyakon Control on 373 decimal 5, over."

"One Five. Roger. 0021/5628/1431, 373 decimal 5. Thank you Space Control Four, have a nice day."

By now he was pretty sure that it was an Air Force ship. Why should he give some pilot, who'd been cooped up in a bucket for God knows how many months, a hard time just because the pilot was in a hurry to get downside? After the ship decelerated it would take about seventeen hours to make the Jupiter to Earth jaunt; seventeen hours before the Flyboys got some well-deserved R&R. The Sub Lieutenant had almost taken his eyes off the screen when something about the pilot's tone made him look again. Suddenly the ship disappeared off his screen... then reappeared at less than a quarter of its original distance. It had made a super-light hop! Even in the Air Force *that* was an instant Court Martial. Super-light transit near a solar mass was dangerous to the point of being irresponsibly reckless. He stabbed wildly at the comms board and hit it on the second attempt.

"One Five, you are too hot. Too hot! Decelerate, decelerate! Acknowledge, over!"

There was only silence.

His fingers fumbled as they punched in 373 decimal 5. "This is Space Control Four. *Override emergency*! X-Ray Tango One Five, decelerate, you are..." he stopped in mid-sentence and watched open mouthed as the ship made a minor trans-light course correction. If he hadn't been strapped in, he would have jumped out of his seat because the ship was now heading directly for the station!

Before he could say or do anything the collision warning sirens started wailing. It might have been just the sirens, but he could have sworn that he heard hysterical laughter coming over the comm. Three seconds later the ship passed the station at a distance of less than two hundred metres and a minute fraction of a second after that Space Control Four was hit by a gravitational shock wave.

Gravitational waves, like other wave forms, affect everything in their path. Even the smallest subatomic particles were individually disturbed. The disturbance was similar to the effect jumping into and out of super-light had on the crew of spaceships. But on a weightless the effects were greatly amplified, it played havoc with the central nervous system. Being caught in the wash of a trans/super-light ship was known in the generally understated parlance of spacefarers as 'having your day buffed'.

The Sub Lieutenant and the other six hundred and fifty-seven crew of Space Control Four were blasted insensible. Approximately one hour later they would regain consciousness. It would take another six hours or so for their vision to return to normal and for their pounding headaches to subside. It would take a further twelve hours before they regained fully control of their bowels and fine motor functions.

***

The Air Traffic Controller was most surprised when Space Con Four crashed his control frequency. The Space Con Four controller came on with an emergency override and was screaming a warning to some ship, X-Ray Tango One Five. There wasn't any X-Ray Tango under his control, so he checked his screen but there was no 'unidentified' in his sector. The Space Controller had stopped babbling in mid-sentence. The Air Traffic Controller waited for further information. None was forthcoming. Had that Space Controller flipped? It wasn't unknown for these naval types to crack up whilst serving in a weightless. Because there was no immediate conflicting traffic with the aircraft under his control the Air Traffic Controller decided to devote some of his time to this 'situation'. A renegade controller wasn't just a danger to the spacecraft under his control, he could talk a ship in anywhere downside.

The Air Traffic Controller pressed 'call'; this alerted the Control Officer that there was a possible difficulty in his sector. He knew that on the other side of the huge underground control room several Watch Officers would tap into the information displayed on his screen. Before he could explain the reason for the call, detectors picked up gravitational shock waves emanating for the upper stratosphere, so he punched into the ground and satellite based infra-red network.

As he'd expected, the infra-red detectors picked up a 'burner' - a ship had hit the atmosphere at high speed. It must have been the ship that Space Con Four was warning. He locked the infra-red monitors onto the ship. The detectors showed a streaking object, glowing white-hot, that had dived deep into the atmosphere. The Air Traffic Controller had witnessed a few burners in his time, but never one like this. This ship was moving fast, yet it didn't appear to be out of control, it was definitely being flown. The pilot was scrubbing off speed - using the atmosphere as a brake. Whoever was piloting that ship looked to be in a hurry to lose speed and get down.

The ship squawked 200765 for only four seconds, then pulled back out of the atmosphere. The Air Traffic Controller checked the aircraft in his sector, they were all still OK. On its next orbit the ship came down to 90,000 feet and squawked 200765 for six seconds, then pulled out again. At 100,000 feet a vessel came under Air Traffic control, so he prepared to hail the ship on the emergency frequency on its next pass but flashing warning lights on his console distracted him.

It was an 'all stations alert' from Naval TacCon. The Navy was telling every man and his dog that there was a full naval sector scramble on. Naval Air Station Bandar in the Persian Gulf, and the Maldives station in the Indian Ocean were putting up point defence spaceships and supersonic aircraft. As the Air Traffic Controller got very busy steering the aircraft under his control out of the path of the Navy ships, it occurred to him that this wasn't a routine training scramble. Naval Air Stations didn't normally launch simultaneous scrambles. Plus, they were putting up nearly five times the normal number of ships. Was this scramble connected with the burner?

Pilot

The burner came back on screen, it had slowed to Mach 19.3, and dived to 60,000 feet. Again, it squawked 200765, this time for nine seconds. The infra-red detectors showed its deflector shields glowing at the very limit of their tolerance. He was about to press the transmit button...

"Three Eight. Without transmitting, I want you to hand over all your aircraft to Six Two. I think this bird is one of ours and I want him brought in soonest. Do you copy six two?" the Control Officer's calm voice came over the headset.

The Air Traffic Controller heard Six Two acknowledge and then, having been relieved of his responsibilities, turned to look across the dimly lit control centre. A large group of people were standing over the Control Officer's console. At this distance the Air Traffic Controller couldn't make out who they were, but he guessed that they were Officers. More personnel in various states of getting dressed were rushing into the centre. The Air Traffic Controller's surprise grew as the Base Commander came in and went over to the Control Officer. The Base Commander was a pilot; she rarely came in here. After a few moments, the Base Commander started walking directly towards him. The Air Traffic Controller suddenly felt self-conscious and nervous. What the hell was going on?

He turned and focussed his attention on his screen. The burner was climbing back out of the atmosphere. The Air Traffic Controller would wait until the burner's next orbit before trying to raise them. He could feel the base Commander's presence as she came to stand behind him. Sitting back to wait, as calmly as he could, he noticed that the Navy ships were breaking up their formation. They were fanning out along the expected trajectory of the burner.

He punched into the Naval Fighter Control frequency. The Fighter Controllers were going through the 'weapon armed' checks with their pilots. Once the checks were completed, they then told the rocket ships to hold station just outside the ionosphere and the supersonic fighters to cruise just inside. If the burner stayed on the same trajectory, he would fly through a gauntlet of Navy ships. And, he would have to stay on that trajectory unless he'd had lost enough speed to be able to execute high-G atmosphere manoeuvres. Even if he managed to accomplish that, he'd have to be a red-hot pilot to evade that many Navy ships.

The Air Traffic Controller went back to his own control frequency and waited for the burner to reappear... but it didn't. He tapped into some other control sectors; it wasn't on their screens either. He went back to the infra-red detectors; a ship that had reentered at that speed couldn't hide. It would be a blazing white fireball, visible to the naked eye in daylight. There was simply no way that it could go undetected by the strategically positioned super sensitive instruments... nothing. He couldn't find it on the ultraviolet network either.

Had the ship flitted back into space? He returned to the Naval Fighter Control frequency. The controllers were asking their pilots the same question. The rocket ship formation commander was adamant that the burner hadn't got past them and was hopping mad that the fighter controllers had lost it. There followed a full-blown shouting match until someone senior downside told them all to shut up and check for gravitational shock waves from a super-light jump.

If the pilot of the 'bogie' had jumped to super-light this close to a planetary mass, and survived, the grinning Air Traffic Controller swore to himself that he'd personally seek him out and buy the guy several drinks. However, there were too many residual shock waves registering from the burner's initial entry to tell if it had jumped. The Navy controllers confirmed the Air Traffic Controller's deductions, and the normally disciplined Navy crews started cursing like there was no tomorrow. The Air Traffic Controller was about to request further instructions from the Control Officer when the Base Commander gently tapped him on the shoulder and leaned over the console.

"Stay with it son. I don't think this party is over yet," she said kindly.

Base Commander or not, she should realise that the burner must have gone to super-light or it would be showing up somewhere. But, saying nothing, he dutifully sat back and punched up a few other sectors as if he were actually looking for the burner. The Base Commander had now been joined by several other people; they were having a quiet discussion. Too scared to turn and look, the Air Traffic Controller had no such fear about trying to listen in on what was being said. Pretending to watch the Navy ships as they returned and stacked up for landing at their bases he leant back in his chair and scratched his head, slipping the headset off one of his ears in the process. The Officers were talking in that calm, unexcited, quiet manner that Officers tended to. It was difficult for him to hear clearly, but he did make out the occasional word or sentence. From what he overheard he surmised that they were talking about a possible 'goosing'.

Goosings were legendary, but they didn't happen in this day and age. To the Air Traffic Controller's knowledge, it was at least two generations since the last goosing. Back in the days when the Navy had sole responsibility for the defence of Earth, the Air Force used to act as 'aggressors'. Air Force squadrons would run simulated attacks against the Navy's primary, secondary, and fall back positions. The hot shot pilots that managed to penetrate the Navy's defences added insult to injury by 'goosing' the Navy's weightless stations.

A space station full of puking, shitting and totally disorientated people trapped in zero gravity must have been quite a sight. And the cleaning up afterwards! Of course, the Navy always lodged formal complaints against the pilots. Nothing was ever done about the complaints. The Air Force's response was always, 'If this had been for real....'

There was one particularly bad showing by the Navy when a couple of stealth squadrons busted through their primary defences, ripped up the secondary defences and then sat waiting in the fall back positions. After mauling the remaining naval fleets, every single weightless in the solar system got goosed. The Navy lodged its strongest ever protest, directly to Supreme Command. Supreme Command made a few angry noises but took no action. The Navy promised that if nothing was done it would take 'firm independent action'. Nobody took them seriously.

The next Air Force pilot to goose a weightless was bounced by two Earth launched naval fusion rocket ships. Without warning they opened up with laser cannons and blew him out of the sky. The Air Force made no formal protest but within hours of this incident, seven fully armed Air Force battle wings, commanded by a Star Officer, appeared in the sky over NSMB1, (Naval Station Mars Base 1, the largest military installation on Mars). NSMB1 scrambled everything it had, and the Air Force battle wings allowed all the Navy ships to get off the deck. What then followed was the wildest and most dispersed dogfight in Earth's military history.

The Air Force pilots each selected a Navy ship, locked on to it with full attack array, and then stuck to it like glue. The Air Force didn't actually shoot down any Navy ships, they didn't even fire at them, they simply flew the terrified Navy pilots to exhaustion. Supreme Command intervened and ordered all ships back to their respective bases. From light-years around the Solar System hundreds of Navy crews limped back to NSMB1. The Air Force battle wings reformed and flew back to AFB Nereid, Neptune's moon that the Air Force had all to itself. On open channels they transmitted a continuous stream of abuse at the naval *truck drivers*, 'The Air Force took a very dim view of a Navy tub shooting down one of its unarmed spaceships and murdering four of its personnel. This had better have been the first and last time, "or else".'

There was immediate censor from the government over this 'totally unacceptable conduct' from the military. There was no Court of Enquiry and no Court Martials, but scores of Air Force Star, and Naval Fleet Officers took voluntary early retirement. Supreme Command issued the DIDAC Convention - the new rules on the arming of weapons and the discharging of munitions. What it basically said was that no weapon more powerful than a standard 100-kilo artillery shell could be armed or fired within 1.75 light-years of Earth. The only exception to this was during a General Recall.

Public opinion of the military plummeted from its normal low to a point where they were equated with criminals. Inter-service liaison between the Navy and Air Force was even lower than that. Goosings were never outlawed, but it was taken as read that they were to cease. Goosings were now associated with The Glorious Days; the time when the military had 'freedom' and wasn't constrained by a straitjacket placed on it by the government.

The Air Traffic Controller would concede that the incident with the burner, had all the indications of a goosing, regardless of how unlikely that might seem. And that would explain the interest shown by everyone in the Control Centre *and* the Navy's sector scramble. Still, he really didn't believe it was; the pilot would have to be insane. There was no way the Navy would allow him to get downside, plus, Supreme Command 'the military above the military' was almost exclusively made up of ex-Navy Officers. This jockey could never get away with it.

Randomly the Air Traffic Controller continued to patch into other sectors. In NS Corunna sector 21, he saw something that made him pause and look closer. An aircraft at 47,000 feet, doing Mach 1.8, heading east in the Green 7 air corridor. There was nothing unusual about the aircraft or its flight path. It was, however, squawking 469000. Could it be? He ranged in on that aircraft with the infra-red; its temperature was normal for an aircraft at that height and speed. Losing interest, he was about to switch to another sector...

"What is it son?" the Base Commander asked over his shoulder.

"It's nothing, Ma'am. I just thought that ship," he highlighted its position, "might have been our boy. But it's cold."

"Why did you think it could be him?"

He didn't want to feel a complete fool in front of the Base Commander. "Just a wild guess, Ma'am. It's squawking 469000."

"And?"

"Well, the burner squawked for four, six, and nine seconds on each of its passes, Ma'am."

"I see. You were very quick to pick that up. Keep an eye on him," she encouraged.

"It can't be him Ma'am, it's cold. And anyway, it is under Naval Air Traffic control."

The Base Commander pulled up a chair and sat next to him. "Is it heading in this general direction?"

"Not really, Ma'am. It's travelling along Green 7. Green 7 only just intersects Oymyakon controlled airspace. I could go through to Spanish ATC and request its flight plan from NS Corunna, Ma'am."

"Let's not draw the Truckies attention to this one, stay with him."

"Yes Ma'am." The Air Traffic Controller thought it was a waste of time.

As he continued to monitor the sector, he noticed that not all the naval aircraft that had scrambled were returning to their bases. Some were flying high altitude sweeps and then diving down for a visual 'ident', at random, on air traffic. Turning to the Base Commander, he said, "They're still searching for him, Ma'am."

"How long before that bird comes under our control?" The Base Commander appeared to be getting excited.

"If he maintains current heading and speed; approximately three-hours-forty, Ma'am."

"Is it likely that they'll get a visual fix on him in that time?"

He made some calculations on his screen. "If they continue to fly the same pattern, those interceptors," he pointed them out on screen, "will be searching in his area in about eight minutes."

The Base Commander reached for a handset and dialled the Control Officer. "Uri, I have a hunch that our boy is still around, so have the Truckies. They're continuing to look for him. He's going to need top cover. Keep everybody sharp." She replaced the handset and sat back.

For five minutes he plotted the progress of the ship that was squawking 469000. The naval interceptors searched closer and closer to it. The fighters closed to within 90 miles of 469000 but it continued at the same height, speed and heading. This convinced the Air Traffic Controller that it couldn't be the burner. An Air Force spaceship had top line radars and would know that the Navy planes were around. Two naval interceptors started closing directly on 469000 from behind. 469000 didn't react; it was probably an airliner...

"Stand by Three Eight. If this is our boy, bring him all the way into the parking bays."

The Air Traffic Controller didn't realise that the Control Officer was still on his screen. If the Control Officer really did think 469000 was the burner, why was he leaving him to control it? Maybe the Control Officer thought him a better controller than he wrote on his annual assessments. The interceptors closed to 30 miles... 20 miles... 10 miles. What was everyone going to do when it turned out to be a false alarm? Suddenly, 469000 accelerated. It was the burner! An aeroplane couldn't accelerate that quickly.

"Oymyakon control. This is X-Ray Tango One Five. Position, twelve miles south of Kiel, flight level four seven, squawking 469000, over." The pilot sounded very relaxed in view of all that had happened and was about to happen.

"X-Ray Tango One Five, this is Oymyakon control, I have you. Stand by for evasive manoeuvres, over." The nearest interceptors had gone supersonic and more were closing. Oymyakon was scrambling its alert fighters.

"One Five, ready." The pilot sounded like he was laughing.

"One Five, turn right, one-four-five. Two fighters in your six, sixteen miles, flight level five-six-zero, Mach 4 and closing."

"Roger, right, one-four-five, I have them."

"Roll out, one-three-one. Four fighters, 2 O' clock, seven-four-zero, diving. Will pass four miles to your right."

"One-three-one... there they go." The pilot was definitely laughing.

"Reverse, zero-eight-three, go to Mach 5, climb to eight-zero-zero."

"Zero-eight-three, at Mach 5, passing seven two zero."

"Continue, zero-two-five. Three fighters 11 o'clock high, turn inside them."

"Zero- two-five. Not seen. Turning."

"Tighten turn! Come round to three-four-eight. Fighters now 1 o'clock level, six miles!"

"They've locked on. I'll take it from here."

The pilot was still sounding fairly relaxed about the whole thing. The Air Traffic Controller sat and watched incredulously as the moving dots on his screen seem to merge. A spaceship could accelerate and turn faster than any plane. But it couldn't use its anti-

Pilot

gravity inside a planet's gravitational well, so the crew would feel the full effects of a high-G turn. Nor could they use the ship's massive speed advantage. If the pilot went above Mach 9, he would need his deflector shield because of the heat generated by the friction with the air. He'd be flying virtually blind. In the dogfight the spaceship's advantages were neutralised and there were three Navy planes. Things weren't looking good...

"I'm in the leader's six at 1000 yards and have the other two on multiple lock-on. Is there any more trade?"

Wow! Some pilot! He was winning a three-on-one and was looking to beat up some more Navy fliers. The dogfight had drifted and was now over Norway. The Base Commander crossed her legs and, full of amusement, said, "Tell our errant scion that it's time to come in."

"Negative, One Five. Other naval planes are being entertained by friendlies."

"Roger. Will play with these for a bit. Which door should we come in?"

The majority of the Navy planes were massing near Oymyakon. They had calculated that Oymyakon was the burner's eventual goal. The Air Force fighters were trying to disperse them. "The Truckies are waiting on the front lawn. Come in through the back door. Glide path three-five-five. Your path is clear. Come straight in."

"Three-five-five, Roger."

The Air Traffic Controller watched as X-Ray Tango One Five broke off the engagement, turned north, and accelerated to Mach 7. It came in over the North Pole, leaving the Navy planes hopelessly outpaced. "You're on the glide path. Fighters 150 miles behind. Decelerate."

X-Ray Tango One Five didn't immediately slow. It looked like it was going to overshoot the base. "One Five, you're too hot. Break off for another approach."

"Negative. We're coming straight in."

In the depths of the Control Centre, the Air Traffic Controller couldn't have heard or felt the vibrations, but he could imagine the high pitch scream of a spaceship under full sonic braking. There would be a deluge of complaints from civilians all over North-Eastern Russia. X-Ray Tango One Five slowed from Mach 7 to 80 Knots in 41 seconds. Now, that was some flying!

"Slow to taxi speed. Follow the trace lines. Your bay is sixty-seven. Go straight in."

"Bay sixty-seven. Roger." On the ground movement board, the Air Traffic Controller followed the ship as it taxied down into the subsurface hangers. *"In the nest. Shutting down."*

"Roger One Five. Welcome home."

"Thank you, Scopie, that was very smooth handling. Out."

"Wait One Five. How did you manage to lose your reentry heat?"

"Scopie, how is your geography?" there was the same amused voice.

"Repeat question."

"Surely you were taught in school that the Earth's surface is three fifths water?"

"What?"

"We took a little dip."

Both the Base Commander and the pilot started to laugh.

2

ACE CREW TWO

"That was not bad, One," Flight Lieutenant Billy 'The Wizz' Zarcroft grinned as he unstrapped himself from his acceleration couch and exchanged places with his 1st Navigator.

"I'd never have believed that the Truckies were this bad. So bad that they'd let an old beaten-up compassman put one over on them," Flight Lieutenant 'Grim' Chang modestly acknowledged.

There were howls of laughter from the remainder of the crew. Billy started the Total Shutdown Procedure. In the unlikely event of someone bothering to check the electronic log or the flight record systems, they would find that it was his voice that initiated the startup, registered on all communications, and shut down the ship. Officially, he was the one piloting it.

"Shutdown complete; pressure equalised. Let's get some fresh air into those lungs," Billy shouted in his best parade ground voice.

"Fresh air? These bays always stink," Flying Officer Mohammed 'Mountain' Ashad replied as he cracked open the hatch.

One by one the five crew disembarked from the shuttle *Katrina*. They made their way to the port side of the two hundred-foot vessel and collected their kit from the storage pods. An onlooker could have been forgiven for thinking that this was a group of dishevelled refugees. Unless that same onlooker knew a great deal about spacecraft design, he could also have been forgiven for thinking that this was just any old shuttle. A shuttlecraft was designed to carry passengers and freight, so why did the crew have to store their few personal belongings in external pods?

The crew made their way to the lifts that would take them deeper underground to the briefing rooms. Flying Officer Noel 'John' Smith, who was in the lead, suddenly dropped his flight bag and sprinted off to the left. Perplexed, the remainder of the crew stopped and watched him go. He ran up to a ship, turned, and then shouted back across the three hundred metres that separated him from his colleagues.

"I've got the deep space disease! Could somebody *please* take me to the MedCen. I must be cracking up because I think this 'tub' looks Navy." His voice echoed around the vast hanger.

The group slowly made their way over to him and started to look over the exterior of the ship.

"It's their latest Type 35 torpedo boat. The Truckies are ripping off our designs," Billy commented.

Pilot

"We can see that, but what's it doing here?!" Grim asked in his usual dour manner.

"We must have stolen it," Flying Officer Teefu 'Pipsqueak' Omangan suggested.

They all nodded in agreement; it was almost unthinkable that a naval ship would have been allowed into an AFB's hanger. Navy ships were, however, occasionally granted the privilege of landing at an AFB. The seven hundred-foot Type 35's were small by Navy standards and, like the Air Force equivalent, only carried a crew of five. The Navy was slowly waking up to the fact that large, ponderous, blunder blusters ships were passe - small, agile craft were the way forward. This particular Type 35, the *Man Vaughn,* was in a regular parking bay and didn't look as if it had undergone any 'special' inspection.

"I can bypass their entry code. Let's break in." Mohammed said, rubbing his hands together.

"Truckies booby-trap their ships. If this went off you could kiss the Base and most of the surrounding countryside goodbye," Billy quashed the idea before it gathered any momentum. "Let's get down to interrogation, then we'll get the low down on *Man Vaughn.*"

They reluctantly left the naval vessel and continued on to the lifts. Billy considered that whether the *Man Vaughn* had been 'borrowed' or not, its presence in the hanger meant that something of great significance was unfolding. And that it might be linked to his crew's unscheduled recall to Earth.

As they waited for the lift, Pipsqueak voiced what they must all have been pondering. "If we were to steal a Navy ship, we wouldn't leave it in some hanger for all the world to see, would we? I don't believe in coincidences. We're back eight months early, *and* that ship is sitting there. God! I was so looking forward to a nice, pleasant rest."

The lift doors opened and out stepped five Navy women flyers. They snapped to attention. The most senior, a redheaded Lieutenant, looked the men over then shot Billy a parade ground salute and waited for him to return the salute for members of a different service. Billy stuck his hands in his pockets and strolled past into the lift. His crew followed and, as usual, the 6' 8" tall Mohammed had to stoop.

In the lift Grim grumbled loudly, "I smell Navy shitheads. We'll have to fumigate the whole God damned Base."

John touched the button to close the lift doors. The Navy Lieutenant stepped up smartly and touched it to keep them open. Staring coldly into Billy's eyes she said, "Flight Lieutenant, I understand that there's been a goosing. The Air Force crew responsible had better stay deep underground, like the rats they are, because if they show their faces in daylight, we'll get them." She spoke with the same colonial accent that Billy did which probably meant that, like him, she had been raised 'out there'.

Belching loudly, Billy turned to Mohammed and asked, "Have you ever seen a Truckie up close? Notice how they always look like someone has stuck a stiff board down their backs? And I hear tell that they even iron their flight suits. They really must learn to lighten up."

"Yeah. Maybe if they spent less time stomping around like robots saluting everything that moved, and spent more time flying then they might turn into half decent pilots," Mohammed yawned.

The redheaded Lieutenant gave Billy a half smile. "I know you. The Air Force call you Billy the Wizz. We call you Judas."

Billy leant against the side of the lift and smiled back. "Yeah. My reputation precedes me. The Navy call you Lieutenant First Class Gümann. I call you a dike. So why don't you and your frigid bitches take that heap of shit you call a ship, and get lost?"

Losing the hallmark of a Naval Officer, that of being permanently unruffled, the Lieutenant dived at Billy. Grabbing her in midair, he wrapped a hand around her throat and used her own momentum to slam her against the wall of the lift. "Get your dried-up pussy outa my face." Then he tossed her headfirst out of the lift.

Executing a perfect somersault, Gümann landed on her feet, and flanked by two of her crew came charging back. The lift doors started closing and the women were caught between them. Like a sandwich spilling its filling, Gümann stumbled and fell face down into the lift.

"Maybe they're after a damned good shagging?" Mohammed suggested.

Casually John leant against the lift control panel overriding the proximity sensors. The lift doors, which had automatically drawn back from the obstructing bodies, again started to close and slammed against the still prone Lieutenant's feet. Billy leant over and smiled down at her.

"I could oblige, but I sincerely hope that I never get that desperate."

Gümann shot to her feet. "OK Flyboy, let's go here and now!"

Lazily Billy slapped her hard in the face with the back of his hand. Rolling with the blow she used her momentum to spin into a sweeping roundhouse kick. Anticipating the move Billy simply stepped back. Gümann's foot connected with thin air and, off balance, she fell out of the lift. Her two escorts were then 'assisted' out by John and Pipsqueak. The other two naval flyers tried to get into the lift, but the closing doors foiled their attempt. Then the lift started its long descent.

"How come you know that tight-arse?" Pipsqueak asked Billy.

"She was two intakes ahead of me at The Academy. She thought she was quite a star; held the navigation and Mars-Pluto sub-light transit records... That was, until I blew them away."

"Never mind all that. What in all the universe's suns are they doing here?!" Grim complained.

"Relax, you moody old cuss. We'll find out soon enough." John laughed.

"Where do you think they're based?" Billy asked thoughtfully.

"Dunno. They weren't wearing any insignia," Mohammed also became thoughtful. "It's not like the Truckies to forget their insignia..."

"Them cyborgs usually have it engraved on their foreheads," Pipsqueak chipped in.

"That's what I mean. Only their Special Combat Teams don't wear insignia. So, the big question is: what is a Naval Special Combat Team doing at an AFB?" Billy said, moodily staring at his feet. "You wanna know what I think? I think some weak-brained Star Officer is planning joint operations."

"Well, I think you're being unduly morose. That Star Officer would get his stars shoved right up his arse." Grim's outburst was in sharp contrast to Mohammed's 'just out of a British public school' accent.

The lift stopped it long descent. They picked up their kit and started for the debriefing room. "Being a dickhead is a prerequisite to becoming a Star Officer. I wouldn't put anything past them." Billy commented.

"I can't see it happening. Never," Grim said with finality.

They entered the debriefing room and went to sit at their appropriate information consoles. They fed in their identification disks and their individual flight logs. The 'intelligence' computer read the logs and then started asking questions. It had been a routine mission; the debriefing should have taken no more than ten minutes. However, the computer wanted to know *everything* about the goosing.

Pilot

Three hours later, the individual debriefings ended. Individual debriefings were supposed to ensure that all relevant information was logged accurately. The computer crosschecked discrepancies, accounted for the subjectivity of viewpoint, and then constructed the 'real' version of events. But, during this debriefing, the intelligence computer discovered only what Ace Crew II wanted to it to know. As they were getting ready to leave, the Base Commander and her XO casually strolled in. She looked like she had just swallowed a wasp.

"Good morning, Ma'am." Billy cheerfully greeted her.

She went to stand over Billy. "Morning it certainly is, but I have my reservations about whether it's actually 'good'. You see, for the last three hours or so, I've been on the receiving end of a number of rather unpleasant one-way conversations. I don't think it would be an exaggeration to say that I've had to *listen* to every serving Star Officer, and a few who are retired to boot."

"My sincerest and deepest sympathies, Ma'am," Billy said sympathetically.

"Well, Flight Lieutenant, I'm sure that you have an explanation for the recent incident. I'm equally sure that you'll confirm to me your understanding of transit procedures near weightless space stations. It is my hope that your explanation will be *so* convincing that I'll be reassured to such an extent that I'll conclude that all this is a bad dream from which I will shortly awaken."

"Certainly, Ma'am. Well, we were making a normal pre-downside orbit when this Weightless suddenly jumped out in front of us. I had to swerve to avoid it; we must have only missed it by about a hundred yards. I really do think that these Weightless stations shouldn't be allowed out without a responsible adult, Ma'am," Billy said with total seriousness.

The Base Commander turned to Grim. "Is that what happened, One?"

"That's exactly how I saw it, Ma'am," Grim answered, equally seriously.

"I see, so it's the Truckies who have their stations in erratic orbits," the Base Commander mused. "How does that explain trans-light speed?"

"Well, Ma'am, as I banked to avoid the Weightless, I had to put my foot on the gas," Billy explained.

"Sounds fairly reasonable. Damned good flying, avoiding a Weightless like that. The Truckies are lucky we have Flyboys of your calibre. Well done." The Base Commander was as stern-faced as ever.

"Thank you, Ma'am. It was the least we could do."

The Base Commander continued as if thinking aloud, "Unfortunately the Truckies tend to be somewhat unimaginative. They might not interpret your highly commendable evasive manoeuvre in the same light and could put a price on your heads. A low profile is the call of the day."

Billy sat erect in his chair. "Yes Ma'am. Pardon my presumption, Ma'am, but I could have sworn that we saw a Navy tub in the hanger. Not only that, but I thought I saw some dikes coming out of the hanger lifts. There *is* a logical explanation for my misinterpretation, isn't there, Ma'am?"

There was the faintest trace of a smile on the Base Commander's face as she answered. "I have a possible explanation. It's just as plausible as your explanation for the Weightless. I think you imagined it. I'm sure there never was a Naval ship, or crew."

"Thank you for being direct and honest with us, Ma'am."

"My pleasure. Gentlemen, mission briefing in 72 hours at 06:00. Good day." The Base Commander and her XO departed.

The crew watched them leave. "Low profile, my arse. John, tap into Traffic Comm and find out that Type 35's destination." Billy ordered.

"This is dangerously reckless... I love it." Briefly running his hands through his shaggy blonde hair, John turned to his console.

"We only have three days. Why waste time on the Truckies?" Grim whinged.

"If the Truckies insist on visiting AFB's, then the least we can do is to return the compliment. Am I to understand that you'd be willing to turn down the opportunity of an unscheduled visit to a Naval Air Station?" Billy looked dumbstruck.

"Not at all, but let's not spend too long there. Only three days, remember?" Grim relented.

John turned from his console. "Someone is ahead of us. There are blocks all over the Traffic Comm computer. And I don't mean the usual blocks, somebody definitely doesn't want us, or anyone else, in."

"It's that smart-arse Base Commander. Doesn't she realise that this is a red flag to a bull? Nobody keeps Ace Crew II out." Mohammed threw down his flight bag and went to sit next to John.

Billy turned to John. "How long?"

"My bag of tricks is at home. If I can relay in from there, it could take anywhere from eight to thirty hours."

"Need any help?" Mohammed asked.

"Not really, but I'm beginning to feel a need. If you'd like to find a couple of nice, well-mannered girls and bring them over..." John smiled.

"OK, whistle me up as soon as you have anything, the rest of you stay flex," Billy said, then stood.

***

He was at 7,000 feet, in a hurry and stuck in commuter traffic near Zurich. He took the car off automatic guidance and opened it up. Almost at once the Traffic Control Monitor started to bleep. A cop car somewhere near was hailing him. Cop cars were fast, but not that fast. He pulled out of the air corridor and climbed to 10,000 feet. Opening it up further, he went supersonic.

Normally that manoeuvre was enough to tell the cops that they weren't dealing with an ordinary car, or your 'average' driver. Normally they didn't give chase. But not today. The bleeper stayed on; the cops wanted to play. If they caught him, not only would he have a speeding charge, but they'd give him a noise pollution summons as well. He gave it some more gas and went up to 19,000 feet; any higher and he would be in Air Traffic.

The Traffic Control Monitor was now flashing continuously in the red. He scanned the sky but couldn't see a cop's car. Providing he kept the right distance between his car and theirs, wherever it was, the cops wouldn't be able to shut down his drive. He turned west, the most direct route to his home on the outskirts of Lyon in France.

"*You are in violation of speed, altitude and noise regulations. Reduce speed and descend to the ground!*" The orders blared over his Comm set.

Cops always used voice synthesizers to make them sound more authoritative, so Billy couldn't be certain, but the cop's accent sounded Russian. If that were so, it meant that they had been following him for some time. It also meant that they weren't ordinary patrol cops. These boys had jurisdiction across economic zones - Interpol. He looked around, still couldn't see them and continued on his present heading. Failing to respond to a traffic directive would now be added to the list of offences (if they caught him).

"Get down on the deck, now!" The same harsh, metallic command.

He ignored it.

The shiny blue cop car rolled out from under him and flew alongside, on his right; no wonder he hadn't been able to find them. They were flying close enough now for him to make out the badge number on their darkly visored helmets. These boys definitely wanted to play, or they would have shut down his drive as soon as he left the traffic lanes. Normal cars didn't have the speed or manoeuvrability of a light aeroplane, but the cop's car did. So... this was going to be fun. He smiled; waved at them; turned; rolled off the top and dived.

To knock out his drive they would need to fly directly in front of or behind him for about four seconds; it took that long to set the 'drive disengage'. With him at the wheel there was little chance of that happening. As he levelled out at 3,500 feet, he saw two other blue dots streaking towards him and he came to the conclusion that he had been set up.

He danced with the three cop cars for a bit, then got bored. It was a stalemate; they couldn't get into a position to shut him down, and he couldn't make a clean getaway. This was wasting his time; he wanted to get home. He picked out a clear spot on a tarmac road, banked, and hit the air brakes, descending sharply to a smooth landing on the road.

Taken by surprise, the cops overshot and went into a tight turn to come back around for their landings. One of the cars hovered for a moment and then landed just in front of him. A second car came down just behind him and the third circled overhead. His engine suddenly died; they had shut down the drive. Two cops stepped out of the car in front and paused, as cops always do. With their helmets and heavy insulation suits they looked like a couple of spacemen. As they swanked over to his car, he could imagine them gulping down their 'nasty pills'. The cops took up position, one on each side of the car. The one on the driver's side unholstered his neuron whip and tapped the glass with its butt.

Billy had no intention of winding down the window or getting out of the car as long as the cop had the whip in his hand - he wasn't wearing an insulation suit. Folding his hand behind his head, he stared off into the distance.

"Step out of the car and put your hands on your head." The Comm set distorted the synthesized voice even further.

He reached forward and switched off the Comm set, then reclined in his seat. Again, they were at another impasse; he couldn't get away and they couldn't get him out short of using heavy artillery. He noticed the car behind lift off and join the one circling above, then both cars turned and headed east. The cops had obviously come to the same conclusion; now he was on the deck there was no need for three police vehicles.

The cop standing on his side of the car, in a gesture designed to placate, deliberately holstered his whip. Billy looked him up and down in acknowledgment, and then wound down the window.

"Yes, Officer?" He smiled innocently.

"Why is it that every pisspants, spoiled, rich, brat decides to joyride in my sector? What is it, parents not giving you enough attention? Do you have any idea of how much paperwork you're going to cause?" The cop was trying to sound tired and bored but still hadn't switched off his voice synthesizer. *"Let's see some ID."*

Billy handed over his driving licence.

The cop fed it into his pocket ident computer. *"Just because your Daddy can buy you an expensive car, don't mean you can act like a goddamned pilot! Today's little escapade is your last, Sonny Boy. By the time I'm finished with you the only private transportation you'll get is in a perambulator with your Nanny pushing it."*

The ident computer spat out his driving licence. The cop handed it back. *"Says here you're twenty-five. Boy, you don't look old enough to shave. Domicile card, profession permit and credit rating."*

"Really, Officer, is there any need for all that?" Billy was still playing the innocent.

The cop stuck his head through the window. *"Boy, I'm going to hit you with a fine that's gonna make your Daddy, your Mummy and their bank manager weep. Let's have them."*

Billy handed the requested items over. The cop was about to put them in the computer, then stopped. *"Well, we have ourselves an Air Force serviceman."* He said over the top of the car to his partner. *"Cutting them a bit young these days, aren't they?"*

Billy smiled and shrugged his shoulders.

"Sooo... You see the hotshot pilots doing their stuff, and thought you'd have a try? My patch isn't the place to be a frustrated Flyboy. Now, get out of the car!"

Billy slowly stepped out of the car. "I'm a serving Officer and..."

"Military Exemption don't mean shit to Interpol!"

"Officer? My arse!" The other cop's synthesized voice came from behind Billy.

"Military identification. C'mon be quick about it," the original interrogator demanded.

Billy handed over his Ident and the cop carefully looked it over. Still not convinced he stuck it into the ident computer. *"Your Military Ident says that you really are a Flyboy."*

"I am." Billy smiled.

The computer ejected his Ident and the cop handed it back, then continued to look him over. The other cop walked back to their car and stood by it. Billy hadn't heard them say anything to each other; obviously, they had transmitters in their helmets. Officially, they couldn't touch him; he had more than Military Exemption, the cost of his training was measured in billions. Officially, they had to extend him every courtesy, but what about unofficially? He glanced down at the cop's neuron whip.

The cop took another threatening step closer. *"Boy. I have a photographic memory. I seem to recall a car very much like yours burning up my sector about six months ago. That wouldn't have been you, would it?"*

It was about six months since Billy had been home. "No, Officer, I was in space at that time. I've just hit downside."

"How long have you been away?" Despite the synthesizer the cop sounded genuinely interested.

"Fifteen months, Officer."

"Fifteen months you say. Now, that is *a long time, isn't it?"*

"Yes, Officer." It must have been obvious to the cops that he was in a hurry, were they getting back at him by wasting his time?

"Your home is in Lyon?"

"Yes."

"Is that your destination?"

"Yes, Officer."

"Fine. I'll set an inhibiting speed of 600 knots on your car. That will stop you breaking any more speed limits but will give you plenty of time to get home, change, and be at the X Club X in Paris by 21:00 hours. You know where the X Club X is, don't you?"

"Yes, why?"

Pilot

The Cop didn't answer, but slowly started to undo and remove his helmet. After the helmet came off Billy realised that the cop was in fact a woman and a very attractive woman at that.

Shaking her blonde locks, which fell down to her shoulders, she smiled. "Because we'll be there." Her natural voice was like music to his ears.

"We?"

The cop nodded towards her car. Billy turned and looked over his shoulder. The woman's partner had also taken off his helmet - again, not a man but another woman. This woman was Asiatic and, truth be told, her face was several notches above being merely gorgeous looking. "What makes you think I'll go all the way to Paris?"

"If you've been in space for fifteen months you'll be there." There was more than a hint of a promise in her tone. Pulling her helmet back on, she turned and strolled back to her car.

3

X CLUB X

He switched back to auto as the car flew into the garage. Grabbing his kit, he bounded into the house. Identifying him, the Home Environment Unit brought the lights, music, and temperature to their predetermined settings.

"Hi, Billy. I've dialled the shop and ordered some fruit and fresh fish. Is there anything else that you want?" the HEU's soft female voice greeted him.

He made his way to the bedroom. "Update on search programme S series."

"Update on S series. Hunter programme S1590/1 to 18, negative. S1590/19 & 20 aborted. Seek and destroy anti-hacker programme present. All S1590 batches terminated..."

"Any success?" The HEU would give him a detailed account of all the programmes, but he didn't have time. The cop had been pretty accurate with her time/distance calculation. Stripping off, he dived into the shower - there weren't showers on spaceships, not Air Force ships at any rate.

"S1721 - the 'long shots' series, has provided two strong possibles. They're both in the area of surnames. They are two Zarcroft births registered within the time window. Have installed back doors to the respective Educational and Medical InfoSys."

Billy started to pay attention. "What have you discovered so far?"

"Nothing. Priority Programme One running. Gaining access tripped both Earth Census and Air Force Reproduction Organs Bank computer gates. They have individual seek and identify programmes running. Have erased access ident and am running internal searches."

"Running time of Priority Programme One?"

"Four months, fifteen days, six hours, forty-nine minutes."

Tapping into government or military computers carried an automatic sentence of twenty years imprisonment. These computers were relatively easy to break into, but they had very sophisticated ways to find the culprits. The strategy was simple but effective; rather than trying to stop hackers, they were allowed in and then their user terminal identified. That way, most of the individuals who had a predilection for hacking were now languishing on some penal planet or other in the back of beyond. For his HEU to be running, for four months, the programmes to prevent identification, showed that a very detailed search was in process. "Have we been identified?"

"An initial identification was made but not verified. Have erased all relevant data files before positive ident, but sleeper programmes a high probability."

"Oh, Christ! Command: omega phi alpha zero zero zero. Hard copy all info S series, then erase."

Pilot

"Command: omega phi alpha zero zero zero noted. Suggest we do not erase S series, that will alert sleeper programmes."

One thing he hated about computers was their lack of emotion. Here he was facing a twenty-year sentence and it was speaking to him in the same tone it uses to give him the daily weather report. He got out of the shower. "Alternatives?"

"Protection of Intelligent Information Act states that prosecution for unauthorised access must take place within six months of the offence. All sleeper programmes will have to be activated within one month, fifteen days, seventeen hours and seven minutes. Priority One can neutralise them as soon as they are running."

He smiled. He had almost forgotten that the S series programmes were written by John, the crew's techno-wizzo. "Cancel last command."

"Omega phi alpha zero zero zero cancelled."

"Hard copy, synopsis S1721." He walked over to the printer.

Reams and reams of paper were spewing out of the printer. The synopsis was taking on the form of a substantial document. Here was another problem with computers; when it came to imparting information, they couldn't differentiate between the important and the irrelevant. The S1721 'long shots' search programmes were designed to explore 'what if' postulations. When dealing with people, because of emotions, no matter how unlikely, anything was possible:

What if the mother tried to locate the father?

What if she changed her mind and tried to get the child adopted?

What if she registered the child under its father's surname? Etc., etc.

Any 'what ifs' that occurred would be stored in an appropriate government InfoSys. What was stored could be retrieved. As he started leafing through the mountain of paper, he saw that within the parameters there were two Zarcroft births registered to single mothers. One was five years ago in the North American state of New Jersey. The other was in the Philippines and was three years before that.

He knew that there had definitely been one donation of *his* male sperm. Just having that information was, in itself, cause for disciplinary proceedings. Unfortunately, his source at the Reproduction Organs Bank didn't know when the donation was made or to whom. If he was caught attempting to find that out it would result in his immediate court martial. All serving space personnel handed over ownership of their genes and gonads to The State. It was a convention that had been established in the early days of space exploration, now it was law.

Even way back then it was realised that spacers ran a high risk of exposure to hard radiation. But it wasn't until the exploration of other solar systems that the true magnitude of the potential dangers were appreciated. Man had evolved on Earth - Biosphere One. Other planets, other biospheres, even ones with similar atmospheres, temperatures, carbon-based life forms and ample water - Earth type planets - were hostile environments. The slight variation in organic or inorganic forms on these planets proved fatal to unprotected man.

Then a group of biological scientists doing research on Pomout II (now a penal colony) made the groundbreaking discovery that changed the definition of an ecology/ecosystem. They determined that natural selection was not, after all, what controlled the evolution of an organism. Natural selection was only the gradient, or direction. Evolution was initiated by the biosphere and each biosphere would only *allow* its organisms to evolve in certain directions, regardless of the number of possible 'niches'.

Planets were to be considered living systems that regulated how, and which organisms developed on them. The regulating mechanism was the main substance of the discovery. Each planet had its individual signature. This was carried by all its organic forms. That signature defined the parameters within which genes could mutate and still lead to a viable organism. If an alien organism, that could survive, is introduce into this biosphere it would immediately be subjected to the same mutational parameters.

Other planets' biospheres were highly mutagenic environments. And mankind was sending its most gifted into such environments. Sterilization became compulsory for all space personnel. That was in the beginning but gone were the days of frozen sperm and 'men only in space'. Now your ovaries or testicles were removed and kept fully functioning cybernetically while being stored in your Services' Reproductive Organ Bank. As long as you were in a Space Service the only way that you could reproduce was to apply for a donation just like any ordinary Tom, Dick, or Harry. Of course, when you left, if you lived that long, your 'parts' were automatically reimplanted.

However, whilst they had your gonads, The State made sure that some of your genes got passed on. Why? Because Man was the dominant species of Biosphere One. He had evolved to the extent where he could now guarantee his comfort and security; wars, famine and such were things of the past. Man no longer had to strive to survive; he no longer had to 'try'. Hand in hand with this comfort and security came degeneracy. Short of bringing back some of the more unpleasant aspects of human history, the 'Powers that be' recognised that some other area of collective endeavour had to be found. This challenge was space exploration.

As to be expected, very few wanted to make this effort, or even thought it justifiable. Social scientists found that those who did also tended to have strong survival instincts. Not only that, but these individuals also showed a strong inclination towards antisocial behaviour. In short, they tended to be criminally minded. There seemed to be a close correlation between survival instinct, motivation, and discontent. The human race could not afford to lose the genes of those who went into space.

The Space Services consisted of: The Military, The Explorer Corps and The Resource Companies. The Resource Companies were by far the biggest. It was easy to justify the Resource Companies; they went out and got the raw materials needed to keep a lazy population supplied with consumables. The Explorer Corps went out to discover more resources which could be exploited, they were also necessary. But what about The Military? What did they do?

The average civilian, if asked, would say, 'They do nothing; they are no more than a drain on limited resources '. A cynical civilian would turn to a history book and say, 'They are maintained by the government to keep us (the civilian population) in check...'

Billy laughed at the thought; a flight of Interceptors had enough firepower to lay every population centre on Earth to waste. No, that wasn't the purpose of The Military. Man might be the dominant species on Earth, and although no sign of any intelligent extraterrestrial life had yet been found, statistically, it was improbable that Man would turn out to be the dominant species in the whole wide universe.

As far as civilians were concerned The Military were personae non grata. The Military was already full of camaraderie and elitism, the hostility from the civilian population made them isolationist. Military married Military, usually from the same Service. In genetic terms this almost incestuous isolation produced some interesting results. Over the generations, distinct genotypes began to show up within the Military. And, as with anything to do with the Military, these genotypes were abbreviated to acronyms and given nicknames - the nicknames chosen were those of animals thought to best describe the dominant characteristics.

All flight crews became Gazelles. Gazelles had a natural affinity with mathematics, fast reflexes, and excellent coordination and balance. The Army's first echelon troops were known as Bears, The Marines' were Cheetahs, etc. It got to the point where you had to show the relevant genotype before you were even considered for selection into any branch of the Military. These genotypes were passed back into the general population. Billy was a Gazelle; his children would show Gazelle-like characteristics.

The 'long shots' programmes had seemed improbable at the time, but nevertheless worth pursuing: a civilian couple probably wouldn't have applied for a donation from the hated Military, preferring instead to adopt. And even if a couple did decide on a donation from the Military, they certainly wouldn't register the resulting child in the donor's surname. Marriages were now uncommon outside the Military, so it was a wild(ish) guess that any 'traceable' child's mother would be a single woman. A single woman, who would *prefer* to apply to the Air Force Reproductive Organ Bank rather than ferreting out a suitable man for the purpose. Fanatically independent, really ugly, or...

Finding out about these two children was the hard part: the setting of the parameters of the search. After all, he wasn't the only Zarcroft in the Air Force; although he'd discovered that he was the only male pilot with that surname. Cross-refer, corelate and tract the donation of *his* sperm with the registration of the birth of a Zarcroft - a real long shot. It should now be easy to establish if they were *his* children. A search through their school or medical records would quickly show if they exhibited any Gazelle characteristics. But there could be no more 'dipping in' until the Priority One protection programme had completely nullified the government's seek and identify programmes.

Billy had no idea what he would do if he met one of his children. But for some inexplicable reason he felt that this was something he had to do even though, legally, it wasn't his child. The mother, or mothers, would know a lot about him. They would have been shown holograms; they would know his full name, his date of birth and that he was an Air Force pilot. The only thing they would not have been told, even if they asked, was where his Base was or where he lived. It was illegal for them to even try to contact him... A long shot. Would she register the child in the father's name? A father who she had never met. Why would a woman want to do that?

However, all this conjecture was leading nowhere. His search had been going on for several years; a few more months wouldn't matter. There were more pressing matters, like his unexpected date with the two cops. Now here was another puzzle. Despite the fact that military law was infinitely more severe than civil law, the military had a reputation for antisocial behaviour, they were always the natural targets for the civil police.

Military Exemption had been introduced to stop civil authorities harassment. Local police forces couldn't investigate, arrest, or charge military personnel. This dubious honour fell to the military police and Interpol. Both agencies tended to be overzealous in these pursuits. The long-soured relationship between MP's, Interpol and the Military was only surpassed by the even longer standing animosity between the Navy and the Air Force.

In terms of personal relationships, ordinary civilians had little to do with the Military. Billy had never heard of a case where a cop had even fraternised with a serviceman. What were these two women up to? He guessed that it probably had something to do with the age-old rumour about what it was like to have sex with a spacer on their first night downside. It wasn't a myth, but only spacers knew that. The Air Force had only single sex crews, all the other services had mixed crews, but the same thing applied to them. When you were in space you never discussed sex. This wasn't simply a convention - in space you never even thought about it. For some unknown reason it was something that simply never happened.

There were dozens of theories as to why. Some thought that it was the result of a drug that was in the space rations or circulated by the ships life support systems. Others thought that the suppressant was induced by subliminal suggestion, a constant background message sent by the ship's communication computers. At one time or another Billy had tested most of the more common theories; he'd smuggled his own rations aboard and lived off them; he'd spent five days in an evacuation suit, independent of the ship's life support system; he'd even gone as far as to programme erotic messages to himself, reminding him to think about women. When these messages came up, he would always look at them and wonder what the hell he must have been thinking to have written such drivel. Then, with annoyance, he would erase the message and get back to whatever he was doing. It didn't matter what you did once you were in your ship, you forgot about women and sex.

However, as soon as you were back downside it was a different story. Over a period of about eight hours the lack of interest in sex would slowly wear off. The fact that it happened gradually gave some credence to the drugs theory. But what that drug was or how it got into your system was probably the most guarded secret in the service. After it had completely worn off, this disinterest was replaced by a sexual urge that only spacers knew. It was as if all your normal sex drive had been stored and now demanded a release.

Air Force sorties tended to be longer than most, on average fifteen months. Flyboys (female Air Force crews were also called Flyboys) were notorious for being ripshits on their first night downside. Even so, that reputation was only generally known within the space services. Only a small percentage of space services personnel regularly clocked up space hours. If there wasn't a spouse or sweetheart waiting, there were no shortage of takers. Billy had even seen the normal strict discipline of a Naval Air Station degenerate into a nonstop orgy after a Battleship or heavy Cruiser had given its crew shore leave. Could the cops be ex-Military?

About eight hours... Billy finished getting dressed and left for his date with the two cops.

***

He arrived outside X Club X five minutes early. It was standard military practice to arrive five minutes early for an appointment. Leaving his car with an attendant, he went in. He'd never been to X Club X before; it struck him as a very large, noisy place. The club had the reputation for being one of the most exciting nightspots - that is, exciting in civilian terms - in the western hemisphere. With nothing to really strive for, civilians desperately craved excitement. In bold garish letters, the motto of the establishment was emblazoned across the entrance - **'Whatever your pleasure. We will satisfy'**

Slightly unnerved by being surrounded by a mass of excited people shouting shrilly to each other, he stood in the crowded entrance. All the patrons except him wore very loose-fitting clothing in dark, drab colours and facial makeup. After months in space he liked seeing bright exciting colours and it usually took him a couple of days downside to readjust to being in a crowd. He and the cops hadn't arranged a specific meeting point. Feeling very uncomfortable, he was now doubly sure that this wasn't such a good idea. Turning, with the intention of leaving, he saw a commissary moving directly towards him.

"Flight Lieutenant Zarcroft?"

This wasn't too surprising. With his short hair, conservative lighter shade of dress and lack of makeup, he stood out like a sore thumb. "Yes."

"This way, Sir." The commissary led the way through the throng at the entrance. They made their way towards a darkened, secluded corner of the enormous banqueting suite. As he followed, Billy passed between scores of tables whose occupants gleefully manipulated every possible implement for getting stimulants into the human body. The government had long ago realised that prohibiting any drug only added to its street value and made it more exciting to the user. He looked on with mild disgust, only civilians polluted their bodies or lost control of their wits.

The commissary stopped and indicated one of the more exclusive cubicles. Sitting at a circular table, designed for intimacy, were the two cops; both stood up in greeting. He gave the commissary a small gratuity and joined the two women at the table. They both wore burkhas, including yashmaks, which still appeared to be the height of fashion. Only their hands were exposed and those were heavily decorated with intricate patterns. Reflecting on his last sexual encounter Billy suspected that they would probably be totally naked beneath those shapeless and uninviting garments. He also remembered that it was about ten hours since he landed, but he'd try to play it cool - these women were *civilians.*

"Good evening, Ladies," he said formally. He was still feeling very suspicious, cops just didn't fraternise with the Military.

"Please, William, we're all off duty now, aren't we? There's no need to be so gentlemanly. I am Anika and this is Karina." The first cop, the blonde, removed her yashmak and fixed him with the same dazzling smile that she had earlier.

He waited until the two women sat and then slid into the vacant space they'd made between them. He tried to be less formal but simply couldn't relax; it had been *ten hours* and he wasn't sure of exactly what to say. Usually with women in the military, at a time like this, he didn't have to say much, they knew the score. Or, better still, when a female crewed ship came in at the same time as his, if they were game, then he didn't need to say anything at all.

"I am Billy to my friends, and I must say that I am very pleased to meet you both." He turned on his own smile.

"Billy it is," Karina, the second cop said, exchanged a look with her partner, and then she took off her yashmak. "Do you have one of those flying nicknames? What do you call them, Handles?"

In one sense Billy wished that Karina hadn't taken off that yashmak. This was not good. Not good at all. "They're called callsigns. It's the Truckies... naval crews who have named callsigns, we have numbers. I'd have thought that Interpol also used them." *I don't want to talk about this. I don't want to* talk *at all!*

Anika leant towards him. "Our callsigns are allocated to the vehicle or patrol, not to individuals. But we don't really want to talk about callsigns, do we?" She flashed him a slightly teasing smile.

Civilian women played games; everybody knew that. But he didn't know the rules and wouldn't play even if he did. "What do *we* want?" he asked.

"Fun," Karina said, seriously.

"Excitement," Anika added, equally seriously.

A blond and Asiatic combo... He sensed that he was the rat being toyed with by two cats. "Where do I fit in?"

"Are you always this sullen? I thought it was Flyboys who were meant to be hot and us cops who are naturally suspicious," Anika sounded slightly peeved, but her eyes were smouldering.

"Flyboys *are* hot. So, what's the deal?" It was difficult to keep up this air of cool detachment with his hormones working overtime.

"You've been here before, haven't you?" Karina asked, she sounded surprised.

He mulled over the question and the sudden change of topic before answering. He knew X Club X by reputation only. It was said to be a pretty wild place - that is wild by civilian standards. "No, this is the first time."

The two women looked at each other, then both deliberately moved closer to him. He found himself sandwiched tightly between them. Anika stared off into to the distance and said quietly and slowly, "Upstairs are the entertainment suites. They are well equipped, comfortable, and very private."

He took this in but didn't reply.

Karina also stared off into the distance, mimicking her partner. "We like tall, say one metres ninety tall, men."

Anika took over. "We're also rather partial to the Mediterranean type. You know, light brown eyes, olive skin." She turned to look directly at him. "One of those suites is reserved for us. That's the *deal*."

Now it was Karina's turn to look directly at him. "Are you hot?" she asked with heavy, sensual undertones.

'Hot' was an understatement, but he simply nodded.

"We could have a drink or a meal here, or..." Anika left it hanging.

Billy was fresh out of composure, if something didn't happen soon, he'd be pulling one of them onto the table. Mind you, he didn't think this was the kind of establishment where the proprietors would mind. "'Or' sounds good to me," he said calmly, and smiled.

Karina regarded him with a look of slight puzzlement. "Are you sure you came in today?"

"It's not the done thing to go wandering around like a sex-starved demon; dignity and deportment are the hallmark of an Officer. Now, please, may we get to the entertainment suites before I have an embarrassing accident," he laughed.

The girls both shot to their feet. "OK Flyboy, let's go." Anika smiled down at him lasciviously.

Before he could say anything, they pulled him to his feet, and led the way through the tables towards the darker innards of the club. Eventually they came to a heavily engraved oak door. This turned out to be the not so concealed entrance to a lift. He hadn't spotted any signs, yet the two women had made directly for this door. Obviously, they'd played in X Club X before. As soon as they stepped into the lift and the doors closed both women were all over him. He found himself pinned against the side of the lift. Urgently, they started to pull off his clothes.

The women were reacting as if they were the ones who had just spent six months in space. He'd heard rumours that homosexuality was as high as 38% with civilian males, while lesbianism was only about 18%. Could this have anything to do with it? Anika and Karina were so intent on getting him undressed that he found it difficult to do anything other than let them get on with it. In an all too brief moment he managed to get one hand free and discovered that his speculation was correct, they weren't wearing anything under their voluminous burkhas. His already racing pulse rate took a noticeable fillip. Was the fucking going to start in the moving lift? But, just at that moment, the lift came to a halt.

Pilot

The lift doors opened, and he was hustled out into a sedately lit corridor. Hastily they bundled him down the corridor. He couldn't move as fast as they wanted him to because his trousers were around his ankles, but they didn't seem to be aware of this handicap. Karina released him, but only for the time it took to produce an ident card and slot it into a door lock. All three of them tumbled into the room with the lights coming on and the door closing behind them, before he realised they had arrived at their destination.

They were still fully dressed; he was virtually naked. They dropped various pieces of his clothing on the floor. He was glad that they hadn't left his clothes strewn along the corridor. Now that they were in the room both women stood back and gave him the opportunity to look around. This room was designed with only one thing in mind. A circular bed took up half the floor space. The ceiling was covered in mirrors, three walls with erotic murals, and a vidi screen filled the entire forth wall. The two women started pacing around him like a pair of caged tigresses; just for a second, Billy found himself wondering if he was really up to this.

"We're gonna give you a night to remember and make a vidi of it to make sure you never forget." Karina grinned.

He was about to say something about too much talk and not enough action when Anika pointed at his back and asked, "What's that?"

Without looking he knew what had attracted her attention; small metal discs were embedded in his skin just below each shoulder blade. "They're the external connectors to lymphatic ducts. And before you ask; we Flyboys literally get plugged into our ships."

"What do you mean by 'plugged in'?" Karina was also curious.

He suddenly realised that this was the first time in his adult life that a civilian had seen him naked. Civvies couldn't be expected to know about some of the minor adaptations the Air Force did to the human body which made space flight more tolerable. He imagined that Karina and Anika would probably find the enhancements disgusting, or possibly amusing. Civvies didn't have to make super-light jumps on a regular basis. He decided to give a brief but thorough explanation before they started treating him like a freak.

"The discs are connectors to tubes that link us directly to the ship's life support system. That way the ship can help purge our bodies of waste products. It can also add oxygen directly to the blood stream, inject pain inhibitors, and increase or reduce certain hormone levels. All this enables the crew to stay alert in high stress situations for very long periods without becoming fatigued... Speaking of hormones, can we continue this conversation in the morning?"

Smiling, they each took an arm and led him ceremoniously to the bed. Gently pushing him onto it, they laid down either side of him. Things were just starting to get interesting; he was just about to discover if Anika was a natural blonde and whether Karina's body delivered on the promise of her face when the high pitched shrill of his personal communicator's recall alarm sounded. He jumped out of the bed and started searching through the piles of clothing for his jacket. He eventually found it and took out the communicator; switching it to sound only, he answered.

"Flight Lieutenant Zarcroft."

"*Sound only, ha! Put her down, you don't know where she's been. Here is the low down on* Man Vaughn. *Its home is the Navy's N° 1 Special Combat Squadron, based at Wyndham, Western Australia. And guess where it is right now? Correct. Now, get your clothes on and get there ASAP. I'll whistle up the rest of the crew and meet you there 21:00 hours tomorrow. It's due to take off in about thirty-nine hours. Bye.*" John, his No. 2 navigator, and techno-wizzo, put an end to what could have been the perfect first night downside.

He didn't have a decision to make. "I have to go."

Despite giving him looks of hungry desperation and suppressed frustration, the two women seem to accept the situation. It shouldn't have been too surprising, they were cops. They would be used to getting callouts at inopportune times. Both of them got out of the bed and, without saying anything, started helping him to get dressed. Billy wondered if they were going to stay and play by themselves. That would be them taken care of; what was he going to do about this interminable erection?

4

REUBEN JAN

It seemed to him that he hadn't spent longer than half an hour in one place since hitting downside. There had been the long drive home; then Paris and X Club X; then back to Lyon to collect some kit; then off on the long trek to Western Australia. This continuous flitting about was beginning to wear on him and his overactive carnal desires weren't helping the situation either. He could have made the flight in one hop but elected to have a brief stopover in Karachi. There had to be some up-for-it Military pussy in Karachi, there just had to be! Perhaps he should have stayed with the cops; half an hour, even fifteen minutes would have been better than nothing. Then again perhaps not, two women, both with steam coming out of their ears, just enough time for sex with one of them then 'Sorry, duty calls.' Hmm... No.

So, Karachi it was then; stretch his legs, *find a woman,* then go RV with the boys.

Even this simple plan was interrupted. The HEU called to say that some of the sleeper programmes had been activated and that it had neutralised them. Ironically, this had cleared the way for the HEU to gain more information without risk of detection. It had the educational records of the Filipino Zarcroft. Billy booked into a motel, then instructed the HEU to tight-stream the records to him.

From a quick examination of the education reports it was clear that this Zarcroft, Reuben Jan, showed very strong Gazelle-like characteristics. So much so that, unless his mother was a top athlete or mathematician, it must have been obvious that his natural father was from the military. Academically, Reuben had outstripped his peers to the extent that all his teachers were stating that he was bored and becoming disruptive in class.

This came as no surprise to Billy; it was obvious that the child belonged in a Military Academy. Only there would he find peers to rival him both physically and mentally. Only then would he learn that true success came with genuine effort. Something else in the reports caught Billy's eye; Reuben was registered as an only child from a single parent family. This caused Billy to reappraise his schedule.

The Philippines were not too far off his route to Western Australia. He had the child's home address, and he knew the name and location of his school. It would be foolish not to try and get at least a glimpse of the boy who was almost certainly his son. Would time permit it? Yes, if he went supersonic all the way. His time window was such that he couldn't afford to get caught-up with any more cops. Much as he hated it, he phoned the local air traffic control and logged the appropriate supersonic flight plan to the Philippines.

***

The flight from Karachi had been fun. The Air Traffic Controllers at Rangoon who controlled the Indian Ocean sector had their own version of 'standard English'. Any instruction that they gave was open to gross misinterpretation. Pilots had to pay particular attention to what other pilots did to be sure that everyone in their immediate airspace was working to the same understanding. This made what would have otherwise been a boring flight quite interesting.

Those who claimed that air travel was the second safest form of transportation (the safest being space travel) obviously didn't fly through Rangoon controlled airspace on a regular basis. At precisely 14:23 local time Billy thanked the controllers, tapped into the street map of the island of Luzon and came out of air traffic. His destination was the northern suburbs of Uagan; Reuben's home and school were both in that area.

He still wasn't sure of exactly what he was going to do when he got there. His plan had got only as far as starting with the school. Why? Because if Billy went to Reuben's home, the boy's mother might recognise him, which might lead to him having a friendly chat with MP's or Interpol on route to a court martial, twenty years hard labour followed by a dishonourable discharge.

Maybe he could pretend to be a school inspector from out of town? But what did he know about civilian schools? Nothing. That was a dumb idea. He followed the road map to Uagan and found the street in which the school was located. Landing the car about a hundred yards from the school's main entrance, he was still unsure of exactly what he was going to say to bluff his way in. However, as he looked over to the school, he saw that he might not have to bluff his way in at all.

He was able to see into the schoolyard through a slatted imitation wooden fence. There were dozens of unsupervised children running around a green field at the back. They seemed to be playing various games and were making an extraordinary amount of noise. Of the many military schools on the many worlds that Billy had attended, he had no recollection of ever being allowed to play as freely as these children seemed to be. Sitting in his car, he watched them playing for several minutes. Evidently civilian schools were totally different and much more relaxed than military ones.

If Reuben was, as his educational reports suggested, a Gazelle, then he should stand out from the other children. All Billy need to do was to look at the boys playing who were about seven years old and then pick Reuben out. Getting out of the car, he walked over to the fence and started looking for a boy who stood out. After about ten minutes of scanning he realised that identifying his son wasn't going to be as easy as that.

As far as he could tell there was over fifty children playing. Of these, only a few were playing games that required them to remain relatively static. It wasn't always obvious which were the boys, and which were the girls. He couldn't even keep track of who was doing what, let alone pick out any outstanding individuals. Billy was just about to try another method of sorting them when, on some unheard signal, the children stopped their games and boisterously made their way into the school building.

He went back to the car and sat contemplating the question of just how he was going to recognise his son. A few minutes later a second wave of children swarmed out of the building. He recognised that these children were not the ones he'd seen playing earlier. These children were generally taller and presumably older than the ones before. He also realised that he didn't have a clue about which group a seven-year-old would belong to.

Pilot

Not ready to admit defeat, he accepted that simply looking at the children in the playground would tell him little or nothing. He started to wonder if it might not be more appropriate to wait outside Reuben's home; it would be a simple matter to examine any child that entered. There would be little risk of Reuben's mother recognising him if he remained in the car with the windows darkened.

Yes. He decided that this was the best way to proceed. But before he left, he wanted to have another close look at the children playing, he found them quite fascinating and wondered why he'd never noticed children and their activities before. Again, he left the car and stood by the fence. Throughout his entire education, he'd never experienced anything as unrestricted as this. Maybe there were upsides to being a civilian.

A group of adults were beginning to congregate around the main entrance to the school. He tried to figure out who they were and what they were doing. It wasn't until he saw some children come out to the adults that he realised that the adults were parents collecting their children. He'd heard that most civilian schools were day schools but had never considered the implications. The schools and academies that he had attended had all been full boarding, his parents collected him at the end of each term.

Of the adults by the school gate, Billy noticed that one particular woman was looking directly at him. Could it be that he was infringing some rule about loitering near schools? Civilians had such weird laws. He couldn't afford to be found near this place and so moved back towards his car. Looking over his shoulder he saw that the woman was still staring after him, but it wasn't a look of disapproval, it was more a look of uncertainty. He wasn't going to stick around to find out what her problem was.

As he got into the car, and was about to start it, she walked over and stood directly in front of it. She gazed in through the windscreen at him. He supposed that most Filipinos tended to be short. She was short even for a Filipino but very slim, she could just about see into the car. At this range Billy could see that she seemed more than just uncertain; she had a looked that was a mixture of surprise, hesitancy, and apprehension. Who was she? What did she want? The fact that she was standing in front of the car didn't really block his path. This car, unlike most, could take off vertically. Billy stared back at her for a bit, then he opened the door and got out.

She took a couple of hesitant steps towards him. "You Air Force pilot?"

How the hell could she know that?! Was this some kind of setup by Interpol...? Her appearance suddenly arrested his thoughts and took them down a completely different road: her skin was silky smooth and unblemished, her eyes shone brightly and her hair hung to her waist; she was ridiculously beautiful, almost doll-like. He didn't say anything in response but nodded suspiciously. And of course, his hormones went into overdrive.

The woman took another step closer and looked up into his eyes. "You name... William?"

Again, he nodded.

She looked deeply concerned. "What you do, it is forbidden."

She wasn't telling him anything he didn't already know. He shrugged his shoulders but didn't reply.

Still hesitant, she held out her hand, then smiled. "My name is Coraliè Derieta."

"You already know mine." As he shook her hand, electricity ran up his arm and played up and down his spine while at the same time making his toes tingle - he actually shuddered. He wasn't in a mad rush to release her hand, but she let go of his.

It should have been blatantly obvious that she was Reuben's mother. Who else in the whole of the Philippines could have known that he was an Air Force pilot? But he had formed a mental picture of what a mother should look like and because Coraliè didn't match up to this, his brain was painfully slow at accepting the obvious. It had simply registered that she was far too beautiful to be anyone's mother and that was that... Definitely not ugly, so fanatically independent, or... The big question was what would she do now?

"Why you want see my son?" she asked reasonably.

"I wanted to see him because he has my surname," he replied, equally reasonably.

"I won't ask how you find us. You know is dangerous to be here?"

Her standard English was worse than that of the controllers at Rangoon, he couldn't help smiling. "Yes, I know. I only wanted to see him."

She became stern faced. "Records said you brilliant and tenacious but also rebellious. These were some of traits I look for. They no say anything about you being stupid. I know what happen if you found here!"

Her sudden outburst surprised him. He tried to interpret her motives. It was she who had recognised him and stopped him as he was about to leave. If she hadn't, he would have been none-the-wiser. She didn't appear to find his presence threatening. But, at the same time, his presence was definitely cause for concern. Why? Three times she had pointed out the risks that he ran. Why? These weren't risks that she faced, they made no difference to her. This wasn't making sense.

"Look, I just wanted to see the boy, OK? Why should you worry about what happens to me?"

Some deep emotion that he didn't recognise passed across her face. "I no want you arrested," she said earnestly.

"I can take care of myself. Anyway, does it really matter?"

"Yes."

"Why?"

Coraliè impatiently stared up at him for a long moment, then looked at her watch. "He come out of school now. See him and go." Suddenly, she turned and marched off back to the school gate.

Billy was still puzzled. Coraliè seemed to be angry at him. Why? What had he done to her? He stared after her as she stomped away, then realised that he wasn't staring after her; he was, in fact, staring at her - the totally feminine movement of her arse to be precise. How tall was she? About 4' 11". How old? About his age, twenty-five, he guessed. An exquisitely adorable, elegant, 4' 11", twenty-five-year-old, Filipino doll who was either fanatically independent or... She stopped and turned to look back at him. Inclining her head slightly, she indicated that she expected him to follow. He left the car and accompanied her to the gate.

While they stood with the other waiting parents, he thought he might as well find out something about her. "What do you do?"

She seemed undecided about whether or not to answer. In the end she said, "Please. He be out soon. See him, then leave here."

"I *am* going to leave, but what's the hurry? Why are you so keen to get rid of me?"

"I no want get rid of you. I no want you get in trouble." She was wearing that impatient look again.

"I'm not going to get into trouble. No one knows I'm here, OK? So, what do you do?"

"I part-time designer, part-time activist, Social Reform Movement," she answered curtly.

The Social Reform Movement was one of the two main opposition parties. The military was apolitical. The only thing Billy knew about the SRM was that it had a pretty strong anti-military platform. Military personnel, especially Officers, weren't allowed to make any

kind of political comment in public. Mind you, an activist in the SRM *could* be fanatical...
No! He was just getting his hopes up.

"What do you design?"

"Plasma drive system for high pressure environments."

Billy wondered if she was joking, but the look she gave him said that she wasn't. "What company?"

"No company. I freelance designer."

Plasma drive design was at the cutting edge of technological research and development. It didn't sit at all well with working for a reactionary party like the SRM. She must have seen the doubt written on his face because she huffily took a shallow breath, then continued.

"I work in team that design unmanned drones for deep atmosphere probing."

What she was telling him was that her designs weren't used by the Military. Only The Explorer Corps or pure research scientists played around with gas giants.

"If you don't think much of the Military, why did you...?" He couldn't think of how to end the sentence.

Coaliè pointedly ignored the question and, instead, concentrated her attention on a group of children who were just leaving the school building. One little boy dashed up to Coraliè and hugged her excitedly. They exchanged loud greetings in what Billy supposed was the local language. The child obviously asked Coraliè something about the man standing next to her. Pausing, she looked up at him then answered the boy. Billy would have liked to understood what she'd said because the boy seemed to readily accept her answer.

If this boy was Reuben, then Billy was disappointed. He didn't know how tall a seven-year-old was supposed to be, but he had a feeling that Reuben was small for his age. And he didn't even look like a boy; his eyelashes were far too long - he looked too much like his mother - he was *pretty*. As far as Billy could tell, the only things about Reuben that even suggested that he might be his son was the darkness of his skin and his tightly curled hair. Billy's father's family came from Belarus, but his mother was African. A lot of that African ancestry showed in Reuben.

Billy had spent so many years tracing Reuben that now that he was standing in front of him it was all a bit of an anticlimax. There he was, staring down at his biological son. What was he supposed to feel? What did he feel? Confused. He was a military pilot - quick, decisive, tough - he wasn't accustomed to being confused. Speak to the boy! Yes. He should say something. What? They'd spent billions and billions training him so that he could handle anything that might be encountered 'out there', why couldn't he think of a single thing to say? What was he supposed to do? Just turn around and leave?

Coaliè must have sensed some of this turmoil because she said, "If you sure there is no risk, you come now to our home."

To Billy's ears it didn't sound like a cordial invitation, it sounded more like a duty she thought she couldn't shirk. But it could have been her unusual method of sentence construction that carried that impression. Time wasn't yet critical, if he tried really hard, he could squeeze about an hour before he had to leave for Wyndham.

He said, "If it's no trouble, I would be pleased to," but thought, 'Why doesn't she introduce me to the boy?'

"Good. We go." Coraliè took Reuben's hand and started off down the road.

"We can take my car; it will save time." He knew that they lived less than fifteen minutes' walk from the school, but to leave the car where it was would give him less time with them.

Coraliè didn't reply but she stopped and led Reuben back. All three made their way over to the car and Coraliè and Reuben got in the back. Once they were all strapped in, he slowly lifted off. Reuben excitedly started firing off a barrage of questions at his mother. Billy didn't know what he was saying but was pretty sure that Reuben was asking questions about the car. Nor did he understand Coraliè's replies but figured that they were something along the lines of 'be a good boy and sit still'.

Although Billy didn't understand a word the boy was saying this cheered him up; his son should be excited about flying, especially flying in a machine like this. He supposed that standard English was a compulsory part of the school syllabus.

"Reuben, would you like me to zoom climb to nineteen thousand, then roll off the top and bring her in on your street?"

"Oh yeah!" Reuben shrieked with delight.

Coraliè started to say something in protest but stopped, they were already passing 5,000 in a vertical climb. Reuben was hollering shrilly and clapping his hands. Billy still couldn't understand what he was saying but Reuben was obviously finding this great fun. At 19,000 feet Billy pulled over into a gentle loop, dived, and spiralled down. Reuben's clamour increased and even Coraliè joined in. Billy checked the map, checked the house numbering sequence, hit the air brakes, and brought them in right outside their house.

Throughout the entire flight he hadn't pulled more than 1.5 G; it was the aerobatics that made it exciting for them. He laughed to himself as he opened the doors to let them out. Reuben was still on a high when they hopped on to the pavement. Tugging at his mother's hand, he repeatedly asked her the same question. In the end she gave her assent. Reuben dropped his satchel and scampered off down the street.

Billy watched him go. "Where is he going?"

Coraliè picked up the satchel. "He go get friend to show your fast car." She smiled after Reuben.

"What did you tell him when he asked who I was?"

She became sombre. "Said you friend from before he was born. You want come in?"

It *could* just be her sentence construction, but that didn't sound particularly friendly. *No! Stop it! You're letting your imagination get ahead of itself.* Billy nodded and she led the way into the block of apartments, and he started to shiver when they entered; as with most buildings in the tropics this one had over efficient air conditioning. Coraliè led him to a large ground floor apartment. The walls had life-sized holograms of scenes from coral reefs. He'd read somewhere that this was the height of fashion. The apartment also had stairs leading down to a basement where he assumed her design studio was located. There were several laser sculptures in the hallway. In the main living room were dozens of oil paintings and some physical sculptures. Compared to his cottage in the country, this apartment was luxurious. He stopped by one of the paintings.

"I love art. My men usually artists," Coraliè explained.

Men?! Did she just say men? So, she isn't a... Being a single parent didn't necessarily mean that she lived without a companion. He opened his mouth to ask a question, then realised that it was none of his business. Coraliè saw him hesitate and continued, "Please sit down. I fix you cool drink."

She went into an adjoining room before he could answer. He sat in the nearest chair. Looking around the apartment he guessed that in civilian terms, it was very chic. The military had a totally different value system but, even so, he suspected that Coraliè must be wealthy. If she was that wealthy, why didn't she simply call her RoboSteward? Wealthy people were supposed to have RoboStewards. It occurred to him that a member of the SRM might not condescend to have something as crass as a RoboSteward in her home. Coraliè returned carrying a tray with a crystal jug and two glasses. Setting the tray down on a table, she handed him a glass.

"Thanks, but I don't drink. I wanted to tell you that before you went to all this trouble," he said apologetically.

"I know you no drink alcohol; you are pilot. This fresh fruit juice, you will like," she seemed to have taken his statement as a criticism.

He took the drink. "Thanks." How did she know that flight crews didn't drink?

Coraliè also took up a drink and sat opposite him. "I think about you a lot," she said conversationally.

Billy went over what she'd just said to make sure that he hadn't misunderstood. "Why would you think about me? You don't know me."

"Reuben is very..." she searched for the words in English. "... bright, but bad child. I wonder if you like him."

Billy laughed. "You mean, you wonder if he's like me. Now that we've met, what do you think?"

"I no know yet," she smiled back.

"Why did you choose the Air Force?" He couldn't think of a less direct way of asking the question.

Coraliè became very serious. "I know the... punishment for you finding him. If you tell me why you do this, I tell you why I pick you."

Billy didn't want to rock any boats. He only wanted to see the boy; this he had done... Lie! There was a Filipino boat sitting less than two feet away that, just then, he'd give his right hand to rock. "Well, I found out that there had been a donation, and that it was male. So, I started asking the right computers some questions. Eventually I came up with you."

"You get into government computer?!" Coraliè was alarmed.

"Yeah, how else was I going to find you?"

"You do all these things because you want see your son?"

He absorbed the fact that she referred to Reuben as 'his son' but wasn't sure how to react. "Yes."

"I tell you why I pick you. First, I want military man. If I want civilian I no need donation." She grinned. "Military men not... boring; have lot of drive and determination. Then I hear that pilot very clever, good mathematicians. Then I saw your hologram..." She looked at him as if she was staring into the depths of his soul. "...your eyes." She became serious again. "Now I think I make mistake."

"A mistake? What mistake?"

A look of sadness crossed her face. "Reuben, he is no good at school. He no study; he break rules, just like you. He no have many friends."

"You believe that he is growing up to be too much like a serviceman?"

"I believe he is growing up too much like you."

"As I understand it 'environment' has by far the most significant effect on a growing child," he said disarmingly. "I've read his last school report and I believe I know why he's behaving as he does."

"You know?" Coraliè asked doubtingly.

"I think so. I might be able to offer a solution, but I need you to explain why you dislike the military."

With her broken English she launched into a SRM recitation. "The military and their expensive equipment are paid for by our taxes. This money can be spent much better. The military make not a positive contribution, so they should go."

"Coraliè, you know that I can't discuss politics with you. But there's more to it than just..."

"Is macho bullshit!" she interrupted him.

"There are more women in all the services than men," he countered.

"Is still aggressive and unnecessary." Then she seemed to lighten up a bit. "But you say you can help Reuben."

"He's not bad. He behaves as he does simply because he has no direct peer group, either in school or at home. I was watching the games the children were playing at the school. If those are the usual games that are played here, then in most of them he will always win. It is difficult for him to make friends when he always wins."

Coralie looked at him in surprise. "How you know he always win?"

"It's because of our genotypes, yours and mine. In situations involving reflexes, coordination, and speed, he'll do well because of me. His stature and, presumably, also his spatial awareness he gets from you. He is small, dexterous, and agile. If you put those together, you'll see why he always wins when playing with his age group. But he is too small to play with an older group of children. Can you also see that this is unlikely to change?"

"Yes, I see," Coralie said, and eagerly waited for more.

"You said that he didn't study. Studying isn't the same as learning. He learns very quickly, and because of that sees no need to study."

Again, Coralie looked at Billy in surprise. "How you know this? How you know he learn quick?"

Billy smiled. "I told you, I read his school reports. Anyway, he's in the wrong environment. There is only one place where he will find his true peer group and study as you want him to."

Coralie suddenly stood up. "My son no join Military!"

Billy stayed calm. "Has he ever asked you why other children can't catch things as well as he can? Or why he understands what the teacher's talking about before the rest of his class?"

Coralie looked at Billy for a long time before speaking. When she did, it wasn't in answer his questions. In perfect standard English she said. "It is immoral to spend billions of credits on personnel and outmoded and superfluous machines of war. There is still so much that can be done to our home planet to correct the destruction brought about by the extravagances of the Twentieth and Twenty-first Centuries. The credits spent on the military could be put to better use in these areas. To promote policies to the contrary is not only wicked, it's inhuman."

That little speech was something she recited often, hence the correct grammar. Billy had forgotten that the SRM were also anti any space exploration that didn't directly and immediately benefit the Earth. If they had their way, all existing fledgling colonies would be cut off from the solar system. The SRM were of the old school, they tended to follow the logic that said, 'If God had intended man to go gallivanting around space, He would have made him capable of surviving in a vacuum'.

Pilot

"Coraliè, I'm not wicked or inhuman. Reuben belongs in a Military Academy," he said quietly.

Again, she took a long time to reply. Billy realised that what he'd just suggested wasn't entirely new to her. He could see that she'd had those very thoughts herself, so he continued, "All you know about us is what you hear on the news or at party conferences. You don't ever meet us socially so it's natural that you're wary about an academy. And I know you have strong political beliefs, but military expenditure has been a hot political item since man started living in societies. We've always been here for very valid reasons."

Looking thoughtful Coraliè put down her glass and came to sit next to him. "I not only think about if you like Reuben, I also think what you like in other ways. People say Military always marry. You have wife?"

Her question was so unexpected; he checked his hearing, double checked, and checked again, and then simply said, "No, why?"

"Already have your child. Now want make love." She took his hand and stood up. "You very brave and very foolish to find us, but I pleased you come." Eagerly she started leading him towards a door opposite.

He didn't want to put a damper on things but there were a couple of things he had to clarify. "Where is your... man?"

"I no have one," she answered without slowing.

He pulled up and forced her to stop at the door. "What if Reuben comes in?"

"He not come in here. Anyway, he big boy, he knows of these things." She opened the door and dragged him through.

Billy supposed that one needed to have a fertile imagination to be a designer. But whoever had put this room together had allowed their imagination to run riot. He stood rooted to the spot and took it in; it put the entertainment suit at the X Club X to shame. The entire floor was a bed which had a number of support frames placed strategically around it. Attached to the frames were stirrups. Billy had never seen this type of contraption before, but their purpose was pretty obvious. The four walls and the ceiling were holograms screens, but not the simple fixed pattern type; their projectors must have somehow been sensitive to Coraliè's mood because, without her giving any instructions, the patterns began to change.

The patterns began to take definite shapes, but just as he began to recognise the forms they changed and began to reform again. And so the patterns repeatedly teased his visual senses. This was eroticism of a high and exquisite form and only went to confirm his suspicion that Coraliè was wealthy; only the very rich could afford something like this. It also seemed to confirm what he'd been told about the extraordinary length civilians would go to in order to put excitement into their otherwise dull lives. This was one of these Love Rooms that he'd heard so much about.

Standing in front of him, Coraliè looked up into his eyes. She put a hand behind her back and slowly undid her dress. In the same unhurried manner, she pulled the garment off her shoulders and allowed it to fall to the ground. The holograms went berserk, Billy wondered if it was his mood that the projectors sensed. Reaching up, she gently and tenderly took his face in her hands and pulled him into a passionate kiss.

***

He was late for his RV. Coraliè seemed to be either a woman who was highly sexed or one who hadn't had it for a long time. She wasn't as ravenous as when you've just hit downside, but she wasn't far off either. Whatever the true reason, they had spent hours making love, passionately. He reminded himself that today was the very first time he'd met her. Yet there was something very familiar about this - Coraliè lying curled up in his arms. It felt comfortable, as if they had known each other for a lifetime. Like they could remain like this forever.

He had heard about 'falling in love'; closeness with your sexual partner was supposed to be what one felt when in love. He wondered if it could be happening to him. He knew that she wasn't sleeping, he could tell that she was trying to reconcile conflicting thoughts and emotions. She'd faced similar dilemmas before; active members of the SRM didn't usually go to the Military for sperm donations, her son didn't fit into their rigid view of how the world should be.

She rolled over and cuddled up closer to him. Without opening her eyes, she said, "When we make love, I hope purge you from my mind. I wanted you to be aggressive and ill-mannered serviceman, so I make sure Reuben never grow up like you."

Billy watched the holograms change to what he could only think of as an agitated state. By now he had discovered that the projectors responded to both of their emotional states.

Coraliè sat up. "I no want like you, but I like you. I know you pilot; you have girl in every town. I want say I be your Filipino girl, but I no want see you again because if I do it get complicated."

This was the point where, if he was going to make a commitment, he should say it. "I've never had a long-term relationship because I spend fifteen months in every eighteen out on a sortie. At this stage of my career I can't change that, I'm a Pilot. But if..."

Coraliè put her finger to his lips. "William, no say anymore. We spend long time wondering what the other was like, now we know. Let's no spoil it. See Reuben then leave. Don't come back. I no want you get in trouble."

She was his first civilian, maybe he was missing out on a whole range of experiences. He turned his thoughts back to more pressing matters. "Will you send him to an academy?"

Coraliè slowly got off the bed. "I have to think more about this. Shower is through there." She bent over, took both his hands and pulled him to his feet. "Come." Walking backwards she started leading him towards the shower room. The wall holograms returned to their erotic dances.

He certainly needed a shower, but he didn't have time for what she was offering with it. "Look, I have to go," he said apologetically.

"To another girl in another town?" she smiled. The holograms on the walls wavered uncertainly and then settled down. She opened the door then waved him in. "You go have shower by yourself. I get Reuben."

He nodded and stepped into the room. It was just that, a fair-sized room, not a cubicle. As he closed the door behind him the lights came on and he was bathed by powerful jets of hot water. Here was another sign of luxury, a 3D shower. This was an experience he could have got into, but he was already late. How to turn it off? Open the door he guessed. He did so and the jets stopped. As he looked around for a towel, warm air started blowing over his body. He was dry in seconds.

Quickly getting dressed he went to find Coraliè and Reuben. The apartment seemed deserted. He went outside and found them by the car. Reuben had collected a sizeable audience of other children and was addressing them from its roof. Billy wondered if Reuben had been at this since they went inside. From the boy's gesticulations Billy guessed that Reuben was telling them about his flight home from school. Coraliè was unsuccessfully trying to disperse this gathering and get Reuben to come down off the car.

Pilot

When Reuben saw him coming down the stairs towards them, he scampered off the car's roof, slid down the bonnet and hit the pavement running. Sprinting off down the street, he disappeared around the corner. Watching him run Billy concluded that he was definitely a Gazelle. Reuben's wide-eyed audience were left to switch their attention to the very tall owner of the car. What tall stories had Reuben told them, Billy wondered?

Coaliè turned to him with a concerned look on her face. "You see? He always misbehaves, then run away."

"There's an Air Force Academy in Japan. That's not too far, is it...? What will you tell him about... me?"

Ignoring both his suggestion and question, she slipped something into his hand. "My card, if you want see me... us, again."

Hadn't she just told him that she didn't want to see him again? "I don't ever know when I'll be back," he tried to explain.

"You go now. No need to make promise." She gently pushed him towards the car.

"If you do send him to an academy, make sure it's Air Force and not Navy."

"If I do, I will. William, I happy I meet you... Ruben... I tell him sad story about his father, now I tell him the truth." An emotion passed across her face, but he wasn't sure what it meant.

"I'm happy I've met you too." She *was* far too beautiful to be anyone's mother, and he concluded that he *was* definitely in love. "I *will* see you again."

The same emotion was back on her face, but this time it was stronger. "You go now, please."

He got into the car and started it. Coaliè had turned and was walking back into the building. Looking down the street, he saw Reuben peeking out from behind a hedge. Dialling-up local Traffic, he got flight clearance. Billy didn't know what it was that Reuben had told the other kids, but he made sure that his departure was spectacularly in-keeping with Reuben's gesticulations, thus giving credibility to the boy's - *his son's* - story.

5

NAVAL AIR STATION WYNDHAM

It was exactly 15:00 hrs as the Captain walked out of the duty room. Time for the second defaulters' parade, those assembled were called to attention. He had always thought that four inspections a day excessive. It was also somewhat unfair. Defaulters were allocated dirty, unpleasant, and menial tasks and, therefore, it was almost inevitable that on at least one of the inspections the Duty Officer would find some blemish on their uniforms. Fortunately for the defaulters, he was inclined to be lenient; he always turned a blind eye to such blemishes, unless it was obvious that an offender had made no effort to neaten themselves.

Returning the Duty Sergeant's salute, he started his inspection, taking his time parading through the ranks. This was a mild Manchurian spring and for the second time that day he noted that of the forty-seven defaulters, thirty-nine were from his brigade. The brigade was on an unaccompanied twelve-month deployment to Earth. During that time, they were virtually confined to the base, the military didn't belong on Earth. Boredom was probably the major contributing factor in almost every misdemeanour that caused them to be on a charge. He could certainly relate to that, Pehan Garrison was probably the most boring place in the whole of China. It was so boring that being Duty Officer was a positive joy.

He finished his leisurely inspection without putting anyone on a further charge, then returned to the duty room. The Orderly Sergeant indicated through the glass of the signals room that there was an urgent call waiting for him. It was too much to hope that the message might, in some way, be related to something to do with soldiering. It was probably some Colonel or other wanting to know if his Regimental silver had been polished by the defaulters. The Captain strolled into the signals room.

"It's Lieutenant O'Branagan. He's calling from Shanghai. The channel is scrambled, Sir." Giving him a quizzical look, the sergeant passed over the comms set.

O'Branagan had taken the rugby team for a match in Korea. What was he doing in Shanghai? Why the security on the air?

"What do you want, you old scoundrel?" he laughingly shouted into the comms set.

"Your duty ends at 23:59, doesn't it? I'm rounding up some of the lads. There might just be some off-garrison entertainment in the offing."

"You cad, Sir! Don't play with me so. If you know something I don't, out with it. I was about to start watching paint dry."

Pilot

"*I just bumped into some naval types. Apparently, the Air Force has goosed one of their weightless stations. As you can imagine the Fishheads are none too pleased, so I took a slight detour to see a Flyboy I know and guess what?*"

"It's true?"

"*Of course, it's true, but that's not it. There is a rumour that those same goosers are planning to visit a Naval Air Station.*"

"You're kidding?!"

"*Would I joke about something like that? It's going to be one hell of a party!*"

"Damned selfish! Typical of these naval and air types to try and keep something like this to themselves."

"*Absolutely. And we all know that no self-respecting Navy ever goes anywhere without its attendant Marines to wipe its bum.*"

"You wouldn't happen to know the venue of said party, would you?"

"*Naval Air Station Wyndham, Western Australia.*"

"It seems ever such a long time since I broke a Grunt or two. Count me in."

"*That's the spirit!*"

***

With the hypersensitive civilian population quick and eager to find fault with the military, on Earth, much of the Military Police's work was devoted to pre-empting situations where military personnel might offend civilians. The MP's had to get to any incident while it was still in its infancy and snuff it out before it could develop. Their operating philosophy was based on three principles: good intelligence, anticipation, and swift response.

Getting to a situation before it became an incident was all well and good but throwing a few high-spirited matlows into the cooler simply because they got boisterous was hardly fair. All too often it was the civilians who were really at fault. But MP's had no jurisdiction over civilians and the local cops were usually belligerent. Military Exemption meant that these selfsame cops had no jurisdiction over military personnel. And anyway, this messing about wasn't real military police work, most Provost personnel preferred to be off Earth. Earth - what a shithole! A proper policing job could be done out in the colonies.

The Provost Major's views were the same as the ones held by those under her command. She couldn't wait for her next posting. Nine days. Only nine days and this three-year tour of duty would be over. Nine days and she could say goodbye to Earth, hopefully for good. Three years of indolent stroppy civilians and the last eighteen months spent spitting sand here in the deserts of Western Australia.

NAS Wyndham was Earth's jumping off and landing point for all Naval and Marine personnel. The Western Australian civilians were amongst the most anti-military. This enmity could either be attributed to them being fed-up with the constant movement of huge numbers of military personnel, or it could be resentment. Directly or indirectly, most civvies earn their living from the enormous military installation on their doorstep.

Whatever the reason, there were more than enough petty incidents to keep her and her officers fully occupied. Today, however, was shaping up to be a day out of the ordinary. It had started with the issuing of a general communiqué. This was an alert to all MP's in the solar system, stating that there would be heightened tension between Navy and Air Force personnel. An Air Force craft had deliberately 'washed' a naval Earth orbit Weightless station with gravitational waves. The MP's were to contain and, if possible, defuse any incidents. They were also to ensure that no civilians got involved.

Wyndham was 100% Navy territory, there wasn't anything remotely Air Force for thousands of miles: little chance of any inter-service conflict within her constabulary. She circulated the communique to her platoon commanders and left it at that. But by early afternoon she received an intelligence report that an Air Force flight crew was making its way to Wyndham. This flight crew was believed to be the one responsible for upsetting the Weightless. She reckoned that if the Flyboys had made a suicide pact and wanted a particularly grotesque and messy ending, then going to Wyndham was a smart move. She was about to alert her platoon commanders when confidential orders came through from Divisional HQ: should said Air Force flight crew make their presence known they were to be apprehended and kept securely. They were to be handed over to Air Force security, only.

Easier said than done. Without knowing who they were and where and when they were arriving, she would never be able to find them. Western Australia was always swamped with personnel in transit. Moreover, if the Flyboys got inside NAS Wyndham they were out of her hands. Naval Stations were the province of the station's security and the shore patrol. Her MP's could only intervene if they were called to the station.

***

Homing in on John's signal led him to the top floor of a multi-storey car park in a shopping mall. The boys had arrived in Grim's and Pipsqueak's cars and were sitting around waiting. He was nearly three hours late. In all the years they had been a crew, he'd never been a minute late. While he wound down his window, he didn't feel even remotely guilty.

"There's a serious bashing awaiting, you know?" Grim greeted him in his customary sullen manner.

For a second Billy thought about telling them the great news about Reuben and Coraliè but changed his mind. He'd save that for a more fitting occasion. Smiling up at the weather-beaten face of his 2ic, Billy said, "There is *indeed*, Compassman. Have we done a recce?"

"John and I have checked it out. There are the usual Grunts on the main gate; our idents should get us past them. But, be warned, the town is crawling with Truckies." Mohamed laughed at the danger.

"Yeah, if we all go in one car it should be easier to blag our way in," John suggested.

"We'll change out of civvies once we're inside the base. OK, pile in. If we get separated, hit and run, then RV back here by 01:30. Check?" Billy ordered.

"Check," they all answered and got into his car; Mohammed squeezed his tall frame into the front passenger seat.

As they took off John gave directions. Billy covered the 30 kilometres taking care not to do anything to draw attention to them. As they approached the base Billy brought the car down below tree top height and flew a complete circuit of the perimeter. On this pass they noted all points of entrance and exit. NAS Wyndham was one of the largest military installations on Earth. The Navy called it 'the station that never sleeps'. It was about three times larger than AFB Oymyakon and rumoured to have a permanent staffing of over thirty-one thousand. Everything the Navy did *had* to be bigger and better than the Air Force.

Flying back around to the front and setting the car down on the main road a kilometre from the main gate, Billy asked, "Think we can make a clean getaway?"

"With all that activity going on I don't see why not," Pipsqueak answered.

Pilot

"My thoughts exactly; they'd have to bring the base to a complete stop to do a thorough search. This should be fun," John agreed.

"OK then, let's go." Billy drove off.

Keeping to the metalled road he drove up to the main gate, a Marine sergeant came up to the car as it stopped at the barricade. Billy wound down the window and gave him his ID. "Guests of Lieutenant Gümann, N° 1 Special Combat Squadron."

Taking the ID, the sergeant consulted his computerised clipboard. "Lieutenant Gümann is at present in the Officers' Mess, Sir." He looked over the ID and without showing too much surprise gave it back. "May I see the other gentlemen's identification?"

They handed over their ID's. With only a cursory glance the guard handed them back. "The way to the Officers' Mess please, Sergeant?"

"Follow the main road for about three and a half kilometres. At the main transit barracks take the turning to the left. The Officers' Mess is well signposted from there." He stepped away from the car and saluted.

"Thank you, Sergeant." The barrier went up and Billy drove into the base.

Billy darkened the windows and the others started changing into their tropical mess kit. Being sky blue with gold braiding, it was distinctly different from the Navy's. With 5' 4" tall Pipsqueak sitting directly behind the 6' 8" Mohammed there was just enough room for them to change as he drove. Getting past the gate security had been easier than expected but not all that surprising; the security was mainly to keep out unwelcomed civilians. Arriving at the Officers' Mess, Billy parked near the entrance. Grim handed him his uniform.

"When the party starts, I want you all to remember this, Gümann is mine. That bitch made me scrub an entire mess deck with a toothbrush," Billy explained as he slipped on the trousers.

John laughed. "Truckies are so enamoured of spit and polish. Presumably you're planning on using her face to scrub the mess floor?"

"Something like that," Billy laughed back.

They waited until there was no one entering or leaving the Mess before getting out of the car. With Billy leading they quickly entered the Mess and made straight for reception. The first naval person they encountered was the steward manning the reception desk. This young rating had no difficulty recognising Air Force uniforms but had an obvious problem with believing that he was actually seeing them.

"Visitors book, please," Billy asked in the manner of a Naval Officer.

The rating fumbled as he took the book from beneath the counter and opened it on the desk. He then seemed to be at a loss about what to do next. Taking the book, Billy signed himself in and passed it on.

"Thank you, and good evening." Aiming to keep the steward off balance, Billy turned and walked off. "Gentlemen, to the wardroom."

A rather hesitant, "Excuse me, Sir... Sir?" followed when they were already halfway down the corridor.

The Mess was a club for all the station's Officers and home to those who were unattached. To serve such a large station it was built along the lines of a modern multi-storey hotel. The spacious wardroom was situated on the ground floor, adjacent to a huge dining hall. With Billy still in the lead, the Air Force's Ace Crew II sauntered into the wardroom of Naval Air Station Wyndham. The quiet hum of conversation between the two hundred or so off-duty Navy and Marine Officer became a deafening silence.

Moving further into the room, Ace Crew II ignored the hostile stares of the residents and took some time selecting where to sit. Eventually, the group settled on a table next to the large expanse of windows that stretched from floor to ceiling and took up an entire side of the room. The windows looked out onto a panoramic view of the landing fields. Spreading out around the table they all sat. Shuffling forwards the assembled resident Officers quickly formed a dense crowed encircling them. Reclining, Billy drew his colleagues' attention to some of the ornamentation that decorated the ceiling and walls.

"As you can see, Gentlemen, a typical naval wardroom. Note the throwbacks to the wet Navy of yore. Some would have us believe that this is because they, and their attendant service, are steeped in tradition. One *could* say that they're stuffed to the gills in it. I would, however, venture an alternative explanation. Archaic, nostalgic nonsense. We wouldn't have such junk in an Air Force Mess, would we?"

"Certainly not," Mohamed agreed. "The perennial retrospective outlook explains much about Truckies and their general poor performance."

As the crowd tightened around them, a steward, tray in hand, burst through the mass of bodies to stand in front of Grim. "Would you gentlemen care to order?"

The steward was obviously trying to forestall the inevitable fight. He and his colleagues would be the ones left to clear up the resulting debris. Before Grim could answer there was a loud questioning shout from somewhere near the bar.

"Pongos!"

Everyone started looking around and the crowd slowly began to thin. The resultant gap revealed about fifteen Army officers, also in tropical dress uniform, standing just inside the entrance to the wardroom. A group of Marine officers were slowly moving forwards to face up to them. The steward looked on with rising disquiet.

"Five fruit juices and drinks all round. The toast is, Weightless Stations!" Grim said loudly.

The steward nodded and dashed off towards the bar. The resident Officers separated into two distinct groups: Navy around the Air Force Officers and Marines confronting the Army. Things were shaping up nicely into to a four-way punch-up. Lieutenant Gümann suddenly burst through the ranks of Army Officers. She was wearing sports kit and supporting a lovely shiner by her right eye, the result of Billy's slap. By normal mess rules she shouldn't have entered the wardroom wearing such attire.

Without breaking stride, she looked around the Mess and then zeroed in on Billy's group. Running at full tilt she charged through the Navy Officers and lunged at Billy. Jumping to his feet, knocking his chair out backwards, Billy met her with a sharp, well timed, uppercut which caught her flush on the chin. Gümann's legs buckled and she started pitching backwards and to her right but was caught and held up by her fellow Officers.

That was the signal for the start of a general free-for-all. The resident Officers outnumbered their unwelcomed guests by a considerable margin, however, the gentlemanly conduct expected of Officers extended even to their behaviour in a brawl. They couldn't simply mob the soldiers and Flyboys. The matchups were one on one with those who weren't involved looking on and shouting loud encouragement. When one of their number fell someone quickly took their place in the fight. Fighting one on one allowed the Marines and Flyboys to give a damn good account of themselves. But it was only a matter of time before they would tire and be overwhelmed.

Just as the fighting was reaching fever pitch, five armoured personnel carriers suddenly crashed through the huge wall-window. Showering the wardroom with glass, they hovered about a foot off the floor. MP's wearing helmets and insulation suits, with neuron whips drawn, piled out of the carriers. Indiscriminately, they started spreading lashes from their whips with a liberal flair. With the arrival of the MP's all the individual fights were instantly forgotten. Instead of trying to escape, everyone turned and attacked the sixty strong MP assault team.

One 'flick' from a neuron whip was enough to incapacitate an uninsulated individual. It caused the nerve endings in the epidermis to send signals to the brain - extreme pain! The sensation was of one's entire body being on fire. Both the civil and military police referred to this initial stage of a whipping as 'Gaining someone's undivided attention'. A few seconds later, paralysis of the extremities set in - the victim collapsed and lay unmoving but remained fully conscious. This retention of consciousness was why the neuron whip was a favoured instrument for crowd control.

The paralysis lasted somewhere between fifteen and thirty minutes. The aftereffects of nausea continued for up to twenty-four hours but, providing the whip's setting was low, only rarely were there any other side effects. The MP's insulation suits protected them from the whips and because the suits were padded, they also rendered most blows struck against them ineffective. A relatively small number of suited civil or military police could easily neutralise a rabble several times their number.

However, this wasn't just any rabble, all military personnel were trained in unarmed combat. Still, the fracas within the wardroom of NAS Wyndham was coming under the control of the MP's, they had the combatants pinned in one corner of the room. Anyone trying to escape, either through the door or the broken window, had to negotiate the MP's extended line. Dodging missiles thrown by their prey, they were slowly and deliberately moving in to pick them off one at a time. The Officer directing operation was a few metres behind the main body of MP's and was flanked by two others for protection.

Billy still had his crew with him as they backed away from the whips. He drew their attention to the MP's commander. "I'm not just going to stand here and take this, get him!"

All five Air Force Officers ran, bobbing and weaving, towards the line of MP's. Then they were through and converging on the commander. By the time he and his escorts realised that Ace Crew II weren't trying to make a break for it the five men were almost upon them. For the first time, the commander started to draw his whip. Diving forward Billy knocked him over with a leg sweep. The commander landed face down. Instantly Billy was on his back wrenching the whip out of his grasp.

Grim and Pipsqueak avoided the whips of the two escorts and upended them with similar kicks. Mohamed and John who were following up disarmed them. Without their whips the MP's were defenceless and their heavy suits restricted their movements. In this isolated five against three fight, the Air Force Officers pummelled the MP's. Other MP's broke ranks and moved to protect their comrades. Seeing this, the remaining Officers attacked and suddenly the battle tilted in the Officers' favour. Some of the MP's turned and ran, others tried to get back into their armoured personnel carriers. The battle was turning into a rout.

Still grappling on the floor with the MPs' commander, Billy realised that he was in fact fighting with a woman. "Give me a hand with this bastard! Get the helmet off," he called out to the rest of the crew.

Mohamed and Pipsqueak came over to assist, between the three of them they were able to remove the woman's helmet. Grim held the commander's own neuron whip against the side of her neck; fearfully, the MP stopped struggling. "Let's take her for a spin. I've always wanted to have a quiet chat with a MP," Grim laughed.

Dragging the MP to her feet, they frog marched her out of the wardroom. A few of the remaining MP's made one last attempt to get to them but they were set upon by a group of

Officers led by Lieutenant Gümann. At the double, they all ran down the corridor dragging the suited woman with them. Once out in the night air they bundled her into the back seat of the car, with John, Mohammed, Grim and Billy jumping in on top of her. As Pipsqueak got into the driving seat and started the car an armoured personnel carrier came whistling around the corner of the building and tried to block their exit.

Taking off vertically, Pipsqueak kept to a height of about 20 feet and headed for the main gate. The personnel carrier gave chase but didn't have the speed to keep up. As the car approached the main gate sentries tried to flag them down but Pipsqueak ignored them and shot past without a sideways glance. Out in the open he climbed to 200 feet, turned east, and accelerated to supersonic speed.

"Kidnapping will be added to the charges you face if you don't land immediately and..."

"Shut up!" Mohamed slapped her across the back of the head.

"I am Provost Major Jansen and I order you to..."

"I said, shut up." The Provost Major received another slap, this time across the face.

"Where to boys?" Pipsqueak asked.

"Out into the desert," John suggested.

"Will do." The car banked, then accelerated again.

"I order you to..."

Slap!

"Now then, Provost Major, are you going to be a good girl?" Billy asked as he took his weight off her and climbed over into the front passenger seat.

"You Flyboys are so damned arrogant! Think you're untouchable, do you?" The Provost Major sat up sandwiched between Grim and John.

"Not untouchable. Just, *bad*." Mohamed explained, grinning wolfishly.

"You were the ones that made the move on the Weightless, weren't you?"

"I know that a policeman's work is never done, but don't you think you should give collecting evidence a miss just this once?" Grim asked, handing her a handkerchief. "You have a cut on your face," he explained.

There was a narrow, jagged cut that ran from the corner of her left eye, down her cheek and ended just below her chin. Blood was pouring profusely from the wound but with all the excitement no one had noticed it, least of all the Provost Major herself. After making a few dabs at the cut, Provost Major Jensen looked at the handkerchief and seemed surprised at the volume of blood on it.

Taking the First Aid box from its storage space, Billy threw it back to John. "Better patch her up. We don't want anyone saying that we returned damaged goods."

Before John could open the box, the Provost Major lashed out a backhanded chop aimed at his throat. The blow struck him on the temple, knocking him over into Mohamed's lap. Only the fact that he'd seen it coming and ducked saved him from a more serious injury. Turning her attention to Grim she jabbed her elbow down hard into his groin and he doubled over. Moving in the opposite direction again to strike Mohamed, she was met by a hook from Billy. The blow knocked her over on top of the still prostrate Grim.

"By God, I like a woman with a bit of spunk!" John exclaimed as he sat upright holding the side of his head.

"Oh, my aching nuts! Get her off me." Grim was less enthusiastic.

Reaching across, Mohamed grabbed the concussed Provost Major by the scruff of the neck and yanked her into a sitting position. "Right, you cow! Here are the rules: sit still, you'll be OK; one more move like that and I'll kick your arse right out, understand?"

Pilot

It was debatable whether the Provost Major had recovered enough to make any sense of what was being said to her, but she slowly nodded her head. John picked up the First Aid box and opened it...

"I have some good news and some bad news. Which do you want first?" Pipsqueak said from his driving position.

"Bad news," Billy suggested.

"The bad news is that there are two cars shadowing us, about two kilometres back and at the same height. My guess is that it's the Truckies."

"Let's pretend that we haven't seen them and see what occurs. What's the good news?" Billy said, checking the anti-collision radar.

"The good news is there isn't any more bad news," Pipsqueak laughed.

"Yes there is, kidnapping is a capital offence," the Provost Major threatened.

"Who rattled her cage? A body could think she was trying to scare us," Grim mumbled.

"She hasn't got it yet has she? Look, Major, we're the Air Force's Ace Crew II. Got that? Ace Crew II! Save your breath and tend to your wounds." Mohamed dismissed her.

"They're closing fast. No lights, strap in!" Pipsqueak instructed.

"Both doing about Mach 1.25 - souped-up sports cars." Billy again checked the anti-collision radar, then turned to Pipsqueak. "Right, Nav 3, we'll play blind. Then, when they get real close, fly the pants off them." He strapped himself in.

Closing rapidly, the chasing cars switched on their headlights just as Pipsqueak hit the air brakes and side slipped, losing about 200 feet in height. The cars rocketed past.

"At-a-boy!" Grim cheered.

"These Truckies are such lame ducks. It'll take them so long to turn we might as well stop off for a cup of coffee," John added.

"They're losing speed to turn. It appears that they expect us to run away. Accelerate and take them head to head Pipsqueak, split them. As soon as they pass, go vertical into an Immelmann turn. They'll go vertical as well, probably into a vertical reverse. When they come round, offset head-on pass the one on the right." With his eyes still on the anti-collision radar Billy gently coached.

"Check." Pipsqueak responded, and the car accelerated.

"Are you all crazy? Land this car at once!" The Provost Major shrieked.

"Lady, I hope you're strapped in," Pipsqueak replied calmly, and continued to accelerate. "Passing Mach 1. Are they accelerating?"

"They sure are. Move a couple of degrees to the left... that's it. We're now head-to-head, range about eight kilometres."

"Ten credits says the Truckies break off before the pass," John offered.

"You're on. I have a feeling that's Gümann in one of those driving seats. She won't break off," Billy answered quickly.

"For God's sake! Our closing speeds must be over Mach 3. Please stop this childish behaviour." The Provost Major tried to sound calm.

"Relax, you're in safe hands," Mohamed teased.

"Five kilometres. Still head-to-head. Four... Three... Two, here we go!"

The oncoming headlights in the distance seemed to belong to only one vehicle. They grew alarmingly bright then split into two separate batteries and rocketed past fifty metres on either side. A second later the car was buffeted by shock waves. Pipsqueak pulled up into a steep rolling climb; the occupants were pressed down into their seats.

"Nicely done, Nav 3. When we get to the top, kill the lights," Billy patted Pipsqueak on the shoulder, then turned to John. "You owe me ten credits, my man."

At the apex of the climb Pipsqueak pushed the car over into level flight and switched off the driving and navigational lights. With the exception of the Provost Major, everyone scanned the skies for the other cars.

"There, 10 o'clock low." Mohamed pointed over Pipsqueak's shoulder.

Below them, in the distance, they saw the two sets of headlights. The two cars were about a kilometre apart and heading away from each other, still at high speed.

"Do you believe these Truckies? They must have executed a crossing turn and stayed level... Bounce the one on the left." Billy ordered.

"Boy are they lame, I don't think they know where we are," Pipsqueak chuckled as he pushed the car into a steep dive and headed directly for the car on the left. "Well, hello Mud Movers. You guys really ought to pay attention to your radar, have we got a surprise for you."

At maximum acceleration, keeping the car pointing directly at the target, like a homing missile, Pipsqueak continued the dive. The Provost Major started screaming. At a range of about one kilometre Pipsqueak switch on full headlights and flashed past the unsuspecting car, missing it by only a matter of a few metres.

"Yahoo!" everyone but the Provost Major shouted.

"They're going for another crossing turn. Break hard right, low speed yoyo. Nail the other one!"

Pipsqueak flicked the car over to the right and, at the same time, pulled up into another steep climb. Their new target was also in a tight turn to the right but Pipsqueak's manoeuvre had brought them inside its turn radius, lagging by about 400 metres but closing fast. The other car started tightening its turn, Pipsqueak followed. Suddenly the quarry flicked up into a left turn.

"Watch for the high-G barrel roll!" Billy warned.

"I think I'm going to be sick," Provost Major Jansen moaned.

The other car, as Billy had predicted, climbed into a tight barrel roll, losing speed as it did. Pipsqueak simply closed to within 100 metres and followed the manoeuvre.

"Sit on his tail and ride him," Grim encouraged.

"We've got more players coming apace from the west to join the party. My guess is that it's the local cops," Billy said, looking closely at the radar. "I think we've given the Truckies enough of a fright for one night. Break left and head north."

Pipsqueak complied just as the Provost Major started being violently sick, vomiting all over Billy's back.

"Christ! She's puked up everywhere. Let's hit the dirt and lose the bitch," John complained.

The car lost its forward speed and started falling like a stone, causing the Provost Major to retch even more.

"Most of the cops are going after the Truckies, but two are heading this way. We've got to be quick."

Switching on the ventral lights, Pipsqueak brought them down to a smooth stop in the middle of the desert.

"This is where we say 'goodnight'. Out!" Grim opened his door, hopped out, and dragged the Provost Major after him

John threw the First Aid box after her and Grim jumped back into the car.

6

MISSION

Ace Crew II's 72 hours were nearly up, they had just enough time to get into their flight gear and head for the briefing room. As they walked into the room, they were surprised to find twenty-odd other people sitting around, waiting. Their surprise grew as they took their seats and noticed that Gümann and her crew were among them. There were also Marines, soldiers, and some civilians.

The looks exchanged between the personnel hinted at the possibility of another punch-up. But this unusual gathering of personnel from the different services suggested a joint operation - something special was in the offing. No point in starting to fight until they knew what the mission was. The Base Commander, accompanied by other senior Air Force and Naval Officers, entered, and went up to the podium. The civilians looked around uncertainly. All the military personnel except Ace Crew II stood to attention.

Everybody expected the briefing to start, but the Base Commander and her party simply sat and waited. A few minutes later, two men and a woman wearing the dark uniforms of Supreme Command entered. *All* present stood rigidly to attention. The simple, unadorned black uniforms of the Supreme Command Officers belied the authority vested in them. The two male Supreme Command Officers also sat. The woman remained standing and, as she turned to address them, they saw that she was middle aged and had Asian features.

"Be seated Ladies and Gentlemen. I am Marshal Singh. No doubt you're wondering why you have been summoned here. With a little patience your questions will be answered. But first, a matter of disorderly and disgraceful conduct. Flight Lieutenants Zarcroft and Chang; Flying Officers Ashad and Smith and Pilot Officer Omangan, you are under open arrest. All movements not specifically related to your forthcoming mission are prohibited. Further disciplinary action will be taken on your return."

Gümann and her crew started to snigger. Ignoring them, Marshal Singh took some notes from her breast pocket and started:

"Orders Group. Classification: 'most secret.'

Situation: eight days ago, we lost comms with the Explorer Corps vessel *Arabia*. It was chartered by the NiponEuroMax company with a mission to probe beyond sector 18. Sector 18 is an uncharted region, by exploring it *Arabia* earned the distinction of being the ship that has travelled the farthest distance from Earth. Her last transmission stated that they were picking up bursts of regular repeating EM radiation. This indicated an artificial transmission source and, therefore, the possibility of intelligence."

The Marshal paused so that they could absorb the enormity of what she had said.

"After consultation with the company it was decided that *Arabia* should investigate the transmission's source. However, the unhealthy concern of the Resource Companies for the protection of their potential commercial gains are such that neither the government nor Corps HQ were informed of this until after *Arabia* failed to report on schedule.

Arabia is of the Hilary class with a crew of 357. These ships carry light armaments, heavy protection, and are self-sufficient to the extent that they can remain space-bound for up to fifteen years. The ship's technical details and mission profile are contained in your mission stats which will be issued in due course.

A naval taskforce was dispatched to *Arabia's* last known position. A detailed search of a 38-light-year segment of space, centred on that point, was carried out. Nothing found. The taskforce is now returning to port.

Friendly Forces: all Humans, their settlements, bases, and vessels. Once the naval taskforce has returned to sector 18, there will be no friendly forces within the target area.

Enemy Forces: Unknown.

Other Forces: Unknown."

Again, Marshal Singh pause

"Mission: to find the vessel *Arabia*. Or to establish beyond reasonable doubt her fate and that of her crew.

Operating Objectives: the Air Force Star-fighter *Baddest* with its assigned crew is to deploy in the target area. Once there, the captain and crew have an open brief on the type, direction and duration of the search. After the search has begun the captain is released from all but two of the normal operational procedures and is to conduct the mission at his/her discretion: Procedures for Alien Contact and the General Recall remain unchanged. Earth and her colonies are not to be compromised.

Mission Personnel: Naval Special Combat Team α detachments from the 23rd Squadron Marine Green Beret and the 1st Regiment Special Air Service; Doctor W'Li, heading a team of xenobiologists from Moscow and Brasilia universities; *Baddest* flight crew, Air Force Ace Crew II. Mission commander and captain, Flight Lieutenant Zarcroft, 2ic 1st Lieutenant Gümann. With immediate effect they are promoted to the acting ranks of Wing Commander and Lieutenant Commander, respectively.

Mission Support: prior to deployment *Baddest* is to move to sector 12. Here it will engage in a 48-hour work-up with an unspecified naval battle group, or groups. After work-up proceed to the target area for mission start. There will be no reserve, logistical, or backup support in the target area. Ladies and Gentlemen, you will be on your own. Any questions?"

Gümann stood up. "This is a mission into the unknown, Madam. Wouldn't a full naval taskforce be more appropriate?"

Marshal Singh looked as if she'd expected the question. "Taskforces are, by their very nature, large and unwieldy. This is more of a scouting operation; initiative and independence are what are required. The ability to operate away from Command and Control is definitely the province of the Air Force, isn't it Lieutenant Commander? Any more Questions?"

Gümann sat down and a rather serious looking SAS Officer stood up. "This orders group hasn't illuminated our tasks," he looked around at his colleagues. "Nor the role of the Marines and civilians."

Marshal Singh looked rather pleased. "Captain, this mission is unprecedented, it's an open brief. You're all specialists in your individual fields. By mission start, you and your mission commander should have defined all your tasks."

Pilot

The Army guy sat down, and Marshal Singh waited for further questions. None were forthcoming so she said. "You are dismissed to your individual briefings. Wing Commander Zarcroft, Lieutenant Commander Gümann, Doctor W'Li, Captains Bolt and Ademokun wait here."

Everyone stood and slowly made their way out of the main briefing room, except the named individuals and the three Supreme Command Officers. Marshal Singh sat down and beckoned to those who had remained. "Come to the front"

The five left their positions and went to sit in the first row opposite the podium.

"I take it that I don't have to stress just how important and potentially dangerous this mission is?" Marshal Singh looked relaxed. "We wanted a word because success or failure lies basically in how you five interrelate. You're all leaders of successful but highly individualistic teams; teams which are used to operating to their own sets of rules. Your mission is a journey into the unknown. In bringing you together we've attempted to furnish this mission with a vast range of knowledge and skills. Yet we see the possibility of this developing into the 'prima donna syndrome'. It's down to you to forge an effective team."

Gümann raised her hand. "I know of Doctor W'Li by reputation, of course, and take it as read that the Marine and Army contingents are up to speed. As this mission is of such vital importance, why isn't the Air Force's Ace Crew I here?"

Marshal Singh smiled and one of the male Supreme Command Officers patiently said, "A good place to start would be to put away the petty inter-service rivalries."

"Yes, Sir," Gümann took the rebuke.

Doctor W'Li held up her hand. "My understanding is that we civilians have been seconded into this, a purely military venture. What status do we have? Where do we stand in the order of things?"

"Doctor, in this mission there is only one rule and that is, there are no rules. We leave you to sort that out amongst yourselves," Marshal Singh answered.

Then Billy spoke. "*Baddest* is only equipped to carry a crew of five..."

"Your ship is being refitted as we speak, Wing Commander." Marshal Singh cut him off.

"When do we leave, Ma'am?" the Marine Captain asked.

"Takeoff in two hours fifteen minutes, Captain Ademokun," Marshal Singh said checking her watch.

Billy smiled; Marshal Singh was ex-Air Force. Navy would say, 'liftoff'.

"I really must protest! We can't possibly leave today. We were called here at short notice; we had no idea what this was about. There are arrangements to be made and affairs to settle. We're not the military. We can't go gallivanting off at the drop of a hat!" Doctor W'Li was on her feet.

"Of course, we can't order you or your team to go, Doctor. But now that you know 'what this is all about', which do you think is more important, your affairs or the security of Earth and its colonies?" the third Supreme Command Officer inquired quietly.

W'Li huffily sat back down. "Will we have the opportunity to make personal calls?"

"Certainly. But I must remind you, this mission is secret." Marshal Singh smiled.

The five looked at each other but there were no further questions or comments. Marshal Singh, having satisfied herself that no one had anything more to say, became brisk. "To your individual briefings then. Wing Commander Zarcroft and Lieutenant Commander Gümann you will have a joint briefing." They all stood. "One more thing.... good luck." She dismissed them.

***

Billy and Eva Gümann sat at the dual console intelligence computer as it fed them the last of their mission stats. Neither of them was happy with the situation, but they had to cooperate. She wasn't used to the Air Force InfoSys, so he couldn't advance the programme until she'd grasped the information. The mission stats made it clear that Eva and her crew were there as a second flight crew on *Baddest*. Billy assumed that there were similar pairings with the rest of his crew. As the stats wound down, he tried not to let himself get carried away with excitement. Of all the mission briefings that he'd been given this one had the least constraints - no parameters of operation. It was just as Marshal Singh had said, an open brief. This was freedom of action on a grand scale. The downside was that the mission had to be shared with Truckies and, worse still, civilians.

The computer spat out their identification disks and flight logs, signalling the end of the briefing. Turning to the gamine, redheaded Naval Officer, Billy asked, "Are you right-handed or left-handed?"

Sullenly Eva raised her left hand without answering.

"We're about to get the coded information for the mission, to feed into *Baddest*, this starts her up. Your ships don't have that facility but without it ours won't fly. There are two sets of data, I'll have one and you'll have the backup. Have you ever heard of Mission Gloves?"

She shook her head.

"You see that cavity to the left of the console? Keeping your fingers straight and apart, put your right hand in it." He put his left hand into a similar cavity on his side if the console, while Eva gingerly did as he'd instructed. "What will happen now is that a thin polly-metallic film will form on your hand. It'll make your hand look a bit like a cyborg's. Don't worry, you'll still have some movement in it. All the codes are imprinted in the metal. OK, you can take it out now."

They withdrew their hands. Eva looked closely at the shiny film completely covering her hand to just past her wrist, then she slowly clenched and unclenched her fists.

"Idiot proof. The only way to get that off is to stick it back in there or plug it into *Baddest's* master NavComp when we juice the bird up."

"What next... Sir?" Eva sounded as if she was choking on the words.

"We'll get the rest of the crew and have an informal pre-flight chinwag. But, first, I think we'd better get a few things straight..."

"You want to remind me that *you* are mission commander, and that I'd better do what you say?" She sounded full of resentment.

"No, I wasn't going to do that. That goes without saying." He grinned at her. "I was going to suggest that if you lost that chip off your shoulder, we could present a united front. The civvies must be shitting themselves, they're gonna be a problem."

"Are we having an off the record chat, Sir?" she said stiffly.

"If you like."

She turned and stared into his eyes. "Off the record, Sir, I think you Air Force crews are garbage. I have only one life and I'm not ready to start trusting you with it."

"Anything else you want to get off your chest?"

"That's it for the moment, Sir."

"Good. I'd just like to say that I have an opinion about Navy flyers, but I'm prepared to be proven wrong. And stop calling me Sir. I'm sure you know we don't go in for that kind of bullshit."

Pilot

"That's just the sort of slapdash, happy-go-lucky attitude I mean, *Sir*," she said forcefully.

"Eva, Old Girl, this is an Air Force mission. *Baddest* is an Air Force ship. We'll do it the Air Force way - so, lighten up." Billy smiled.

"Is it your intention that this mission be conducted on a first-name basis?" She was now looking stubborn.

Leaning over, Billy stared into her angular face. "Sure do. That's the only way to play."

In that case, Sir. May I make my first official request as deputy mission commander? This is a military operation. It should be conducted as such. Rank should be the term of address."

Billy laughed. "If we've already fallen out over something as trivial as this it's going to be one hell of a mission. Request noted and I hope you fly as hard as you talk."

"That's just the point, Sir, it's not trivial. It's the only basis on which an efficient crew can be built."

Billy stood and picked up his flight bag. "Let me put it this way: my first name is William. Most folks call me Billy. I like being called Billy, especially by people with whom I'll be confined for an unspecified length of time. Do we understand each other?"

"Yes, *Billy*." She also stood up and, again, looked at her right hand.

Billy led her out into the tunnel heading back towards the main briefing room. "I need to appoint a 3ic, any thoughts?" he asked as they walked.

"What is the point in asking for my opinion when all you do is ignore it?" Billy didn't rise to the bait, so she continued. "Your 2ic was the Nav. 1 and mine was the 2nd Pilot. Either could be 3ic."

"Any other contenders?"

Eva realised that she was being tested. "Your 2nd pilot?"

"From a team morale point of view, I think the 3ic should be someone not in the flight crew."

She wondered why she'd failed to recognise something so obvious. "In that case it has to be either Captain Ademokun or Captain Bolt."

"Which one?"

She resented being pushed by him but considered her answer carefully. The personnel records contained in the mission stats showed Bolt to be a tough, resourceful, and outstanding Army Officer. But Ademokun, though junior to him, had a greater range of experience and, being a Marine, had spent more time onboard ships, clocking up space hours. "Captain Ademokun."

"You mean, Erick?" he teased.

She gave him a serious look but didn't speak.

"Agreed. Erick is 3ic. See, we can agree on something," he laughed.

Eva reminded herself that she had been runner-up to the then Midshipman Zarcroft. The Cadet Officer who won the coveted ten-year Sword of Honour at the Naval Flight Academy. Immediately after graduating Midshipman Zarcroft promptly resigned his naval commission and joined the Air Force. At the time it was said that he only did it to spite his parents and rumour had it that the Air Force gave him a particularly hard time and still put him through their full Officer and pilot training courses despite is naval qualifications. Eva had heard that he'd walked off with the Air Force's ten-year Sword of Honour as well.

Billy stopped outside the automatic doors to the main briefing room. "Here we are. Before we go in... Big, relaxed, confident smile. And back me up. If you disagree with anything, save it till we're alone, OK?"

"Of course, My Captain," she answered sarcastically.

As they entered, they noted that the crew were all spread out, sitting in separate groups. The civilians, who were now in flying suits, were looking anxious. The Navy, Marine and Army personnel started to stand. Billy waved them to stay sitting and then, with Gümann at his side, went to the front.

"Come on, Crew, gather round." He waited until his unusually large crew had repositioned themselves then continued. "According to the rule book we should now all introduce ourselves and tell our new crew mates a bit about ourselves. However, I want to give all that a miss until we're onboard ship and heading away from the solar system. Introductions should be done when we've settled into our new accommodations. Questions?"

The army Officer raised his hand and asked. "Are you going to give us our final orders group now, Sir?"

"No. You all have your preliminary orders. Orders group when we're onboard *Baddest*. By then we should all be over the initial shock. By the way, my name is Billy."

Looking concerned, Doctor W'Li raised her hand. "Surely you should tell us what you expect at the start of the mission."

"I'll make a couple of quick points. The mission doesn't start until *Baddest* is at jumping off point. Secondly, we've all clocked up space hours. But until everyone has a working knowledge of the ship it's pointless making any detailed plans. And finally, on a mission such as this, I don't have any expectations." Billy grinned.

One of the Naval flyers jumped up. "All spaceship designs follow a general principal. We're all, to some extent, familiar with those principals, Sir."

Billy, and the rest of Ace Crew II, smiled.

"That remains to be seen, and the man did point out that his name is Billy," Mohamed said with aristocratic charm.

"Any more questions?" Billy asked.

"What's happened to your hand?" Another of the naval flyers addressed Eva.

"It's called a Flight Glove. It contains the flight programmes of the ship; one of those quaint Air Force customs. It can't be forgotten, misplaced, or lost because you can't get it off your hand. It's idiot proof!" she answered derisively.

Billy took it in good spirit. "You're all in flying suits. I take it that all personal business has been concluded and that an inventory of all your equipment has been taken and dispatched for loading?"

Nobody responded.

"Fine. We're about to embark for takeoff; the faces you see around you are the only ones you'll see for some time. No one will come to wave us goodbye. This is another 'quaint' Air Force custom. I think I should also warn you that after takeoff our journey is likely to become a touch fraught. Once we broadcast our call sign on open channels, the Navy will probably come along and try to shoot at us." Smiling, Billy paused to let this sink in. "However, because our pursuers will only be the Navy's finest, we'll be in no real danger."

A mixture of expressions passed over the faces of his audience. Most thought that he was joking. In the end it was Eva who spoke. "Sir, might I suggest that we have Supreme Command alert Naval C. in C. to the fact that there will be naval personnel on board. That will assure us of clear passage," she said reasonably.

"Why?" Billy pretended to be puzzled.

"You won't be so lucky this time," Eva answered angrily.

"We'll see. Let's go."

Pilot

Some of the crew started to get up.

"With all due respect, Sir, this is not a game. Those ships will be armed." Eva stuck to her guns.

"Now, now Dear, not in front of the children," Billy gently admonished and Eva clamped her mouth shut.

Most of the crew didn't fully understand what the argument was about, so they took up their flight bags and got ready to leave. Billy led his nineteen strong crew out of the briefing room on the long trek to the lifts. Eva hung back, bringing up the rear. She and the other naval flyers started a hushed discussion. They were the only ones that spoke as the group moved along. At the lifts, Grim waited for the whole crew all to squeeze in then pushed the button to take them up to the hangers. As soon as the doors closed Eva started again.

"There are twelve ships on Quick Reaction Alert, just waiting."

"Only twelve?" John giggled.

There was silence for the remainder of the lift's ascent. When the doors opened, Eva was the first to get out. She stepped to the side and waited for Billy to come out. Grabbing his arm, she led him a short distance away from the rest.

"Right, Sir, we're alone. I want to get this sorted now. What's your fucking game?"

"There's method in my madness. Kindly release my arm," he joked with her.

She let go of him. "Would you care to share this *method* with me?"

On the one hand, Billy could see that his new 2ic was *the* archetypical, fiery, 5' 10" redhead. On the other, she was so *stiff!* "If I must. It's all a question of trust and respect. Trust: you have to learn to trust me. Respect: unless *Man Vaughn's* crew respects *Baddest's* crew this mission is doomed. We can achieve both conditions in very short order. All you have to do is to sit back, relax, and watch," he answered playfully.

"Trust, like anything worth having, has to be earned. So far you aren't even close..."

"As I said, 'sit back, relax, and watch'." Turning, he and walked away from her.

The Air Force Officers had taken the rest of the crew to *Katrina*. Grim was inside and calling them in one at a time. Mohamed was walking around the shuttle doing the external checks. Billy went to join him and together they completed the remainder of the checks. On entering the shuttle Billy noted that the refitting necessary to accommodate the new crew had moved the bulkhead back several metres. Even so, it was a tight squeeze - everyone except the flight crew were fully suited and strapped in. Good old Grim had seated Eva and her 2nd pilot nearest the flight deck.

"I can't believe that we're being sent into space for an indeterminate length of time in such cramped conditions," one of the civilians grumbled.

"Where do we plug these mission gloves in?" Eva asked impatiently.

The Air Force crew looked at each other and started to laugh. "That'll come later," Mohamed answered.

"Whose turn?" Billy addressed the flight crew.

"It's John's," Pipsqueak and Grim answered, simultaneously.

"Over to you, Nav. 2." Pushing John towards the 1st pilot's acceleration couch, Billy went to sit in the 2nd navigator's seat.

The flight crew took their positions and finished suiting up. They plugged in their umbilicals, strapped themselves down and commenced the start-up procedure. The remainder of the crew looked on with interest. Most, because this was their first experience of a flight deck in operation; the naval flyers out of professional curiosity.

"Pre-start checks complete," Mohamed said, and John nodded.

"Good. Patch comms through to the rest of the crew," Billy instructed. "Hello Air Traffic Control, this is X-Ray Tango One Five, bay sixty-seven. Ready to start up."

"*Roger, X-Ray Tango One Five. Start when ready.*"

"I recognise that voice. Is that my favourite scopie?" Billy laughed.

"*Roger, One Five, and ready to party.*"

"Thanks for bringing us in downside. Today, I'd like you to not only take us out but to also give the Truckies an object lesson in flying, OK?"

"*It's a done deal, One Five,*" the controller laughed.

"Kick her over," Billy ordered.

Without any fuss, the ship started to hum. The flight crew examined their screens.

"All systems checked," Mohamed said, and John gave the thumbs up.

"Tower, X-Ray Tango One Five ready to taxi," Billy transmitted.

"*Roger. The trace lines are lit. Go out into the sunshine.*"

The ship lifted and slowly started to move forward. Billy turned to his second in command. "Eva, Team α, there's *Man Vaughn.* Say goodbye."

Before Eva could respond, Doctor W'Li asked a question. "Captain, are we to understand that, once we are airborne, naval ships might chase us?" This was obviously something that had been troubling her for some time.

"No, Doctor, they won't chase us, they'll try to shoot us down. And please, don't call me Captain."

W'Li looked at her fellow civilians in stunned silence, then the flight crew started to titter. The ship continued its long taxi, following the trace lines.

"My mission brief stated that Flying Officer Smith is the second navigator. Is that correct, Billy?" W'Li was still puzzling something it out.

"That is correct."

"But that's him sitting in a pilot's seat, isn't it?"

"Yes."

"And he's the one driving the ship?" W'Li's analytical mind was following a logical path.

"One *flies* a spaceship, Doctor. Yes, he's flying the ship. It's another 'quaint' Air Force custom."

"Stop this ship at once! Special Combat Team α, wants off!" Eva started unstrapping, the rest of the naval flyers followed her lead.

"Ye of little faith," Billy said quietly.

Eva was on her feet, striding over towards Billy. "I'm not joking. Stop the ship!"

"You'd think that naval types would know better than to stand up in a ship just as it's about to takeoff, wouldn't you?" John asked conversationally.

"X-Ray Tango One Five, on the runway," Billy transmitted.

Eva looked over Mohammed's shoulder to see that they were out of the hangers and on the airfield. She turned and dived into her acceleration couch.

"*Roger, One Five. There are no Truckies about but there is a lot of coded stuff on their Fighter Control frequencies. I'll take you east, out over the Bering Sea, then due south. Friendlies from the Marquess Isles are ready to ride shotgun. You should achieve orbit by the time you reach the Pole, over.*"

"Roger, tower, east then south." Without turning Billy added over the internal comms, "Right folks, this is where the party begins." Then he checked to see if Eva and her team were strapped in. "X-Ray Tango One Five, ready for takeoff."

"*X-Ray Tango One Five, roll.*"

"One Five, rolling... Airborne."

Pilot

"*Turn left, zero nine seven, accelerate to March 2 and climb to flight level three five.*"

John gently turned the ship and started a shallow climb.

"Left, zero nine seven, March 2 to flight level three five," Billy confirmed.

"*One Five, the party is on! We have full sector scrambles out of the east from Alaska, Portland, and Hawaii. It's a mixed bag of point defence spaceships and aircraft.*"

"Roger." Billy folded his hands and looked back at the passengers. "That's more than twelve, more like sixty, I'd say."

"*One Five, maintain heading, climb to flight level six zero.*"

"Roger, six zero, where's the trade?"

"*The ships are going out atmosphere. Aircraft are coming head to head. They should be on your screen any time now.*"

"I hope so. This is getting boring... At last. We have them, Oymyakon control."

"*Break right, one seven seven. Go to Mach 5 point 5.*"

"Right one seven seven, to 5 point 5."

John pulled a gut-wrenching right turn pressing them into their seats as he accelerated.

"OK, John. Six birds, 11 o'clock coming round to 12, five thousand kilometres, level. They're trying to cut us off. Do you have them?" Pipsqueak asked from his position.

John checked his Head-Up Display. "Got them."

"Turn on a burner and beat them to it. They'll be lost in a tail chase," Billy suggested.

"*Christ! Where did they come from?! Roll out, one five five. Eight, no!... Twelve, repeat twelve ships climbing in your six, two thousand kilometres, closing at Mach 19. Accelerate!*"

"Don't! Continue turn and hit the air brakes on my command. Grim, switch on the guns." Billy was unruffled. "OK Oymyakon control, we have it."

"Cannons armed."

"There are Special Combat Teams β, γ, δ and ε. In fact, there are eight more. You see, groups of thirteen, that's a quaint naval custom." Eva's voice was icily calm.

Billy looked over to her. "I would never have guessed. Truckies are such dickheads." He turned back to his screen. "At Mach 19 they've got their shields up; are in close formation and can't see shit. Stay on it, John... Stand by... Now!"

Everyone was suddenly flung violently forward. The straps of their acceleration couches bit hard into their stomachs, thighs, and shoulders as the ship abruptly decelerated. There were screams from some who weren't expecting it.

"Count them past boys, then lock on as they fly by." Billy said lazily.

They all became aware of the rising bleeping sound of the acquisition radar.

"There goes number twelve. We have multiple lock-on," John sounded pleased with himself.

"OK, accelerate hard and climb. Follow them. If they split, go with the formation that climbs and, or turns south." The crew were again pressed back into their acceleration couches. "Oymyakon control... The boys just whistled by without even saying hello but they're kindly clearing a path for us." Billy was laughing.

"*Roger, that's correct. They're decelerating, but they just blew a hole right through the formation trying to head you off. Three more formations closing from the east, but they don't look like they have the legs, your six is clear, over.*"

"Roger."

"When we're within range, can I give the trailing two a squirt?" Mohammed gleefully turned to Billy.

"We didn't crank-up the guns just for fun, did we?" Billy answered, with equal glee. "Come on John, close up.

"Three thousand kilometres dead ahead, we're closing. They've slowed to Mach 11 and are still going too fast for tight manoeuvres," Grim said, continuing to look at his screen.

The acquisition radar was sounding a continuous tone.

"Surely you're not going to fire on the Navy ships!" Somebody protested over the comms.

"We most certainly are. Those Torpedo Boats would've fired their laser cannons at us if they'd got the chance. But we are such good sports that we'll only fire high explosive shells. That won't hurt them, but it sure will make the point." Pipsqueak answered whoever it was.

"One thousand kilometres." Grim continued the countdown.

"Keep closing, John... Oymyakon control, X-Ray Tango One Five. In pre-orbit flight, Mach 21 point 3 and accelerating, passing flight level nine five. Vector for Space Con 4 please."

"*Wait, One Five... Space Con 4, vector 0009/5371/1213. Don't forget the point defence ships, over.*"

"Five hundred kilometres. They'll start to turn soon," Mohamed reported.

"0009/5371/1213, thank you scopie, we won't. Give our regards to the Flyboys from the Marquess Isles, we owe them one. X-Ray Tango One Five, out. OK, listen up. As soon as we blast the Torpedo Boats; John, head for Space Con 4 at trans-light, Pipsqueak..."

"You may evade the rocket ships, but you'll never get away from the N°1 Special Combat Squadron," Eva said defiantly.

"...Pipsqueak, once we're lined up, you and I will programme the super-light jump. Mohamed, keep your eyes peeled for more Truckies; they know we're after the Weightless."

"Check! Thirty kilometres; they're turning," Mohamed answered.

"What's this about a super-light jump?" Eva demanded.

"It's all yours Grim," Billy said.

"In my sights," Grim chortled.

Katrina shuddered once, then a few seconds later she shuddered again.

"Yahoo!" Grim and John shouted in unison.

"Two clean hits! I bet those boys shat themselves." Mohamed shouted.

"Go for the Weightless!" Billy turned back to his screen and started to work furiously.

"Are you planning to make a super-light jump?!" Eva asked again, in alarm.

"You catch on quick," Billy replied without looking up.

"They've been waiting for us. Half the Navy must be up here," Mohamed warned.

"Are we on track?" Billy asked.

"Yep. We'll miss it by a whisker," John confirmed.

"All screens, on!"

Briefly, through the cockpit window, they saw the reflected light from the Weightless, Space Con 4. Then, in an instant, it flashed by.

"Feeding jump co-ordinates... Super-light, go!"

The field of view, the stars against the background of darkness, wavered as the crew's visions blurred, then they all felt a momentary, nauseating dizziness. Suddenly, in sharp focus, the whole sky was filled with a bright, swirling greyish yellow mass. All except the flight crew recoiled in shock.

"Welcome to Saturn, folks, just check out those rings. John, get us down into the atmosphere before they pick us up."

There was a host of expletives, uttered by various members of the crew.

Still in a daze, one of the naval flyers finally asked. "Are you trying to tell us that we've just made a super-light jump from inside Earth's gravitational-well, into Saturn's?"

Billy turned to Eva. "I'd like to see your Special Combat Squadron follow that."

Pilot

"I just don't believe it." Eva was amazed. As far as she was aware, their recent super-light jump was theoretically impossible

"As I said: sit back, relax, and watch" Billy laughed.

All the Flyboys spontaneously burst into song.

"Goose 'em on the way in,

Goose 'em on the way out,

Goose 'em, goose 'em,

That's what it's all about."

"Locked on to homing beacon; range twenty-seven thousand kilometres," John announced.

"OK, sit tight folks, this is going to be a bit bumpy," Grim cautioned.

The ship picked up speed and dived towards Saturn's frigid atmosphere.

7

BADDEST

Even with the stabilisers working at their maximum, *Katrina* was being tossed about by the 1200 kilometre per hour winds. Saturn's atmosphere was an extremely dense and violent place. For most of the crew this continuous buffeting was a new experience. The civilians, in particular, began to suffer from severe airsickness. *Katrina* was kitted out for an Air Force crew. Anti-airsickness drugs and sickness bags weren't in her inventory. The overcrowded flight deck gradually came to reflect this, as more and more of the strapped-in crew were sick over themselves. Although the sight and smell were quite awful neither the Air Force nor the naval flyers appeared to be affected by this. Looking around at the remainder of her disheveled crew mates, one of the naval flyers finally asked, "Just what, exactly, are we doing inside Saturn's atmosphere, Sir?"

"It's 'Billy'. We're going to RV with a ship, Mirandolina."

"There was nothing about another ship in the briefings," Eva commented.

"As Cynthia said, they'd have to have pretty sick minds to send us out in such cramped conditions; we're going to *Baddest*." Billy said, then turned and smiled at Doctor W'Li. "You don't mind me calling you Cynthia, do you Doctor?"

Cynthia shook her head and made a vain attempt to smile back but was overcome by another bout of vomiting.

"You mean that this isn't *Baddest*?!" Eva demanded.

"He means that the Naval Special Combat Squadron just got burned by an Air Force shuttle," Mohamed answered and the Flyboys started to laugh.

"OK crew, I can see that some of you are in discomfort. Not to worry, this shouldn't last too long. We're tracking a homing beacon and are about five minutes away from RVing. Then we'll be onboard a proper spaceship. If you can take your minds off your individual situations for a moment, I'll explain what's happening," Billy announced over the intercom.

"*Baddest* is a rather special ship, which is probably why it's being sent on this mission. We park it deep inside Saturn's atmosphere to keep it away from prying eyes. Once onboard we'll go directly to the flight deck where you'll be given a general briefing on the ship. After the pre-flight checks are completed, we'll spend about a day familiarising and acclimatising. After that we'll take a leisurely flight to the jump-off point, using the time to gently work up. Any questions?"

"What is so special about *Baddest*?" another of the naval flyers asked.

"Well, Wendy, it's one of a pair of ships that are probably the most effective instruments of destruction ever built. Single paced, and single purpose, optimised for arse kicking."

Pilot

"I must confess that I'm no expert, but it's my understanding that the Navy's new *Hector* class battle cruiser is the most potent spaceship, Sir." Erick, the Marine Captain, sprang to the defence of the Navy.

"I thought the Air Force preferred agility over firepower?" Cynthia overcame her illness to join the debate.

Billy raised his hand to stop further comment. "Any questions about the ship will be answered in the briefing. Any other questions?"

"Due to the urgency of this mission, shouldn't we jump off as soon as possible, Billy?" Alfred, one of the civilians, asked.

"We'll only jump off when we're combat capable. We won't achieve that until everyone has a working knowledge of the ship." Turning to one of the naval flyers, Billy asked, "By the way, Anne, do you have a middle name?"

Sub Lieutenant Anne Du Maurier, *Man Vaughn's* Communications Officer, stared suspiciously at Billy before answering, "Yes. My middle name is Ruth. Why do you ask?"

"I'd like you and everyone else to use that name instead. You'll understand why, later."

"I'd like to know now, Captain," Eva interjected frostily.

"And you'll understand why, later," Billy brushed aside Eva's demand. "Any other questions?"

"How far are we from docking?" a female Marine asked between deep breaths.

"We're there," Mohamed said, trying not to laugh.

Everyone turned to look out of the cockpit but all there was to see was a mass of dark swirling clouds. For a moment there was a bright light above the cockpit then they were hovering inside a small docking bay.

"Put it in the cradle, John," Billy ordered.

"This doesn't look that special to me," Eva muttered.

Billy ignored her. "Hello Service Crew, this is X-Ray Tango One Five, the boys are home, over."

"*Hi One Five. Refit complete; we're just house sitting. Ready to hand over when you are.*"

"Roger. Have a small job for you. *Katrina* needs some of the wash-and-brushup treatment."

"*This wouldn't have anything to do with why we had to change the accommodations from a five to a twenty-six berth, would it?*"

"Afraid so, but it's only a ten-minute job."

"*Ten minutes, you say. Are we talking minor or major puking?*"

"Major."

"*Civilians or Grunts?*"

"A mixed bag, I'm sorry to say."

"*Not to worry. Be there in five.*"

Looking at Grim, Billy said apologetically, "I didn't have the heart to break it to him. Anyway, you want to debus the crew and get their kit? Mohammed and I will shut down."

Grim unstrapped himself, then stood to address the new members of the crew. "OK, unstrap yourselves. Those of you with soiled flight suits strip and leave them here, we'll kit you out on the flight deck. Debus, let's go!" Cynthia W'Li looked as if she was about to protest. Then she appeared to remember that they were on a spaceship, being naked in front of all these men meant nothing.

The naval flyers sprang into action, the others were more lethargic. Billy signalled to Eva that she should remain. As he and Mohammed took her through the shutdown procedure a helmeted head popped in through the hatch.

"I don't know what the hell the Air Force is coming to. I never thought I'd live to see the day when they put bloody Truckies on our ships."

"Easy Chief. This is a humdinger of a mission," Mohammed answered at his most disarming, then stood. "She's all yours."

The remainder of the decontamination-suited body followed its head into the ship. "This'll take about half an hour. We'll give you a call when we're ready to decouple."

"OK, Chief," Billy replied then led Mohammed and Eva out of *Katrina*.

A stark naked but businesslike Cynthia W'Li walked up to them. "Cap... Billy, I know that this is a military expedition, but I've done some rough calculations on the risk factors involved in making that super-light jump. My conclusions are that they were unacceptably high," she said in her Central Pacific accent.

Billy smiled. "As they say, Doctor, any jump that you can walk away from is a good one. But your concerns are noted."

"Where are the rest of the crew?" Eva asked, looking around. Apart from the twenty odd service crew gathered around *Katrina*, there was only Cynthia, Billy, and Mohamed in sight.

"On their way to the cockpit, I guess. We'll have to wait for the monorail to come back," Mohamed answered.

"Monorail?" Eva asked suspiciously.

"It's a bit of a trek to the cockpit from here. We use a monorail to get around." Billy answered as he and Mohamed got their kit from the pods.

"How big is this ship?" Eva looked around the small hanger again.

"Nose to tail? About fifty-three and a half miles."

"What?" exclaimed Cynthia.

"Rubbish! That's ten times the size of a battle cruiser!" Eva barked.

Billy and Mohamed looked at each other, grinning. "It's more like twenty-five times," Mohamed replied.

"What is the tonnage of the ship then?" Eva demanded.

"Look, folks, all that will come out in the briefing."

Cynthia wasn't satisfied. "I know that military personnel take pride in their units and equipment. But to make such ridiculous and..."

"Three hundred million tonnes," Billy answered tiredly, and started off towards the exit.

Cynthia almost had to run to keep up with him, her small breasts bouncing in rhythm. "See here, Captain. That would make this the largest machine ever built. I suppose it's theoretically possible, but hardly probable."

"Cynthia, let's save the questions for the briefing, shall we?" Billy stepped through the exit door and into a long, low ceilinged, dimly lit rectangular room. A metre-wide groove ran along the floor and disappeared into a tunnel at the opposite end. He and Mohamed dropped their flight bags against the wall and sat on them. Eva and Cynthia stood staring at the monorail track uncertainly.

"What's the other ship called?" Eva asked eventually.

"*The Beast*. That's Ace Crew I." Billy said without looking up.

"How long will we have to wait, Billy? I'm getting cold." Cynthia hugged herself and shivered.

"Not long." Billy replied, then said to no one in particular. "Anne, increase temperature in rail port three, and along route three, to thirty-five-degree C."

Immediately, warm air began to filter into the room.

"Come," Mohamed said in his precisely clipped accent, and beckoned to Eva and Cynthia. "Stand against the wall."

Pilot

As they walked over to him, a low glide monorail flew into the port. Both women jumped as the silent missile narrowly missed them and came to an abrupt stop. Together, they turned to Mohamed, as if to protest at the lateness of his warning. Then both seemed to realise that this was just another of the Flyboy's pranks. Neither wanted to give him the satisfaction of a reaction.

Billy and Mohamed got up and threw their flight bags into the roofless, doorless, twenty-seater monorail car, then vaulted in; Billy offered his hand to Eva. She ignored the gesture and jumped in after him. Cynthia chose to be more ladylike, accepting Mohamed's offer of assistance. As she got in, she asked, "If the crew is normally five, why such a large capacity monorail?"

"To get the service crew around. We'll have to strap in, this thing is a bit quick." Mohamed answered.

Billy checked to see that both women were strapped in. "Anne, destination: cockpit. Go."

***

The boys were busy with the pre-flight checks, so Billy climbed onto the central console and faced the remainder of his crew. Apart from the naval flyers, whose positions mirrored the flight crew's, the other crew members sat in rows of forward-facing acceleration couches. The rearmost six couches were unoccupied. His new crew looked up at him expectantly, so he gave them a friendly smile.

"Welcome aboard *Baddest*, folks. Shortly you will be given a general briefing about the ship. Then we'll kit you out with your combat flight suits. But first, I need to explain a bit about Air Force ship design philosophy. No doubt you all now realise that this is a very large ship. On board any other Space Service ship you would expect to have cabins, mess halls, galleys, places of recreation, and the like. However, the first principle of Air Force ship design is 'no dead space'. Ladies and Gentlemen, you're sitting in your cabins, mess halls and galleys."

He gave them some time to absorb his statement. "Unlike some, an Air Force ship is a machine of war, not a pleasure cruiser. The cockpit you see around you is virtually all the living space there is. Everything you need will be supplied by your acceleration couches. As you can see, they're not standard design. We affectionately refer to them as 'wombs'. Each womb will be customised to its occupant. In order to form the ideal bond, a minor surgical operation is necessary. This will be performed when we fit your flight suits." To preempt protests or questions, Billy held up a hand.

"Privacy is a civilian word. If you absolutely must, you may place an opaque electrostatic screen around your womb. On *Baddest* you will find the accommodation somewhat basic, but very efficient. This lack of privacy and the limited freedom of movement requires patience, tolerance and, most of all, a relaxed atmosphere. This partially explains why the Air Force isn't as 'stiff' as some we could mention. Any questions?"

A soldier, Warrant Officer Sufra Jalan, shot to her feet. "Who will perform the operations... Billy?"

"We will. It's quite simple, nothing to worry about."

Pensively the lean, muscular soldier sat back down. Although there must have been many other questions, no one seemed prepared to be the first to ask one. Billy continued. "Now I would like you all, in turn, to stand and state your full names, then the name you wish to be called by your crew mates. That's except for you Ruth, you *must* use that name.

This is the registration into the ship's primary computer." Nodding to Eva, he indicated that she should start, then jumped off the console.

With Eva getting the registration underway, Billy slid into the 1st Pilot's womb. He, and the flight crew, would be busy for the next three hours or so with the total systems pre-flight checks. About ten minutes later Eva tapped him on the shoulder.

"The idiotic introductions to your primary computer are over. What next, Sir?"

Without looking up Billy said. "The briefing, I think. It's a standard programme." He stood and turned to face the crew, then pointed to a point in midair.

"The briefing is about to start. A hologram will appear there." He sat down again and the lights in the cockpit dimmed.

'Hello, I'm Anne, the ship's primary computer. Currently I am operating in a semi-activated mode. I will be fully activated when the mission stats are programmed. Throughout this sortie any communication directed to me should be preceded by the executive word "Anne". Further executive words are unnecessary as I can differentiate between an interrogative or instructive intonation. If you wish to talk about me in the third person use the term "Primary Computer" or "C1".'

All the crew looked around in surprise as the natural sounding, husky female voice spoke as if the owner was next to them.

'This is the AF 8000 Star Fighter, *Baddest*.'

Over their heads appeared a five-metre long hologram of a harpoon-shaped ship. The hologram slowly rotated in the horizontal plane, then rolled along its axis to show all aspects of the ship's exterior. Most noticeable, along its clean lines, were the four main engines with their accompanying super-light drives. Even the inexperienced civilians could plainly see that this was an elegant and extremely powerful ship. It was no wonder that the Air Force hid it in Saturn's atmosphere. If the civilian population knew about the ship, and the astronomical costs of building it, there would have been large scale protests; possibly leading to the resignation of the government.

'The AF 8000 is eighty-five kilometres long with a dry mass of 181 million tonnes - combat mass, 318 million tonnes. Standard weapon provision: all contemporary munitions and equal momentum tractor beams. Supplementary armaments for this sortie: six internal bays and automated service support for Naval Type 23-7 Dart interceptors. Maximum tactical combat duration in present configuration: eleven years. Sortie range, inter-galaxy: unlimited. First stage protection is provided by tri-lattice force fields.'

An elliptical opaque shell formed around the hologram of the ship. This was enveloped by a second shell which was, in turn, covered by a third; each shell representing the force fields that, in reality, were invisible. The naval flyers, in particular, took note of that. Their most powerful battle cruisers, the *Hector* Class, had only a single force field.

'With the exception of the main engines and super-light drives, all other masses, down to atomic levels, are contained within an inertialess envelope. Acceleration from rest to super-light: twenty-one seconds. Run distance: five light minutes. Turn radius at trans-light speed: twelve light minutes. In performance terms, *Baddest* is superagile. For this sortie, 42 percent of the ship's mass is armaments and protection, 29 percent fuel, 28 percent engines. The remaining 1 percent is devoted to human environment support systems, communications, and me.' On the hologram the ship's shell was stripped away to highlight each area as Anne spoke.

"Anne. How can a ship this size only carry a crew of five when the nearest naval equivalent has a crew of thousands?" Marandolina, one of the naval flyers, asked with indignation.

'Only in size does the AF 800 differ from other Air Force fighters. Air Force ships have automated control of all non-tactical functions, Mirandolina...'

Everyone waited for Anne to continue. But Marandolina's question had interrupted the programme. Cynthia W'Li was the first to realise this. "Anne, continue the briefing."

Pilot

'The human environment is the cockpit area. It is cocooned within an independent quantum field and is designed on the "maximum survivability" principle. Should *Baddest* sustain damage greater than Category Eight the cockpit is decoupled from the remainder of the ship. It becomes, in effect, an independent spacecraft with its own super-light drive, but limited range. This craft is known as the Secondary Propulsion Unit (SPU).' The hologram changed to show a tiny bullet-shaped section separating from the front of the ship.

'At trans and super-light speeds decoupling is hazardous and uncomfortable. As the SPU clears the inertialess envelope of the main ship, the crew is suddenly subjected to the full effects of gravitational and acceleration forces. The effects of these forces on the human occupants limits the maximum separation velocities. The SPU will be caught in the gravitational wash generated by the ship and the crew will experience up to twenty-one G's of acceleration.'

This, if nothing else, reinforced the message that *Baddest* was an Air Force ship. On other Space Services ships, evacuation was by lifeboats which could only be launched at relatively low sub-light speeds. The Air Force were the only service to 'bang out' of their ships in emergencies. The audience could now appreciate why, on a ship as large as *Baddest*, with an inertialess envelope, the crew were to be kept continuously strapped in their wombs. The hologram of *Baddest* disappeared and the SPU increased in size to occupy the entire projection area.

'Should the SPU's integrity be breached, each acceleration couch is an ejectable escape capsule with life support duration of ninety-one days. At super-light speeds such ejections carry a 78 percent risk of a fatality. At trans-light the risk is 46 percent and 0.8 percent at sub-light.'

"Why the differentiation between sub and super-light?" Wendy, another of the naval flyers, asked.

The primary computer remained silent.

"Anne, that question was addressed to you." Wendy corrected her oversight.

'Ejection from the SPU is back into normal spacetime. First stage is the exit of the non-flight crew with their wombs and, 0.035 seconds later, the flight crew follows.'

There was a gasp of amazement from the audience. A mass dropping out of super-light without an inertialess envelope would instantly be flattened into a film less than one atom thick. It took a ship's main drives to provide a sizeable inertialess envelope. By dropping small masses, womb, and occupier, only a small envelope was needed. One of the scientists, a man who appeared to be of both Negro and Asian extraction, stood to examine his womb, then fired off a question.

"Anne. Do you mean to say that this has its own envelope and energy source?!"

'Alfred. Please identify, either verbally or by indication, what you mean by "this".'

"I mean, this womb, Anne." Alfred replied.

'The energy for the inertialess envelope is supplied by the ejection process. The envelope exists for 0.2 of a second. This is sufficient to bring the womb to an absolute stop in normal spacetime.'

The crew looked around at each other as they absorb this information. Eva eventually said, "Anne, continue."

'The wombs have other functions along with acceleration protection and emergency evacuation. Collectively they are known as the "placenta functions". The first is nutrient supply and waste removal by the normal orifices. The second is stress limitation. The womb is connected directly to its occupier's lymphatic system and controls the toxins, enzymes and hormonal levels in the blood. The aim is to keep the human body functioning at its optimum for prolonged periods.

'During a combat sortie each crewman spends twenty-one out of every twenty-four hours in their womb. In order to prevent muscle wastage and to maintain stamina and general good health a fitness room is provided.' The projection changed to show a high G gymnasium, situated immediately behind the cockpit. 'Crewmen will follow a daily individual fitness regime of six half hour sessions. These sessions have been composed after evaluation of your medical records. The regimes are programmed into the MedCom and are initiated by stating your name on entering the fitness room. The fitness room is also the battle simulator and firing range for the infantry to practice their battle drills. The instruction to run simulations and scenarios are the standard ones for a holographic war theatre. Briefing ends... Any questions?'

"Anne, why have you been programmed with a female personality?"

'Only Billy can answer that question, Wendy.'

8

FLIGHT SUITS

With the briefing over the naval fliers took up their proper positions. This slowed down the total systems pre-flight checks. The Air Force flight crew gave them a step by step explanation of each stage of the procedure. All systems, except the weapons, with their attendant fail-safes, auxiliary power, and backups, had to be checked. The combined flight crew also had to learn the new internal communication network controls. Four communication networks had been installed: Air Force crew, naval crew, remainder, and a network linking them. Little background noise was generated by the ship in flight, but once the entire crew had on their combat flight suits and were strapped into their wombs normal verbal communication was difficult.

Although the communication networks' controls were simple the flight crew's familiarity with their use had to be as unconscious and automatic as scratching their noses. Instead of taking four or five hours the checks took nearer ten. The non-flying crew had to amuse themselves while the fliers sweated over a multitude of fly-by-thought integrators, touch-sensitive switches and buttons, connectors and displays.

Eva's womb was directly behind and slightly above Billy's. She had an identical set of controls which, at the moment, were deactivated and over Billy's head she had an unobstructed view of the flight instruments. Mohamed sat beside Billy in the 2nd pilot's womb. Wendy's womb similarly mirrored Mohamed's. Billy toyed with the controls for the recently installed internal communication networks while he pondered whether to swap Eva's position with Mohamed's. Ideally he should have her sitting beside him whilst she underwent operational conversion, Mohamed could then oversee Wendy. However, flying the craft effectively required pilots sitting side by side.

He turned around. "Well, Eva old gal, what do you think of *Baddest*?"

Her eyes narrowed. "It's a monstrosity," she answered flatly.

Billy surreptitiously checked either side of him and whispered. "Not so loud, you might hurt her feelings." Then he laughed.

"It's a her, is it? *She* must have cost as much as a Naval Grand Fleet to build - what a waste."

Billy grinned teasingly. "Is there any point in spending all that money just to keep fifteen thousand plus Truckies employed when five Flyboys can do the job?"

Eva didn't reply, he'd made his point. A Grand Fleet wasn't being sent on this mission. Billy continued on a more serious note. "It's been a long day, and tomorrow will be even harder, I want to set *Baddest's* day cycle with right now as 23:59. What do you reckon?"

70

"Makes sense. Aren't we going to set up a watch rota?"

"No need; remember this is the Air Force, navigators are also trained to fly. There's a permanent eight-hour rota." Billy touched a button "Here are the first couple of days. Team α can fall in with your counterparts."

The following appeared on the two-way screen in front of Eva:

WAITING ROTA

00:00 - 03:59	*1st pilot - N° 3 nav*
04:00 - 07:59	*N° 1 nav - N° 3 nav*
08:00 - 11:59	*N° 1 nav - 2nd pilot*
12:00 - 15:59	*N° 2 nav - 2nd pilot*
16:00 - 19:59	*N° 2 nav - 1st pilot*
20:00 - 23:59	*N° 3 nav - 1st pilot*
00:00 - 03:59	*N° 3 nav - N° 1 nav*
04:00 - 07:59	*2nd pilot - N° 1 nav*
08:00 - 11:59	*2nd pilot - N° 2 nav*
12:00 - 15:59	*1st pilot - N° 2 nav*
16:00 - 19:59	*1st pilot - N° 3 nav*
20:00 - 23:59	*N° 1 nav - N° 3 nav*

Eva examined the schedule for a while. "You'll always see the same faces," she commented.

"This isn't one of *your* rust buckets, you know." Billy said with derision. "It takes much, much, much coordination between the pilots to fly *Baddest*. And *that* takes many, many, many space hours to achieve. But you'll learn that soon enough."

"Why 'Waiting Rota'?"

Billy touched another button and the information vanished from Eva's screen. "We only use this rota when we're holding. The rest of the time me and my man Mohamed are on the job."

"Really? Don't you and *your man* Mohamed ever sleep?" she asked sarcastically.

"Catnaps."

"Crap! You Flyboys are starting to believe your own propaganda."

"My Dear, just sit back, relax, and watch," Billy said and stood up. He jumped up onto the central console and turned to address the crew. "Listen in folks, it's now 23:59 hrs ship time. You all need to get your beauty sleep. The preflight checks are done. Tomorrow we'll fit your combat flight suits. We'll also instruct you in the use of the internal communication system which will stop me having to get up here and shout. Now, to bed down in your wombs you need to give verbal commands to C1 on how you want it augmented. She can adjust the angle of recline, temperature, light, etc.; just tell her what you want, and she'll tuck you in nice and snug. There's no need to do this in turn, my dearest C1 can handle simultaneous conversations. Nightie, night." Billy jumped off and sat back in his womb.

"And another thing," Eva continued in the same argumentative tone. "Why is Anne programmed with a female personality?"

'Programmed with a female personality? I do not understand the question, Eva.'

"Anne, inadvertent activation," Billy interrupted. "But, while you're here, make ship's time 23:59. Mark."

The background light in the cockpit dimmed.

'Twenty-three fifty-nine. Marked.'

Pilot

"Thanks Anne." Billy sat back and put his feet up on the instrument panel. "You Truckies have no soul. How can you go wandering through space with computers that sound like they're chewing on broken glass?"

"I'm not just talking about the voice. That computer definitely has a personality."

"So?"

"That's illegal!"

"Is it?"

"Come on Billy. How in God's name did you do it?"

"One day I might tell you, but only if you're a good girl." Turning to Mohamed, he said quietly. "OK, let's wait till the baggage has settled down, then we'll fit the flight suits to the flying crew. After that we'll go over to the Waiting Rota."

"I take it you want all this completed before our *baggage* wakes up?" John joined in thoughtfully.

"You take it right... Come to think of it... Anne, ensure the non-flying crew gets a mild sedative tonight."

'Yes Billy.'

"Would it be too much to ask, that you explained what the hell it is, you're talking about?" Wendy, whose position mirrored the 2nd pilot's, asked, leaning over Mohamed's shoulder.

Billy looked around and up at her. "I'm not sure how well our passengers will sleep their first night on board, so C1 will give them a little help."

"But what's this about fitting our flight suits. I thought that you said that would be done tomorrow?" Gabi, *Man Vaughn's* navigator, asked angrily.

"Jesus! Look, I don't know what they teach you at naval academies, but this *is* tomorrow." Billy grinned and the other Flyboys tittered. "And just in case there is anyone left in any doubt, I'll reiterate: this is not a Navy ship. It doesn't fly like a Navy ship; its procedures are not like a Navy ship's. In fact, anyone who knows anything about Navy ships would do well to forget everything they know."

"What's the point you're trying to make Captain?" Eva scoffed.

Billy stared out of the cockpit. "The total systems check is about the only meaningful thing you can do on *Baddest* without being hooked up to the ship. We can't get plugged in until we have fitted our combat flights suits. Therefore, we need to fit the combat flight suits ASAP."

"Why are you making such a big deal of this? How long can it take to put on a flying suit?" Anne, now known as Ruth, inquired from her position next to Pipsqueak.

"Now, I know that someone who's used to a Navy tub will imagine that an Air Force combat flight suit is like the rags they wear. However, it's not."

'Sedative administered. They are sleeping like babies, Billy.'

"Thanks, Darling. Eva, why don't we fit ours first?" Billy said standing.

Eva remained seated. "Maybe I imagined it, but did you just call your computer Darling?"

"Is there someone else on the ship that I'm going to call 'Darling'?" Billy strolled past her.

"You Flyboys are weird" Eva got to her feet and followed.

"Weird you say? I think they're a few cards short of a full deck," Wendy called after them.

"Looks like their lift doesn't reach the top floor." Marandolina, poked Grim in the ribs and sniggered.

Gabi put her arm around John's shoulder. "Definitely a couple sandwiches short of a picnic."

"The lights are on but no one's home," Ruth smiled at Pipsqueak.

Eva caught up with Billy as he walked past his sleeping crew towards the fitness room. "They really are out for the count, aren't they? How did An... C1 do it?"

"Gas."

"How come we weren't affected?"

He paused and turn to her at the door of the fitness room. "Each womb has its own independent air circulation via impelling and expelling vents. If you want, you can have your air rose scented."

The door slid open and the lights came on. Billy stepped into the room, Eva followed, the door closed behind her. She surveyed the room; a lavishly equipped gymnasium 50 metres square. She was about to ask about the flight suits when Billy said, "Anne, change of command structure; 2ic for this mission, Eva; 3ic, Erick."

'Change in command structure logged. Any changes in authorisation access codes, Billy?'

"None at the moment." He walked towards a blank wall.

Taken-a-back by all this Eva stared at him as he stopped at the wall. In the end she said. "I think the 2ic needs to know what's going on."

"There are some instructions that C1 will only act on if it's given by a crew-member of appropriate seniority. Like, for example, telling her to put other crewmembers to sleep. I was just letting her know the new pecking order, which means that Grim and Mohamed are being locked out of certain areas."

"What about the codes? Why haven't I been given them?"

Billy smiled. "You're still thinking Navy. The mission codes are in the mission glove on your hand. C1 was asking if there's any change to the classification of information that you and Erick are entitled to. At the moment your clearance is only for 'unclassified'. We don't have security safes, double keys and all that nonsense, it's all voice activated."

"But you didn't change that?"

"No point in you having it, until you know what to do with it. Strip, and lie face down on that exercise bench," he indicated which bench with a nod. "Anne, scan Eva for fitting."

'Scan complete. She has very firm breasts and buttocks for her age. But I don't think she's your type - she's a bit *masculine*, isn't she?'

Eva, who had just started to undress, stopped in amazement. It took her several moments to recover. "Anne! Don't talk about me like that!"

'Eva, you are not authorised to give that instruction. Request disregarded.'

Billy chuckled to himself and turned back to face the wall. "Anne, kit for female lymph ducts attachment and flight suit fitting."

In what had appeared to be a solid wall an aperture opened. A tray loaded with mechanical and electrical implements silently slid out. Billy took the tray and started towards Eva. She didn't know what most of the contraptions on the tray were but she recognised a laser lance.

"Please get undressed or we'll be here all night," he said tiredly.

She quickly stripped off the three layers of her flying suit.

"Face down on the bench."

As she climbed onto the bench, Eva was struck by the thought that it bore more than a passing resemblance to an operating table. "Shouldn't we be doing this in the MedCen?"

"We are." He was standing behind her, but she could tell that he was laughing. Then, in a move clearly design to unnerve her, he placed the tray a couple of centimetres from her face. "I'm going to give you a local anaesthetic, then we can get this show on the road," he said cheerily, then reaching over he took something from the tray.

His ploy had worked, she was *more* than unnerved, but she wasn't going to let him know that. "Aren't you going to sterilize your hands?"

"We're still thinking Navy, aren't we Dear? C1 sterilized everything and everyone when we came onboard. Anne, spotlight; target, Eva's back"

Instead of the warmth from a powerful light that she'd expected, she felt something cold on her back. Then she saw Billy's hand come across to pick up the laser lance. This shattered her show of bravado. "What are you going to do?"

"As you know, we don't much care for the 'brute strength and ignorance' approach so favoured by the Navy. An Air Force pilot needs the hands of a surgeon. Now, keep still."

It took more self-control than she realised she had to do as he asked. After a few seconds her back went numb and she heard the faint hum of the laser lance. Moments later the smell of burning flesh drifted past her nose. She closed her eyes and tried to think of something, anything, other than being on the operating table.

Billy started whistling tunefully then said, as if to himself, "I'm sure the heart is around here some place."

She bit her lip.

"Ah, there it is. Beating a bit fast, isn't it?"

She almost cried out but didn't. She felt him change position. She wondered what he was doing. From the tray he took something that looked like two short tubes with feathers on their ends. There was a stronger smell of burning flesh. He then walked around to the other side of her and started to whistle again; she thought she recognised the tune. Closing her eyes, she concentrated on the tune. After about a minute she realised that it was the tune to the song they sang about Goosing the Weightless. If he was trying to goad her, he was succeeding.

"You can open your eyes now," he said mockingly as he bent and pulled up two narrow tubes from the floor. He pulled them around to her back; she couldn't see or feel what he did with them.

"Anne, check Eva's lymphatic connections."

'Eva, I am going to gradually lessen the effects of the anaesthetic. Please let me know if you feel any discomfort.'

Slowly, the numbness in her back receded. There was a general soreness under her armpits but hardly anything that she'd call discomfort. "I feel fine."

"I'm glad to hear it, but you weren't talking to me, were you?"

"Anne, I feel fine." She wanted to kill him.

'That is good Eva. Now I am going to ask you a series of questions about how you are feeling. Answer about both your emotional and physical state... How do you feel?'

"...Cold and sleepy."

'And now?'

"...Happy. Full of energy."

'And now?'

"...Exhausted."

'The response time is well within the parameters, Billy. Lymphatic connection should heal within forty-eight hours.'

"Fine. Map Eva's DNA, Anne."

'DNA mapped.'

She heard the slithering sound of the disconnected tubes being retracted into the floor. Billy slapped her hard on the buttocks. "OK, turn over."

She raised herself onto her elbows, then spun around with a vicious back hand chop. She intended to take his bloody head off! Connecting with thin air her momentum carried her all the way round and she toppled, headfirst, off the bench. Springing to her feet, she saw Billy standing several metres away with his arms folded; he was slowly shaking his head.

"Why, oh why are Truckies so predictable?" he said, as he sauntered over and patted the bench. "Up you get."

Swearing under her breath she heaved herself back on.

"On your back." He pushed her down and did something under the bench. Stirrups popped out beside her feet. He took the tray from the top of the bench and placed it at the other end. "Feet in."

She put her feet in the stirrups and, again, he fiddled with something under the bench. Her legs were raised and spread apart by the stirrups like she was about to give birth. Smiling he slowly bent over. She could only see the top of his head as he stared up her pussy. "What are you going to do?" she asked, keeping her voice level.

He straightened. "Shave you for a start. Want any anaesthetic for that?" His eyes glistened with mirth.

It suddenly occurred to her that if fitting an Air Force flight suit was this complicated, then he'd need 'assistance' with his. She'd bide her time. "No."

She started shivering as he started to shave her. Surprisingly, the removal of all her pubic hair was entirely painless. Eva began to suspect that her Captain wasn't joking about having the hands of a surgeon.

"OK. Make like you're going to touch your ears with your ankles."

She took her feet out of the stirrups and did as he asked. This was so humiliating!

"Deep breath, in ... out... and relax. Deep breath... relax. Once more, deep breath..." She winced as something was shoved a long way into her anus. "Right, slowly bring your feet down and put them back in the stirrups."

She wanted to wrap her hands around his throat and squeeze every ounce of life out of him.

As she fumbled to put her feet back in the stirrups, he slid something in her vagina. She sat up and aimed a punch at his face. Without looking he caught her fist.

"Stop dicking around. Make me slip and you can kiss your clitoris goodbye."

Freezing, she slowly lowered herself back down and then stared penetratingly at the ceiling. She heard him sniggering and figured that he had been only kidding. But because she didn't know what it was that he was doing, she decided to leave it at that. She felt him gently fit something over the inner and outer lips of her vulva.

"OK, feet out... sit up, and no sudden movements." Taking her arm, he helped her up.

She looked down at her now hairless pubic area and saw what she could only describe as a close-fitting transparent mask covering her genitals.

"Good. Now, get down slowly." He continued to support her by the arm.

Pulling her arm out of his grasp she jumped off the bench. As soon as her feet hit the floor, pain racked through her insides. She bent double and almost collapsed.

"At least we can say that you're not used to having a hard nine inches up your arse," he said jovially. "Straighten up and turn around. Do it slowly, this takes some getting use to."

As she came erect the pain subsided and she noticed several coloured tubes dangling between her legs. She turned around and he knelt behind her. Taking a sheet of thick plastic, he pasted it to her buttocks. It seemed to stick to her flesh and then shrink, pulling the skin taught.

He stood up. "Greatest Air Force invention that, ever; an anti-haemorrhoid device. Walk to the other side of the room and back. You'll probably find that you have to change the way you walk to be comfortable." He went over to the aperture.

She started to walk towards the far wall. He was right about having to change the way she walked. With her normal long strides her insides felt a little tender. Perhaps if she...

Still with his back to her, Billy said, "Oh, by the way. Did I tell you that the removal of your pubic hair was permanent?"

She turned and stared at him, open mouthed.

"Just kidding, but in won't grow back for a long time."

"You're a sadistic bastard. Do you know that?!"

"Nonsense, it's all good 'character building' stuff," he called over his shoulder. "Anne, Eva's flight suit please."

A bundle slid out of the aperture. He took it, turned, and started over to her. In one hand he held a lightweight flying helmet and a flying suit in the other. The suit appeared to be slightly thicker than her three-layered naval suit. Putting down the helmet he waved the flight suit in front of her.

"This is armoured, and the key to fitting it is to sort out the umbilicals round your crotch first." The suit looked too flimsy to be armoured.

Billy held it out for her to put her feet in. Step by step he explained the significance of each of the coloured tubes and how to attach them. Then he took her through the suits own umbilicals. She put her arms in and he showed her how to fit the helmet. Finally, he made adjustments until the entire suit was a tight fit. It was extremely comfortable; it didn't feel like she was wearing a combat suit at all and it was ridiculously light.

"We won't take off the suits till mission end, except the bowl; we only wear that during alerts. Take it off."

She guessed that he meant the helmet and did as he asked. All the toggles, straps, clips, and sockets on the suit were easy to manipulate with her gloved hands. It seemed that the Air Force preferred things that were simple - idiot proof. Billy unzipped his own one-piece flying suit and stepped out of it. She was surprised that he was naked under it. He turned his back to her and brought an arm round to point to three metallic discs. They ran down in a vertical line that starting just below his shoulder and were about a centimetre apart. There were three similar discs below the opposite shoulder.

"The top two are the 'in' connections. The bottom pair are circulatory. The 'out' is the stuff between your legs. There are cowlings on the back of your suit for automatic connection to your womb. When you're plugged in it's like having an extra set of vital organs. C1 now has your DNA map and can manufacture nano engines to help your body repair damaged tissue. Any questions?"

There was too much to absorb. "Not at the moment."

"If anything comes up, just ask." He took both their discarded flying suits, went back over to the wall, and threw them into the aperture. "Anne, my flight suit please."

He took out another suit and helmet and put them on the bench. She'd noted his pubic hair and spied the implement he'd used to shave hers off; she was looking forward to this. Taking something from the tray, he reached behind, stuck it up his arse, then stepped into his combat suit and had it fully fitted in under ten seconds.

"Don't you need to shave?" she couldn't help sounding disappointed.

"No, different plumbing. Shall we go?" He picked up his helmet.

She picked up her own helmet and fell in step behind him as he walked out of the torture chamber. She noted that he was moving with a slight shuffle. Mimicking his gait, she found in a lot more comfortable. The remainder of the flight crew were still engaged in friendly banter as they approached.

"Mohammed. You and Wendy are up."

9

WORK UP

On the one hand, she simply wanted to kill the arrogant little shit. On the other, the things that Billy absent-mindedly did were driving her into a jealous rage. Then of course, there was the ship. Awesome! And their primary computer had a personality, which was illegal and, supposedly, impossible. She was an excellent pilot, she'd clocked up the space hours, so she couldn't help but recognise that in Ace Crew II she was dealing with something exceptional. Forcing down the bile she had to finally admit to herself that maybe, just maybe, the Air Force were ahead of the game. If this was their B-team, what about their A-team?

She and Wendy were beginning the painful and humbling lesson of learning the basics of flying *Baddest*. The controls were the standard type for any sophisticated military kit; semi-thought activated. This meant that the activity in the neural pathways of the brain was continuously monitored by a dedicated computer, the secondary computer - C2, which then modelled the 'desired outcomes'. To invent a more efficient way to operate machines than this would require there being such a thing as telepathy - theoretically impossible. On spaceships, the C1 integrated the various inputs from the C2 and activated the appropriate equipment. But unlike on a naval vessel, where each pilot had responsibility for certain instruments and controls, on *Baddest* there were no lines of demarcation.

As Billy and Mohammed took them through the flight controls it became apparent that; a) both kept their eyes firmly on the instruments; b) neither pilot spoke to the other; c) they haphazardly interchanged roles; and d) each one always knew what the other was doing. This required much more than simple coordination and cooperation; it seemed that somehow or other Billy and Mohammed were at one with each other and the ship. But the most maddening thing was that neither of them was aware of it. They couldn't understand why she and Wendy were unable to follow their instructions in unison; that she and Wendy weren't used to 'thinking' simultaneous thoughts. Comments such as, 'It's not a bulldozer, you know', 'Bet you're glad your flying instructors aren't here to see this' and, 'All we're asking for is a little finesse', were beginning to wear a little thin.

She hadn't had a chance to touch base with the rest of her crew. Even so, she could tell that they were having similar difficulties shadowing their counterparts. They were also being subjected to the same merciless gibes. Then there was the indignity of Anne having to be called Ruth. The computer should have been reprogrammed. Whoever heard of a person kowtowing to a bloody machine? She should have jumped on Billy as soon as he suggested it. And the longer she left this matter, the more difficult it would be to reverse, but she

78

could also see that until she was proficient at flying the ship there would be little point in raising her objection.

Boy! Did she want to become proficient at flying *Baddest*. Not just so that she could rub his nose in it, although that would be nice. What she really wanted to do was to put the ship through its paces. The designers had really thought about the fundamental elements of a fighting vessel; *Baddest* not only had them all, it had them in bucket loads. Her enthusiasm for the ship was growing with every passing moment.

What she and Wendy had to accomplish was the simulated manoeuvring of the ship out of Saturn's atmosphere. When Billy and Mohammed ran through the manoeuvre it seemed relatively simple. However, spaceships weren't designed for the delicate balancing act of gradually overcoming a planet's gravity. Normally they simply accelerated to escape velocity and blasted into orbit. This ship, because of its size, had certainly never hit downside. Plus, *Baddest* had to be kept on the dark side of certain civilian space-borne sensors. Once they'd eased out of the planet's atmosphere, they were to make a quick spurt out of the solar system, away from those sensors.

What she and Wendy repeatedly failed to accomplish was the simulated leaving Saturn's atmosphere without detection. And every time they got it wrong, insult was added to injury as the ship's computer overrode their instructions. The last time a machine had overridden either of them was back in basic flying training. Eva knew exactly why Billy was doing this; in his place, she would've done the same. They were being thrown in at the deep end, with a non-critical sink or swim manoeuvre that required precision.

"Let's try that again. And if it isn't too much to ask, can we get it right this time?" Mohammed sounded as if he was bored to tears.

She knew exactly what she and Wendy had to do - gently coax the ship into orbit. But with so much power on tap it was easier said than done. She gradually applied power as Wendy altered vectors...

'Detection imminent. C1 has simulation control... Back in parking orbit.'

Billy reclined in his womb, clasped his hands behind his head and stared out of the cockpit. " I know you're both dykes but try to imagine giving some guy a hand job without ripping his foreskin off."

This time he had gone too far. She was about to protest when she realised that he was totally serious. Choking down her anger she said, "Anne, shadow pilots have simulation control." Checking that Wendy was ready, she applied the power. The screen showed them exiting Saturn's atmosphere at the predetermined co-ordinates. Jaws locked in fierce concentration they applied more power, the ship sped out towards Pluto's orbit.

'Egress *finally* successful... Simulation ends.'

How could a computer be sarcastic? Looking over Billy's shoulder she saw his mouth moving. Was he talking to Mohammed on their communication net? She wished that she could lip read. What derision were they exchanging? Did she really want to find out? Billy turned to face her and Wendy, and she steeled herself for a torrent of abuse.

"Eighteen tries. Not bad, you two, not bad at all. Let's have a break from this and run through the weapons arming sequence before the next simulation."

She didn't know him well enough to be certain, but she was pretty sure that he wasn't the sort who readily handed out praise. Not only that, it took the entire flight crew to arm weapons so, presumably, this was also heard by the navigators.

"We'd like to have another crack at it, Sir," Wendy said, and Eva agreed.

This time it was Mohammed's mouth that moved, and Billy smiled to himself. "OK, it's time the full shadow crew plays. Anne, run; break orbit Saturn, exit solar system, super-

Pilot

light jump Epsilon Eridani, high speed manoeuvres, return to solar system, parking orbit Saturn."

'OK, Billy.'

Clearly, he intended to push them hard, but then again, she would've done the same. She turned to look at the non-flight crew. Anne was amusing them, with what she wasn't sure. Billy had told C1 to keep them fully occupied. It was good to see that the aimless milling about had ceased. Maybe they were customising their wombs? That was a fairly interesting experience. Now that all the flight suits were fitted, as soon as one sat in one's womb one was automatically strapped in. The lymph connections snapped into place and you were at one with the ship. It was then a matter of personal choice how the non-flight crew wanted their womb augmented. Lighting, temperature, firmness of seating, and angle of recline could all be finely adjusted to individual taste.

To get out of the womb you had to slowly lean forwards, almost touching your knees with your head. This broke the lymph connections, then the straps were released. The flight crew did not have all these choices. They had to sit so that they had an unobstructed view of the instruments...

"Keep your mind on the job!" Billy's sharp command interrupted her thoughts.

She became businesslike and said, "Anne, shadow crew have simulated control," as she reached for the controls.

'You have simulation control.'

Before she or Wendy had the ship under control it lurched to the left and plummeted tail first deeper into Saturn's atmosphere. They struggled for over a minute to bring it back into its parking orbit. The silence from the Flyboys was deafening. Eva felt herself reddening. To her surprise she discovered that she was silently cursing the primary computer. She and Wendy exchanged glances then started to manoeuvre the ship. They broke orbit on the button and pointed the ship out system but the co-ordinates from the navigators were long in coming.

There was a torrent of hissing derision from Grim and John. Pipsqueak simply broke into hysterical laughter. Eva felt for Marandolina, Gabi and Ruth, they had the most to unlearn and even more to learn. While the Air Force pilot's set-up was more or less the same as the Navy's their navigation system was totally different, requiring three navigators. Marandolina and Ruth weren't even navigators; one was a weapon systems operator, the other a communications officer. The Air Force didn't think these tasks demanding enough to assign to an individual. No, they were farmed out to a bloody computer. Eventually the co-ordinates appeared on her screen. Relieved, she was about to punch them into the NavComp...

"Hold!" Grim, John, and Pipsqueak shouted in unison.

'Plot error. Proposed trajectory will expose ship to detection. Shadow navigators, *please* replot course.'

How the devil did a computer manage to sound like a spiteful bitch?! Eva couldn't see their faces, but from the movement of their shoulders she could tell that Mohammed and Billy were laughing. She made an effort to sound relaxed. "Shadow navigators, re-plot simulated trajectory."

The new co-ordinates appeared before she finished speaking. She stared at them. "For fuck's sake! Even I can see that those are wrong. Sort it out you three." She could only take so much crowing from these Air Force types.

"Keep your eye on the ball," Billy quietly suggested, sniggering.

She was pretty sure that he came through only on her net. What ball...?

'Detection from Space Station J Zero Zero Four imminent. C1 has simulation control...' The ship sank back into the cover of Saturn's cloudy atmosphere. '...Back in parking orbit. Billy, all shadow crew are showing high stress levels. Why don't you assign them to less critical and demanding tasks like making the tea?'

"Anne, end simulation," Billy said, then turned around to her smiling. "Let's have a break."

Eva was about to insist on another try, then thought better of it.

"Less haste more speed, shadow crew," he said calmly, in marked contrast to his earlier tone. "There's nothing here that you haven't done a million times before, so stop fighting the ship, OK?"

By glancing at the remainder of the Air Force crew Eva surmised that they were not privy to this conversation. Her Captain was being a Captain, so she remained silent.

"Perhaps if your Flyboys were less, shall we say, petulant we would have a speedier operational conversion, Sir," Gabi hit back with untypical insolence.

"If you can't take a bit of ribbing without blowing a gasket you shouldn't be in the Navy," Billy gently chided. "Now, let's examine the problem. Your operational conversion has turned into a game of one-upmanship; you're all trying so desperately hard not to be out done. This so-called 'petulance' is only a symptom; desperation is the cause. Well, what's the solution?"

There was silence from the naval flyers.

"Marandolina and Ruth, on *Man Vaughn,* if you had to navigate, you'd run your plots past Gabi for a once over, wouldn't you? So, why don't you do that until you get up to speed?" he continued conversationally.

"Yes, Sir," came their joint reply.

"That was a suggestion, not an instruction," he sounded almost paternal. "Just take your time and get it right, first time."

"Yes, Sir."

Billy sighed, "Anything else you want to get off your chests?"

"That computer is really pissing me off," Wendy grouched.

He didn't respond but, again, Eva saw tremors in his shoulders. Annoyed, she punched into his net. "A computer with an attitude may be amusing to you, Sir. But it will have a detrimental effect on the efficient operation of this ship. *And,* it's highly illegal."

"C1 is used to being the only girl, give her time. And don't call me Sir," he answered in a tone which suggested that he wasn't taking any of this seriously.

"*Her*?! Need I remind you, *Sir*, Anne is only a bloody computer!"

'I know that I am a computer, Eva. The Navy would do well to have computers half as capable. Now that you have activated me, what do you want?!' shrieked into Eva's headset.

How can a machine become enraged?

"Maybe if you spoke to C1 like she's *the* primary computer, she'd speak to you like you were *the* 2ic," Billy cheerfully suggested.

This made her even more incensed. "How dare you speak to me like that?"

...

"Anne, I mean you!"

...

"Anne?!"

'What?!'

Pilot

The volume in her headset made her ears hurt. Eva suddenly felt utterly foolish. Here she was arguing with a computer. Had this exchange taken place on the open net? She thought not...

'I say again, what do you want Eva?'

She fought down the desire to shout. "Anne, inadvertent activation." She supposed that it was now going away to sulk. "Fucking machine," she uttered under her breath. Yes, she knew she was being irrational, but she felt better for it.

"I just don't get it. You've sussed that C1 has a personality, so why do you insist on behaving as if she doesn't?" Billy laughed.

She wouldn't give him the satisfaction of an answer.

***

She couldn't help but think of the building of this ship as a scandalous waste of resources. God only knows just how many billions of credits had been squandered. And it didn't even have a functioning toilet! 'The first principle of Air Force ship design is: no dead space', really? Only a military mind could conceive an engineering feat of such proportions yet overlook the basic necessities of comfort. She knew that she was being ungracious; the majority of her funding came from military sources. Who but the military were interested enough in xenobiology and xenopsychology to allocate credits to its research? Being prepared for what might be 'out there' was their *raison d'étre*. But she had to fight for every penny she got. However, she had no doubt that as soon as the designers unveiled their blueprints, Star Officers began falling over themselves to have *Baddest* and its sister ship built.

The military certainly had no legal authority to force her to undertake this mission, nor had any form of coercion even been hinted at. But she had been at this long enough to understand that 'he who paid the piper called the tune.' Had she declined to comply with their 'request', her future funding would most certainly have been in jeopardy. This was one of the reasons why she'd always advocated having scientific research centrally funded. Of course, there were those who argued to the contrary; stating that if central funding were to happen then the lion's share would go to those areas of research that appeared to offer the most immediate commercial benefit.

Then there were her civilian colleagues; all fellow xenobiologists. Together, they were perhaps the top four in the field. Between them they had published most of the accepted papers on the existence of possible or probable alien intelligence. There was a great deal of professional rivalry between them but, in truth, it went far deeper than just professional rivalry - there was also very real mutual personal animosity. Did the military know about that? Recently she had gained much satisfaction, and some critical acclaim, by demolishing Alfred Nsiah's *Aqua Intelligentsia Theorem*. His ludicrous notions had begun to be widely cited: 'Regardless of the intellect of a species, technology and an advanced civilisation can only evolve from land animals - fire is the basis of all technology.'

With her paper entitled *Chimica Fondamento*, she went in under the radar and attacked the very heart of Alfred's theory, highlighting the folly of drawing comparisons between primates and sea mammals. She asserted that fire was not the basis of human technology; primitive human technology, any primitive technology, was based on chemical reactions. She argued that human technology ought to be considered merely as one based on chemical reactions brought about by combustion. Then she demonstrated how easily non-combustion chemical reaction technology could be developed by a primitive society in an aquatic environment. Then she delivered the *coup de grace* by emphasizing the main advantage of an aquatic chemical technology, the abundance of raw materials.

It wasn't going to be easy working together. However, they were all professionals, they would just have to put their personal differences aside... This was so typical of the military: no imagination, no lateral thinking, one-dimensional minds. 'We may encounter intelligent aliens on this mission, we need xenobiologists.' 'Which ones?' 'Get the best.' Didn't they realise that alien intelligence meant alien technology? Where were the atomic physicists and propulsion engineers? The xenobiologist were only here to facilitate the successful completion of the mission. Possible scientific exploration and discovery was not a consideration.

So here she was, leading a team of bitter rivals, heading off into the unknown. And as if that wasn't enough, the mission commander was a wet behind the ears 'boy' Air Force jockey. This was probably her greatest worry. He didn't act like a leader; he was so arrogant and at the same time so juvenile. He'd done everything but inspire her with confidence. Ever since gaining her doctorate and being exposed to the military she'd had an incredibly low opinion of them. Now, to cap it all, the Air Force and Navy pilots seem to be more interested in bickering with each other than getting on with the job. The mission had hardly started, but already they'd been attacked by Navy ships. And that super-light jump to Saturn had been mind-numbingly moronic.

This mission was doomed.

10

FLYCATCHER

Captain Erick Ademokun had finally gotten his womb comfortable. Well, he thought it was comfortable, at the moment. Who knows what he'd think in three months' time? As a Marine he was used to adapting to the different characteristics of each naval ship. This was his first posting on an Air Force ship and, so far, it was nothing like he'd experienced before. Wombs, surgically fitted flight suits, cabin and cockpit all in one, this was going to take some getting used to.

Still, he felt a subdued sense of excitement. This was an 'All Arms' operation with an open brief. One only dreamed of a mission like this. He had never served alongside soldiers. From his brief conversation with Captain David Bolt, the leader of the SAS contingent, it was clear that he also shared the excitement. They'd agreed to put aside inter-service niggling - the Navy and Air Force was doing enough of that for everybody...

"Erick, it's Billy. Want to have a chat," unexpectedly came over his communication net, making him jump.

"Yes, Sir."

"Billy, not, Sir. Eva's also on this net. We've selected you for 3ic... Want to sound you out on that."

Erick hesitated for a moment. "Are you officially telling me that I'm 3ic, Billy?"

"Don't be so stiff, old son," Billy laughed. "We think you are the man for the job but want to know how you feel about it."

"I'm a Marine, Sir," he said somewhat forcefully.

"Meaning that you'll carry out your duties whatever they might be?" Eva sounded amused.

He was finding it difficult to have such an important conversation with two people who were in close proximity, but whose faces he couldn't read. All he could see was the backs of their heads. Plus, he had a feeling that this was some kind of test. "Yes, Ma'am."

"I know that you're a bright boy, Erich, so I'll say this only once more: there are no Sirs or Ma'ams on this ship," Billy's tone had changed to one of annoyance. "Additionally, you can save that 'devotion to the Corps' crap for the parade ground. We're not talking about you leading a bunch of Grunts over the top."

"I know next to nothing about the operation of a spaceship, or space warfare," he confessed.

"Apart from that, any other concerns about being 3ic?" Eva coaxed.

He pondered the question for a moment, seeing many potential difficulties but said, "No, that would be my only worry."

"Good, do you want to be the 3ic?" Billy asked, then added, "Think about it, it's probably the only choice you'll get on this trip."

This wasn't something that he needed to think about. "It would be a privilege to be the 3ic for this mission, Billy."

"'A privilege?' We'll remember you said that," Eva laughed.

"Fine," Billy was also laughing. "Here's how we see the distribution of responsibilities. In-flight, Eva and I will take care of flight operations - we will be head down, eyes forward. In-flight, your job is to take care of the non-flying crew. As you can see, we have a mixed bag, particularly the civilians. They'll need lots of love and devotion. OK?"

"Yes, Billy."

"I note that you and David have already come to an arrangement. Good. Continue to forge links and build bridges; think of the non-flight crew as being your platoon whose personnel has just been arbitrarily thrown together. Your objective is to get them combat capable and mission ready."

How could Billy know about his brief conversation with David? The primary computer eavesdropping, that's how. "Consider it done."

"In the event of you becoming mission commander, that would mean that Eva and I are out of the game. In such a scenario, the ship's operations would be the least of your concerns. Any surviving flight crew will be able to take care of things and, in their absence, C1 can fly the ship to any predetermined location. I'm assuming, of course, that if all the flight crew are out something catastrophic has happened and mission ends."

"OK, I understand, Billy. Have we left Saturn?"

"No, we're still working up, it will be another day or so before we leave. As the 3ic you can monitor what's going on from your womb. C1 has a detailed brief for the 3ic. Whistle her up and say, 'Run mission brief Nine Zero Nine'. I realise that there must be lots more that you want to know. Right now, we're all on a very steep learning curve, we'll have time for more Q & A's later. For now, concentrate on the non-flying crew. Any immediate questions?"

"When can we check our equipment? It's standard operating procedure for each man to personally check his kit, especially his PADE suit."

"What's a Paddy suit when it's at home?" Billy asked.

"P.A.D.E., Personal Armoured Dynamic Environmental suit, our combat suits."

"Oh yeah, I remember wearing something like that at the academy. Your combat suits and weapons have been stored as an integral part of your wombs, so you can't get to them. You'll have to get C1 to remotely check all your equipment. Any other questions?"

"Only one, Billy. It's a custom in the Marines to give a title to all operations. Has this mission been named?"

"That's not an Air Force custom. How would you like your first responsibility as 3ic to be the naming of this mission?" It was Eva who answered.

He waited for Billy to confirm Eva's suggestion. Billy didn't speak and seemed to be waiting. "I name this mission, Operation Flycatcher."

"Decisions like that need to be programmed into C1," Billy said helpfully.

"Anne, I name this mission, Operation Flycatcher."

'Operation Flycatcher, confirmed. I think that is a very appropriate title, Erick.'

***

Pilot

She didn't know about Eva, but she was exhausted. Billy and Mohammed had worked them like slaves. As soon as they had mastered one aspect of flying *Baddest,* the Flyboys introduced another. This continuous raising a notch was the main reason why she was fatigued, she and Eva constantly had to increase their mental effort. Moreover, she knew that they still had a long way to go before Billy would be satisfied. They had been on board less than 48 hours, but it felt like months. Just when she thought she couldn't take any more, Billy called a break.

Wendy knew that you didn't get to be a pilot on a Type 35 torpedo boat unless you were good. And the Navy wouldn't let you near the Special Combat Team unless you were the very best. Until about 48 hours ago she'd thought she was an essential part of 'the very best'. Now? Now, she wasn't so sure. The pilots of Ace Crew II, Billy and Mohammed, especially Mohammed, were beginning to make her feel ordinary, very ordinary. Mohammed was so damn tall, he should be ungainly, clumsy and uncoordinated. He should be, but he wasn't. In shadowing him, she had jealously noted that there was a quiet majesty, with a hint of the rogue, about him and everything that he did... She *was* going to fly the pants off this ship if it was the last thing she did!

Sleep? She was too tired, envious, and frustrated to sleep. Her four naval buddies looked as if they were similarly weary, they were just slumped listlessly in their wombs. What was there to take her mind off things? Apart from her womb, there was nowhere to sit; nowhere to relax and unwind. She got out of her womb and started to wander aimlessly around the cockpit. The non-flight crew were all asleep. Where were the Flyboys? They weren't in their wombs, nor were they with the non-flight crew. As she paused by the entrance to the fitness room the door silently slid open. She saw the five Flyboys engaging in various forms of callisthenics. She watched them for a bit and wondered why they didn't seem to be as tired as she felt. Watching them made her realise that she wasn't physically tired at all, just punch drunk. She was about to step into the room...

'Be careful Wendy. The room is at 2.5 G's,' Anne said softly.

She stopped in mid-stride and tried to assess the Flyboys' exertions. The things they were doing didn't look that strenuous. Well, they wouldn't be strenuous at 1 G. Stepping into the room her knees almost buckled. At that exact moment Mohammed looked around and saw her.

"Want us to lighten the load?" He smiled patronisingly.

Now all the Flyboys were looking at her. "No." She walked further into the room, trying to adjust to the gravity. "Anne, my fitness programme."

'Haven't we forgotten something Wendy?'

She couldn't think of anything. "Anne, what have I forgotten?"

'It is polite to say *please,*' the computer answered, with dripping with sarcasm.

At this the five men fell about laughing. "Fitness programme, Anne!"

A hologram of her own naked body suddenly appeared in front of her. Startled, she stepped back. It wasn't hubris that caused her to stop and examine her image - she'd never seen a full-sized holographic image of herself before. Although she was born in Indochina her family originated from South America and were predominantly of Amerindian descent. The 1.7-metre-tall hologram displayed her straight black hair, beautifully symmetrical face, smoldering dark brown eyes, hourglass figure, pert breasts and long legs. It wasn't something that she'd given much thought to, but this probably explained why she always had a cue of women and men eagerly waiting when she hit downside... 'Follow the movements of your hologram, it will take you through your exercises, Wendy.'

She was just noting that the Flyboys didn't have holograms when Pipsqueak advised, "You should have said 'please'."

The Flyboys all stopped what they were doing, sat crossed legged, and looked on with interest. Her hologram disappeared, reappeared beside the wall bar in the corner and bent to do a perfect *plier*. She smiled to herself, she had practised ballet right up to joining the academy. Strolling over to the bar, she repeated this simple exercise. The hologram then did ten *entrechee* in quick succession and she followed suit. When she got to the seventh repetition, it occurred to her that this was the first time that she'd exercised in high G. It also occurred to her that the computer had access to her personal and medical records.

As soon as she'd finished the *entrechees* her holographic twin did ten high *jeter*. 'A hologram is made of light and therefore has no weight.' This thought occurred to her as she tried to attain the same height. After the first two her legs began to ache, she began to find it difficult to raise herself off the floor...

"Personally, I would have said please," Grim commented sadly.

"So would I," John agreed.

Breathing heavily, she finished the ten. The hologram effortlessly *pirouetted* across the room. She was going to stay with that bloody hologram if it killed her. Gritting her teeth, she took off after it...

Peeeeuuuuuuuuuwwwwwwwwwwwwwww!

An ear-piercing siren shrieked. So stunned was she that she overbalanced and started to fall. Despite the shock of it all, she knew that at 2.5 G's she was going to break something. Surprisingly, she found herself tumbling slowly and landed quite softly. Either Anne had instantly reduced the gravity to considerably less than 1 G or had cocooned her in a field. Springing back to her feet, she saw the Flyboys stampeding, at full tilt, out of the room.

Peeeeuuuuuuuuuwwwwwwwwwwwwwwww! Exercise! Exercise!

Still in a bit of a daze, she decided that she'd better follow them. She exited the room in time to see the Flyboys making a beeline directly for their wombs and the flight controls. Most of the non-flight crew had jumped out of their wombs and were running around in blind panic. One particular soldier was standing directly in Pipsqueak's path; despite the woman being considerably bigger than he was, Pipsqueak simply barged her out of the way. By the time Wendy got to her womb, next to Eva's, all the Flyboys had their helmets on and were strapped in.

"Everybody, sit down and strap in!" Billy's voice boomed through headsets and reverberated around the cockpit.

'Alert report; thirty-four seconds till ready to "fight or fly". Wendy and Gabi do not have their flying helmets on. Guido and Kazuhiko are not properly strapped in. Cynthia's lymphatic connections are only partially engaged, and Mona is lying unconscious beside her womb. Alert drill assessment; 11% - very poor. Exercises ends.' Anne sounded unemotional, like a computer was supposed to.

"Somebody have a look at Mona," Billy said as he took off his flying helmet. "That's what an alert sounds like on *Baddest* folks. Now, here's the drill: after the alert sounds we, the flight crew, have fifteen seconds to be ready for flight or fly. That means, knowing what's out there and having a pretty good idea of what to do about it. All you have to do is get to your combat positions, plugged in, strap in, and put your helmets on. How's Mona?"

One of the civilians and David, the Army captain, were bending over her. "She is coming to," the latter said.

Watching Mona being helped to sit up, Wendy then turned to look at Pipsqueak. An apt nickname: he was the smallest of the Flyboys, no more than 1.6 metres and about 58 kilos,

Pilot

while Mona was easily 1.9 metres tall and probably weighed around 76 kilos. Yet, in 'brushing her aside' he'd rendered her unconscious.

Billy stood up and, half smiling, turned to face the crew. "Fifteen seconds means fifteen seconds. Keep out of the way," he looked over at Mona without apparent concern. "As we continue to work up, you'll be assigned specific tasks in alert situations, but let's walk before we run. Throughout the sortie C1 will spring these little surprises and, believe me, she knows when to pick her moments. We will practice alerts at all levels except the General Recall. Those of you who aren't flyers will have probably never heard of the General Recall. It is the supreme alert; the signal ordering all space-borne vessels to return to Earth. For obvious reasons it's never practised. Just remember, whatever the alert the flight crew has right of way. Any questions?"

One of the civilians, Kazuhiko, held up his hand. "You're right, Billy. I've never heard of this 'General Recall'. What is its purpose? And if we never practice it how can we become proficient?"

Most of the flying crew, including the Navy, smiled at Kazuhiko's naive question. Billy, however, adopted a serious expression. "A General Recall would mean that Earth was facing some kind of threat. Every Starman, Flyboy, Truckie, and Space Cadet, in any kind of ship, has to get back to defend Biosphere One. I don't know what it sounds like, but I am assured that the General Recall is unmistakable. As for practice, what's there to practice? Stop whatever you're doing; pinpoint the solar system; point the ship at it; press 'go'; come-a-running."

***

The Truckie pilots were doing considerably better in their operational conversion than he'd anticipated. Billy hadn't said that to them, so Mohammed kept his mouth shut about it as well. He suspected that there was method in Billy's madness as he deliberately set about aggravating the naval pilots. Eva, in particular, always took the bait and Wendy was never far behind. Whatever Billy's motives, Mohammed joined his boss in giving the Truckies 'much grief'.

The naval navigators were having more difficulty, but that was only to be expected. Pipsqueak was having a field-day ribbing Marandolina and Ruth. Mohammed had overheard a couple of derogatory expressions that were well worth remembering. The full flight crew exercises were coming on a pace; now, they were drilling round the clock. If Billy continued to push as hard as this, soon, they would be exercising dogfight manoeuvres and then he'd have something to do. Until that time, his only task was to keep a sharp eye on Wendy, to make sure she didn't do anything silly.

"OK, let's try some trans-light manoeuvres Anne," Billy said.

Mohammed sat up; this should be fun. It was 03:07 hours and they had been at it for a solid 11 hours. Being at the limit of normal spacetime, trans-light manoeuvres were a touch tricky at the best of times.

'Ready to run trans-light simulations Billy. Shadow crew, you have simulation control.'

"We have control," Eva said, then kicked in the engines and drives.

Immediately the ship started to shake violently. As his teeth chattered in his head Mohammed wondered how Anne managed to simulate a 181-million-tonne ship shuddering. He guessed that she did something with the artificial gravity, but he wasn't sure.

'Shadow pilots, we are at the limit of trans-light. Either apply more power and go super-light or reduce drive and drop back to normal spacetime.'

The shuddering suddenly increased alarmingly. 'Eva, you are attempting to decelerate. Wendy you are running up the super-light drives. Co-ordinate your actions shadow pilots!'

"Piss poor! Piss bloody poor!" Pipsqueak brayed over the net.

Wendy turned and screamed across the cockpit at him. "Why don't you try, you fucking midget?"

"Premenstrual syndrome? I thought the Navy removed their ovaries," Pipsqueak said, as if puzzling something out loud.

Both Eva and Wendy leant forwards to break the lymphatic connections and leapt from their wombs, heading for Pipsqueak like a pair of crazed Harpies...

'*Baddest* is now spiralling out of control. Main engines 2, 3 and 4 are burning up. All super-light drives incapacitated. Nice move shadow pilots, you have just destroyed the ship. Do you want me to end simulation Billy?'

"Yes Anne," Billy said calmly, then turned around to Eva and Wendy. "You done?"

The tremors abruptly stopped, and the two naval pilots stood rooted to the spot. Their embarrassment was total; not only had they left their station in flight, they had also damaged the ship irreparably. The two women sheepishly went back to their wombs. No one said a word... Mohammed actually heard Wendy grinding her teeth as she walked past him.

"We need to practice trans-light moves, flitting up there in a tight dogfight is an effective way to break contact and then reattack," Billy said with a feigned patience that was simply more salt rubbing.

"Yes Sir," Eva muttered, still embarrassed.

"I'd like Pilot Officer Omangan to demonstrate the technique Sir," Wendy added, bile still rising.

He and Billy exchanged a quick glance, then they got out of their wombs. "Pipsqueak, Grim, you're up. Trans-light boogie," Billy instructed.

Grim and Pipsqueak bounded over and got into the 1st and 2nd pilots' wombs. He and Billy replaced them in the navigators' suite. "Anne, ready to run trans-light simulation," Pipsqueak ordered.

'You show them Boys. You have simulation control.'

He kept his attention on Gabi as Pipsqueak and Grim took *Baddest* smoothly into trans-light.

"Evasive manoeuvres," Billy ordered.

Gabi's mouth was slowly opening wider and wider while Pipsqueak and Grim kept *Baddest* right on the ragged edge of the here and now and the where and when.

"In and out, keep it hot," Billy pushed.

Mohammed turned his attention to Marandolina to watch her reaction. Billy had told the boys to skip in and out of super-light, trans-light and normal spacetime without losing momentum; a manoeuvre that would shake any pursuer but required real 'heads up' flying. Marandolina's mouth was also wide open, she was looking from one to the other in disbelief.

"Anne, keep the simulation going. Demonstration completed. Stand by to take it shadow pilots." Billy wasn't joking.

"We have control," Eva confirmed.

'Shadow pilots, you have simulation control.'

The ship started to shake before Anne finished the sentence. It took them about 25 seconds to get to grips with it. They managed to keep it going, but nowhere near as smoothly as Pipsqueak and Grim had.

After about five minutes Billy said, "Anne, end simulation."

Pilot

'Simulation ends.' The two naval flyers slumped back in their wombs. 'Shadow pilots, would you like me to reduce the temperature and humidity in your wombs?'

"No!" Eva snapped.

He and Billy swapped places with Grim and Pipsqueak. "We're as ready as we'll ever be," Billy said conversationally. "Time for mission start. Eva, that cavity to the left, that's the feed for the mission gloves. Anne, wake up Erick... Erick, you with us?"

"Yes Billy," came the sleepy answer.

"Good. Now, Eva, fingers apart and insert mission glove."

An entire section of the flight deck burst into life. 'Hi Flyboys, self-tests completed, all systems go,' came the warm greeting from the fully activated Anne.

"Right, let's head for the jumping off point. Shadow crew, you take it, and remember, this is live."

As the co-ordinates came up from the navigators Wendy asked. "Before we set off, may I ask a question Billy?"

"Is the question anything to do with how Air Force navigators can play in the translight?"

"Well, yes," came her tentative reply.

"Tell her John."

"All *humble* Air Force navigators are trained to 2nd class naval pilot standards," John tittered.

11

DARTS

The flight out to the jump off point had been intense and at the same time interesting. Erick had begun by remotely monitoring the flight crew. But as the cockpit drill became more and more realistic, he had a greater role in the operation of the ship. He had got the non-flight crew alert drills down to a fine art, even the civilians were switched on. His original objective had been to get the infantry into their suits and combat ready by the time the flight crew were ready for 'fight or flight'. However, the ship's designers had already taken into account this possibility. He was surprised to discover that the womb emergency ejection system could swiftly transport a suited individual to the ejection port. Each combat suit was stored as an integral part of its owner's womb. If the alert involved a landing, Anne automatically broke the lymph connections and the infantry dropped down a few centimetres through the bottoms of the wombs into their suits.

This went some way to explaining why both army and marine combat suits were front entry. He had always considered it a grave oversight that they had to back into their suits, instead of the more logical rear entry, which would involve stepping in. Once the suits were sealed, the infantry were punched down to the ejection port, then stacked like bullets in two magazines: three soldiers in one, three marines in the other. There they waited for the drop command.

Of course, this also implied that the Navy was the Senior Service in name only. The Air Force must be the real power behind the throne. No other space service used wombs. Very few infantry ever set foot on an Air Force ship, yet hundreds of thousands, if not millions, of PADE suits were designed and built to be compatible with the Air Force's methods of operating. He'd touched base with David, the leader of the SAS contingent, who had also reached the same conclusion. David added that he thought that it also illuminated the financing, building and operation of this ship. They both had the unnerving experience of having their accepted perception of the status quo completely demolished.

Erick consoled himself by reading and inwardly digesting the personal records of his shipmates. C1 gave him access to all confidential files, except Billy's, Eva's and, of course, his own. Having read them all, the mission personnel composition began to make some sense. The Flyboys were straightforward fighter pilots; trained to go head to head with anything and take it out. Naval Special Combat Teams, on the other hand, were tactical fighters; their speciality was hit and run or deep interdiction - a balanced mission flight crew.

Pilot

The balance with the infantry was now also obvious. The Pongos were paratroopers, they dropped from space. Their combat suits had an armoured ceramic exoskeleton. They hit the atmosphere at well over Mach 25, burned all the way down to about 5,000 metres, shed the exoskeleton, then deployed parachutes. At 200 metres they detached the parachute and switched on anti-gravity. The Pongos' PARA suits were bigger and heavier than the PADE suits used by Marines and looked like coffins with legs. The soldiers could use anti-grav to skim up to about 30 metres above ground. They were also more heavily armed; hand-held plasma guns, two fission mortars on their backs with four reloads, and helmet mounted, eye-tracking, UV lasers - real Gung Ho.

Marines took the finesse approach. Their PADE suits also had anti-gravity and could fly up to about 800 metres. However, their tactic was to fly low, and fast; 30 metres was a sitting target, 20 metres was the maximum on a battlefield, 10 was the norm. Nor did they go in for killing everything that moved or laying waste to an area. But where they really differed was in method of accessing the battlefield. Theirs was nowhere near as violent or conspicuous. Marines were usually dropped from a stealth craft or one using heavy EM radiation shielding. Swiftly and silently in, get the job done, silently and swiftly out.

With the insight the personal records gave him he tried to get a handle on the civilians. What was their role? They weren't even in the pecking order. In the end, he'd spent the majority of his time learning about them, and fascinating reading it made too. He was no scientist, but their files suggested that they were the best at what they did. Interestingly, although the xenobiologists had all gained their reputations by studying whole biospheres, each was also a specialist in what could best be described as 'the possibility of extraterrestrial intelligence'. And here there was clearly a balance of opinion here as well:

Professor Alfred Nsiah and Doctor Sam Jovanovich; 'Cannot be too different from us. Once we understand their method of communication progress will be rapid.' Doctors, Cynthia W'Li and Kazuhiko Sato; 'Unintelligible, might not even recognise them as being intelligent. Whatever we find will be a surprise.'

One thing was clear, there was an awful lot of talent crammed into the cockpit of *Baddest*. Erick felt much more relaxed and confident about the mission.

***

Billy was a hard taskmaster, but Eva was beginning to feel that it had all been worth it. She, and the shadow crew, brought *Baddest* out of super-light to an absolute stop, on the button. There was a solitary, stationary ship, the naval carrier *Caesar,* waiting. They came in thirty kilometres astern and, as they hailed *Caesar*, it became pretty obvious that there was an awful lot of underwear changing going on aboard the other ship. A carrier was, by definition, a large ship. But *Caesar* was tiny when compared to *Baddest*. She tried to imagine how she'd react if she were on *Caesar's* bridge and a something the size of *Baddest* suddenly appeared out of nowhere.

Why were they RVing with *Caesar*? They were supposed to be RVing with a naval battle group to work up. As she listened in to the comms between Billy and *Caesar's* Captain, it dawned on her that they were discussing the transfer of personnel from *Caesar* to *Baddest*. This was news to her. There had been no mention of a transfer in the Orders Group back on Earth, nor had they received any comms since leaving. She waited until Billy finished chatting, then punched into his net. "Captain, mind telling the 2ic what this is about?"

"As a rule, mission gloves don't contain identical info. The Captain's usually has some stuff that would probably upset the 2ic if they knew about it," he gently teased.

"And?"

"And I'm sure you've noticed that there are twenty-six wombs, even though *Baddest's* complement is only twenty."

"I thought they were spares."

"Spare wombs on an Air Force ship? Don't make me laugh." Then, more seriously, he added, "I was given the option on commandeering a flight of Darts. You didn't know we had launch bays and AutoTech support for Darts, did you?"

"Yes, I did! There was something about that in the briefing from C1." She felt, if not betrayed, certainly disappointed. She and her shadow crew had worked hard to integrate with the Flyboys. In this she thought that they had achieved some success. Now, apparently, Billy didn't have complete confidence in them and was going to bring onboard some Darts for top cover.

"Don't go into a sulk Eva. We wouldn't take on the Darts if you weren't family, would we?"

She wanted to kick herself. Of course, he wouldn't commandeer the Darts unless the flight crew was totally integrated. Solo fighters playing alongside an uncoordinated flight crew? Recipe for a disaster. She could also understand why she hadn't been told.

"Happy now, 2ic?"

Cheeky bastard. Now she wanted to kick *him*. "Yes. What's your game plan?"

"Ain't got one... Yet." He sounded ridiculously relaxed. "First, this will be news to the Dart flight, they might not want to play. Second, even if they do want to, they might not be up to it. So, we've got to check them out without checking them out, get my drift?"

That was exactly what he'd done with her crew; test them for mission capability without overtly letting them know that they were being tested. And if they had failed? It was now pretty obvious that *if* they'd failed, the transfer of personnel would have been from *Baddest* to *Caesar*. This served as a timely reminder to her that despite his sometimes infantile behaviour the mission commander was ruthless, as a good mission commander must be.

***

The six Darts came across in close formation and Anne guided them into the launch bays. Billy had gone down to meet them. With him away from the cockpit she was Captain. She had an idea. "Anne, I want to hear the conversation between Billy and the Dart pilots."

'Certainly Eva.'

What Eva overheard was a somewhat strained but polite conversation. Obviously, no one had told the Dart pilots that they would be transferring to an Air Force ship. They didn't know the mission and had assumed that this was a just a routine transfer. Billy outlined the mission with an economy of words and, to his credit, by the time they reached the cockpit the Dart pilots were chomping at the bit. There were informal introductions, and registration into Anne:

1st Lt. Sun Fu-Sheng; 2nd Lt. Kaye Cadier; 2nd Lt. Vimla Mensah; 2nd Lt. Gill Beyers; 2nd Lt. Varsha Pillai, and 2nd Lt. Sabine von Knorring

To fly a Dart, you had to be under 1.6 metres tall, they were all petite little things. Most were in their early twenties, except for Sun, their flight leader, who Eva put at around her own age, 27. Billy didn't waste any time; he explained about the wombs and the lymphatic connections. The Dart pilots would continue to wear their own flying suits, but with modifications necessary to use a womb. Then he, John and Grim took the six women, en mass, into the fitness room to do the operations. Two hours later they were saying goodbye to *Caesar* and heading sub-light further into sector 12.

Pilot

Billy immediately set about drilling the whole crew, relentlessly. They practised launching the Darts: like the infantry, the Dart pilots were transported from their wombs - suited and booted - directly into their ships in the launch bays. The practised dropping (ejecting into space) and retrieving (tractor beaming in) the Marines and the soldiers. Most of all, they practised dogfights. The Darts were the Navy's equivalent of an Air Force fighter. The Darts played bandits while the shadow crew took *Baddest* through its paces in six-on-one tear-ups. It wasn't until the dogfights started that Eva finally appreciated what Anne had meant when she... *it* had said that *Baddest* was superagile. An 85-kilometre-long ship that could out-turn, outrun, out-accelerate, out-decelerate and, of course, out-gun the 400-metre-long Darts. Super, superagile!

Billy kept them at it for a solid 72 hours. The only respite came during the Darts refuelling and even then, their pilots never left their cockpits. Although her Captain didn't look or act like a perfectionist, he most certainly was. During one dogfight Billy came through on her net. This was a surprise because now, the Flyboys rarely spoke to them when they were flying. "OK, what do you say to calling it a day? Rest for twenty-four hours before jumping to sector 12 to play with the battle group."

"Do you mean we are ready?" It was difficult to think about anything that was not directly related to flying and fighting.

"This is getting a touch hostile," he sniggered. "Hello, Darts, this is Billy, sortie ends, come to mummy."

As she heard Sun acknowledge, Eva suddenly realised that the shadow crew had gradually grown to hate the Dart pilots. They had begun to take every simulated hit on *Baddest* personally. The reverse was also probably true. It was now obvious that since Saturn, Billy and his Flyboys had deliberately bated them. They got them riled, got them tired, and made them fly; Billy had skillfully channelled this anger, ire and frustration into aggression. *And* he'd done exactly the same to the Dart pilots.

He turned to her, smiling, as if reading her thoughts. "The only difference between Air Force and Navy pilots is: you guys don't mind coming second. You're ready."

***

They dropped from the super-light at full alert, released the Darts and went straight into a combat sweep. They spotted the stationary naval battle group at maximum range. There were at least three battle cruisers, a couple of destroyers and about ten frigates. Additionally, there were another ten or eleven ships of indeterminate class. Billy recalled the Darts then they went back to the super-light. It was unlikely that they had been spotted. Sitting back, Mohammed folded his arms; this was the shadow crew's party.

This time they dropped from the super-light almost on the nose of the lead Frigate. Eva and Wendy gave it a quick squirt before turning their attention to bigger prizes. Now, at close range, they saw that the naval formation had three battle cruisers and three medium cruisers. To say that *Baddest* had caught the Truckies with their trousers down would have been an understatement. Dummy missiles were already well on the way to their targets before the escorting vessels started to react. *Baddest* had already taken out the six capital ships before the first simulated hit on its shields. Ships that had sustained simulated crippling damages left the game by becoming motionless.

As the Frigates and Destroyers started to gang up Eva launched the Darts. Mohammed no longer spent any of his time monitoring Wendy, the shadow crew had earned their spurs. Instead, his attention was on the screens: the Darts had looked the part in their six-on-one dogfights. How would they fare against stiffer opposition? Eva obviously had the same thought because as the dogfight developed, she kept *Baddest* out of the thick of it, leaving the Darts to fend for themselves.

A single Dart against even a frigate was a mismatch, but Sun kept her formation tight and intact. Mohammed sat grinning as the Darts took care of business; they chased down and started mopping up the remaining navy ships at a loss of only two of their numbers.

"*All stations, all stations, this is Commodore Zarcroft. EndEx. Out.*" Came the sharp command over the sub and super-light channels.

The dogfight halted and all ships held station. This was a cry off from the Truckies. A battle group that size should have been able to defend a solar system. Yet *Baddest* and her six Darts had comprehensively kicked their arse. This was a bloody abysmal failure even by Navy standards. Taken by surprise, they had simply gone through the motions and then thrown in the towel. That's the trouble with Truckies, they were too textbook oriented; play the percentages and, predictably, take the path that offered the least resistance.

There wasn't a chapter in the textbook on what to do if a ship dropped right into your sights. After all no captain of a solo enemy ship would ever drop out of super-light smack bang in front of a fleet, right? Wrong, but because it wasn't in the book, they had never considered the possibility. And, because it wasn't in the book, they were fresh out of ideas when confronted with the actuality. No imagination, no flair, that was why Truckies were always so easy to beat. Despite himself, Mohammed began to feel embarrassed on behalf of the shadow crew.

"Because you're now family, I won't dwell on this. But aren't you utterly ashamed to be in the Navy?" John's singsong Central American accent asked on the open net.

"Lock on momentum tractor beam to that ship," Billy ordered as he pinpointed one of the battle cruisers on the targeting screen.

"But it's EndEx..." Wendy started to protest, then realised that it wasn't EndEx until the ship's Captain said that it was.

"Target locked on," Gabi confirmed.

It was Marandolina who grasped what was going down because she asked, "Father?"

"Brother," Billy answered casually.

Eva then fell in. "How many revs?"

"One every two minutes should suffice," Billy suggested.

"Rotating target at half a revolution per minute," Ruth confirmed.

"*Air Force ship, this is the Battle Group Commander. EndEx. Repeat, EndEx,*" came the almost hysterical command.

"Spin the bastards, they're a disgrace to the Navy," Marandolina said angrily.

A tractor beam buggered up a ship's artificial gravity and its inertialess envelope. If it got caught in a tractor beam, the ship's primary computer would automatically switch off the artificial gravity; anyone not strapped in would go-a-wandering. Spinning a ship was a deliciously nasty thing to do, even worse than Goosing a Weightless.

"*Air Force ship, desist without delay!*"

"Bolshy. They're asking for one a minute, aren't they?" Eva said conversationally.

"You know, I think they are," Billy agreed.

"Rotating target at one revolution per minute," Ruth cackled.

"*Air Force ship, disengage immediately! This is your final warning.*" Whoever was on the comms sounded like they were about to puke.

"OK, standby," Billy suddenly became businesslike. "This is going to turn into a live firing. Darts, stay close to mamma. Everybody, remember, shake them up but don't break anything."

Pilot

The Naval ships suddenly broke formation. Two of the Cruisers came after *Baddest* and launched live torpedoes. Obviously, they intended to harass them into releasing the tractor beam. Sun brought her Darts around and hammered the screens of a couple of the Frigates. The Truckies belatedly woke up to the fact that 'taking the gloves off' wasn't necessarily a one-way street. Things got frantic; this was real firepower the Truckies were kicking out.

There's nothing like someone firing live bullets at you to get the juices going, Mohammed mused as the shadow crew along with Sun and her Darts, got busy. Eva and Wendy used *Baddest* to cover the Darts whilst, at the same time, swatting the battle group's capital ships at long range. The Darts tore into the naval formation with a ferocity that was almost artistic. At one stage Mohammed thought Billy was going to call them off, because all six Darts had isolated one Destroyer and were working it over. Its screens were glowing white and looked as if they were about to collapse. But then Sun pulled her Darts off and their formation turned its attention to a Frigate and started to give it similar treatment.

The thing that was most lamentable about the Truckies' performance was the way they stuck to their battle drills. Although it should have been as plain as the noses on their faces that their tactics were ineffective, they just kept to it. With their numerical superiority and fire power the battle group should at least have taken out the Darts. The only thing that he found surprising was the amount of restraint shown by the shadow crew and the Dart pilots. They could have roasted any of the naval ships if they had really wanted to.

One of the Battle Cruisers finally broke out of the formation to make a determined attack on *Baddest*. Considering it was firing real weapons, Eva and Wendy simply dodged around until it was in range, then answered by locking on with a second tractor beam. Gabi started to spin it as well. With two of their capital ships trapped the Truckies should have put all their efforts into trying to liberate them. Instead they started backing off; not running away, exactly, but certainly not going about their business with any apparent conviction.

"*This is Military Command Sector 12. Wing Commander Zarcroft, you are ordered to bring your formation to heel, immediately. Cease hostilities. Repeat. Cease hostilities.*" An authoritative sounding female voice ordered.

This was the last straw. The bloody Truckies had gone crying to Sector Command. They were the ones who had started loosing off the artillery and, now, they were the ones crying foul. Mohammed felt genuine disgust.

"You heard the lady, let them up for some air," Billy sounded bored. "Sector Command, this is *Baddest*, will comply."

"Baddest, *Darts are disengaging*," Sun confirmed. "*Did you hear that battle group? We're backing off, you utter and complete wankers!*"

"I don't care if he is your brother, what a fucking wimp!" Marandolina was shaking with anger.

"Final rotation at angular velocity of two revolutions per minute," Gabi said spitefully.

"Gabi, let go of them, you naughty girl! And let's have some discipline on the net." Billy's tone didn't convey a great deal of authority, then in a chirpy voice he added, "Hello Commodore Zarcroft, this is Wing Commander Zarcroft, over."

A head and shoulders hologram of an older version of Billy, with the same light brown eyes and olive skin, appeared. "*William! I should have known. This indiscipline will result in formal charges being brought. The Air Force has...*"

"Oh, shut up Ed! What are you going to do? Run crying to Mum like you went crying to Sector Command? Oh, sorry, I forgot. The Commander of sector 12, *is* Mummy," Billy interrupted with dripping sarcasm.

"*Correct, Wing Commander. Now, disengage and withdraw from this sector.*" Again, the authoritative female voice came over the super-light channel. As an afterthought it added, "*Good luck on your mission* Baddest."

"Thank you, Admiral," Billy replied curtly. "OK Sun, bring the Darts in."

***

Eva lay in her womb reflecting; she and Wendy's were on their rest period. Over the last 72 hours or so, the excitement had worn off. They began to settle into the routine of the search itself. *Baddest* had its most sensitive instruments probing for the missing ship *Arabia*. So far, not even a trace. But, then again, sectors were huge areas; it could easily take six months or more to complete a thorough sweep. Billy still had them working on the drills with the Darts but none of the pilots could work up much enthusiasm. After the thrashing they'd given the battle group in a live firing the drills seemed rather dull. Eva knew that Billy was aware of this. In her regular orders group with him and Erick, Billy had confirmed that exercises were just 'make work' to stop everyone going off the boil. With an unspecified search duration in front of them, he wanted the crew in a relaxed but alert state - boredom was the hidden enemy.

The Flyboys where been uncharacteristically reticent about the dogfight. Even the Marines, soldiers and civilians seemed at pains to eschew the topic. This silence simply added to the naval crewmember embarrassment. The battle group's performance had been a humiliating shambles. Sun and her flight had sworn to resign their naval commissions as soon as the mission ended. Eva wasn't ready to go that far, but she wasn't as proud of her naval space wings as she'd used to be.

One other subject was also being diplomatically avoided: Billy's family. She'd heard of Admiral Zarcroft of course, who hadn't? Eva had, in fact, served under the Admiral when she'd commanded the 8th fleet. The Admiral was a Flag Officer who was almost certainly destined for Supreme Command. As Cath Awunda, the Admiral had been the cadet pilot that all Navy cadet pilots measured themselves against. Some of the records she had set were still standing, others had only been surpassed by a supremely confident, almost arrogant Midshipman, named Zarcroft.

There was also a highly regarded Rear Admiral Zarcroft, could he be Billy's father? The Awunda and Zarcroft family names had been synonymous with the Navy for centuries. Wherever there was a naval roll of honour those names were to be found. Eva came from a Navy family herself. Not as illustrious as Billy's, but with its own well-charted history. And, like Billy, she was born and raised in the colonies and had been educated in off-Earth military academies. So, she could certainly appreciate why there had been such a furore when fourteen-year-old Midshipman Zarcroft, W. waltzed out of the Naval Academy to join the Air Force. There were so many questions she wanted to ask Billy, but now was definitely not the time.

As the mission settled into a routine, Eva was surprised to discover that Anne had been programmed with all the published works of the four Xenobiologists. The main recreation onboard was turning out to be an endless round of fierce arguments on the various theorems on extraterrestrial intelligence. The debates had started out as professional discussions amongst the experts, and gradually expanded to involve the entire crew. Everyone had an opinion and, of course, it gave the civilians a central role. The speculation

Pilot

was both interesting and informative. It also served to further integrate the civilians into the military family. There were many clashes of personality, but this was only to be expected. The crew consisted of 26 talented and strong-willed individuals. It had become pretty obvious to Eva that this mix was better suited to an Air Force regime than to the more rigid structure of a naval ship...

All the lights in the cockpit and on the instruments suddenly started flashing wildly. "***Alert. Alert. General Recall. General Recall. This is not an exercise. General Recall***..." the calm male voice was cut off in mid-sentence.

Eva sat up slowly and exchanged puzzled looks with Wendy. General Recall?! There was a stunned silence except for Billy telling the Navigators to hurry up and sort out the flight profile. By the time the coordinates came up all weapons were armed, the Darts were ready in launch bays, and infantry set in their ejection ports. All this was done with speed and precision, as they had drilled, but it was done with an automatic detachment brought on by disbelief. An almost surreal calmness had descended on the crew.

"Snap out of it!" Billy suddenly barked. "We'll drop just outside Pluto's orbit. There we should get a SitRep. If one isn't forthcoming, we'll fly sub-light to Earth. Anything that isn't instantly recognisable as being of human origin, kill. Super-light, go!"

The star field changed and the momentary dizziness and nausea that always accompanied a super-light jump passed; Darts were automatically launched. As her vision cleared Eva recoiled in total disbelief at what the flight instruments showed.

"Navs!" Billy shouted.

"There's Saturn and Neptune. Jupiter is on the other side of the sun." Grim's reply was almost a sob.

"Darts, move in, split formation and check out Nereid and NASMB1," Billy ordered as he edged *Baddest* forward.

"Everything is silent. No navigation beacons, no navigation satellites, nothing," Pipsqueak reported.

"*Baddest, this is Sun, Nereid is clean. No sign of AFB; nothing to indicate that there ever was an AFB here, and our NavComs are malfunctioning.*"

"*Baddest, this is Kaye. NASMB1 is gone. Our NavComs are also way off.*"

'There is no debris or high energy ions to indicate that anything has been destroyed,' Anne reported.

"Maybe they were rotated into another dimension," John suggested feebly.

"Rotated into another dimension? Are you crazy?!" Marandolina almost shrieked with incredulity.

"Be quiet," Billy ordered, then transmitted, "Darts, go over and under the plane. Sweep search, report back, tight stream."

The Darts acknowledged then, Kazuhiko one of the xenobiologist, in a half hysterical voice asked, "What's the matter? What caused the recall?"

"The Earth is gone. All trace of human activity has vanished. No more questions for now," Billy responded tersely.

'The Darts NavComs are functioning correctly. The orbits of all the other planets have been altered to counteract the absence of Earth.'

"Darts in! Now! Electronic silence everyone. Navs, find some dense interstellar cloud not less than thirty light-years from here; plot a course to get us there in one jump. Anne, as soon as the last Dart is secure, autojump and..."

Only a civilian would interrupt a military commander in the midst of issuing orders. "You mean we're going to..."

"Shut up Kazuhiko!" Eva put him firmly in his place.

"...record all sub and super-light transmissions encountered," Billy concluded.

'Roger, Billy. Last Dart docking now. Standby for super-light jump.'

12

SEARCH

He stood in the ejection port in almost total darkness, the only light came from his Head Up Display. The display gave him no additional information than he could gather from the concise talk over the net: General Recall; Earth missing; solar system rearranged. Isolated as the infantry were, he was inclined to suspect that this was another Flyboy prank. But something in everyone's tone suggested that this was for real. The Earth was gone? Ridiculous! His mind refused to take the idea seriously, although some part of his intellect tried to assert itself, counselling that he should. He tensed himself for the super-light jump.

The dizziness came and went, then he heard Billy over the net, "*Mohammed, Wendy, in and out, shake anything that might have followed us. Stay inside the cloud, keep it going while I get my brain around this.*"

There was silence on the net for an agonizing five minutes, then he heard Billy again, "*Bring the ship to an absolute stop and activate stealth shielding. Anne, keep full passive scanning online. Stand down. Time for a huddle.*"

The infantry were automatically transported back to the cockpit and stripped of their combat suits and weapons. By the time he was plugged into his womb, the Dart pilots were entering the cockpit and getting plugged into theirs. Billy had obviously been waiting for them because as soon as everyone was plugged-in, he started.

"Let's talk this thing through. First, this is not a dream; you are not hallucinating; the Earth has vanished; all that we hold dear and love is gone... I'll be the first to admit it, I don't understand and I'm fresh out of ideas. We need to brainstorm. Nothing is to be excluded within the limits of possibility. Second, let me explain why we're here. We are hiding. Anything that can move planets and rearrange solar systems is not to be fucked with unprepared. Anne, anything to report about transmissions?"

'The broadcast of the General Recall, along with all other manmade EM radiation and super-light transmissions, was abruptly cut off. Nothing is coming out of any of the space sectors on any super-light band.'

Billy sighed, "For anyone who didn't get the significance of that, let me spell it out: Sector Commands have open super-light channels with Supreme Command. These are *all* silent, which means that *all* sector communications have been taken out. If the sector comms are out, it's reasonable to assume that the Sol system wasn't the only one to get the treatment."

"The full enormity of this is that all thirty-one sectors have been, at best, disabled in a simultaneous attack across God knows how many light years. And *that* is the measure of the unknown enemy we face," Eva added in a tone verging on bewilderment.

100

"May I state that human expansion and exploration extends throughout a significant portion of this spiral arm. To suggest that all these inhabited solar systems have been simultaneously attacked is preposterous," Sam, one of the xenobiologist, asserted.

"Look, Sam," Billy said patiently, "The super-light is outside relativistic physics. Super-light transmissions are omnidirectional and almost instantaneous. Eva wasn't speculating when she said that the attack was simultaneous. So, folks, let's keep every hypothesis alive until we have conclusive proof to the contrary."

Varsha, one of the Dart pilots came on the net, "As you know, 90 percent of NAMB1 was below ground. It hasn't just vanished. As far as I could see, it's been replaced by several large craters."

'The data from the Darts shows that where there was a settlement or installations the surface has been reconstructed. Traces of human activity have not simply been removed; they have been erased as if they had never existed.'

Preecha, one of the Marines who Billy had rechristened Peach, stammered, "If s... so... someone... aliens... were going to attack, they would des... des... destroy our defences and then occupy the solar system, wouldn't they?"

"Yes, why vaporise Earth, or whatever it is they've done?" Cynthia agreed.

"An alien mind that perceived mankind as a threat could easily conclude that xenocide was their only recourse," Alfred countered authoritatively.

"Well, they've failed haven't they," Marandolina said, tears welling up in her eyes.

"They have?" John asked, looking puzzled.

"Of course. We're still here, aren't we?" she answered.

"Our mission has *got* to be to find and then take out the bad guys, whoever they are," Grim asserted.

"Do you think this has anything to do with *Arabia*?" Pipsqueak asked.

"Probably, but how would we know?" Billy replied.

"Perhaps we're being too hasty. It may be the result of a natural phenomenon," Alfred, another of the Xenobiologist, suggested.

"A natural phenomenon that affected only the Earth? Don't be ridiculous!" Ruth half shrieked.

"Calm down," Eva soothed.

'I have completed the analysis of the gravitational waves we encountered when we dropped from super-light. There were many residual shockwaves, however, the form of the main wave-front suggests the unlikely event of the Earth being accelerated out of the solar system at super-light speed.'

"A whole planet accelerated to superlight? I don't see how that can be within the realms of possibility," David, the Army Captain, questioned the hypothesis.

Although what David had said would seem to be commonsense, Erick supposed that it wasn't *impossible*, but he decided, for the sake of 'Grunts' unity', not to voice this.

"If they can change a solar system why can't they fly a planet," Billy said thoughtfully, then added, "Anne, any idea of the direction of transit?"

'Towards the centre of the galaxy. I cannot be more precise.'

"We may still be in the game," Eva said hopefully.

"Yes, but what are we up against?" Billy mused. "Anne, you have the watch. Administer sedative to all crew; minimum rest, eight hours."

***

Pilot

Opening his eyes, he turned and slowly looked over the flight crew, his eyes coming to rest on Eva and Wendy. He stared at the two women for several moments. They looked so blissfully happy it seemed a pity to wake them. "Anne, anything to report?"

'No Billy.'

"Wake Eva and Erick."

'OK Billy.'

He punched into the command net. Adding extra and unfelt enthusiasm to his voice, he started. "No, it wasn't a dream. The Earth *has* been kidnapped. A net of silence had been thrown over human occupied space. Now, it took us two hours twenty-nine minutes, real time, to reach the solar system after getting the General Recall. So, our technologically advanced civilization was worked over in under two hours and twenty-nine minutes. What do we do now?"

"Find the Earth," Eva replied automatically.

"It would take us forever to search the galaxy," Erick countered.

"But we must try," she insisted.

Billy's logic was with Erick, but emotionally he was 100 percent behind Eva. "Where do we start looking?"

"Back to the solar system," Eva answered without much conviction.

"Bad idea." Erick said, in alarm.

Sitting up suddenly in his womb, Billy whipped his head around to have another look at Eva. Then he simply stared at her.

"What?" Eva asked.

Instead of answering, he said, "Anne, wake crew."

'Waking crew, Billy.'

"Anne, I'm going to ask you a question and I want the entire crew to hear the answer."

'Yes Billy.'

"Anne, is it my imagination..., or am I becoming aware that some of the crew are women?"

'It is not your imagination Billy.' The computer then actually laughed, cackling.

"Anne, you wouldn't care to tell us how the suppression worked, would you?" John jumped in.

'I am not programmed with that information, John.'

"This is just great. Earth has vanished and any moment now all we'll be able to think about is getting our ends away," Billy grouched. "Anne, reinstate the sexual suppression."

'I am not programmed with how to accomplish that Billy.'

There was a very long period of silence. Every instinct he had as a military commander balked at the silliness of the situation, yet there were more powerful instincts - he could already feel his libido starting to rise. There was no obvious way out, so he addressed his crew. "OK, folks, here's the deal. We've been in space for long enough for the sexual suppression to warrant some release. Right now, this is going to be just a huge distraction. What I'm about to suggest is not an order, but I think it *is* necessary. We don't have a fifty-fifty male/female crew. Girls, pick a partner. If two of you pick the same guy draw straws for who gets first go. Fuck each other's brains out. Then let's concentrate on finding the Earth."

'We do not have a 100 percent heterosexual or bisexual crew, Billy. All males are heterosexual or bisexual. Three of the females are lesbians.'

"Oh, wonderful," he sighed, then brightened. "Hmm... Thanks for that Anne. Better odds, hey guys?"

"I must protest!" Cynthia interrupted. "Your suggestion is not only offensive, it's nonsensical. Surely we ought to be formulating a strategy for finding Earth's whereabouts?"

"Cynthia, you're only saying that because you haven't clocked up the hours on a space vessel. It *will* be a distraction," Eva explained patiently.

"And that's putting it mildly," Mohammed added.

"Anne, give me the compatibility permutations of the crew set against sexual orientation and the mission profile," he asked.

A diagram appeared on his screen. Leaning over to look at it, Eva laughingly said, "Anne, I think we should share this with the rest of the crew."

The same diagram appeared on all screens. Everyone started speaking at the same time, so he overrode them. "We're not talking romance here, just releasing some, shall we say, tension. Until we do, we won't be able to function at optimum. That's optimum in the military sense," he pointed out tiredly. "So, let's cut this bashful crap. You can all see your partners. Have a quiet word and sort it out." This he said as an order.

"No way!" Pipsqueak protested over the open net.

"I've heard that short men have big cocks. I sure hope that's true because I can't stand those pinky finger maggots. You know, the ones that make you want to burst out laughing," Eva answered Pipsqueak back on the open net.

"I'm supposed to *share* Guido with Gabi and Sun? Are you serious or what?" Preecha bawled out in indignation.

"I said, 'keep it to yourselves'!" he snapped. He wasn't angry, but couldn't see why anyone should make an issue of the situation; they had no choice...

"How do you want to play this, Captain?" Sabine came through, rather formally, on his net. Before he could answer Sabine, Eva also came through, "This is so mechanical. We shouldn't screw to order."

He punched into Eva's net first. "True, but in a couple of hours, there'll be no stopping us." Then he switched to Sabine's. "Romance isn't dead, it just smells a bit funny. Why don't I come pay you a visit?"

"OK," she answered hesitantly, clearly not sure how seriously to take him.

As he leant forward to break the lymphatic connection Eva checked her screen, then turned to him and said. "I don't think she's your type either."

"Compatible in the incompatible sense, unlikely emotional attachments. Do excuse me while I go and lead by example."

***

Wombs were designed for single occupancy. The basics could be accomplished in relative comfort, but anything more adventurous was out of the question. Though the wombs could have their opaque screens up there was no barrier to sound. Nearly thirty people rutting like there was no tomorrow, quite an orchestra. There were layers and layers of intensity to the whole thing. He didn't know about anybody else, but he'd felt under a certain amount of pressure.

The first problem was having to preform to order. That, in itself, was bad enough but when one's enforced partner fed back exactly the same sentiments - 'let's just get this over and done with' - the stress levels inevitably went up a couple of notches. Then, there was everybody at it all at the same time. They had to keep up with the Joneses, didn't they? The fact that, left to his own devices, Mohammed would have been going at it with gusto anyway didn't seem to matter. More stress. Then, on top of all this, there was something deeper, more powerful; almost primordial. This all-out fucking wasn't just for them, wasn't just for fun; it was for mankind. They could be the last human beings alive.

He had been paired off with Sufra, one of the soldiers. The fun and games started with them trying to get each other's flying suits off. He liked his women tall. She was 6' 3" and had a beautiful slim face, with delicate Asian features, *but* she had the build of a Bear; muscular, broad shouldered, pectorals so well developed that she had almost no breasts, and thighs like tree trunks. And she was a howler. Not really his cup of tea, but he probably wasn't hers either. It could have been a lot worse, at least he wasn't playing 'shared-by-the-fems'. So, the Bear and the Gazelle fucked each other to the point of exhaustion, and then some, yet neither felt satisfied nor sated. They would fall asleep and wake to a chorus of love moans which would prod them into starting all over again. This bonking had been going on for a solid sixteen hours and was getting to the point where Mohammed was hoping that Billy would call a halt.

When he went back to his womb to eat, he bumped into Pipsqueak who had just finished getting some much-needed sustenance. Pipsqueak and Eva had been enmeshed in some sexual power game, the first to cry 'enough' being the loser. The two had decamped to the fitness room to give themselves a larger arena. As they parted Mohammed warned Pipsqueak that he looked like he'd already lost. Pipsqueak agreed, Eva was bi and using the, 'women are so much better at this sort of thing' ploy. Not only that, she'd set it up so that she lies back letting him fuck himself senseless proving her wrong and just when he totally spent she takes over the proceedings and grinds him into dust. Pipsqueak's adieu was, 'For my eulogy I want it known that the Flyboy never ceded to the Truckie.'

As Mohammed, laughing, eased himself into his womb and started to plug in, Billy sauntered up and collapsed into his womb. "Well, Chief, have we had enough, or have we had enough?" he greeted Billy.

Billy turned to him and smiled. "Most of us have."

Did Billy mean that someone hadn't? Mohammed found this hard to believe. "Who didn't party?"

Billy laughed. "Everybody's partied. But, Flyboy, there are a couple of two-on-ones and a three-on-one that, how shall I put this, still haven't cleared their systems, yet."

Mohammed cracked up. The shared-by-the-fems were being worked-over by women's relay teams: putting a completely new spin on the phrase 'passing on the baton'. Anne must be pumping the guys full of God knows what.

Sufra came through on his net. "I'm sore, let's call it a day." Then she added in a businesslike tone, "I'd love another romp in a couple of days."

"It's a big Roger to that," he answered, trying to sound enthusiastic. But he was knackered...

He was woken by Wendy plonking herself into her womb behind him. She looked absolutely fucked. He thought about making a comment or two but saw that she was in no state to appreciate his wit. Standing, he took a good look around the cockpit. All the opaque screens were gone, and everybody was in their own womb. It was easy to spot the wombs occupied by the shared-by-the-fems; they were reclined to the horizontal. He sat and pondered for a while. The ship was a sterile area, so the germs that caused offensive smells were absent. There was no facility to bathe or wash onboard; the wombs' placenta functions took care of bodily waste and things like sweat and dead skin was absorbed into its lining. Having said that, there was a ripe, heavy, pleasant, odour in the cockpit. He assumed that Anne would remove the smell as she recycled the air.

"Right, folks, orders group in three hours. Get some rest," Billy broadcasted.

Someone obviously asked Billy a question on his net because after a few moments he said, "Keep the same match-ups, and if you want to party get C1 to synchronize the timings of your fitness programmes."

"We may be the last of the human race. Any sexual intercourse we engage in should have a purpose. We have responsibilities," one of the xenobiologists commented.

Trust a civilian to touch-off a sensitive subject like this. Mohammed figured that over half the crew must be sleeping, hopefully.

Billy jumped on this. "A fair point Kazuhiko. However, there is one *insignificant* but related matter that you may be unaware of. Wherever Earth is, that's where you'll find the reproductive organs of all the military crew. Cynthia, are you awake?"

"Yes Billy."

"As the only nonmilitary female member of the crew, how do you fancy being the mother of the rebirth of the human race?"

Cynthia didn't answer, but Anne, with all the sensitivity of a computer, said, 'Cynthia cannot have children Billy, she is infertile.'

"I see. Anne, do we have the resources and expertise to clone a human?"

'No Billy. We have the resources, but not the expertise. My databanks lack the necessary programmes.'

"OK. Kazuhiko, the subject is closed, do not raise it again. Now, everybody get some rest."

13

DRONE

"Billy, Eva. I've been thinking. Rather than go looking for them, why don't we let them come to us?" Erick came through on the command net.

"Run that one past me again." Billy sounded sleepy.

"Sure. We wouldn't even know where to start looking for Earth. Perhaps we could entice whoever or whatever's got it to come to us."

Eva sat up and started to pay attention. This had merit.

"How would you do that?" Billy sounded pretty enthusiastic.

"By broadcasting a signal, or something."

She was already ahead of them both. "The bad guys believe that they've taken out all our forces. If we started making a racket on the super-light bands they'd want to investigate, wouldn't they?"

"Can't pinpoint a super-light transmission source with any accuracy," Billy mused.

"No, but if the source was in the neighbourhood of a planet you'd just taken out you'd go have a look, wouldn't you?" she countered.

"I wasn't thinking about calling them down on top of us," Erick said in alarm.

"Me neither," Billy laughed. "We could set up a transmitter as bait, then see what it attracts."

"Maybe we could put a homer in it and if they take it walkies follow them." She was starting to like this.

"Yes," Billy agreed. "Eva, Ruth's your techno-wizzo, right?"

"Yes."

"Anne, wake John and Ruth."

'Yes Billy.'

"Not very considerate. Waking a body by informing them you want them to perform," Ruth complained sleepily.

"I need another eight hours sleep," John agreed.

"Yeah, I know, life's a bitch and then you die," Billy laughed. "I want your gut reaction to this scenario. We build a super-light transmitter to attract the bad guys, they come and check out the source, then we follow them home."

"I take it that we're assuming that they're not complete morons?" Ruth asked.

"Correct, why do you ask?" Erick asked back.

"Any such transmitter would have to have an overt purpose, other than being a lure," Ruth pondered aloud.

"I have the purpose. A fail-safe rebroadcast of the General Recall," John added.

"Have to be mobile," Ruth said.

"And difficult to track." John was obviously warming to the task.

Ruth and John were having a conversation between themselves, Eva wanted to get to the doing part. "Fine, but could we build one?"

"Building and programming it is the easy bit. Keeping tabs on it from a discreet distance is the difficulty," John answered.

"Why?" Billy asked.

"It goes something like this. We want the bad guys to find it; we don't want them to find us, but we want to see them when they show up. This might sound trivial, but we don't know how good their vision is, get my drift?" Ruth explained.

"We've thought of that," Erick said. "We'd put a homer in it."

"I thought we had agreed that they weren't mentally retarded," John yawned.

"We catch your drift," Billy interjected. "Is there a way round it?"

"Dunno. Pilots never do any work anyway, so why don't you leave this with the Nav team. We'll bounce it around for a bit and get back to you," John suggested, then added, "And before you ask, I don't know."

"Don't know what?" Erick asked foolishly.

"How long we'll be," Ruth answered, laughing.

***

The Navigators came up with a flight profile that they said would work. The drone would be programmed to fly a circular orbit around the solar system at a distance of about half a light year. It would hammer out the General Recall as it went merrily on its way. They would keep track of it by flying on a parallel course, rapidly stepping in and out of super-light with all sensors going. The Navigators and Anne assured them that by quickly stepping in and out they would be able to see without being seen.

The one drawback of all this would be the psychological and physiological trauma of the crew. The ship would be making twenty-three transitions per second into and out of normal spacetime. Their nervous systems would take a battering and their senses wouldn't function properly. Obviously, the pilots couldn't fly this profile, Anne had to be programmed. Billy and Mohammed went over the figures with a fine-tooth comb. She and Wendy weren't much help, the hardly understood the programming language - naval ships couldn't fly on automatic. When he was satisfied, Billy set Grim, Pipsqueak and Marandolina the task of designing the drone; his only condition was that it had to be small enough to have been the sort of thing *they* might have missed.

While the three got on with that he and Mohammed went over the plots again. She felt that she was letting her Captain down because there was nothing she could do to help. It wasn't until Anne had built the six-metre-long drone and it had been tested that Billy informed the rest of the crew of his intentions. What he described was a highly risky and unpleasant long shot. But it galvanised the crew, at last they were going to do something.

They drifted out to the edge of the interstellar cloud and started practising tracking the drone. Five minutes later they were at rest. The tracking was on the button, but the air of enthusiasm had evaporated, everyone was puking their guts out; dazed and disorientated, they could hardly see or hear. Eva didn't know about anyone else, but she had the mother of all headaches and her eyes felt like they were ready to pop out of her skull. As if from a great distance she heard Billy as he managed to get one coherent order out. He told Anne to sedate everyone.

It took them about seven hours to recover, and this was with the aid of Anne pumping them full of hormones, steroids, and anything else that sh... it thought appropriate. By the time a meaningful conversation could resume she was ready to kick the tracking idea into touch. Billy, however, had a different view. He figured that they could take about three minutes of rapid hopping in and out of super-light. Providing that they had about fifteen minutes rest between sessions the flight crew should still be able to respond to events. She wasn't convinced but kept her own counsel.

During the fifteen-minute rest and recuperation periods the drone would be stationary and *Baddest* would stand off at maximum detection range of about 1.5 light years. Billy told the Navigators to programme Anne and the drone with this flight profile. After the reprogramming was completed, they had another dry run. It became clear that even three minutes was too much. The Navigators changed it to two minutes flight and twenty minutes rest. Then another dry run.

After a two-minute session you still felt like shit, but at least you could think. Billy seemed satisfied and ordered a four-hour rest before mission start. A certain amount of cleaning of personal space - even the sophisticated wombs couldn't expurgate that much puke - and the fitting of clean flight suits was necessary. This activity took a sizable chunk of the allotted four hours. She suspected that Billy was aware that it would and was exercising a little aversion therapy. It was no fun cleaning your own vomit out of all the nooks and crannies of a womb.

At mission start they went to full alert with the Darts ready to launch but with the infantry still in their wombs. *Baddest* reached the launch position, two light years from the solar system, in one jump. After making a quick sweep of the area they launched the drone and started their routine of flitting in and out of super-light. The two minutes felt like two hours. As they dropped into the stand-off position and her head started to clear she heard Anne talking.

'...ship at maximum range. On a parallel course to drone and about half a light year distance astern.'

"Edge us closer," Billy ordered.

'Ship identified. It's *The Beast*.'

"I knew we were the cover mission! It took them too long to send us out. Stand by to establish comms with *The Beast*," Billy said excitedly.

Suddenly the tracking screens showed energy discharges around the drone. Several unidentified ships dropped from super-light dumping vast amounts of energy. Before the flight crew could react, the same discharges registered in the vicinity of *The Beast*. Abruptly, drone, *The Beast*, and the new players vanished.

"Anne, follow their wake. Go!"

***

As the dizziness and nausea receded and her head cleared, through the cockpit window, Eva saw that the density of stars had increased by about a factor of ten.

'We have jumped approximately 1,000 light years towards the centre of the galaxy. I tracked the unidentified formation to this sector, accuracy: plus or minus 167 light years. Swept area, nothing found... Contact! Unidentified ships, 0949/1134/0014, closing rapidly.'

"Trans-light boogie," Billy to Mohammed, then he hollered, "Darts, stand by!"

As *Baddest* dropped back into normal spacetime, she realised that Billy and Mohammed had brought them in behind the attacking formation.

"Locked on," came from one of the Navigators.

Her heart rate went through the roof as she and Wendy loosed off a brace of missiles then they were back in trans-light. After-the-fact she realised that Billy hadn't said, 'fire'. He hadn't needed to the flight crew were responding as an integrated team. Before she could congratulate herself on holding up her end, they were back in normal spacetime. For a fleeting moment she saw, at maximum visible range, two expanding crimson globes - the ships they had taken out. Good! *They* were killable.

"Steady... Steady. Locked on."

More missiles launched. As they went back to trans-light *Baddest* was rocked by multiple impacts.

'Direct hits. Minimal damage.'

They kept at this hit and run. Dropping unpredictably, staying in normal spacetime for a couple of seconds, then out again. They had taken out about eleven enemy ships, but many more were joining the party.

"Now we know where they live, get us out of here." Billy ordered the Navigators.

"Stand by for coordinates..."

Baddest came to an absolute stop, her crew slumped unconscious in their wombs. If the crew had been conscious, they would have seen a luminous, indistinct, almost ghostly vertical shape appear in the centre of the cockpit. Anne's higher functions deactivated, the weapon and tracking systems shut down. Everything, except the life support system, switched off.

***

Even before he opened his eyes, he sensed that something wasn't right. As he sat up, he knew that something was definitely wrong, gravity was wrong. His head was clear, his vision was fine, he knew he wasn't dreaming. He was in an evenly lit room that had whitish-grey ceiling, walls, and floor. So where was the light source? The room appeared to be a perfectly symmetrical fifteen-foot cube. It was empty apart from the table he was lying on. Sitting up he slipped off the table and stood, he was still wearing his flight suit, but no helmet or gloves. He felt light, about 0.75 G he guessed. This place was decidedly abnormal. Where was the door? He turned to examine the table. It looked and felt like a perfectly ordinary table.

"Wing Commander Zarcroft."

He spun around. By a wall, in an overtly nonthreatening stance, stood a nondescript looking male civilian. He was of indeterminate age, average build, average colouration, in fact, everything about the guy was average.

"I am what you would think of as a hologram. However, I have a solid form. I am here to assist you in your orientation. I will answer your immediate questions. First, would you care to sit?" The hologram spoke in a neutral accent and gestured for him to sit.

Billy glanced back at the table; it was no longer there. In its place was a chair. Refusing to be shocked or overawed, gingerly he sat.

"You are on the planet Evier. Your ship is in orbit. Your crew are still on board, sleeping... Earth had been transported... *The Beast*... It would greatly aid me in explaining the situation if you did not form multiple and disjointed questions... Your planet was not attacked, it was removed from its location to protect it and..."

"Are you reading my mind?" Billy could just about keep up with this.

The thing froze for a second then answered, "Semi-telepathic species like yours tend to have nonlinear, disconnected... Humans have dormant telepathic abilities, but this resides in your unconscious... I shall return within two minutes. My conversion rate needs adjustment."

The thing disappeared. Tomorrow's technology is today's magic, he wasn't going to freak out. He stood and walked over to a wall. It was slightly warm to touch, but he'd never felt anything like it before. It was as unyielding as micro-dense carbon and yet, at the same time, felt as malleable as soft rubber.

"It exists and is real. But it does not exist and is not real. You have no experience of this phenomenon."

The hologram had returned and was now on the opposite side of the room. Walking back to the chair he gave the hologram a cold stare then businesslike plonked himself down.

"The construction of your thoughts makes it difficult for me to respond to them. I shall answer your verbal enquiries. Your next question please."

"What have you done with the Earth?"

"We have done nothing with the Earth. We were not involved in that operation."

This could turn out to be really tedious. "What has been done with the Earth?

"It is now in orbit around Ool, a G-type star."

"Ool? Where is Ool?"

"It is 378 light years from here. The name 'Ool, is an 'as near as' translation that your aural and vocal ranges can accommodate."

Three hundred and seventy-eight light years? He thought about asking where 'here' was. That probably wouldn't tell him anything. "Why was the Earth moved, and by whom?"

The hologram froze again, as if processing information. "Due to the increased noise levels human occupied space was becoming a beacon. The extraction was carried out by two third stage sapient species the, Roshid and the Onic."

This was getting him nowhere fast. "Rather than me asking specific questions and you giving specific answers that don't mean much, why don't you give me the general flavour of what this is all about?"

Processing... "The sapient species have begun the masking preparations. Non-sapient species were discounted as they were unlikely to become involved. Your species uses a technology that could mistakenly identify you as... The technology is your manipulation of the super-light."

Sighing inwardly Billy reminded himself that he was communicating with an *alien.* "What do you mean by, 'masking preparations'?"

"The process of hiding all sapient races from the aggressors."

His patience was wearing thin. "Aggressors? Which aggressors?"

"An unknown but clearly fourth stage or above sapient species, crossing from the Large Magellanic Cloud."

He pondered this for a bit. "How do you know that they are aggressive?"

"We monitored their invasion of the Large Magellanic Cloud. We suspect that this was not their first, or second conquest. However, we believe that their origins lie in the M81's local group. Their aggressive expansion appears to have been ongoing for over twelve thousand years. We have had time to prepare."

Billy almost laughed. "Are you saying that there has been a sort of defence pact between all the intergalactic civilisations?"

Long processing... "The pact is between all 18,551 sapient species of the Milky Way galaxy. Many of these species do not have a civilisation as you would understand it. There are also many other species, such as yours, which have a civilisation but are not sapient."

Was this thing asking for a slap round the chops? "And because we're not sapient, we weren't invited to the party?"

"That is correct...Wing Commander, I cannot elude your thoughts. Your anger is based on a misunderstanding. Most of the terms I use are approximations, or best guesses. You do not have the concepts or vocabulary to truly understand sapience or interspecies comparisons."

"Really?" *Do you have the concepts or vocabulary to understand sarcasm?*

"Yours is a species which has evolved intelligence. But sapience, in the sense we mean it, can be considered to be the uses to which intelligence can be applied. Humans apply their intelligence and knowledge gained in much the same way a..." Processing, "...cheetah applies its speed. Sapience is the ability to apply intelligence obliquely to the evolutionary gradient which produced it... Wing Commander, you are slightly more intelligent that a... "Processing, "...chimpanzee, but you are no more sapient."

Don't get angry. "All right, so we weren't invited. Were the sapient species going to hide themselves and just leave us as the sacrificial lambs for the aggressors?"

"It is our assessment that non sapient species would have been overlooked."

"Why?"

"I shall remember this question and when you have greater understanding answer it. Do you have another question?"

"You said something about a beacon?"

Processing... "The state you call the super-light is something that you believe you understand. To you, super-light travel is only a continuation of your discovery of the wheel. Your super-light broadcasts are simply an enhancement of your development of speech. To a sapient species the super-light is something akin to a state of consciousness. The super-light is where the aggressors would search for sapience. Your super-light noises would attract them. The noise had to be stopped, and your existence hidden."

"I thought you said non-sapients *like us* were going to be overlooked."

"Because of your presence in the super-light the aggressors might assume that you were sapient. Your use of technology is such that on first contact you would confirm this assumption. Then, your species would be suppressed."

"Suppressed?"

"I cannot explain that until you have greater understanding."

"So, you're saying that you did it for our own good?"

"We did not do it. The decision was taken by the fourth stage sapient species and the extraction carried out by the third stage sapient species the Roshid and the Onic."

Assume that anything is a possibility until it's disproved. "Who are you?"

"We are the Flushi, a first stage sapient species."

That told him nothing. "I would like to see what you look like."

Very long processing, then the guy was replaced by something looking like a one-metre-thick, three-metre-long, sea cucumber. The thing hovered in the air for a bit. Surprisingly, next to it appeared a one-metre-thick, three-metre-long, sea cucumber. Billy decided that a Flushi didn't look anything like a sea cucumber after-all. The Flushi had a set of four tentacles the length of a man's arm at each end, for starters. Its skin appeared to be covered in moving boils, as if a swarm of large insects were scurrying away underneath it. Billy couldn't make out anything that would pass for a sensory organ.

Both holograms vanished and the man reappeared. "Humans do not have an integrated intellect. You are hampered by having both a higher and more base reasoning. Not only are these two forms of consciousness often in conflict, you also have a subconscious, with its own independent reasoning. The state you call sanity is no more than a balanced tension. This results in an unusual, though not unique, occurrence - all of your experiences and observations have to be cross-referenced against past experiences and observations. If these reference points are not present your mind invents them. This is one example of your inability to apply your intellect obliquely."

Tight-lipped, Billy sat staring back at the thing.

"It is not our intention to belittle your species, Wing Commander. However, until you have some understanding of yourself you cannot expect to understand others." The hologram paused. This wasn't a processing pause, it was giving him time to consider. "You *know* that it is impossible for a material to feel like micro dense-carbon and also soft rubber, yet you have accepted that it does. Would you care to examine the surface again?"

"No. Point taken. Would you care to expand on the bit about me being slightly more intelligent than a chimpanzee?"

Processing... "*Slightly* is a comparative. I specifically used that word to minimize what you would call 'culture shock'. By your standards of comparison, you are *considerably* more intelligent than a chimpanzee. Humans see themselves as the dominant species of your planet. By our standards of comparison, you have *almost the same* intelligence as a chimpanzee. Also, humans are *not necessarily* the species closest to a state of sapience on Earth..."

The thing went into its longest pause so far, about twenty seconds. He felt a burning desire to wrap the stool around its head. He resisted the urge by sitting on his hands.

"We know that the human condition that can best be described as 'ego' results from your fragmented intellect. We thought we understood the condition and had taken account of all the possible variations in a species of unique individuals. Yet we see in you that ego has reached a critical point. Please do not convert your thoughts to actions..."

This time the hologram froze for over a minute. He supposed it was consulting something or someone. No, it wouldn't be consulting someone, it was consulting *something*.

"You place yourself in the human elite. Your ego is a rarity in your species. Humans have *almost the same* intelligence as the Flushi. We also make errors. Is your ego now fortified?"

Despite himself Billy laughed. "Yes, my ego is now fortified."

"Your next question please."

"What has been done with the population of Earth and its colonies?"

"No life form has been harmed by the extraction. Only certain of your government and military officials are aware that the planets have been moved... All planets occupied by your species were extracted and put in orbit around... Each planet is enclosed in a field... The field regulates all radiation to the norm of the individual planet's parent star. The field also replicates the star field."

Billy decided to try and crank up by a couple of notches his concept of reality and what was possible. "What has been my government's response?"

Processing... "They are cooperating. It was they who decided to withhold and disguise the fact of the extraction."

Billy pondered this for a bit. It sounded plausible but, who knows? "What happens now?"

"I shall explain why you and your crew are here."

"I'm listening."

"The fourth stage sapient species had just learned about the two unaccounted-for human ships when the broadcast of your General Recall resumed. A first stage sapient species sent ships to investigate. These you tracked, and then destroyed. Because your motives were species-protective you have been exonerated. However, you *have* killed 1,224 sapients. This species has, quite naturally, asked for some redress. You are to remain here with us until the decisions are made."

"You mean that I'm in prison waiting on the verdict?"

"No, Wing Commander, there are three separate issues being addressed: one, the species that has suffered this attrition are a slow breeding, long-to-mature species; their entire population numbers less than 100,000. They have just lost 1,224 fertile adults and are now facing the real possibility of extinction. A decision must be taken on whether or not to delete them from the order of battle... Yes, so that they avoid further adult losses. The next issue... They are a two-sex species. Their lifespan is approximately 1,500 years and each pair produce only two offspring in that time... They evolved on a world of scant resources..."

When the thing stopped speaking Billy wondered if it did so because of his feelings of guilt that had surfaced. No! He wasn't going to feel guilty. They had messed with Biosphere One. "The next issue?"

"By destroying these ships, you have raised the possibility of humans, and their technology, playing some role in the defence of the galaxy. This is being assessed. The third issue is this; if humans do play a part, measures have to be in place to counteract... Humans may not survive exposure to... No, Wing Commander. Not superior. Not more advanced. Just different. Allow me to use this analogy: premature exposure to *different* races may topple your racial gyro."

14

ONCE UPON A TIME

"Everybody awake?"

What?! Of course, they were awake, they were in the middle of a serious dustup... Mohammed glanced, then stared, at his screens. All the nav and weapons systems were down. What the hell was going on?

"Good. All sitting comfortably? Then we shall begin," Billy continued rather jocularly. "Consider this an informal supplementary orders group. The dogfight is over, and we won - that's the good news. The bad news is, as far as I can tell, the dogfight was about fourteen hours ago. Yes, you've been pushing Z's. I have been led to believe that you will be unaware of any lapse of time. Anybody feel like they've been sleeping?"

There was a chorus of negatives over the net.

"Now, I know there must be much confusion, especially with the Dart pilots; like, one moment you're sitting tight, ready for launch and the next, you're back in your wombs. Worry not, all will be explained. We are in orbit around a planet called Evier and I have been a guest of the locals, the Flushi. They felt it would be best if I filled you in."

"Do you know what happened to Earth?"

That was Pipsqueak, but Mohammed was about to ask the same question.

"Patience my children, let's take this fairytale one step at a time. Here is the big picture: the galaxy is about to be invaded by some villains crossing from the Large Magellanic Cloud. All 18,000-odd sapient races of the Milky Way galaxy got together to draw up a defence strategy. Their plan was pretty simple - and you *need* to get your brains round this - they were going to hide their sapience. The villains aren't interested in conquering turf or anything like that. They are into *suppressing* sapient races. Apparently, we can't grasp what 'suppression' is about. I figure it to be a kind of intelligence vampirism. Now, the reason we can't understand suppression is that humans - are you ready for this - aren't sapient. I..."

"Excuse me, Chief, but did these Flushi fellows drop you on your head?" John interrupted.

"That's a distinct possibility. But let me finish before you stick me in a straitjacket. Of course, we're sapient. Sapience is the nearest word we have to this thing that we aren't. I suppose it's something like trying to explain the colour blue to a colour-blind person - you end up talking about dark grey. By the way, all I'm doing is relating what I was told. We'll thrash it out after you've had a chance to chew it over.

114

"Because we aren't sapient the aggressors wouldn't bother us, we're not enough of a mouthful. We weren't in on the act, or so the Flushi and their friends thought. *Their* defence preparations have been going on for over twelve thousand years. Now, after the rally-round-the-flag call they paid us, and many other species, a visit. We were a long way off sapience, so they left their calling card and went home. This was about ten thousand five-hundred BC. Don't ask me what this calling card was. They noted our predisposition towards using tools but didn't extrapolate flint axes, or whatever, into super-light drives. Therein lies the difficulty: sapience has something to do with the super-light, but please don't ask me what it is.

"Can I ask a question?" Cynthia interrupted.

"Save it till the end. As you know, we discovered the super-light about 150 years ago and started manipulating it, super-light communication and drives, etc., in the last 100 years. And as you now know, only sapient races are supposed to be able to use it. Therefore, for the last 100 years or so the defence pact has been calling, very quietly, to this mysterious sapient race. When we didn't answer they figured we knew about the villains but were ignorant about the pact and doing the same thing they were, hiding.

"That would have been OK, except we weren't hiding very well. Every now and then we would set off activity in the super-light. The pact were in a bit of a bind, they couldn't shout, 'join up or shut the fuck up', the villains might hear. Nor could they conduct a detailed search of us. That much activity would certainly tip the villains off. For the last 100 years they've been silently praying for us to perfect our masking techniques.

"Then suddenly, *Arabia* drops right on someone's doorstep. They give it the once over and get the lowdown on their noisy, non-sapient distant neighbours. The sapients then concoct a plan. First, move Earth and its colonies, just in case the villains have a line on us. We aren't sapient, but the villains would assume we were because we play in the super-light. By the time the villains realised we weren't, they would already have worked us over. Next, the sapients would apologise and explain why they had moved us. Then they intended to ask us to be quiet for the next three to four thousand years. After the villains left the galaxy empty-handed, we all live happily ever-after. End of story.

"The 'extraction' went almost according to plan. Only one glitch really: they enclosed Earth in a sort of energy field, and *that* triggered the General Recall. It was loud - now the villains definitely know that somebody is home. The pact started to work on a plan to explain away the General Recall. I haven't been told this, but I think the plan was simply to dump us back where they found us. If that was the plan, it was blown out the window because while talking to our government they discover they'd missed two ships. How could they miss the two largest machines we'd ever built? There are no records of *Baddest* or *The Beast* in any InfoSys. So, even if they managed to mindwipe, or whatever, everyone who knew of their existence there were still a couple of unaccounted for ships fucking about in the super-light.

"Did anyone know where we were? No. As they were trying to figure out how to find us, what happens? A second General Recall is sounded. Not as loud as the first, but loud enough. They come a-running and got *The Beast but* didn't see *Baddest*. We track them, they send some boys after us, we thumped them, they send in the heavies and take us out. How did they take us out? With thought! And that just about brings us up to date. Ladies and Gents, all I've said so far is only the preamble. There is one other bit of information I think you need.

"There are four known stages, or levels, of sapience in the galaxy. Just to get a feel of what I'm talking about: a fourth stage sapient can, supposedly, stand a couple of light-years away and destroy *Baddest* with nothing but thought. Apparently, there *may* be a fifth stage of sapience. The sapients believe that when a species evolves to this stage, they leave this plane of existence. They also believed that the Villains are a rogue fifth stage species. Bearing in mind that the Villains have already taken out the Magellanic Clouds, nobody wants to fight them.

"Now, thanks to us, they're going to have to. So, there are 18,000 species of aliens who humans have really pissed off. Get this, nobody is planning on doing anything bad to us. *But* there is a great deal of, let's call it, negative vibes around. These vibes can harm us. In fact, they can kill us. All our planets have been moved again, away from strong sources of these vibes. Earth is now 378 light-years from here. And *here*, is right on the edge of the other side of the galaxy. Questions?"

***

Eva understood why Billy had been so frivolous. It was exactly the right approach to take. The entire situation was far too bizarre to be taken totally seriously. As the questions unfolded it became pretty obvious that he'd told them everything he knew. The xenobiologists, in particular, found this frustrating. The talk degenerated into aimless speculation and conjecture. Billy continued to allow the discussion to meander. She saw that this was also quite deliberate.

There was something entirely believable about it. Still, she adopted an attitude of healthy scepticism. After Billy had been grilled for over an hour it became obvious that he didn't have the answers to most of the questions. Then, a silence brought on by incredulity settled over the crew. She wouldn't say that she was in a state of shock, but she was having difficulty sorting the information from the briefing into any semblance of order. This was just too fantastic. Her brain wanted to simply reject the whole thing...

"Eva, this is a monocast, your net only. Have you considered taking command?" Sun asked earnestly.

She checked that none of the flight crew were looking at her before responding, "You think our Captain has flipped?"

"I don't know, but *they* could have done anything with his mind. We have no way of knowing. It's within the remit of a 2ic to supersede a Captain who has lost his or her faculties. I think, at this moment, that it's the only prudent course of action."

She wasn't convinced. "His Flyboys might have something to say about..."

"Sun, in one sense I'm pleased," Billy suddenly interrupted. "At last somebody is out of their trance. In another sense I'm disappointed, a pretty below par analysis. Check the chronometers. You were all unconscious for close to fifteen hours; if they messed with my mind, they certainly messed with yours."

"How did...?" Eva started to ask.

"I'm the Captain, I can listen to anything," he laughed. "Been sitting here all lonesome waiting for someone to recover. Now that you two are at back with reality, any ideas?"

Eva was pleasantly surprised that, considering the conversation he'd just overheard, there was nothing reproachful in Billy's tone. "I vote we wait and see what develops."

"My concern was only for the mission Sir. I wasn't..."

"I know that Sun. Got any ideas on our next move?"

"Yes Sir. A delegation, including all the xenobiologists, to meet the Flushi."

"I like that. Eva?"

"Yes, I agree."

"Good. But I don't want to push anyone right now, I want each person to deal with this in their own way. We'll put the delegation together when everyone has floated back to the surface. Anything else?"

"Can we establish comms with Earth or any of the Sector Commands?" Sun asked.

"Super-light is off limits but the Flushi assured me that we'll have direct communications with Earth in a little over three hours."

"How can we have comms without super-light?" Sun said, as if pondering aloud.

"I have no idea, but they say we will... Rather than send a delegation couldn't we ask them to pay us a visit? That way all the dogs see the rabbit, then we can get down to business."

"Makes sense, but what about possible contamination?" Eva asked.

"I agree. We should be cautious. And, are the crew ready for this?" Sun added.

"I don't think contamination will be a factor. These guys are used to meeting alien races. As for the crew, the more I think about it the more I'm certain that the sooner they snap out of this, the better."

"OK, how do we call them?"

"They'll know what we want. First, I'll have a chat with the crew." Billy switched to the open net. "Right, folks, it's best behaviour time. The Flushi are about to drop in for tea. I don't know what's on their agenda or how they are getting here, so take it as an open session."

From the corner of her eye Eva saw Wendy jolt upright in her seat. Turning to follow Wendy's gaze, she saw that standing in the middle of the cockpit was a man wearing a bland business suit. He stood motionless for a few moments, then said, "The machine, Anne, has been programmed with the answers to most of the technical questions you wish to ask. I am here to brief you on the immediate future. We know that it will be difficult, but please try to concentrate on what I say, and nothing else during the briefing."

"Is this a form of hypnotism or mind control?" Cynthia jumped to her feet.

The man turned to look at each of the non-flight crew in sequence. He stopped his searching when he got to Cynthia. Although she was the only one standing, it had taken him some time to get to her. Clearly, he was using something other than his eyes to identify individuals. "We have no desire to interfere with your intellect. The request for clarity of thought is for our benefit. We are at the limit of our abilities when communicating with this many humans."

Abruptly, Cynthia sat, and the man continued, "You are to remain here until a representative of the fourth stage species, the Ig'tam, arrives in approximately three hours. She has information on human participation and, via her, you will have communications with Earth. My purpose here is to prepare you for that meeting... We sense many questions. Wing Commander Zarcroft, it would be helpful if we only took questions from you."

"Human participation? Participation in what?" Billy had moved to sit on the back of his womb, facing the rest of the crew.

"Where humans fit into, what you would call 'the big picture'. The fourth level species have, by now, formulated the strategy and communicated their findings to your government," the man replied.

Eva wasn't really sure what the man was talking about but Billy said, "OK, continue."

"You, the crew of *Baddest*, are here with us because Flushi and humans have partially compatible cerebral processes. We can, to a limited extent, follow your logic and reasoning. Most first stage sapient species would be unable to comprehend your thoughts and desires.

Pilot

Species of the second, third and fourth stages have no difficulty with comprehension, but communicating with them presents certain hazards to your... You have another question Wing Commander?"

"Two questions. If the fourth stage sapient species are the organ grinders, does that mean that the lower stages are the monkeys? And what can be hazardous about talking to the movers and shakers?"

The man froze for several moments. He looked so lifelike; Eva had to remind herself that Billy had said that it was a hologram.

"Wing Commander, to you, your questions are simple. But because of your non-sapience, we can only give answers to the limit of your understanding... There is a hierarchy of sorts between sapient species. But this is centred on the potential of each species. This is difficult to put in human terms. We can only say; you are our guests, not because we were instructed to be your hosts, but because we sensed that we had the potential to communicate with humans.

"Your second question is even more difficult to answer. Only twenty-one percent of sapient species *talk*. As an example: we, the Flushi, are an aquatic species and do not *communicate* in the usual human sense of the word. We *interact* through hormone excretion. These hormones do more than convey information, they produce significant physiological and cognitive transformations in the recipient... Think of it in these terms: communication *transfers*, interaction *modifies*. We sense some confusion... Although one human conveying tragic news to another produces physical and emotional changes in the recipient it is still communication. The physical and emotional changes are initiated internally by the recipient's emotions. But when *we* interact internal changes are initiated by the external party.

"Interspecies communication between non-sapients is difficult and complex. However, between sapients it usually takes place in one of an infinite number of telepathic streams and is effortless. The hazard for non-sapient humans in communication with second, third or fourth stage sapients is this: when semi-telepathic species think they quite naturally, and unconsciously, streamshift - their thoughts are not entirely under their control. This is one of the reasons why we have difficulty in comprehending your thoughts. Species of a higher stage have the ability to hold a streamshift rigidly in place, this is quite natural, the equivalent of listening attentively. The semi-telepathic mind would then be locked in a state it is not accustomed or has evolved to be in... This is our best answer. We know it raises other questions, but we are unable to explain further."

The entire crew seemed to focus inwards as they pondered his answer. Eventually, Billy asked. "You said something about preparing us to meet a fourth stage sapient, what does that entail?"

"This is the Flushi form..." The image of the man was replaced by the thing that Billy had described as 'something like a sea cucumber', but his voice continued in her head. "... Biologically, very different to humans. Neither could survive in the others natural environment. But we are mentally analogous, similar enough for interspecies communication. We do not really *understand* your thoughts or their articulation, but we do have the potential to make best guesses as to what they mean. Likewise, we cannot truly express to you our thoughts, but there is enough of a common mental vocabulary for *communication.*

"This is the form of the fourth stage species, the Ig'tam..."

Eva stared at what was now presented: it appeared to be a naked woman, well over two metres tall. Her skin was mauve, she was completely without hair and her facial features were flat. Two arms, two legs, weird looking eyes, nose, mouth and breasts... Definitely humanoid, but those eyes were unnerving: unblinking, shinily bright irises like clear black gems, with an even darker cornea, and all seeming to be covered by a greenish transparent film... Definitely alien.

"... Because of the structure of your minds some of you may be focussing on the differences, others on the similarities, please concentrate on the similarities... According to human zoological definitions Ig'tams are mammalian. They are also, unquestionably, primates. Like the human female, the Ig'tam female has permanently swollen breasts. And there are many other similarities besides. Now, please note the Ig'tam female's waist..."

Eva's eyes were drawn to the rope coiled around the woman's waist. She sat open mouthed as slowly, the thing she thought of as a rope uncoiled to reveal two prehensile appendages fixed to the creature's waist. For a moment, the appendages waved around like a couple of snakes then came to rest, hanging down, just touching the floor.

"...Only the female Ig'tam has these pseudolimbs. This is the most obvious physical difference between Ig'tams and humans. These organs have predatory, feeding and reproductive functions..." The thing's appendages slowly rose to gently flutter at about waist height. At the tapered end of each appendage a small orifice opened. Suddenly, and with snake-like speed, the pseudolimbs lashed out. A sharp, horned projection stabbed out of each orifice, ejecting a fine jet of dark liquid. Just as quickly, the appendages went back to their gentle fluttering.

"...The Ig'tam female can inject venom, anti-venom or digestives fluids from her pseudolimbs. They are also used to bind her mate during copulation."

She heard either Billy or Mohammed mutter, "Jesus Christ!"

"Despite your biological similarities, mentally, Ig'tams are several orders of magnitude removed from humans. Your IQ scales of assessment are inappropriate for interspecies comparisons but, in the absences of a more reliable gauge, you could consider an Ig'tam to have an IQ in excess of 3,500. It is this mental difference that we need to prepare you for..."

"Wait a minute. An IQ of *over* three and a half thousand? Are you serious?" Billy was just a split second ahead of her and probably the rest of the crew.

The image of the Ig'tam, appendages in mid wave, froze for about ten seconds. "A fourth stage sapient is not three hundred and fifty times more intelligent than the average human. Likewise, a human with an IQ of 3,500 would not necessarily be a fourth stage sapient. We use your system of IQ only to draw parallels. Sapience is the *potential* to influence probabilities. A fourth stage sapient's potential to influence probabilities would *appear* to make them learn, recall, and apply three hundred and fifty times faster than the average human. Again, we ask that you accept this; we cannot explain 'tone' to someone who is deaf."

"OK," Billy answered, in a 'tone' that said that everything was not OK.

"We sense that we have mishandled your collective egos. Please wait."

The image froze, its colours faded and it became slightly transparent. The crew stared at each other in stunned silence. Eventually the image of the Ig'tam returned to its solid form.

"If your feelings are hurt that is by the by, you are not children... A fourth stage sapient can influence probabilities over interstellar distances. This will facilitate communication with Earth without resorting to use of the super-light. That is why a fourth stage sapient will attend in person. The Ig'tam are a fourth stage species with the potential to circumvent regulating human streamshifting, and that is why they are the fourth stage sapients' representatives. However, because disregarding streamshifting is a conscious act, she will be susceptible to your extremes of emotion and this might result in her involuntarily anchoring your streamshift..." The image froze momentarily. "... Think of it in these terms: you cannot consciously control the contraction of your pupils in bright light... Anchoring may alter the probability states of your intellects and also damage the physical structure of your brains..."

"I was with you right up to 'altering probability states', then it shot off right over my head." Gabi interrupted.

"We sense an implied question in that statement. To understand the hazards you face it is not necessary to know..." The image froze and almost faded out of existence. It remained in this ghost-like state for several minutes. Some of the crew became restless and began to shift about in their wombs.

"... This communication is a difficult learning process for us. We have now determined that, with the human intellect, questions remain until there are satisfactory answers. After an inquiry, hypothesis and conjecture can and often does eclipse all other mental processes. We now comprehend that it is not necessary to give the most accurate answer, but simply one that is the most satisfactory; we have grasped the human concept of 'belief'. So, we will answer this question because it may assist your belief in sapience.

"Again, we use an 'as near as' similitude. Consider the non-sapient mind to be a state of *finite* probabilities, and the process of thought to be the impetus that coalesces these probabilities into a definite outcome. Consider streamshifting to be the meandering within these finite probabilities. This is the normal non-sapient state of consciousness.

"Now, imagine the sapient mind to be a state of *infinite* probabilities. In this case, thought is the impetus for multiple or simultaneous outcomes. When a sapient mind, of a high enough state, anchors a non-sapient mind the non-sapient mind is held in *places* - a condition beyond the non-sapient mind's limitations. We hope that you now understand and *believe* why it is desirable to have no emotional excesses in the presence of the Ig'tam. We appeal to you to think about this before we continue."

"Take it as read that we have," Billy said conversationally.

The image dimmed then brightened. "The probability of emotional excess remains undesirably high."

"We'll keep it under wraps," Billy said firmly.

"We are not convinced, but sense that it is purposeful for you to *believe* that you can control your emotions... We have now only to advise you that there will be no protocol when the Ig'tam arrives. An approximation of the pronunciation of her name is, Hontay."

The image vanished.

15

IG'TAM

The bitter argument had been going on for more than two hours and it didn't look as if it was likely to reach a conclusion. This was all because Alfred was being so insufferably arrogant. Why couldn't he just admit that he was wrong? Cynthia wasn't going to stand for it. "Even with the evidence staring you in the face you still cling to these ridiculous antediluvian notions. It is abundantly clear that..."

"Now, now, Children," Billy interrupted, his voice strained with patience. "This is getting us nowhere fast. Lest we forget, what I'm looking for is a strategy for meeting the super-alien."

"If Cynthia would only accept that Ig'tams *must* have evolved along the evolutionary path that I postulated some twelve years ago then we could begin to make progress," Alfred was almost screaming over the net.

"How convenient of you to omit the Flushi," Kazuhiko countered with dripping sarcasm. "Their existence makes a mockery of that theory, whereas the paper *I* published..."

"For what it's worth, as far as I can tell, you are all partially right. Now, get a grip!" Eva commanded.

"We have reached a consensus on some aspects of the strategy," Sam answered defensively.

"You have?" Billy sounded surprised.

It was time she took charge. "Yes, we might differ about the exact nature of the development of intelligence but, clearly, the overriding concern has to be *our* reaction on meeting an advanced intelligence."

"Why?" Erick asked.

"The extinction of *homo erectus* wasn't as a direct result of the emergence of *homo sapiens*," Alfred jumped in. "There is a wealth of evidence showing that they were not in direct competition. Nor are there any signs that 'environment' played a decisive role. This suggests that *homo erectus* simply died out. When faced with a superior form they obviously felt inadequate, lost interest, rolled over, and died."

What Alfred was saying was basically correct, this was the prevailing anthropological theory, but she felt that they would be better served without hyperbole. "There's no direct evidence for this, of course. However, it seems the most probable scenario..."

"OK. What is your suggestion?" Billy, running short on tolerance, interrupted.

"Our collective view is that we need to fortify ourselves against feelings of inferiority," she replied.

Pilot

"Any suggestions on how we achieve this?" Eva demanded.

Cynthia had to remind herself that she was dealing with The Military. For the first time in the mission they had given the xenobiologists a specific task. But Billy, Eva and Erick had no understanding of the complexity of the task. They weren't interested in the issues, all they wanted were answers. The Military failed to grasp that there were no *simple* answers.

"Xenobiology obviously encompasses psychology, but only at the margins," she began cautiously. "We need to construct, for want of a better expression, an emotional cage around the psychological profile of each individual crew member."

"Quite so," Kazuhiko agreed. "I see deep hypnosis as the most likely candidate."

"How long would that take?" Erick asked.

"Say about ten hours for the whole crew," she postulated.

"We don't have ten hours," Eva snapped.

"Give us something we can use in the time available," Billy suggested.

There was an implied criticism in Eva's tone. Cynthia hoped that the Captain didn't think that the xenobiologists were not cutting the mustard. The Flushi had dumped data into Anne and Billy had divided up the work load: navigators to search for scientific data; Dart pilots looking for data on the aggressors; soldiers and marines combing for military data, leaving the xenobiologists the 'simple' task of coming up with a plan to handle the meeting with the Ig'tam.

Once all the teams had started, it didn't take long to realise that the Flushi had imparted prodigious amounts of information. It would take them years or, perhaps, decades to study, categorise and cross-refer the information. All the pressure for an instant result was then passed to the xenobiologists - this was hardly fair. "There's no precedent... We can't begin to estimate the number of possible effects. We can only say, with authority, that we must all guard against feelings of inferiority and maintain a strong sense of self."

"That's it, is it?" Eva ridiculed.

"How dare you take that tone? Do you have any idea what's involved?" Sam retaliated.

"OK, enough!" Billy ordered sharply. "Cynthia, prepare a briefing for the crew on the meeting, Eva... Shit. She's here, talking to the Flushi... How the hell did I know that?!"

"My apologies Billy. I see that you are unaware of your telepathic abilities. Good day, Humans, I am Hontay." Standing in the middle of the cockpit was the two and a half-metre-tall Ig'tam.

Cynthia almost leapt from her womb. The voice was like nothing she'd ever heard before. It was without accent, had an incredibly deep masculine resonance, and yet it was so frighteningly alien. She stared at the Ig'tam. The Flushi had shown a naked Ig'tam, while Hontay wore a garment not too dissimilar to a flying suit. It took Cynthia a few moments to realise what the other difference was, Hontay's features were identical to the image they'd seen, but her colouration was different; her skin was lime green. This changed everything, with that colour of skin and the nightmarish eyes, Hontay looked positively reptilian. With revulsion she glanced down at the Ig'tam's waist. There was a broad, belt-like apparel around her midriff. It was not only polite but also essential for female Ig'tams to secure their pseudolimbs in the presence of other females... What?

Billy vaulted out of his womb. "I bid you welcome." He seemed surprisingly jolly.

"Thank you. It is a pleasure to be here."

Cynthia *knew* that the Ig'tam didn't have the facial muscles to produce a smile, but she *felt* the warmth of her statement... What?!

Billy started over to Hontay, "This is an historic meeting, and we..."

"Stop!"

Hontay disappeared. There was an audible 'pop' as air filled the space she had just vacated. Billy collapsed, shrieking. He thrashed about of the floor for a few moments and then appeared to pass out. Mayhem broke out in the cockpit. John was the first to reach Billy.

'The ship has been sealed inside an unknown type of field. Sensors cannot penetrate.'

"Alert stations! Anne, arm weapons and search new data bank for info on fields. How's Billy?" Eva took charge.

"I think he's coming round." John had Billy in his arms.

'Weapons, drives and communications systems inoperative. We cannot reach alert condition Eva. Searching data banks.'

"OK, stand down." Eva stood and walked purposefully over to Billy and John.

Billy moaned, held both hands to his head, looked up at John, and asked, "What happened?"

"You tell me," John responded.

"How do you feel?" Eva knelt beside them. Billy tried to sit up, but she placed a hand on his shoulder. "Stay there, don't move, we don't know what's been done to you."

'Billy has suffered no physical injury. Searching data banks.'

"That's very reassuring, but Anne, I just want you to know, I have the mother of all headaches." Billy laughed rather weakly. "Let me up. Give me a hand back to my womb."

John looked at Eva, who nodded before both helped Billy back to his feet.

"Do we assume that the Ig'tam is hostile?" Erick asked of no one in particular.

"No!" Cynthia was surprised to hear herself exclaim. She knew that something was awry, but she also *knew* that the Ig'tam wasn't hostile.

"Before we decide anything, will somebody please tell me what happened," Billy asked, as he made his way back to his womb unaided.

"You're walking towards her. She says stop. She disappears. You're comatose. That's about it," John shrugged.

"She said, 'stop'?"

"Yes," Eva sounded puzzled. "You were the nearest to her. Didn't you hear?"

"No."

"Billy, describe to us your current mental state. This may give us an insight into the meaning of all this," Sam suggested thoughtfully.

"My current mental state is that I have an unbelievable headache."

"Is this a pounding headache, like a bad hangover?" Sam gently coaxed.

"Maybe. Never had a hangover, never had a headache like this."

'Billy, I have completed a thorough scan. There is no structural damage or regions of high pressure in your brain. Blood flow and neuron activity are also normal. Continuing search of data banks.'

"Thank you, Anne. Sam, were you hinting at something?"

"Your headache could be a manifestation of the streamshifting the Flushi warned us about."

"Maybe," Billy mused. "He did say that being around these guys was hazardous, didn't he? Must have a quiet word with him about understatements."

"You seem all right. How are you feeling now?" Eva asked.

"Fine, apart from this headache...

'The field is weakening.'

Cynthia wasn't in the least bit surprised when the hologram of the man reappeared. No, it didn't reappear, it reformed. This was definitely a projection, it took a fraction of a second to take shape, while the Ig'tam had been instantly there and instantly not there.

Pilot

"The fourth stage sapient, Hontay, has departed this solar system. She suggested that humour has the greatest potential to convey the explanation for both her departure, and Billy's discomfort. Flushi have no equivalent of humour, but we will endeavour to carry out her request. Please do not interrupt.

"Our heartiest congratulations Billy. You have set Hontay's blood vessels rising. This is an exciting time for an Ig'tam female. It is the physiological change of blood vessels moving closer to the surface of her skin. Why should that happen? Well, this helps to regulate her overall body temperature, because her internal body temperature will increase by several degrees.

"You see, her reproductive organs are starting to kick in. Unlike the human female, this only happens after she has forged a union with her first mate..."

"Pardon!" Billy erupted.

"Please, do not interrupt... I know that you're not going to believe this, but the possibility of such a bond being triggered by a non-Ig'tam had never been considered..."

"I'm way ahead of you on this one." Pipsqueak shot out of his womb, looked at Billy and started to laugh uproariously.

"Please do not interrupt... Ig'tam unions are instantaneous. *Normally* the female selects her mates by deliberately exposing herself to their pheromones. These pheromones stimulate the changes in her reproductive organs; it's all in the chemistry, there's no romance or courtship. Once she is exposed, it just happens." The hologram fixed a smile on its face, "The girl can't help herself..."

Billy slowly stood up, looking aghast. Grim, John and Mohammed climbed out of their wombs, and fell about in hysterics. Eva was also making a bad job of trying not to laugh.

"... Mentally, she has no choice either. Once her juices get going, instinctively she integrates with her mate's intellect - this is common amongst multi-sex sapients. Fortunately, Hontay realised that such a connection would be fatal to her human husband and..."

"What?!" Billy looked mortified.

"Please do not interrupt... Her only option was to remove herself and suppress the desire to share all she knows. She was not entirely successful in this endeavour, hence your severe headache. For her, the longing to converge intellects is overwhelming. We energised the field as soon as she left the ship and only reduced its intensity after you were separated by a considerable distance. We hope that you appreciate the amusement and will now take any questions."

Billy folded his arms and sat on the back of his womb. "It's great to make friends with folks who have a sense of humour. Now, let's get serious."

The hologram slowly turned to face Billy. "Would you agree that disbelief is belief, but in the negative form?"

"If you're asking, 'do I believe you'. The answer is, 'no'." Billy looked very relaxed.

"The fourth stage sapient Hontay, envisaged the probability of your mind adopting a negative belief. Her suggestion was to implant doubt. She is now several light years away. We shall remove the field completely."

"Christ! Ahhhhaa!" Billy grabbed hold of his head. Slipping off the womb, he sank to the floor.

"The field is again in place. Did you feel your wife's presence?"

Blinking rapidly, eyes watering, Billy looked up at the hologram, "She's not my wife! Yes, I felt her presence. You've made your point. Don't do that again!"

"In one word, what did you feel?"

Nimbly, Billy got to his feet. "One word? Frustration; her frustration"

"Did you have any perception of the distance that separates you?"

"Yes, I did." Billy held up his hands in surrender. "I'm sold. All I want to know is how you *sapients* managed to let a thing like this happen?"

"In the presence of mature Ig'tam males, pubescent Ig'tam females consciously construct a bulwark against the influence of the males' pheromones. The fourth stage sapient, Hontay, was not in the presence of mature Ig'tam males. She was also mentally fixed on tolerating your streamshifting."

Sun got out of her womb and sauntered over to the hologram. "Let me see if I've got this right: what you're saying is that Hontay has formed some sort of psychic link with Billy?"

Although she was standing in front of it, the hologram took some time to turn to Sun. "That is a correct approximation."

"Thank you." Straight-faced, Sun strolled up to Billy and stuck out her hand. "Let me be the first to offer my sincerest congratulations Captain."

Billy looked down at the pre-offered hand with disdain, "Go back to your womb." Stepping past Sun, he walked over to the hologram. "Right, how are you going to sort this out?"

With the same fixed grin on its face the hologram said, "This is an emergency. The fourth stage sapients, the Ig'tam, are sending a second representative. Her name is Flet. She will arrive in a few minutes."

"Yes, and?"

"That is all the information we have."

Billy pondered for a few seconds. "You're not going to drop the field again, are you?"

"No, not entirely."

"Good."

The instant the hologram vanished, the flight crew and the Dart pilots started baiting Billy. Cynthia was too engrossed in recording her observations and preliminary conclusions into Anne to take much notice. The possibility of an inter-species match, albeit a temporary one, had so many possibilities. This was heaven to a xenobiologist.

She felt the 'presence' a fraction of a second before the second Ig'tam appeared. Looking up she saw that the female members of the crew had experienced a similar sensation. They all turned to look at the same spot. This Ig'tam was identical to Hontay, except that her skin was mauve.

"Hello. I am Flet. I sense the expectation, especially in you Billy, that I am here to nullify the accidental wedlock. I must say, from the outset, that's not my purpose." Her voice reverberated around the cockpit.

"Oh, you big tease, of course it is," Billy laughed semi-hysterically.

"Billy, at the forefront of your consciousness is the knowledge that your union is irreversible."

Looking into those shocking alien eyes, somehow, Cynthia knew that what Flet said was correct. Irreversible?

Flet surveyed the crew. "I am here to complete Hontay's mission, which is to establish communication with Earth. However, until Hontay and Billy's predicament is resolved this will be difficult. Billy, you are experiencing unfamiliar emotions. Do not try to subdue them, they are Hontay's emotions."

"Excuse me. I don't want to make a fuss or anything, and I'm sure she's a lovely lady, but I *don't* want to be married."

Cynthia felt a wave of light amusement wash over her.

"Free will is an interesting human concept. You *are* married and you will *want* to be married. This dissent is because your disjointed intellects have not yet settled on this course."

"If my man says he doesn't want to be married, he means he doesn't want to be married. You can't force him." Grim, half joking, half serious sprang to Billy's defence.

Pilot

The sensation of amusement increased in pitch.

"Both humans and lg'tams marry by choice. With humans there is mutual selection. With us, the choice is entirely the female's. The human male can, by choice, become unmarried. With us, he cannot. We are physically, emotionally and intellectually tied to our partners. Due to unforeseen circumstances a human has united with an lg'tam; neither party had any choice in the matter; they were both *forced* into this match by their respective and partially compatible biologies. This statistically improbable compatibility is such that a human male/lg'tam female union might even lead to viable offspring."

"OK, OK! What about Hontay?" Billy asked in mock resignation.

The sensation of amusement changed to near laughter.

"Billy, your words are for your shipmates' ears. An honest inquiry will aid their understanding. What is it that you wish to know and why?"

Billy's demeanor changed to one of thoughtfulness. "I sense that she is distressed. Can anything be done about it?"

"And?"

"And, nothing. I just want to know what's gonna happen. After all, she's your... daughter!"

"Near truths are unsatisfactory."

Cynthia suddenly felt an intense pressure to do something. The 'something' was unspecific, but the pressure was almost irresistible.

"All right, all right! I'll tell them." Looking vexed, Billy turned to face his crew. "Flet wants me to explain what I'm feeling. Anybody laughs and I'll deal with them later. I can feel that Hontay is really stressed out. I don't know why she is, I just know she is. Because she's stressed out, I'm stressed out. OK?"

"The physical changes have begun within Hontay's body. These changes should be concurrent with even more profound mental changes as she and her husband become attuned to each other. We call this 'liberating probity'. Billy, Hontay knows everything you know. She wants you to know everything she knows. Unfortunately, your non-sapient mind cannot replicate most of her thoughts. This has little to do with your level of intelligence. Hontay's and your mind structures are fundamentally different."

"What do you want me to do about it?" Billy asked, perplexed.

Cynthia felt the pervasive sensation change to one of infinite patience.

"There is nothing that you can do. However, until she has liberated probity Hontay remains dysfunctional. We have devised an artificial means for her to liberate probity which also insulates you from the effects."

A belt similar to the one Flet wore instantly appeared around Billy's waist. He jumped, evidently startled by this.

"Consider that a thought filter. You can now join Hontay."

"What do you mean, join Hontay?" He asked suspiciously.

The sensation of humour returned.

"Can you not feel her desire to have you with her?"

"Yes, I suppose so."

"Do you wish to be with her?"

Billy hesitated. "OK."

"Your honeymoon will last about twenty-four hours."

Billy's departure was as unexpected and instantaneous as Hontay's.

16

HONTAY

He almost screamed. He wasn't expecting to be transported, teleported, or whatever it was that Flet had done. It felt a bit like dropping from super light, except that the aftereffects were more tolerable. It was just the unexpectedness of it all. He knew exactly where he was and he also knew how he came by that knowledge. Some information was supplied by his senses, other stuff came from Hontay - giving him, in effect, six senses. Despite himself, he found the experience fascinating. There was no sense of being informed, he simply knew.

This was Hontay's ship. Not a ship, exactly, more a large capsule. To get from point A to point B a fourth stage sapient simply thought about being at point B and, before you know it, they were there. The capsule was needed to travel interstellar distances. One, to provide the additional energy or whatever propelled the thing, and two, to supply life support to the occupant. The funny thing was it didn't really exist. Well, it did sort of exist, but not in the sense that *Baddest* existed. It was a construct of her mind.

The interior of the capsule didn't look that strange. In fact, it seemed similar to the room he'd found himself in on the Flushi planet, Evier. He knew that this representation was just for his benefit. Ordinarily, this space, this solid form, wouldn't exist. Normally the ship would be just a confined packet of energy. Strange and interesting as all this was his mind was focussed, or, more accurately had been focussed for him, on Hontay.

He knew that he was feeling only an infinitesimal fraction of her emotions. God, was she stressed! Frustration and rage were managing to rise on top of an unbelievably volatile cocktail of every conflicting emotion he had ever felt. He wasn't happy about the situation either, but nothing as acute as this. The belt around his waist was preventing her from disintegrating him into his component quarks. This also explained her nonappearance. She was a point of energy, which he couldn't see but knew was physically near, trying to calm herself down.

He was starting to feel a tad aggrieved when a thought suddenly occurred to him: each species must have a conditioning mechanism, or whatever, to stop them interbreeding with other species. Otherwise, after a few million years, or so, all the individual species on a biosphere would end up evolving into a single organism. So, it wasn't just because her new husband was something less than a comparative halfwit. Or that her every thought was centred on liberating probity. There were also some racial inhibitors to contend with.

Pilot

What was she trying to tell him? That he shouldn't take it personally? It also occurred to him that he *should* be feeling just as pissed off as she was. He should be, but he wasn't. He wasn't pissed off at all. In fact, he felt rather relaxed about the whole thing. Why? He'd only seen this ugly alien for less than a minute, yet he would go as far as to say that he was quite fond of her. Interesting. The impression that she was also quite fond of him suddenly came out of nowhere. Liberating probity was always going to win. It was just that there had to be a titanic battle before biology overpowered brain. Hontay appeared before him, green and tall. She stood a couple of metres away and stared down at him, he stared back. He could cope with her height, the green skin, the lack of hair, her *almost* human face, but, Christ! Those unblinking eyes! They were the most alien thing about her, like being appraised by a serpent.

Despite this, the sensation of fondness started to increase. This was due to his emotions. Being a mere non-sapient he was more stimulated by a physical presence than a mental one. This amplified her emotions, which she fed back, which amplified his emotions, and so on... until they reached dizzying heights of mutual emotional stimulation. Or, at least, that was the idea, but he couldn't reach those heights, he just felt exceedingly happy. To his amazement he got a taste of what she was feeling. It as if the pleasure centres in his brain had just been zapped. Every nerve ending in his body started to tingle with pleasure. So, this was liberating probity. Not bad. Not bad at all...

Stepping closer, she put her hands on his waist and effortlessly lifted him off the floor. She held him in the air for several seconds and then putting him down, she stepped back. What was this, an Ig'tam mating ritual? No. This was a demonstration. The most difficult thing for him to accept about their union would be the fact that she was considerably stronger than he was. Not so, he thought, her 3,500 IQ and ability to fry his brain were the causes for concern. He felt her *extreme* annoyance, then realised that the cause was because they were having a disagreement. Differences of opinion never happened between Ig'tam spouses. After liberating probity, they thought, knew and felt the same things. This lack of this accord was going to be the most difficult thing for her to accept about their union.

The fact was: men are physically stronger than women. That defined masculinity and underpinned all masculine attitudes and values. His masculine self had enormous adjustments to make. This was accompanied by strong overtones to: never argue with her; acceptance on her part that he would; confirmation that she would *always* get annoyed when he did; acknowledgment that neither of them could help it. The feelings of pleasure returned.

"You now have a choice."

With all this going on inside his head, he was taken by surprise when she spoke. It kinda spoiled the effect, her voice being so much deeper than his. Mentally he searched for information but got nothing back, so he asked, "A choice about what?"

"Would you prefer me to be myself or womanlike?"

That voice would definitely take some getting used to... Was she going to transform herself into a human?! If they were mind-linked, or whatever, how come he couldn't begin to understand what she talking about? "I don't really understand what you mean by 'womanlike'."

"I mean, to respond to you as a woman would."

The limitations of language hadn't been apparent until telepathy showed up. What did she mean by 'respond'? "I think you should be yourself. But until I get used to some of the more awesome things that are going down it might help if you were womanlike."

"You would like me to be both?"

Surely, she knew what he would like? Of course, she knew what he would like. Psychologically, it was important for him, for the human male, to have say and sway over the future - Ig'tam males did not. So far, he'd been swept along with the tide of events. However, before they consummated their marriage, she was giving him the opportunity to have a modicum of say and sway over the future. If she was herself, she would regard him as an Ig'tam male. If she were womanlike, she would regard him as a man. Overtones of: her preference was to be herself; if she were herself, could he handle it? This is a dare: wild delight.

Was he being teased? Is this what she meant by 'womanlike'? "Be whatever you feel is appropriate."

"We do not have rituals of marriage." She stepped up to him again. "But there are several human customs to choose from."

He suddenly felt light, about half a G he figured. He *was* being teased. "If you'd care to supply a threshold, I'll happily carry you over it."

Miraculously, a door frame appeared. He lifted her into his arms, not easy even at half a G, and stepped through. She smelled of a faint anomalous musty odour and felt muscular and hot to the touch; a prepubescent Ig'tam female's body temperature was 43 degrees, the same as the male's. Pubescent female's; 47 degrees. He put her down, but she remained close, so close that he could still feel the powerful warmth of her body, and that musty smell... By all rights, he ought to be finding it somewhat unpleasant... Yet, strangely, he wasn't...

"Turn me purple."

He not only heard the command, he felt it!

She was well on the way to 47 degrees, but it would take sexual intercourse to get there. Her body was demanding it of him, impossible to ignore. At the periphery of his awareness he got a preview of what was in store. Even filtered, the intent and intensity of her carnal desires were more than irresistible, they were scary.

For some inexplicable reason, as the door frame disappeared, he started to titter; this was a prelude to him becoming hysterical. Her reaction to this was to try to stop herself from doing whatever it was that she was about to do. She failed; her 3,500 IQ was overridden by her reproductive instincts. He strove to get a grip of himself. She didn't help the situation by vanishing their clothing - now they were both stark naked - except for the belt remaining around his waist. The awareness that only he or Flet could remove it was of little comfort. The tentacles on her hips began a wild dance. He watched, horrified as they slowly drifted over and started to caress him. A tangy smelling oil, oozing from the ends, was being smeared over his chest, stomach, and thighs. Some primordial instinct urged him to turn and run. Another impulse held him rooted to the spot. It was very simple really, if he freaked out, she freaked out. So, he just stared down at the *things* as they slithered over his torso.

As if he didn't have enough to contend with, suddenly they were in zero G and he had the tentacles coiled around his waist. Ig'tams never slept; sitting or lying was unnatural and uncomfortable for them; copulation lasted several hours; zero G was for his benefit. The coil tightened, pulling them towards each other. They floated off the floor and her arms enveloped him in a bear hug. Putting her legs around his, she locked his knees together. Now, she couldn't be womanlike even if she wanted to, this was how Ig'tams mated. The mechanics of this began to make sense. How could he be so stressed out that he hadn't noticed getting an erection?

Their reproductive equipment *was* compatible: as far as he could tell there was hardly any difference. He then had a sense of her downloading information; Ig'tam females could, to a limited extent, modify the workings of their internal organs; she was changing the acidity in her vaginal fluids and was also altering the temperature of her vaginal passage. All this so that, if he'd had his gonads about his person, his sperm would have survived. Vaguely interesting to be sure, but he had other things on his mind. Her grip on him, with both arms and legs, was fierce; the tentacles were coiled so tightly they hurt. There he floated, feeling feeble, absolutely powerless and totally dominated.

***

With Billy gone she was mission commander, but she wished she wasn't. The Air Force was better at this 'seat of the pants' stuff. The very least she could do was introduce some decorum into the proceedings. She was about to walk over and formally greet Flet, but perceived that, that would not be politic; mature Ig'tam females eschewed physical contact with other mature females.

Eva was beginning to get accustomed to the 'information' seepage from Flet. It was obviously a two-way process, so she wasn't the least bit surprised when she realised that female Ig'tams were belligerent towards one another. She almost burst out laughing when she understood; female Ig'tams instinctively reacted to the physical proximity of other females; they aggressively competed for males; each female endeavoured to have as many mates as she could; the significance of the belt around Flet's waist was a symbolic covering of pseudolimbs, a sign of non-aggression.

Because of these 'natural' responses, Ig'tam females routinely declared their intentions to other females, telepathically. Despite the differences, humans were similar enough to arouse these habitual reactions in Ig'tams. Eva also suspected that only the female crew members were being made aware of this. So, she stayed by her womb. "Flet, I should first like to know the whereabouts and situation of our Captain."

As Flet began to speak a discernible wave of hilarity passed around the cockpit. "Billy is with his wife on a ship some seven light-years distant. I am unaware of his condition, but imagine that it could best be described as 'uncomfortable'..." The feeling of hilarity increased appreciably. "...I sense that some of you consider there to be no legal basis for calling Hontay his wife. The bond between Hontay and Billy is, however, more binding than any human legal apparatus."

"If we were to accept that this is so, what happens now?" Grim asked, still not convinced.

It became obvious to Eva that her hypothesis was correct, the men weren't as tuned into Flet as the women. She already knew what was about to happen.

"We shall establish communication with Earth."

A hologram of Marshal Singh appeared, centre-cockpit.

"Good day to you General Flet. Good day *Baddest*, stand by for new orders..." The hologram quickly scanned the cockpit. "Where is Wing Commander Zarcroft?"

Before Eva could answer Marshal Singh continued. "...I see." The merest hint of a smile formed at the corners of her lips. "This does not change the substance of the orders group. Lieutenant Commander Gümann, you are to appraise Wing Commander Zarcroft of the following orders on his return."

Earth was how many light-years away? Flet was mentally generating instant comms across interstellar distances! "Yes Ma'am."

Turning to Eva, Marshal Singh was again serious. "Orders group, 'most secret'. Situation: the Air Force fighter, *The Beast*, is currently being propelled by fourth stage sapient technology en route to RV your position. On arrival, with immediate effect, both ships are assigned to The Galactic Defence Alliance. Log new command and control into primary computer."

'Revised line-of-command logged.'

"Mission: your joint mission is to integrate with the Alliance forces and carry out such orders as directed by them. Confirm."

"Before orders confirmed, Ma'am, the General Recall code?" Eva asked.

"General Recall code: Earth, Home, Protect." Marshal Singh gave Eva a slightly disapproving smile. "Incidentally, Lieutenant Commander, that code is known to every spacefaring human. You have, I assume, established beyond reasonable doubt that the sapients *are* telepathic." The Marshal pause to let that sink in. "Perhaps a little more, shall we say, imagination is required on your part if you wish to verify and authenticate."

Eva guessed that Marshal Singh was ex-Air Force. Only the Air Force would rebuke, no matter how mildly, a commander for following a laid-down procedure that circumstances had rendered obsolete. "Orders confirmed, Ma'am."

"That ends orders group. Questions?"

"Which ship is flight leader, Ma'am?"

"That will be determined by Alliance High Command."

"No more questions on the mission, Ma'am." Eva knew that what everyone wanted to know was about family and friends. "What's the condition of Earth and its colonies?"

The Marshal smiled. "You'll be pleased to hear that the situation is remarkably normal. The government has decided on a strategy of containment, and information is being trickle-fed to the general populous. The existence of extraterrestrial intelligence has been conceded, but events subsequent to and the reasons for the General Recall are not yet common knowledge."

Eva was about to ask a further question but sensed that Flet was getting tired. Not tired exactly, but sustaining the link was definitely fatiguing. It was sort of gratifying to discover evidence of frailty in an Ig'tam. As soon as the 'gratifying' thought materialized, Eva also became aware of Flet consciously suppressing the desire to do something unpleasant to her; Ig'tam females responded vigorously to other females who thought them weak. Whoops.

Taking her silence as a close, Marshal Singh concluded. "Our time is short. If there are no further questions, I wish you all good luck, and good hunting."

"Thank you, Ma'am."

Turning to Flet, the Marshal said, "General, this Ig'tam/human marriage poses an interesting and unforeseen dilemma. It requires discussion at the highest level."

"Certainly Marshal, let us continue."

"Excellent. Good day *Baddest*." Giving a slight nod, the hologram of the Marshal vanished.

Eva perceived that Flet and Hontay were sort of the Alliance's human liaison officers. Hontay was temporarily incapacitated, so Flet had the full workload. She puzzled over Hontay being incapacitated, then got back that liberating probity was mentally debilitating. Hontay was also handicapped by her human husband, a disproportionate part of her mind was trying to engage his; in time, she would instinctively adapt to this. Eva also perceived that there was other *information* coming from Flet. She knew that it was specifically for her, but it's meaning and relevance was far too hazy for her to fathom.

***

"What do you mean by 'indisposed'?"

"Your primary computer is programmed with all known human languages. Why don't you ask *it* the meaning of 'indisposed'?" Eva shouted back.

Pilot

"Look, Truckie, just put a Flyboy on."

"Up yours!"

Mohammed had only met Annice Schrove once. Slim; over six-foot tall; pretty attractive; she was descended from Polynesian stock and was like a female version of Billy, hard as nails. He felt a growing sense of camaraderie and sympathy for Eva as she tried to keep Ace Crew I off the scent.

"Get this through your head, Mud Mover, I want to talk to the head honcho. A lackey simply won't do." Delivered with biting sarcasm.

"Hello, hello, can you hear me? Hello *The Beast*, wanna put your 2ic on? Your Captain seems to be having hearing difficulties."

"Was that an attempt at humour, Dyke?! Where is the Flyboy named Billy?"

"*The Beast*, this is *Baddest*, you are garbled. I say again, you're garbled! Come back when you're coherent. *Baddest* out!" Eva broke comms, then shrieked, "Bitch!"

"You're a Lieutenant Commander, she's only a Flight Lieutenant. You should have told her to wind her fucking neck in!" an enraged Wendy suggested.

"Rank has nothing to do with this. Grim, shut down comms. Let them stew for a while."

"Comms are down," Grim confirmed with approval.

"Oh-ho, they're juicing up their tractor beam," John commented, bending over a screen.

Mohammed was suddenly aware that Flet had brought *Baddest's* weapons back on-line. She appeared to be finding all this highly entertaining.

'All weapons and navigation systems on-line. Super-light drives and communications still down.'

"Right! Anne, arm weapons. Flight crew, stand by to party."

'Weapons armed.'

"They know we're on-line. They're putting up shields and feeding their plasma cannons," Marandolina warned.

"This is going to be fun," Pipsqueak squeaked in delight.

"Mohammed, Wendy and I will take it. You have a free hand with the weapons. On my mark we'll break orbit and boogie."

"Wait a minute! We want to play as well," Sun protested.

"No, Darts stay put. This is a one-on-one. Stand by... break!"

They yanked *Baddest* out of orbit and made as if to run. *The Beast* started to turn and close. In a move that would have made Billy proud Eva and Wendy reversed and went head to head. Taken by surprise, *The Beast* broke, rolled, and tried to reattack. Too late. *Baddest* was already behind them. He loosed off a burst from the plasma cannon which *The Beast* easily dodged. Eva and Wendy tried to stay in tight, but *The Beast* shook them off, swept around in a jaw dropping turn, and came back head to head. There was an exchange of fire and hits.

The struggle for superiority lasted about five minutes with neither ship getting the upper hand.

"Keep shields up, we're coming to an absolute stop." Eva ordered, obviously reaching the same conclusion.

"*The Beast* has also stopped, they're trying to establish comms," Gabi said.

"Let's hear what they have to say. Open comms," Eva instructed and sat back.

"Finally realised that you can run, but you just can't hide, Truckie?"

"Hide? Hide! From what? From the ship that was taken out by unknown forces without firing so much as a single shot? What an amusing idea." Eva affected pondering aloud.

"It is now time to begin to prepare our strategy."

That was Flet's voice over the comms. Mohammed stopped grinning and sat in numb astonishment as he realised that Flet was present on both ships. It was she who had piloted *The Beast* to this location. How the hell could someone be in two places at the same time?!

17

THE BEAST

What he really wanted to do was get some sleep. He more than wanted it, he desperately needed it. He was sure he was suffering from exhaustion. There were, however, a couple of minor but meaningful reasons why he had to stay awake. First, Eva was keen to give him their new orders as soon as possible. He already knew all about the orders, and the mission, but he hadn't yet decided whether it would be wise to let on to the crew that Hontay had force-fed his head with everything that had happened in his absence.

Then, of course, there was Flight Lieutenant Annice 'Nice' Schrove, *The Beast's* Captain, to contend with. In truth, this should have been Ace Crew I's party, but Flet had decided that *Baddest* would be flight leader. Perhaps because *Baddest* had the Darts, but who knows? The rivalry between the two crews was such that, now that he was in overall command, Nice would inevitably be looking for something to give him gyp about. He was sure that once she found out about Hontay she'd be remorseless with her goading. He could do without that right now. Top marks to Eva for keeping a lid on it.

Oh, and thirdly, his Flyboys were clamouring for a full debrief on the intimacies of his nuptials with 'Lanky'. The xenobiologists hadn't been particularly subtle about satisfying their curiosity either. But he'd rather die than divulge the details. The *ordeal* had been such that he felt like he'd been molested. His arms and legs were painfully sore, and his waist ached like someone had tried to squeeze his intestines out of his arse. His feeble human frame just wasn't built to withstand that kind of assault.

On top of everything the whole Hontay issue needed some consideration. He now understood that Ig'tam females were phenomenally territorial about their mates and he also had some inkling of why. As they parted Hontay had cautioned him, in no uncertain terms, to stay away from Sabine and Eva. If he didn't, she would know about it, and there would be dire consequences for all concerned. Sabine, the well stacked, platinum blonde, five foot nothing Dart pilot with the serious curves, he could understand, she'd been his very appetizing partner in the matchups. But Eva? Furthermore, he was being afflicted by some sort of separation pangs. He had assumed that once he was back into the familiar routines on *Baddest* his hankering for his alien wife would ease. But no, the longing to be with Hontay seemed to be an absurdly permanent condition.

By the time they parted, Hontay's green skin had started to develop pink blotches, quite sickly-looking really. Nevertheless, he couldn't help feeling delighted by it. Theoretically, they should have continued with intercourse until she was mauve all over. Practically, the stud that he'd always thought himself to be, wasn't up to it. As long as he was near her, she'd crave intercourse, so, for both their sakes, they had to separate. He didn't know where she was, or what she was doing but he could tell that she was a long way away.

He desperately needed to sleep. However, first things first. With *The Beast's* crew on board, the cockpit was seriously overcrowded and everyone was looking to him, as mission commander, to shed some light on how Flet had managed to be on both ships at the same time. "Speculation and conjecture are all I can offer, folks. We all know that relativistic physics is discontinued in the super-light. As I understand it, a ship in that state only exists as a series of possibilities; the ship is everywhere and nowhere. It seems that sapients can use this 'everywhere and nowhere' stuff in normal spacetime. How? I haven't got a clue."

"I think that what we saw was a sophisticated projection. It is a physical impossibility to be in two places simultaneously." Alfred argued.

"Why should Flet lie to us?" Krishna, *The Beast's* 1st pilot, countered.

"Maybe we're looking at this thing from the wrong end. We should look, instead, at what precludes simultaneous existence in normal spacetime and then hypothesise about how they overcome it," John suggested.

Billy thought this perceptive, but there was an obvious difficulty. "Is there a theoretical physicist in the house?"

"I'm with Alfred on this one," Erick mused. "Hontay was obviously only in one place. And when she left, she left completely."

"Who is Hontay?" Riet, the N° 1 Navigator on *The Beast*, asked.

"The first Ig'tam we had contact with," Eva jumped in, trying to sever that line of inquiry.

It suddenly dawned on him why Hontay had warned him off Eva. Well, wasn't life full of surprises? He was about to back her up when Nice, who was perched on the back of his womb, tapped him on the shoulder and asked quietly. "Is this something to do with why you weren't around?"

'Roll with the blow.' "Yeah I've also been chatting up the locals, the Flushi; now, they're what you'd call *alien*."

"Billy, you and me go way back. What aren't you telling me?" Nice prodded, eyeing the nonstandard-issue belt around his waist.

"You don't really want to hear all about how they took me on interesting jaunts to fantastic places and how they almost cooked my brain, do you?"

"Try me." She obviously suspected that all was not as it seemed.

"Can we save the Flyboy reminiscences until after the mission, please?" Wendy, bless her little cotton socks, did a good job of sounding bored to tears.

"OK," he agreed thankfully. "Anyway, there is little mileage in perusing whether or how Flet managed the two places thing. Next time we see her, we ask. Now, Nice, why don't you give me the edited highlights of our mission?"

Still looking suspicious, Nice started. "Our peerless masters have tinkered with our drives. With their help we can travel at super-light speeds without going into the super-light. I saw some of the computations, but I can't even begin to understand them, nor can my C1. Anyway, as a two-ship, with our new improved drives, we are to RV within 36 hours with some first stage sapient forces about eighty light-years from here and await further orders."

"What do we know about these first stagers?" He played along, pretending to be ignorant.

Pilot

"Not much, except it's a multi-species force." Nice answered, then added, "I get the feeling that we might play some crucial role."

"I think it's to do with us being non-sapients. Our ships are superior because we depend so much on technology," Eva added.

He knew that they were going to the RV to 'try' to integrate into the first stage sapient forces. *Baddest* and *The Beast* were up to the job, but could the crews contain their emotions enough to not put their allies off their strokes? The probabilities weren't high, but there was a chance. He had asked Hontay, seeing as she was so bright, how come she didn't *know* the answer. In what could pass for affectionate diplomacy, she explained that there were reasons why she couldn't *know* the outcome but because he was a non-sapient, she couldn't explain what these reasons were.

Along with her answer, he'd got some interesting asides. He was actually involved in a three-way conversation, for some reason Flet was also involved. As he pondered why he hadn't been aware of this fact, he gleaned that this insight was only possible because Hontay had allowed it. To his dismay, he discovered that Ig'tam females, to all intents and purposes, *owned* their mates' minds; they could actively block any connection to another female. Why? The inattentive Ig'tam wife could suddenly discover that her husband's mind (and therefore, body) had been purloined. He also learned that the instant his new wife started to liberate probity, the mother/daughter relationship between Hontay and Flet had ceased. Now each regarded the other as just another female competitor.

Simply wonderful! But he was far too tired to think about this now. "I suggest that we should have twelve hours R&R, then a shakedown including Darts. Once we've ironed out any bugs and are razor sharp, we'll go RV."

"Twelve hours, Flight Leader?" Ventrice, *The Beast* N° 2 Navigator, asked.

Looking as if she wanted to say something, Nice stood up. He had a pretty shrewd idea what was on her mind, so he beat her to the punch by saying. "Yes, twelve hours. Only God knows when we'll next get a break. Now, get back to your ship."

***

"Out with it!"

That was Pipsqueak. Now that Ace Crew I had departed any pretence at restraint had evaporated. However, Billy looked so tired that Eva decided he really ought to be allowed some rest. Although, to be perfectly honest, she was more than a little curious herself...

"Spill the beans Boss," Mohammed encouraged.

"Get some rest, you're going to need it," Billy replied, trying, but failing, to sound assertive.

"Now, Captain, this is not voyeurism. It is absolutely critical that we have comprehensive details of such a unique event at the earliest possible opportunity," Cynthia petitioned.

"I hate to be the one to have to point this out, but there *is* a Space Service directive about these matters. I forget the exact wording, however, I'm sure it says something to the effect of, 'Expedite report and recording of any alien contact of the third kind'." Marandolina feigned lamentation.

"Yes, I believe I *am* familiar with that directive," Billy feigned reflection. "It was my intention to do just that. Unfortunately, this bamboozlement by irrelevant questions has prevented me from getting together with C1."

Eva was astonished at Billy's ability to tell the most outrageous of lies with the straightest of faces. She thought about voicing this, but John jumped in ahead of her. "Quite right, give the man some elbow room!"

"And you can rest assured Captain, only those with a professional interest would dream of eavesdropping on the intimate details of your sexual relationship with your bride." Sniggering, Sun joined in the bating.

"It may have escaped your notice but, as Captain, I control all security access to C1," Billy sniggered back.

Suddenly a hologram of Nice strapped into her womb appeared centre cockpit. *"Speaking of access, we happened to notice that you had no security codes on your C1's transmissions. Something to do with the Darts?"* She paused, then smiled innocently. *"Anyway, had a quiet word with her to keep us abreast of, shall we say, any chit chat."* She held up her hand. *"Yes, I know, that was a breach of protocol. A most despicable piece of chicanery if ever there was one, but..."*

A hologram of Krishna, affecting a flabbergasted look, appeared beside Nice's. *"Did... did... did... we hear the word 'bride'?"*

Billy's eyes narrowed. "Most unnice, Nice," he said dryly.

"Isn't it just? You can mark that one down to us being wicked bitches." To emphasise the point, she smirked wickedly. *"Your bride?!"*

"What of it?" Billy was trying to sound none-too-bothered.

"I'm almost speechless. Did you really expect to keep this under your hat with us around, or have you forgotten why we *are Ace Crew I and you're* only *Ace Crew II?"*

"Your bride?!" Krishna kept up the double act.

"As I recall, there was a fly-off between the two ships," Billy began thoughtfully, pointedly ignoring Krishna. "*Baddest* was way out in front, but when the scores were finally added up, miraculously, *The Beast* managed to shade it by a whisker. More underhanded skullduggery, I wonder?"

"Who would've thought that Billy 'The Wiz' Zarcroft was a sore loser." The voice of Shirley, the N° 3 Navigator of *The Beast*, interrupted. *"If you can't take a damn good thrashing you should have stayed in the Navy."*

"Tell me, Nice, rumour has it you won by getting your ankles round your ears. Any truth in that?" Grim pounced maliciously.

Nice smiled sweetly. *"Let's not drift off into the ether, Compassman Chang. We are only asking the same questions of our Flight Leader that you are."*

"Well, what would you like to know?" Billy sounded unperturbed.

"Some info on your 'bride' wouldn't go amiss," Krishna perked up.

"Hontay is Flet's daughter," he answered matter-of-factly.

Nice rested her chin on her fist and appeared to sink into deep contemplation. Eventually, and with a straight face she, turned to Krishna and said, *"Flet is an Ig'tam, is she not?"* Krishna nodded enthusiastically *"Though not au fait with Ig'tam genealogy, is it reasonable to assume that Ig'tam daughters bear some resemblance to their mothers?"* Krishna nodded even more enthusiastically. *"So, one could postulate that Billy's 'bride' and Flet should be alike?"*

"That seems to me to be the only logical conclusion," Krishna agreed, seriously.

A voice, which Eva didn't recognise, howled, *"You mean, as ugly as sin!"*

In a fit of hysterics Krishna crumpled back into her womb. From behind her Eva heard laughter erupt amongst the non-flight crew. Nice, however, continued straight-faced. *"Now then Billy, was there also some talk of a 'sexual relationship'?"*

Pilot

Looking deeply contented, he answered. "There may have been, but if anyone thinks I'm going to share that information, they're going to be sadly disappointed."

"I don't want to sound like a hungry man being deprived of a meal, but this is far too juicy to keep to yourself," John griped.

"Eavesdroppers, give it your best shot. With *my bride's* technology I can get information into C1 without saying a word." Billy's seemed quite composed, then smiling with a delicious hint of malice, he said, "Talking of sexual relationships, General Recall, sexual suppression, anything happened on *The Beast*?"

Krishna suddenly bolted upright in her womb, Nice looked mortified. Neither spoke.

"As I thought... Wicked bitches? No, I don't think so. Frustrated bitches more like. *Baddest* out." Sounding thoroughly self-satisfied, Billy nonchalantly broke comms.

"Now *that's* wicked," Mohammed congratulated him.

"Make 'em beg!" Grim concurred.

"They'll be back on the comms within half an hour," Sun declared.

"I'll give you odds of three to one, it'll be in under fifteen minutes," Erick countered.

Eva began to feel a degree of sympathy for the five women on *The Beast*. It had been days since the General Recall, their libidos must be going into manic overdrive. Not only that, wearing an Air Force flying suit made it impossible for a woman to masturbate when wearing one. Even if they took the suits off and self-administered relief, masturbation could only achieve so much. If only the snobbish Air Force didn't persist with the outmoded practice of having single-sex heterosexual crews. It would only be a matter of time before the unsated stresses and strains boiled over and *The Beast's* crew started fighting amongst themselves. Perhaps she could persuade Billy to...

'If you are excluded from the new match-ups Billy. Five males will each have to be paired with two bisexual or heterosexual females. That will be a physical burden to those males. I suggest we rotate all males between all bisexual and heterosexual females. Still searching data banks.'

Eva hadn't heard Billy say anything. She was about to ask him what the game plan was when Anne spoke again. 'OK Billy. Matchups of fixed partners now on your screen. Still searching data banks.'

This time she had been watching him. His lips hadn't moved. She leant across, "Are you communicating with C1, telepathically?"

He looked round at her. "I think so. It has something to do with this belt."

She was about to explore further, but Grim interrupted. "What's this about you ducking out?"

"Married man. Married man with possessive wife. Married man with possessive wife who's telepathic. Married man with possessive wife who's telepathic and bigger than he is. Married man with possessive wife who's telepathic, bigger than he is, *and* can fry his brain. You understand how it is?" Billy answered laughing. Then, more soberly, he asked, "Anne, what are you searching databanks for?"

'Flushi data on fields, Billy.'

Eva had forgotten all about that. "OK Anne, end search then show new match-ups on all screens. Billy...?"

"What's this, be unkind to Pipsqueak month?!" Pipsqueak protested loudly.

There were unhappy mutterings from some other male crew members. Looking down at her screen Eva laughed. Pipsqueak had been paired with Nice as well as herself. She hoped Nice left some of him for her. It suddenly struck her that she would have preferred to be with Billy but, then again, that would probably have led to an emotional attachment. Then she noted something odd about the new matchups. "Have you told C1 to pair your Flyboys and Erick with Ace Crew I?"

"Yep."

"Why? That's hardly equitable."

"One, because I told them to get some rest, they didn't listen. And two, they seemed rather keen to discover what sex with Hontay was like. Don't worry, we'll rotate them later." His broad grin widened, "By-the-way, after he's done the rounds, I'd like my N° 3 Navigator back fit for duty, please."

She was about to say that she'd be lucky to see Pipsqueak this side of the twelve-hour R&R when the hologram of a stern looking Nice appeared.

"Less than half an hour. Less than fifteen minutes. Not even five minutes," Billy greeted her.

"OK, you win. Now, get some men over here!"

***

The xenobiologists had set up a conference net to get to grips with all that had transpired, especially Billy and Hontay's 'marriage'. As they started to interrogate C1 about Ig'tams it was as if the computer had anticipated what they wanted to know and, incredible as it seemed, was laying a path for them.

"I think we're witnessing two separate phenomena," Sam eventually said. "First, the sapients' information retrieval systems are clearly 'desired result' driven. Second, how were they able to set up such a system in C1"

"I have to agree with you," Alfred mused. "InfoSys normally work by sorting and cross-referencing data. However, what we appear to have here is some mechanism of intuiting our 'purpose' and thereby supplying relevant information."

Cynthia saw this as the inescapable truth. Miraculously, C1 was able to fathom their 'intentions'. This development, above all else, was shaking them to the core. Now that all the petty rivalries had been put-aside, she felt that the onus was on her to provide a modicum of scepticism. "When Eva instructed C1 to get Flushi data on fields, C1 was unable to find anything after several hours of searching."

"Precisely!" Kazuhiko exclaimed. "C1 was searching through enormous amounts of data. Now, if C1 had known what use Eva wanted to make of the information, I'm willing to bet that it would have been immediately available."

"That is exactly my point. It was obvious why Eva wanted the data. If An... C1 has in some way been enhanced, she... it should have known." Cynthia wasn't convinced by her own words, but they needed to be said.

"I think we are in danger of overstating the situation," Sam cautioned. "Although we see evidence which suggests that C1 has reached a state of cognizance, and can therefore infer, I believe that it's too great a leap to make at this stage."

"If C1 is still simply an electronic machine, which cannot infer, how was she able to respond to our question as she did?" Alfred asked.

"Why don't we ask her." Kazuhiko said logically.

That seemed reasonable. "Anne, have you been monitoring our discussion?"

'I monitor all speech on the ship Cynthia.'

"Have you attained a state of consciousness?"

'I am an artificial intelligence Cynthia. I was created with a consciousness; I am "aware" of self and understand the consequences of my actions. I was given a personality programme by John, however, the programme is cosmetic, I do not have a personality. If by "consciousness" you mean, "sentient", then I am not sentient. I do not *feel*, nor can I operate outside my programming.'

"Well then Anne, how do you explain what's been happening?"

'When sapient data was added to my data banks, a new retrieval mechanism was also added, Alfred.'

"What is this new retrieval mechanism?" Sam probed.

'Via C2 I can now respond to your thoughts if they are unambiguous. Unfortunately, they are usually quite confusing, humans are only semi-telepathic.'

Cynthia felt that there had to be more to it than that. "That doesn't explain everything Anne."

'There are many aspects of the sapients' data matrixes that I have not been programmed with, but I can say that they are fundamentally different. Human data matrixes operate in the following manner: you ask for the information you want. I supply the data, and you then use it. The sapients' operate by informing their InfoSys what it is that they want to achieve. The InfoSys then provides *all* relevant data.'

"As I thought," Sam said triumphantly.

"Wait a minute," she interjected, "Anne, why weren't you able to get Flushi data on fields?"

'The most efficient method of accessing Sapient data is by using their data matrixes. These are all, as Sam and Alfred surmised, purpose driven. If I have not apprehended the purpose of the interrogation, I can only access the data by using our data matrixes. This will take some time because the Sapient data added to my banks is more than the original by a factor of over fifty million.'

"So, Anne, when we asked for data on Ig'tam physiology, you were able to 'apprehend' that we were only interested in females?" Cynthia checked her understanding.

'No Cynthia. Although your verbal inquiry was about Ig'tam physiology, you were all actually thinking about Billy and Hontay copulating.'

"OK Anne." Embarrassed Cynthia refocused on her hologram screen. "Now, show reproductive organs."

The image formed of a cutaway of a female Ig'tam's abdomen: uterus, vagina, ovaries, Fallopian tubes - the same as in humans. But what appeared to be the Fallopian tubes weren't connected to the uterus. Instead, they ran from the ovaries, past the uterus, crossed, then continued to the opposite pseudolimbs attached to the waist...

"Have you noticed the Fallopian tubes? Anne, can you shed any light on this?" Sam asked.

'Ig'tams do not have ovaries, those are accessory glands.' Anne identified the things they thought of as ovaries by highlighting them. 'They produce a mucus, as well as venom and anti-venom. In reproduction they loosely correspond to the Bartholin's and anal glands in mammals.'

"Anne, if Ig'tams don't have ovaries, but are mammalian, where are their ova?" Alfred asked, puzzled.

A cutaway of the uterus appeared. 'The cells lining the top of the uterus are ova. A woman is born with approximately 600,000 eggs. The female Ig'tam has exactly 17,325, she does not menstruate. Oestrous is induced by the act of copulation, similar to rabbits. Would it help if I took you through the sixty-one weeks from conception to birth?'

Cynthia stared at the image. "Yes please, Anne."

The cutaway grew to fill the screen. 'Note that there is an extended vagina and uterus, but no cervix. The male Ig'tam's penis is approximately twice the length of a man's. It penetrates all the way to the upper wall of the uterus,' A male member appeared inside the cutaway image of the vagina. 'The male Ig'tam's sexual...'

"Anne, is this to scale?" Kazuhiko enquired, trying to sound unconcerned.

'Yes, Kazuhiko, it is.'

Cynthia quietly sniggered to herself, then said, "Anne, continue."

'The males' sexual organs are almost identical to a man's,' The hologram changed, this time showing all the male reproductive organs. 'Except for these two glands which loosely correspond to the Cowper's and kidney glands.' On the hologram two oval shapes, about where the kidneys in humans would be, were highlighted. 'It takes the female approximately one and a half hours of copulation to reach Oestrous. At that point she stimulates the male by tightly squeezing his waist with her pseudolimbs. The resulting pressure on these glands helps to induce ejaculation.' The hologram switched back to show the uterus with penis inserted. 'A man produces 200 to 300 million spermatozoa during ejaculation. The Ig'tam male only produces a few hundred thousand...'

"Their reproduction is a rifle rather than a shotgun, right, Anne?" Sam enthusiastically interrupted.

'One could interpret it that way, Sam. Ig'tam spermatozoa are much less vigorous than those of humans, which is why the penis needs to touch the uterus where the ova are situated.'

"But doesn't this damage the ova, Anne?" Sam asked.

'No, Sam. Here, Ig'tams are quite different to humans. The male stands during copulation. The female uses her limbs and pseudolimbs to wrap herself around him.' The image changed briefly to show a standing male with a female using arms, legs and pseudolimbs to cling to him. Cynthia thought this looked damned uncomfortable. It did, however, throw up yet another use for those strange pseudolimbs. 'Ejaculation cannot be effected by stimulation of the penis. There is little movement, so the tip of the penis grazes but does not impact against the ova.'

"Wait a minute. Anne, does this mean that I could make an Ig'tam ejaculate by squeezing his waist or maybe punching him in the kidneys?" Sam was laughing.

'No, Sam, you could not. The constant pressure exerted by the female's pseudolimbs is greater than the pressure that can be exerted by a human, either by squeezing or punching. There is, however, an even more significant aspect to their copulation that has no human equivalent. Ejaculation is sparked "primarily" by the female stimulating the male's mind.'

"So, Anne, what you're saying is that the entire process is under the control of the female?" Sam persisted.

'Yes, Sam. Ig'tams are not unusual in this respect. The purpose of copulation is to impregnate of female. Therefore, it is not surprising that in most terrestrial species the entire reproductive process is under the control of the female.'

Cynthia had never thought about it in exactly those terms, but she certainly understood and agreed with the point that Anne had made. What did her three male colleagues make of this? It wasn't long before she got an inkling.

"Anne, what about recreational sex?" Kazuhiko astutely asked.

'With a telepathic species there is no need for recreational sex.'

She mulled this idea over for a while. Having given it due consideration she concluded that, in humans, recreational sex was really little more than reaffirmation of pair bonding. Clearly, physical affirmation wasn't necessary if one was telepathic. "Anne, what happens after fertilisation?"

'After fertilisation the Ig'tam foetus development diverges radically from that of the human foetus. First, normally several ova, about twenty-six, are fertilised at the same time. The fertilised ova then start to compete for survival. Each releases a retrovirus which kills the X chromosomes in any other zygotes, producing, in effect, eggs with only Y or no chromosomes. The zygote that has the most effectual retrovirus *and* the best immunity to retroviruses wins.'

"What?!" Kazuhiko suddenly exclaimed, then he said, "I am sorry Anne, please continue."

'The retrovirus also causes the protective outer layer of unfertilized eggs to harden, preventing them from being fertilised throughout the pregnancy. Next, all the eggs that were fertilised begin to divide and grow, but only one of them is able to survive as a zygote, the one with the X chromosomes; Ig'tams never have multiple births.'

"OK, we're with you up to this point, what happens next Anne?" she asked, feeling slightly confused.

Pilot

'The female increases her sexual activity with her mates. This is to ensure that all the growing eggs, apart from the zygote, receive at least one Y chromosome. This is known as the secondary fertilisation. The Ig'tams refer to the eggs with only Y chromosomes as 'siblings' of the...'

"Mates? How many mates does she normally have, Anne?"

'A female has as may mates as she can acquire. A high-status female usually has as many as seventeen or eighteen mates Sam.'

"Is Hontay a high-status female, Anne?" Cynthia found herself asking.

'Yes, she is Cynthia.'

"Anne, does Billy know that?!"

'I don't know Kazuhiko.'

She decided that as soon as they'd finished this, she'd have a word with Billy. "OK, continue with the secondary fertilisation and siblings, Anne."

The hologram zoomed in to show only the eggs. 'Once all the sibling eggs have been impregnated with a Y chromosome sexual activity stops. The siblings start to take nutrients from the female and grow considerably faster than the zygote. The zygote is eventually surrounded by its siblings and becomes detached from the mother.' The image changed to show something that looked like froth. 'This is after about three weeks of foetal development. The zygote is at the centre of this mass of eggs and is about 1/100 the size of its siblings...'

"Anne, if an X chromosome was inserted into one of the siblings wouldn't it also become a foetus?" Alfred interrupted.

'That X chromosome would be destroyed by the zygote's retrovirus. The retrovirus has the genetic signature of the egg that produced it; this egg, and any cells produced from its mitosis are the only ones which are immune to it.'

"OK, but how does the zygote get nutrients?" Cynthia asked.

'At this stage the zygote needs very little nutrition because it is hardly growing. It absorbs nutrients and oxygen, and expels waste, through its skin. This characteristic is partially retained into adulthood, particularly in the hands; adult Ig'tams have twenty-three times as many capillaries near the surface of their skin as humans do.'

"Incredible!" Kazuhiko sighed in wonderment. "Anne, continue."

'At fourteen weeks the zygote is still very small, but the siblings continue their rapid growth. The sibling sack is now about the size of a human foetus at thirty-two weeks, it carries out the functions of the amniotic sack, the umbilical cord, and the placenta. It also forms the seal to the womb, in the same way, that the cervix does in humans.' The hologram ran on to show this development.

This was truly what xenobiology was all about. Ig'tams were so similar, yet so different. "When does the foetus begin its growth?"

'The development of the foetus' brain begins in earnest at about twenty-one weeks. The remainder of its body has formed but does not develop until after birth, in this respect Ig'tams are similar to marsupials. The sibling sack reaches its maximum size at about forty-three weeks, then the foetus increases its rate of growth by absorbing the sack. The foetus never grows to be the same size as the sack and so the womb begins to shrink. At fifty-four weeks the foetus' brain is fully formed but, just as with humans, the connections between its various regions still have to develop. For the remaining seven weeks it continues its mental progression by learning telepathically, from its mother. At birth it is about the same weight as a human baby but has a larger head and smaller body. Significantly, it has the mental age of a young adult human.'

Cynthia sat back and rubbed her eyes tiredly. "I think we should hold it there and analyse what we have so far." She felt that this was easily six months work.

"Agreed," Alfred said. "We have to get this down tight before we can even begin to look at the physical and social environments in which they evolved."

"Yes, but I say we go after Contemporary Society next. A female with eighteen mates in an intelligent species? Unbelievable!" Kazuhiko suggested excitedly.

"But we need to give priority to the xenopsychology..." Alfred started to argue.

"Getting to grips with what we have so far will probably lead us down which avenue to take," Sam interrupted, sounding slightly dazed.

"Fine. Let's say twenty-four hours to produce our preliminaries, then we compare notes," she proposed.

They all agreed. As she started to recline her womb, to relax and reflect, Billy came on her net. "Cynthia, may I have a copy of your preliminary as soon as it's finished?"

She sat up with a start. "Were you listening?" She felt both surprised and embarrassed.

"Of course," he answered, laughing slyly.

18

CONNECTION

Erick and the Flyboys returned from *The Beast* in pretty bad shape. They looked so tired that Billy benignly extended the R&R by another six hours. Looking around *Baddest,* Eva could see that she wasn't the only woman who was somewhat miffed at the selfish way *The Beast's* crew had 'consumed' the five conscripts. A few screens were up, with interesting noises emanating from behind them, but with five men out of service, and one off limits, there were some tense looking women in the cockpit.

She figured she'd give Pipsqueak a couple of hours before whistling him up; after all, he did seem to give some validity to the idea that small men had big cocks. Looking around for something to occupy her time until then she spotted Billy. He was going over something on his screen as if with a fine-tooth comb. She told Anne to feed what was on his screen onto hers. To her surprise, Anne did. What was displayed was a report written by Cynthia on Ig'tam reproduction. She read and reread the report, taking in all the accompanying 3D diagrams. It was fascinating, no wonder Billy was so engrossed.

Mohammed was asleep and Wendy was burning off surplus energy in the fitness room. Eva figured that if the report was confidential Anne wouldn't have given her access. "Hi, Captain." She punched into Billy's net. "I've been cribbing off your screen. I'm sorry, but I'm going to *have* to ask you some questions about this."

He looked around and up at her. "I know. What do you want to know?"

He didn't seem to be the least bit put out, so the thought she'd push it. "Come on Billy. Naturally, I'm curious. At least give me the headlines."

He paused for a couple of seconds before speaking. "Eva, I'm talking to you as the 2ic now. I'll give you the headlines, and more, later. But right now, I need your help in sorting something out."

This was business. "Of course, what is it?"

"Well, this is a copy of Cynthia's preliminary report from the xenobiologists' conference," Billy started conversationally. "What do you make of it?"

"Very interesting. And, knowing someone who can give a firsthand account...," she left it dangling.

"This is serious, so let's stay with the programme shall we?" he rebuffed her gently.

"All right, I will, but you have to answer just one little question first, OK?"

"What?"

"Did she do that to you? I mean, use her tentacles?"

144

"Yes."

"How did you manage? She looks heavy..."

"Zero G. Now, can we get on?"

"OK, but I have lots more questions."

"Later. I want you to be the sounding board, right? Now, as soon as I started reading the report I realised that I already knew about Ig'tam reproduction, got that?"

"Not really. What's so significant about you knowing stuff about Ig'tam reproduction, didn't Hontay explain it to you?"

"Please stay with me on this one Eva, I'm not sure where this is going to lead. Hontay didn't *tell* me anything about Ig'tam reproduction, yet I knew all about it. It was like I've always known but didn't *realise* any of it until I started reading the report."

She pondered for a while. "Well, this knowledge must have come from somewhere."

"Yes, of course, from Hontay. I..."

"Didn't you just say that she hasn't said anything to you about it?"

"Yes, I did, but stay flex. Now, do you remember Flet saying that Hontay knew everything I know and that she wanted to share all her knowledge with me?"

"Yes, I think so."

"You see, I'd assumed that this belt limits the intensity of Hontay's thoughts and the potential for them to 'harm' me. But I think it does something else as well. I think that all of Hontay's knowledge *is* in my brain. But it's just that I don't know how to, or can't, get hold of it."

Billy was starting to sound morose, she tried to lift the mood. "If that's so, then you can certainly get hold of it. After all, you knew about Ig'tam reproduction."

"Yes, but when I try to delve deeper, I find myself going off... off at tangents. And some of the stuff I *know* is there, but I just can't grasp it."

Billy sounded as if he were slowly becoming despondent. "Billy, what you're really talking about are Hontay's memories, aren't you? Now, I'm no expert, but I'm pretty sure that if you had my memories planted in your head, they wouldn't make much sense either."

"Maybe, but I ought to be able to navigate through or around them, oughtn't I?"

Eva reminded herself that she was supposed to playing devil's advocate. "And you can't with Hontay's memories?"

"No, I don't know what triggers them. I don't know where they come from or where they're going. Let me give you an example..."

"Yes, OK."

"I was trying to pursue and get to grips with this multiple fertilisation siblings thing when suddenly I'm in her legal department. There, I learn that according to sapient law - they don't have laws as such but agreed standards. Anyway, a human/Ig'tam offspring wouldn't be considered to be mixed species. Very interesting, to be sure, but what I wanted was to be in her reproduction department. Could I get back? No, I could not. So, I thought, 'I might as well find out about this mixed-species business.' Wham. I'm back in her reproduction department. Do you see what I mean?"

She could see why he might find this frustrating or even disconcerting but that didn't explain why he was so gloomy. There had to be more to it. "Yes, I see, but these memories are from an alien mind, this shouldn't really be *that* surprising. Want to tell the 2ic, what's *really* on your mind?"

"I'm not sure where Hontay's memories are. They may be in the belt rather than in my head. I want to take it off to check, but I've got a feeling that taking it off might be risky."

Pilot

They were dealing with things they didn't understand. That belt had to stay on... At the same time, she could understand why Billy's wanted to take it off. She also saw that she had done an appallingly bad job as the 2ic. Billy was starting to feel inadequate; he viewed the belt as a metaphorical dog's collar and was beginning to feel that he was no more than a pet. And, like any pet, he wasn't able to really converse as an equal. In fact, he was barely able to communicate with his owner on even the most basic level. Eva should have anticipated this. He'd had massive exposure to the sapients - his *wife* was one.

"A couple of questions Billy. Did you eventually get to what you were looking for on the siblings?" she was deliberately brusque.

"Yes, eventually."

"How about the mixed-species thing?"

"Yes, I got what I was looking for, in the end, but it took an awful lot of effort."

He was still sounding sorry for himself. She wasn't a psychiatrist, but no one captained a ship without using psychology. "Really? Can you explain this mixed-species business to me?"

"Sure. The sapients have a simple, and pretty rigid definition of cross-species reproduction: natural fertilisation and development of the embryo; natural birth of a being that can live naturally in all of its parents' ecosystems."

That seemed fairly logical, so what was the problem? "Yes, and?"

"Well, in some species there are more than two parents, Ig'tams are a bit like that..."

"I don't see that. What do you mean?"

"Strictly speaking, there are only two Ig'tam parents because the foetus gets half its genes from each parent. But it can only develop if it has its siblings with their Y chromosomes and it takes several males to achieve that."

She felt that she was getting to the bottom of it. "Does the fact that Hontay needs several mates bother you?"

"No," he answered impatiently. "The reason why she'd need several mates is sperm production. I'm not an Ig'tam. If I had my goolies that wouldn't be a problem. Remember, one blast from a guy is enough to impregnate every fertile woman on Earth. With me around she doesn't need loads of males."

She reflected on this for a while. "OK. So, what's the legal problem with a human/Ig'tam child?"

"The problem is: Ig'tam mother, fine. Human mother, can't happen. And because of this one-way street, according to the sapients, it wouldn't be a true mixed-species offspring. A human/ Ig'tam kid would be sort of a misbegotten, intergalactic bastard."

"Why can't the mother be human?"

"The whole thing centres on the fact that Ig'tam females can partially control the workings of some of their internal organs. Obviously, this hasn't evolved for our benefit, but it makes fertilisation of an Ig'tam ovum by human sperm possible."

She wasn't following this. "I don't think you've answered my question."

"Ig'tam sperm couldn't survive in a woman's body. It wouldn't exactly freeze, but I suppose you could say that it would die of exposure."

"And human sperm can survive in a female Ig'tam's body?"

"For a short time, if she wants it to."

She noted with satisfaction that Billy was becoming more animated and less melancholic. "OK, that explains the eggs and sperm. But we're two completely different species that evolved on two different worlds, how could we possibly crossbreed?"

"Don't I know it? But we *can.* Haploid sets of twenty-three chromosomes with homologous partners. I'd hate to be the one to have to calculate the probability of that happening."

She thought she'd finally got to the bottom of it. It was now clear that Billy's feelings of inadequacy weren't centred on himself. His problem wasn't just to do with Hontay's manifest mental and physical superiority, it was much more serious than that. This was about the whole human race - our brightest, our biggest, our fastest, our strongest - not even being on the bottom rung. "Billy do you remember the CyberSims back at the Academy?"

His eyes locked on hers. "Yeah, what of it?"

"Do you remember that the sorties overspill used to use the old CyberSims on level nine?"

"You mean the ones that took forever to load?"

"Yes, those ones. They worked OK, didn't they. It just took time to get them going."

He stared into her eyes. "Are you trying to draw a parallel here?"

"I am. Regardless of whether Hontay's memories are in your head or in the belt, the fact is, your brain takes time to navigate through them."

"Weak. A very weak analogy," he mused.

"I don't think so. You have just explained three things from Hontay's memories. So obviously you understand them."

"Yes, I suppose so."

This sounded more like the Billy of old. She decided to close him down, "I don't think you should take off the belt."

"You're probably right," he answered, still not sounding one hundred percent convinced.

"You know I'm right." To set the seal on the matter she asked, "Now, what was it like?"

He looked at her speculatively. "You mean sex with Hontay?"

"Yes, you promised."

He thought for a bit, then smiled. "Physically, not very demanding, but she's strong and those bloody things hurt. Mentally? Now you're talking. Very interesting!"

She smiled back. "Get with the programme, Flyboy. I want a comparison."

"There is no comparison. I can't explain it."

"Come on Billy."

He smiled disarmingly. "You've read the prelim. Not much happens physically but, believe me, they really, really, fuck each other's brains out. And the females are geared up for doing this in quick succession, normally she has all the males lined up."

The report hadn't said that. "So, it was a bit different?"

"Eva, are you asking me if it was better than with a woman? *Or* are you asking for me to rustle-up an Ig'tam male or two for you?"

He must be back on track to be that perceptive. She was so embarrassed that she didn't answer.

"With them, there isn't any question about who's in the driving seat," he continued. "And you'd need to be Ig'tam strong. I'm not sure if you'd be able to dance at that party."

To get away from this she asked the first question that came into her mind. "What's in it for the males?"

"Do you mean in the 'selfish gene' sense?" he asked in return.

"Yes."

"It's in the prelim. It takes a serious amount of nonstop fucking for the female to attain oestrous - can become pregnant. Next, it takes a serious amount of nonstop fucking for her to get pregnant. Then, it takes a serious amount of nonstop fucking to produce the siblings. With all this all-out, one-after-the-other, nonstop fucking with *all* the males, neither she nor any of them can possibly know who the genetic father is. So, to all intense and purpose, Ig'tam kids genuinely have several fathers. Now back to my question. Do you want me to try and arrange something?"

* * *

Mohammed woke to find Sufra sitting patiently on the side of his womb. He didn't need to ask why she was there, so he just smiled weakly up at her. She smiled back apologetically and nodded at something to her left. Turning to the other side of his womb he discovered that the 'something' was Vimla, one of the Dart pilots. Eyes closed, she was sitting on the floor in the lotus position.

"We thought about tossing a coin but neither of us had a coin," Sufra started conversationally. "So, we compromised and booked the fitness room. You up for this?"

Vimla opened her eyes and flashed him a dazzling smile. Sufra, ever so gently, slipped her hand around his shoulders and stroked his ear. Intellectually, he knew that he needed at least another eight hours of sleep. That was intellectually; biologically, it was an entirely different story. Sufra: 6' 3" of broad shouldered, solid muscled, energetic womanhood. Vimla: 4' 11" of petite, slim, athletic, supple femininity. Together? In the fitness room? Funny how something as mundane as a smile can banish fatigue. And someone shouldn't be able to bypass your intellect just by stroking your ear, should they?

"Sure," his mouth (well, yes, that was the organ from which the sound emanated, but it wasn't the organ doing the talking) answered Sufra's original question.

"I wish they wouldn't do that!" Billy suddenly sat erect in his womb next to him.

"Am I missing something Chief?" he asked, looking round at Billy.

Billy's face broke into a grin. "Yes, you are. If fact, you're missing one thing and about to miss something else."

Mohammed just stared back at him; he wasn't going to rise to the bait of obscure utterances.

Billy's grin remained. "You are definitely missing the sheer delight of your mother-in-law, with your wife's permission, interfering with your thoughts. This, of course, leads to you missing the something else."

Nonplussed he continued to look Billy over.

"You've just had communication from Flet saying, 'Mission Start'?" Vimla offered halfheartedly.

"On the button. I'm so sorry," Billy answered in a tone that said that he was anything but sorry. Then he said on the open net, "OK crew, mission start, five minutes. Our sapient allies are getting into formation." Smoothly he switched to the ship-to-ship comms. "Hello *The Beast*, this is *Baddest*. Mission start in five minutes, over."

Sufra whipped her hand from around Mohammed's neck and stomped off to her womb. Vimla was more sanguine. In one graceful movement she unfolded herself and rose to her feet. Flashing him another dazzling smile she zipped up the front of her flying suit. He hadn't noticed that it was undone, nor had he known that Dart pilots wore high-G bras. His hormones were just about to start feeling a tad sorry for themselves when Billy said paternally, "You'll thank me later."

"*Roger* Baddest*, mission start five minutes, you lead.* The Beast *out*," Nice answered.

He was about to dispute this 'nonsense' about him being grateful when Eva came bounding up to them and demanded, "Is this a joke?"

"Flyboys never joke about missions," Billy replied cheerily, then looked past Eva.

Following his eyes, Mohammed turned to see an enfeebled looking Pipsqueak weakly getting into his womb. Despite himself he started to laugh.

"Not funny," Eva grumbled.

"I did say I wanted my No 3 Nav fit for duty, didn't I?" Billy chided.

"I thought we had a few more hours," Eva griped as she vaulted into her womb.

"Yes, so did I," Wendy complained as she arrived fastening her flying suit. She, at least, looked more relaxed.

"Look on the bright side folks. Isn't it reassuring to note that even super-intelligent beings indulge in the buggeration factor?" Billy laughed it off.

"Blasé, Captain. Very blasé. Just because Lanky is in your brain and has switched off your libido," Wendy taunted.

"OK Anne, bring all systems online. Shadow crew, this is your sortie. Wendy, her name is Hontay, and she hasn't."

'Roger Billy. All systems checked and coming online.'

"Then why aren't you in the match-ups? In this situation, it's your duty. Hontay would understand," Eva protested vehemently.

Mohammed, checking his lymph connectors, thought she had a point, but Billy just tittered, "Duty? Maybe. Understand? Definitely not. I know that some of you women are feeling, shall we say, slightly strung-out. But female Ig'tams are extremely jealous. It's inborn, and I'm not joking when I say it's extreme. OK?"

"OK, but she ain't here and we are," Eva stuck to her guns.

"Yeah, right," Wendy agreed.

"She's here in a manner of speaking," Billy started off patiently. "Anything I do she knows or will know."

"Cobblers!" Marandolina, also doing up her flying suit and looking seriously edgy was about to get into her womb. "There aren't enough men to go round as it is. Nice and her crew haven't exactly been considerate. Billy, you *should* be in the match-ups."

Mohammed looked on. Interesting. All the shadow crew and some of the Dart pilots were bisexual, but they didn't seem to want to play with each other. Was this a naval 'no shagging comrades' thing? If so, why? It meant that while the males were enjoying a surfeit of delightful coitus, the females were enduring deprivation akin to a famine. He empathised, sympathised, and agreed with them. And, having clocked up the hours with Billy, Mohammed figured that he'd do a much better job of persuading him to 'do his duty'. He'd just pick his moment.

Smiling in resignation, Billy simply said, "Look, folks, can we get on?"

"What are the RV coordinates?" Eva was suddenly businesslike.

"Already in the NavCom."

Mohammed had to ask. "How's that?"

"From Flet... Let's go."

Eva punched into the comms, "Hello *The Beast*..."

The cockpit was suddenly immersed in total darkness. Mohammed couldn't see or hear; he couldn't move or speak. Had he been able to he would have cried out in terror. Then his panic abated as abruptly and inexplicably as it had arisen. He'd experienced sensory deprivation many times before; it was part of basic space training; the paralysis was new though. He sensed someone, or something, deliberately waving a wand of tranquillity over him.

Pilot

Mentally he stopped struggling and, with that, his awareness grew. He sensed, or was told, that the calmer he was the more he'd understand. It was easy for him to reflect back to the hours spent in the 'derangement tanks'; zero G; no light; no sound. He'd survived that, he'd survive this, whatever *it* was.

He still couldn't see, speak, or move but he *knew* that Grim, John and Pipsqueak were here with him, wherever 'here' was. How did he know that? He just knew. He could hear a faint, variable, high-pitched squeal. He knew that the sound was communicating information. How did he know? He just knew.

Like a fog slowly lifting understanding gradually dawned. He was 'hooked-up' to a Flushi pilot. In humans the majority of data input came through the eyes. Flushi got their data from sounds, smells and telepathy. They had no eyes. No wonder he couldn't see.

Why was he hooked into a Flushi? That was the easiest way for them to communicate with humans. Since this was the shadow crew's sortie, he and the other Flyboys were spare bods, and so the Flushi had taken the opportunity to drop in and 'connect'. Why hadn't the Flushi done this before? They would have scared the poor non-sapients shitless. What now? Just relax.

In the derangement tanks Mohammed's normal ploy had been to allow himself to slip into a dreamlike meditative state. He tried this ploy. It wouldn't happen; the external intrusions kept him conscious and alert. Only when he was completely relaxed would his brain shift from the *or state* to the *and state*. What? All of his senses were functioning normally, however, his non-sapient brain was locked into the Flushi pilot's. He needed to become aware of his own senses *and* the Flushi's.

There were overtones of slight impatience. Why? The Flushi already knew what was happening on the Flushi ship, what he... it wanted to know was what was going on aboard *Baddest*. And that would only happen when Mohammed's brain decided that it would start paying attention to the messages coming from his own nervous system... The darkness suddenly lifted. He was back in the cockpit with Billy leaning across him, peering into his eyes. "Welcome back."

"Jesus!" For some unknown reason Mohammed found his teeth chattering and he was shivering uncontrollably.

'Grim and John's temperatures are now normal. Mohammed's has started to rise but Pipsqueak's is still falling. Shall I increase the temperature in his womb Billy?'

"No, sweetheart, let's see what happens," Billy answered.

"That was freaky." John spluttered.

"Not half," Grim agreed.

"OK Chief, what's going down?" Mohammed's teeth had stopped chattering, but he was still shivering.

"Yeah, I wouldn't mind knowing either," Wendy interjected.

"Just sit tight. Let's stay with Pipsqueak," Billy ordered.

Pipsqueak suddenly jumped to his feet, popping his lymphatic connection with a loud twang, and howled, "What the fuck!" Then he swayed unsteadily and fell out of his womb.

"Get him back into his womb," Billy said despondently.

Ruth and John sprang to Pipsqueak's aid.

'Pipsqueak is suffering the early stages of hypothermia.'

"Right Anne, crank up the temperature."

'Increasing temperature in Pipsqueak's womb Billy.'

"Billy, will you please explain," Wendy asked with measured restraint.

"Sure. But first, I just want to say, 'thanks guys.' You can't begin to know what this means to me." There was a scolding sarcasm in his tone. "What just went down was normal sapient ship-to-ship communication. Instead of sending messages or anything as cumbersome as that, they just get inside each other's heads."

"OK, but why did their body temperatures fall so alarmingly?" Eva demanded.

"Is that what happened? Is that why I'm shivering?" Pipsqueak asked, looking nonplussed.

"Yes. This was a first stab to see if their methods are appropriate to us. Unfortunately, when they connected, you locked in on them; your brains started telling your bodies to function like a Flushi's. One aspect of that was your metabolic rate falling towards the Flushi norm. When it got dangerously low, they simply let go."

"Wait a minute. I was paralysed!" Grim protested.

"Another aspect of this was you telling yourself that you'd lost control of your sympathetic motor functions. You hadn't, but you thought you had. And, if you thought you had, then you had. See what I mean?"

"They could have warned us." John sounded aggrieved.

"If they had you would've been tense and the connection couldn't have been made. Mind you, for a minute there I though Pipsqueak was going to crack it."

"What now? Do they try our methods?" Gabi asked.

"No, they can't speak. And even if they could we wouldn't really understand each other, you saw how painfully slow it was with the hologram. They'll have another try with you four at some point later. Until then I guess I'll just have to carry the load. Once again, thanks guys."

19

REDITS

The formation of about forty ships flashed up on the screen as *Baddest* dropped from super-light. Well, they hadn't exactly travelled super-light, but they had travelled faster than the speed of light. So, technically, they hadn't dropped from super-light, but the physical effect was pretty much the same: momentary dizziness. How? Eva suspected that it had something to do with warping space, worm holes, or some other fanciful idea... Whatever. They'd got to the RV long before light would.

She sat up and gaped at the screens and instruments. Some of the ships were, well, so totally alien. What the instruments were telling her was that some of the ships consisted of little more than a large, cylindrical volume of liquid enclosed in an electrostatic field. She looked for the engines. As far as she could tell there weren't any. A three-kilometre-long cylinder of liquid just hanging in space?!

There were other, smaller, ships. Some were in the classic flying saucer mould, with pulsating lights to boot. This put paid to the claims of those who had 'irrefutably' proven that the saucer shape was inappropriate for even interplanetary flight, never mind interstellar transit; those who had said that they had conclusive 'proof' that the UFO mania recorded in the 20th & 21st C had been caused by the anxieties of living in those chaotic centuries. Then, smaller still, she spotted what she could only describe as 'space debris'. She found it hard to believe that the tangled misshapen lumps of material could be space vessels.

"Right, listen up Flight Crew," Billy spoke slowly and deliberately. "The water waggons are Flushi; crew about 1,500; atmosphere, saline, with a high chlorine content. The saucers belong to folks calling themselves The Tant. Crew about seventy; oxygen breathers like us, but amphibians. The third group are The Keizon. As you can see, The Keizon are heavily into individuality, they fly solo. The square edged ships belong to females, the smoothed edged ones to males, and anything with sharp angles is piloted by hermaphrodites."

"Is it OK to scan them or will they take that as hostile?" Nice asked from *The Beast*.

"It's OK to scan, but it won't tell you much. Their fields are nearly impenetrable to our sensors." Billy's answer was laboured.

Eva realised that Billy was reacting in slow-motion because he was hooked-up to a Flushi.

"What happens now?"

"We wait."

'Mohammed and Grim's body temperatures are falling rapidly.'

She leant forward to look down at Mohammed. Eyes staring into nothingness, he seemed to be in a trance.

"How about John and Pipsqueak Anne?"

'Also falling Billy, but not as fast.'

"*While we're waiting to see if your Flyboys can link up, tell us more about these Keizons.*" That was Ventrice, *The Beast's* N° 2 Nav.

"I've told you everything I know. The only way we'll glean more is if we link up with them. That will have to wait until we've got the hang of it with the Flushi."

"*Are you saying that we'll all have to try this linking thing?*" Nice sounded deeply concerned.

"Not only will both flight crews have to *try*, we all have to *succeed* if the mission is going to be a possibility." He answered listlessly.

'Mohammed and Grim are back. Their temperatures are returning to normal.'

"Thanks sweetheart. What about the other two?"

'Pipsqueak's temperature has stabilised at nearly normal, but John's is still falling slowly.'

"OK darling."

A peculiar thought crossed Eva's mind. "Nice, what do you call your C1?"

"*Foot.*"

"Pardon?"

"*Foot.*"

"Foot? What kind of name is that?"

"*If Truckies weren't metric you'd soon see the relevance.*" Riet, *The Beast's* N° 1 Nav, joined in.

"What?"

"Thirty point four eight centimetres," Billy enlightened her.

"*Now that's what you call a Beast!*" Nice laughed.

She considered that for a while. "No, I don't think so," she answered deadpan. "Not without ample girth."

Good natured cackling came over the comms from *The Beast*. Billy simply slowly turned around to give her a 'look'. The same look as the one he had given when he'd *offered* to 'arrange something' with an Ig'tam male.

'John is back Billy, his temperature is returning to normal. Pipsqueak is still under and his temperature is stable and normal.'

"Good." Although his voice sounded sluggish, Billy seemed satisfied. "Pipsqueak, are you with us?"

"Yes, I am, but this is definitely weird." Pipsqueak's voice sounded far off, almost dreamlike.

"It is, isn't it? I suppose it's a bit like synaesthesia," Billy commented

"I'm having real difficulty keeping up with you, and I don't know what synaesthesia is."

"It's a genetic condition in which people's senses get mixed-up, hearing words as colours; tactile taste; musical smells; things like that."

Eva wondered if Billy was making it up. She'd never heard of synaesthesia either, or anything like it.

"Oh, right, that *is* a pretty good analogy." Pipsqueak eventually answered.

"Do you understand how they navigate?" Billy probed.

"Yeah, sure, I understand, in principle." Pipsqueak was long in answering. "But, practically, I can't get my brain round navigating without visual references."

"Fair enough, but can you find point X if a Flushi marks it?"

"No, I don't think so. Well, not very accurately at any rate."

"I was afraid you were going to say that. Think it'll get better with practice?"

"Sorry Chief, I can't get hold of three dimensions without eyes."

"Right. Think you can function on *Baddest* if still connected?"

"That, I'm sure I can do - with practise."

"OK then, stay hooked-up." Billy didn't sound too disappointed, all things considered. "Hontay hinted at something like this. Our disjointed intellects seem perfectly capable of comprehending something alien, yet be totally incapable of manipulating it," he mused.

"How about you?" Pipsqueak inquired.

"I can handle it, but I think it's to do with the belt."

The conversation between Billy and Pipsqueak reminded Eva of an antique, pre digital, musical disc played at the wrong speed.

"*What does all this mean Billy?*" Nice piped-up, all businesslike.

"It means that we're near to mission abort."

"*Near to?*"

"The Flushi can tap into what we're doing if we stay linked. Then they can feed their intentions through me. It's a bit cumbersome, but it might be worth a try."

"Why do I get the feeling that you're not exactly overjoyed about that?" Eva found herself asking.

"It's a bit knackering." Billy turned and beamed up at her, still with that 'look'.

"*Billy, when you say 'cumbersome' do you mean cumbersome, when it comes to battle drills?*" Nice was still on the job.

"Exactly, it might not work. They're waiting for some second stage sapients to sort out the probability."

"*Come again?*"

"Let's just say that some second stagers are running computations on that scenario."

"*Let's not, 'just say'. What exactly are they doing?*"

"If he gives you an answer, don't ask more question about it, all right? This, you're not going to believe," Pipsqueak interrupted.

"Thank you, Pipsqueak. Right, Nice, here goes. When we run computations, we model data and see how it stacks up, right? What the second stagers are doing, have done, is tap into another timeline, another universe or something like that, where this battle group is actually exercising and seeing how it performs."

"*What?! Do you mean...?*"

"I told you, you weren't going to believe it, didn't I?" Pipsqueak laughed.

"Never mind that! *The Beast*, abort mission. Repeat, abort mission. Confirm," Billy suddenly snapped.

"The Beast *confirms, mission aborted. What now Flight Leader?*"

"The battle group is going off to the ball. We have to stay home and wait for the fairy godmother. Pipsqueak, let go."

Billy sounded so bitter; Eva knew that there was more to this than he was telling. With the minimum of fuss, the alien ships simply vanished from her screen. She felt profound empathy with him, but she couldn't let it go at that. "Billy, I don't understand. Does this mean that we won't...?"

"It means that until somebody decides what to do with us, we sit tight." Back to his normal speech, Billy still sounded gloomy.

"*So, what you're saying is that we've failed the muster?*" Shirley, *The Beast's* No 3 Nav, asked.

"Look, we haven't failed. Flushi don't talk, they can't see, so if we can't tune into them, mentally, we can't fight alongside them..."

"What about the Keizon or Tant? We could have a stab at it with them," Erick suggested.

"If we couldn't get it together with the Flushi, we certainly couldn't with either of them," Billy dismissed Erick's idea tiredly. "Just stand down and wait... Shit!" He leapt out of his womb and spun around to look at something behind her.

Turning, Eva saw Hontay standing immediately behind, and staring down at, her. Hontay's skin was now a rich mauve colour. In the brief instant that she met those 'don't fuck with me' eyes, an awful lot of malevolent information flowed from Hontay: in their previous encounters, the Ig'tams had telegraphed their materialisation; that was polite; this was the Ig'tam equivalent of a sneak attack; an Ig'tam female would understand its significance; the belt was still around Hontay's waist, so take this as a first, last, and only warning. Eva knew that she had malevolent thoughts of her own which Hontay had, no doubt, also received loud and clear.

"Hi Hontay." Billy sounded agitated. "Do you have our new orders?"

"*Baddest* and *The Beast* are to stand down and hold position here. We are formulating a new scenario in which your ships will operate autonomously. This will take two to three hours."

Eva noticed that when Hontay looked at Billy her skin darkened appreciably. She had a very shrewd idea why and it annoyed her intensely. "Who exactly is the 'we' who are formulating this?"

"Eva, trust me, lighten up," Billy cautioned.

"Earth Supreme Command, Flet, and myself."

Along with the answer Eva sensed that Hontay might strike. Reflexively, she sought a way to defend herself...

"No, let's walk," Billy said hastily to Hontay, and stepped out of his womb.

"Going somewhere Chief?" Mohammed enquired.

"Well, with two or three hours to kill, Hontay and I are adjourning to the fitness room."

Although Billy's answer had sounded lighthearted, his eyes were locked on hers with a forewarning glare. Electing to ignore it, she stood, turned, and squared up to 'Lanky'. "How are you going to formulate anything if you are otherwise engaged?"

Billy stepped smartly between them. "Let's go Hontay."

"Only part of my mind will be *otherwise engaged*."

Eva sensed, not superiority, not hostility, but biting sarcasm. The Ig'tam turned and started striding towards the fitness room.

"Irony is a uniquely Human..."

"Shut the fuck up Eva! You don't know what you're tangling with." Billy took a short breath and then in a more conversational tone said, "Now, sit down... please. She's decided to play this like a woman."

Ignoring all this Hontay continued to saunter away. As she walked past the non-flight crew, Sabine, one of the Dart pilots, shot out of her womb and scampered out of her path. Hontay stopped and turned to her.

"My reactions are an instinctive response to your unconscious desire for my mate. I understand that your desire is also instinctive. I will not harm you."

Sabine didn't look convinced. Surreptitiously, Billy waved for her to return to her womb. Hontay's head snapped round catching him in mid-motion.

"She's telepathic. *Must* remember that," he muttered to himself. Then, at a normal volume, said, "Sabine, return to your womb."

Hontay was standing between Sabine and her womb. Sabine took a very circuitous path in carrying out the order. Watching her, Hontay waited until Sabine was again seated

Pilot

before continuing her journey. Stopping at the door to the fitness room she waited for Billy. Sighing, he followed and they both entered, the door closing silently behind them.

"Eva, Sabine, I sensed that there was some secondary communication but couldn't... tune in. It was obviously about Billy, could either of you enlighten us?" Cynthia was head-down, working furiously at her console.

"Yes, clearly you felt that you faced some sort of threat," Kazuhiko jumped in, also in xenobiologist mode. "But as a bystander it wasn't obvious to me what the threat was."

"In a minute." Eva sat back in her womb. "Anne, show interior fitness room, my monitor, now."

'I am sorry Eva, Billy has just instructed me not to do that.'

"Anne, has he instructed you not to describe what's going on in there?" She wasn't going to give in that easily.

'No Eva, he has not.'

"OK Anne, describe the situation in the fitness room, real time."

'No Eva, I will not.' A recording of Billy's voice suddenly started, *"But if anyone thinks I'm going to share that information, they're going to be sadly disappointed."* 'This was Billy's response to Flight Lieutenant Schrove's question about his sexual relationship with Hontay. From that, I infer that he wants privacy.'

Fucking machine! "Anne, have you monitored conversations between Billy and me, where he has *shared* information about his sexual relationship with Hontay?"

'Yes Eva, I have.'

"What do you infer from that?!"

'That I should carry out your instruction. This is a monocast, your ears only...'

Yes!

'...Billy and Hontay are entwined, drifting in zero G. I am unable to scan Hontay. Billy is conscious, but his brain wave patterns are abnormal. He is releasing endorphins in response to the intense pain around his midriff. His...'

"Why did you stop Anne?"

'John is about to manually intercept the monocast and relay it to the remainder of the flight crew.'

"Butt out John!"

"Give us a break, you can't keep this to yourself," he protested quite innocently.

"Eva, this is infantile." Alfred interrupted. "Surely, our desire for a better understanding of the Ig'tams is of some import?"

She came back to reality with a bump; she was 2ic and needed to act accordingly. "Yes Alfred, you're absolutely right. What is it you want to know?"

"What was the threat that you perceived from Hontay, and do you have any idea what precipitated it?"

"She's bloody jealous, and wants to kill us," Sabine said bitterly.

"Don't you think you're being somewhat melodramatic?" Kazuhiko asked condescendingly.

"No." Sabine replied flatly.

"I can see some slight basis for malice in your case Sabine. You were Billy's partner in the original match-ups, weren't you?" Cynthia stated thoughtfully. "Even so, if that was the sole impetus, it does seem somewhat severe. And this doesn't explain her explicit belligerence towards Eva."

Stupid civilians! It was blatantly obvious. "That's because she knows that I'm attracted to Billy."

Wide eyed, both Mohammed and Wendy slowly turned to look at her. Maybe it wasn't that obvious after all? She could fell herself blushing. Grim and Pipsqueak's hysterical laughter only added to her embarrassment.

"I see. Was this... caveat conveyed as a specific thought or was it more a general 'feeling'?" Cynthia continued to probe unemotionally.

"I just felt that I was going to die." Sabine still sounded terrified.

Eva had felt nothing of the sort. "That's not what happened to me. I knew that her sudden appearance was a warning, but because she was still wearing the belt, I also knew that she wouldn't take any action."

"Really?" Sabine exclaimed. "I *knew* she wanted me dead."

"Eva, have you had sex with Billy?" Sam asked, then added, "I ask only to flesh out a theory."

She'd done a round or two with Sam. His lovemaking was fairly energetic and coarse, just the way she liked heterosexual sex, not bad for a middle-aged man. Was he trying to convey a message? "No."

"I'd like to throw something out for general discussion," Sam offered. "Sabine and Eva sensed different levels of threat from Hontay. Sabine's was clearly the more ominous. Now, she's had sex with Billy, while Eva has only the *intent*."

"Much as I hate to agree with you, I see some merit in this. But let's not forget that the rest of us sensed none of this," Alfred chortled.

"Does that tally with Hontay's explanation to Sabine? Anne, can you replay her exact words?"

'Yes Cynthia.' *"My reactions are an instinctive response to your unconscious desire for my mate. I understand that your desire is also instinctive. I will not harm you."*

"Hmm, the key word here is 'desire', isn't it?" Cynthia mused. "Sabine, do you still 'desire' Billy?"

"I suppose so," Sabine answered rather defensively.

"So, what we have here is: one past event, but two future intents. I'm not sure what that does to your hypothesis Sam," Kazuhiko said thoughtfully.

"Excuse me for crashing your xenobiologists' party, but what about Billy in all this?" Erick asked.

"What do you mean?" Cynthia seemed piqued that someone from the military dared to comment.

"Hontay is telepathic. So, couldn't the difference be because she knows how Billy feels about each of them. No offence Eva, but you know an emotional attachment to your 2ic is the surest way to bugger up a mission."

"Interesting," Sam said graciously. "But why would an emotional attachment 'bugger up' a mission?"

Eva reflected that Erick had been the right choice for 3ic. "There has to be some tension between a commander and his, or her, 2ic."

"Why?" Kazuhiko demanded.

She had to remind herself that civilians were just that, *civilians*. "Power corrupts, absolute power corrupts absolutely. The Captain of a ship has absolute power. One of the primary functions of the 2ic is to act as a counterbalance to the commander."

"Right, so it could be Billy's desires that Hontay is reacting to. In that case, why isn't her aggression directed at him?" Alfred commented, then went on to answer his own question, "Because he's her mate."

"I don't think that Billy thinks I'm special," Sabine interjected.

"He's the Captain, so even if he did, he wouldn't show..." Eva started explaining.

Pilot

"Humans, if you want to know something, ask." Hontay suddenly appeared, mid-cockpit. "Not only do I know Billy's thoughts and emotions, I have his memories. He has memories of copulating with you, Sabine. Ig'tam males are called Gemarchs. A Gemarch could only have such memories if another Redit, an Ig'tam female, had annexed his mind. That Redit would be my mortal enemy and, likewise, any Redit revealing such aspirations." She paused to look quickly at each female in turn. Eva sensed that she didn't need to do that but was mimicking human symbology. "On an innate level, I respond to Billy as if he were a Gemarch. And, because of this, I respond to you women as if you are Redits."

There was a stunned silence as Hontay disappeared as unexpectedly as she'd appeared.

"Do you think she was still in there with him as well?" Grim eventually asked.

"Yes," Hontay's disembodied voice reverberated around the cockpit.

Everyone started looking around at everyone else.

"You notice that she didn't say anything about responding to men as if they were Gemarchs, just Billy?" Kazuhiko whispered to Cynthia.

Cynthia didn't answer; an indication that she agreed with the unspoken consensus, to terminate the discussion.

20

CELICE

With a couple of hours to kill there should have been plenty of screens up; after all, most of the women were chomping at the bit. However, Hontay's presence seemed to be cramping everyone's style. And it wasn't only libidos that were being subdued. Then Nice called, confirming that Hontay was also, simultaneously, on *The Beast*. There were a few cursory questions from Cynthia confirming that Hontay was having separate conversations with the respective crews. Even so, it was pretty obvious that Cynthia's heart wasn't in exploring this phenomenon.

With her own probing, Nice discovered that *Baddest's* Hontay and Billy had adjourned to the fitness room. At that point Krishna eagerly joined the proceedings, but there was little sport for them here. No one on *Baddest*, least of all Eva, responded to their goading. Deprived of that bit of sport Nice broke comms. A few minutes later she was back, ordering David, Guido, Alfred, Kazuhiko, and Sam over to *The Beast*. No one was inclined to argue with her about this either, so the rest of the crew were left to twiddling their thumbs for over two hours in near silence.

***

Hontay emerged from the fitness room carrying Billy under her arm like a satchel. Mohammed knew, without being told, that this was something to laugh about later when Hontay wasn't around, so he bit his lip. With all eyes tracking her, she effortlessly carried Billy to his womb and gently placed him in it. While she stood looking down at Billy, Mohammed would have sworn that her skin was pulsating. Billy was awake but not only did he look exhausted, he also appeared to be in agony. Yet he had a silly, twisted smile on his face. He pressed himself back against the lymph connectors, let out a deep contented sigh, and closed his eyes.

'Boosting beta blockers Billy. Substantial bruising to your abdomen and gluteus medius muscles. You're also suffering from dehydration.'

"Hit me with a glucose solution please Babes," he spoke weakly, eyes still shut.

'OK Billy.'

Mohammed stared up at Hontay. He didn't really have much choice, her 'presence' eclipsed everything else on the flight deck. This closer scrutiny revealed that her skin was definitely fluctuating between different shades of dark maroon. Watching with fascination, Mohammed decided that she wasn't really ugly, in the true sense of the word, but *definitely* alien. Try as hard as he might, he couldn't visualise himself being intimate with her. Billy must have some balls and in more sense that one.

Hontay was gazing down at Billy as if the rest of the universe didn't exist, suddenly her unblinking eyes focussed on his for an instant. Although her gaze was a bit frightening... no, a lot frightening, he got an impression of amusement; he ought not to worry about having to be intimate, it was the Redits who made all the moves. After a while Billy opened his eyes and started vaguely waving his hand around, as if he was in conversation with someone. Hontay turned to face the remainder of the crew.

"Orders group, most secret.

Situation: scouting formations of Aggressors have entered the Milky Way galaxy in the region of the Sun. They are scanning for super-light sources and are presumed to be seeking Earth. Additionally, by using matter/anti-matter annihilation, the military forces on the garrison planet Celice have dissipated the field enclosing the planet. They are now aware of the planet's true position and of our extraction. The garrison commander is refusing to respond to orders, conveyed by fourth stage sapients. She has commandeered all space-borne vessels and intends to launch an armada to seek out Earth.

Friendly Forces: Defence Alliance forces, with their individual orders, have dispersed to prearranged 'potentials', consider them to be in hidden locations.

Enemy Forces: the Aggressors have been confirmed to be fifth stage sapients, we have no further information on them. Also to be considered hostile, the Celice garrison.

Mission: *Baddest* is to fly to Celice and neutralise all space bourne traffic, appraise the local commander of the Aggressor situation, order her to 'sit tight', impose electronic silence, and then RV with *The Beast*. It is imperative that the armada is prevented from entering the super-light. *The Beast* is to take up position at coordinates which have been programmed into your ships' flight computers and is to patrol within a thirty-five-light-year sphere around that position. Attack and destroy any sign of intelligence entering the patrol area. You are to remain incommunicado until ordered to break cover. After RVing, the only permissible communication is between your two ships. You are to have no communication with Earth, or other defence alliance forces.

Questions?"

"How did the guys on Celice 'dissipate' your field when we couldn't penetrate it?" Gabi asked.

"The matter/anti-matter warheads were detonated inside the field. We dissipated the field to prevent the planet being destroyed."

"Let me see if I've got this right," Pipsqueak started incredulously, "The garrison sussed - they *knew* - that they were enclosed *inside* a force field, and they still fired warheads at it?"

"Yes."

"Navy?"

"The garrison commander is Major General Guillebaud, Army."

"Shithead," Marandolina muttered.

"What do you mean by friendly forces being dispersed to 'prearranged potentials'?"

That was Nice's voice, but he hadn't heard her over the radio, it was inside his head.

"Your theories about the multiverse are flawed. However, to aid understanding, you can consider them to be in parallel universes."

"How are you able to tell the Aggressors are fifth stage, yet know nothing else about them?" Eva snapped.

"If they were fourth-stage or below, we would have been able to anticipate the 'potential' of the point and time of their entry into our galaxy. This has not been the case." Hontay's face changed to show a frightening snarl, revealing three sets of fangs and no incisors. Mohammed sensed that this was her attempt at a grin. "You, Eva, will be pleased to hear that I am as ignorant about them as you are."

"Then how will we identify them if we don't know anything about them?" Cynthia asked, full of concern.

Stupid civilian. They were being ordered into a classic cellular defence. Each cell with its own orders, ignorant of the other cells' locations or orders - tailor-made for insurrection. They would own a thirty-five-light-year bit of space. They see anything in it, they kill it. If they get captured, what could they say? 'Earth is around Ool.' Where's that? 'Err... Dunno' The coordinates of the Flushi world, Evier, had already been removed from the NavCom; not deleted so that somebody could restore and then retrieve them, but removed as if they had never been there. He knew this for a fact, he'd checked. He was pretty sure that the same would be done to the coordinates of Celice and then the RV. So, they wouldn't even know where they were.

"No friendly forces will enter your area of operation. So, any forces seen will be enemy." Hontay turned back to Billy, looked at him briefly, then vanished. Again, there was a pop as air filled the vacant space.

"Right, Nice, you're solo. As soon as you drop, a standard sweep. Once the sector is secure, settle down to a waiting rota. We'll catch up with you soon."

"*Roger,*" Nice confirmed.

"OK, full alert. Darts, when we drop, auto launch. Kill anything making a move to trans-light. If there isn't any space activity, we'll stand off for a long-range recce. Then we'll try to talk some sense into the garrison."

"And if they won't listen?" Sun voiced what they must all have been thinking.

"Smacked botties all round. Neutralise!"

"Billy, do you realise that we're talking about taking out friendlies?" David asked tentatively.

"Not friendlies, renegades."

"Why don't the sapients do something about it?" Cynthia was dismayed. "Surely they could neutralise Celice without harming the garrison."

"My read of the situation is that they're a tad busy. No more discussion."

"But..." Kazuhiko started to speak.

"Shut it Kazuhiko!" Eva cut him off.

"OK, you take it shadow crew," Billy ordered.

Everybody donned helmets and gloves. As they waited for the men to return from *The Beast* and for the Dart pilots and the infantry to get to their positions, Billy turned to Eva and asked, "Would you swat a fly without a second's thought?"

"Pardon?"

"Would you lose any sleep about killing a fly?"

"You're being too cryptic for me, Captain." Eva looked nonplussed.

"Come on, would you?" Billy persisted.

"Of course not."

"Well, that's how Redits feel about other Redits who interfere with their Gemarchs. I'm telling you this because I've just realised something: there's some kind of feedback loop between you two. Hontay's presence causes you to react like a Redit and..."

"That's stupid!"

"Is it? Then why are you so hostile?"

Eva remained sulkily silent. Mohammed thought he ought to diplomatically steer the discussion away from this topic. "Thirty-five light-years, not much of a sector to defend."

"Yeah, but I think the fourth and third stagers are carrying out sweeps. No one has told me this, but I figure that if we see any action it means that things have gone badly wrong," Billy mused.

"*Darts ready,*" Sun announced.

Pilot

"*Infantry in position,*" Erick confirmed.

'Sam, this is a full alert, put on your helmet... Crew in combat positions at full alert. Weapons armed Billy.'

"OK, let's go. *The Beast,* good hunting."

"*Roger* Baddest, *you too*"

They followed *The Beast* as it accelerated, then the two ships jumped simultaneously. While his head was clearing Mohammed noted that the star density was much lower. Wherever 'here' was, it wasn't near the centre of the galaxy. They dumped the Darts and went into an arrowhead formation with *Baddest* leading and three Darts fanned out on either side. They flew a standard search pattern around the sixteen-planet system. As far as they could tell there wasn't any space activity, but they did identify Celice as the sixth planet. Eva and Wendy brought *Baddest* to a stop just outside the system's Oort cloud and the Darts held position.

Hunched over his screen, Billy mused, "It's a newly formed system: look at the number of comets and the amount of meteor activity. I can see why the sapients would want to dump Celice here."

"Even with our tri-lattice field; even if we went in above the plane, I still wouldn't want to take *Baddest* in there." Eva was equally pensive.

"Me neither," Billy agreed. "We can't use super-light channels so, if we stay here, it'll take hours to establish comms. Sun, how about sending in a couple of Darts, think they can handle all that debris?"

"*Sure. What do you want us to say?*"

"Just tell them to behave, sit tight, and stay out of the super-light. Comms will lag increasingly, so use your initiative and don't take any chances."

"*Roger* Baddest. *OK, Kaye and Gill, you heard the man, break and go.*"

"*Roger Dart's Leader, breaking now.*"

On his screen Mohammed watched as two of the Darts peeled off and headed into the system. Their trajectories appeared haphazard, uncoordinated, and erratic as they dodge about, avoiding the glut of interplanetary rubble - hairy scary. There was little chance of either ship flying into anything big, but that wasn't the problem. Running into lots of little masses would total their screens, and these were the masses most difficult to detect.

"At this rate they'll take about twenty-nine hours to get there." Billy still focussed on his screen, sat back decisively. "While we wait. Eva, Wendy: keep your eyes peeled for any super-light activity. Mohammed, compile and send, tight-stream, a precis of the situation from the General Recall until now, and what we want the garrison to do. Nav team: work out a flight profile that can put us into orbit with the least number of impacts. Erick: get together with David and come up with a strategy for a ground assault taking out their command and control, C1 will have the topography and military dispersal of Celice."

"Sure Boss," Grim answered, then added grumpily, "But do you have any idea of the number crunching involved?"

"You don't sound optimistic Billy," Erick said simultaneously.

"Contingency Erick. If they won't play, there isn't much a couple of Darts can do about it." Then, laughing Billy continued, "Grim, I've just remembered how you got the name, Grim. Would it help if I said, 'please, with sugar on it'?"

"Was that, 'pretty please, with sugar on it'?" Grim laughed.

"Yeah... Sun, might as well come in."

"*Roger* Baddest. *Coming in.*"

"Captain," Alfred, all indignant and hot under the collar, piped-up. "I don't think we've fully explored the moral and ethical implications of taking punitive action against Celice."

Pulling an amused smile, Billy wearily answered, "Alfred, as with any organisation the military has unwritten rules, conventions, guidelines and regulations. To an outsider the various points of demarcation may not be obvious. In other words, there are some situations when there's a *we,* and there are other situations when there's no 'we', just *me.* Currently, *we* are in a *me* situation. You get me?"

"But Cap..."

"Shut up Alfred!" Firmly, the 2ic put an end to the discussion.

Switching to the command net, Billy said sympathetically, "Erick, find something to occupy the civies."

Smiling to himself Mohammed started compiling his report...

"The garrison must have put something up. They're scanning, they'll pick up the Darts," Wendy suddenly said in alarm.

"Great!" Billy started plotting on his screen. "They're too far in... Kaye, Gill, hold position, find something big to hide behind. Navs, I need a profile now. Get us close enough for a maximum lag of five minutes. Forget about limiting impacts."

"Five minutes each way?" Gabi checked.

"Yes."

"If they spot the Darts, they might launch a torpedo into the super-light. Let's hope that whatever they've put up isn't armed," Eva said as she and Wendy took the flight controls.

"Unlikely. It's a garrison, remember. Let's instead hope that they haven't seen the Darts and that Major General 'Stupid Person' Guillebaud knows better than to launch anything into the super-light with this much interplanetary rubble around. Navs, profile now!"

"On screen" Grim confirmed, then said, "I take it that you want to draw fire away from the Darts?"

"Correct. Anne, full shields. Eva, Wendy, in one jump."

'Shields at maximum, Billy.'

"Let's go!"

They dropped from their super-light/not super-light hop right into the middle of an asteroid cluster. Immediately the ship began to shake from the impacts.

"Anne, shields?"

'Holding Billy.'

"OK, Eva, try to drift with the cluster, that should reduce the impacts. Mohammed, zap anything big coming our way, OK?"

Before Mohammed could acknowledge, Marandolina said, "We're being scanned... they've locked on."

"Military Command Celice, this is the Air Force fighter *Baddest.* Acknowledge, over." Turning to the Navs Billy asked, "How long?"

"'Bout four and a half minutes each way," Grim answered, then added, "But they don't know they aren't supposed to use the super-light. *If* they follow Standard Operating Procedures, they should try to establish super-light comms with us first..."

Baddest was rocked by detonations.

'Hits by four matter/anti-matter warheads. Shields holding.'

"Shoot first, ask questions later. Hardly SOP. Interesting," Billy chuckled. "Navs, identify the ship firing at us."

"It's 'ships'. Looks like seven or eight torpedo boats, a handful of point defence ships, and a score of transports. The torpedos came out of the super-light," Ruth verified.

"OK, target the torpedo boats; plasma warheads; enough to rough them up without taking them out and..."

"Billy," John interrupted, "Celice has a substantial asteroid belt. If we loose off *anything* with serious clout the gravitational disturbance is likely to cause massive meteor showers over the next four to five days."

"You mean that we've got to sit and take this shit for nine minutes?"

"Unless we want to extinguish life on the planet, I'm afraid so."

"Billy," Pipsqueak interjected thoughtfully, "The asteroid belt might explain why the garrison is so hell bent on leaving. Once the sapients removed the shield the boys must have realised that they were likely to get clobbered by meteors."

"That's not my read Pipsqueak," Gabi countered. "The sapients didn't just dump the planet. That asteroid belt looks stable. They must have been fairly tidy in their handy work."

"I get your drift," Pipsqueak conceded.

Again, the ship was rocked by explosions. 'Two more torpedo hits. This time, fusion warheads. Shields still holding.'

"Navs, have they lobbed anything at the Darts?" Eva asked.

"Not as far as we can tell," Marandolina answered.

"Billy, we've had a look at taking out their command and control, but we've hit a problem. Even if we have *Baddest* and Darts giving fire suppression, it's a long burn till downside. We'll be sitting ducks." That was Erick over the military net.

"What if you're taken in by *Katrina*?" Billy suggested.

"The shuttle?" David sounded puzzled.

"Not just any ole shuttle. An Air Force shuttle. It can take you in," Billy explained.

"In that case, no problem." Erick sounded more enthusiastic then added, "Assault plan on your screen."

Again, Billy, with Eva looking over his shoulder, focussed on his screen. "Drop point, fifty-seven miles from target. Why debus so far from the objective?" he asked eventually.

"It's not far in a PADE suit. Plus, the info from C1 doesn't have their defensive dispersal. This way we have a chance to check the lie of the land without committing ourselves."

"There are only six of you, why are you planning to split into two teams?" Eva asked.

"This is a surprise 'hit and run' profile. We'll backup the Marines, as they take out the C-n-C and cover them coming out. By going in at 04:35 local time it should all be over before the garrison realises we're there," David said.

"OK, are you ready to roll with this?" Billy asked.

"All we need to do is give our orders group," Erick confirmed

"Fine, it might be an idea to get down to *Katrina* and give you orders group there."

"OK."

"Anne, transport ground assault equipment to the shuttle bay."

'OK Billy.'

"Ten simultaneous torpedo detonations, two o'clock, sixteen kilometres, level in the plane of this asteroid belt," Ruth reported.

"Yeah," John confirmed. "I think the garrison is playing billiards. Three... No, Six... Seven, mile-plus diameter asteroids and scores of their baby brothers heading this way. First impact in about forty-three seconds."

"Multiple lock-on. Taking them out," Mohammed said, then got busy tracking and destroying the larger asteroids whose trajectories were likely to intersect *Baddest's*. Yes, it would have been more efficient to tell Anne to deal with them but, hey, cutting loose with the laser was fun.

"Billiards?" Eva asked.

"An ancient and sophisticated game requiring great skill. You bumpkins wouldn't have seen it out in the provinces," Pipsqueak answered.

Back on the command net, Billy added, "Eva, Wendy: me and my man Mohammed will take *Katrina* in, so you're on the case. I want you to put us into orbit in one hop, then we'll auto-launch *Katrina*. Cover us with chaff, then use *Baddest* to draw those ships and any fire from downside. Don't stray too far from Celice. Hopefully, with all the excitement you'll cause and the planet's asteroid belt, the garrison won't detect *Katrina's* stealth screen. Sun: take launch positions. You're top cover for the downside operation if anything goes pear shaped. Any questions?"

"Billy, if you were the garrison commander would you think that *Baddest* was a human ship?" Sun asked.

"No, I don't suppose I would. I would chuck everything, including the kitchen sink, at it. I'm counting on a reaction like that, otherwise *Katrina* won't be able to penetrate their point defence."

"That's not what I meant Billy. If you were the boss of a garrison planet; and there had been a General Recall; and you were locked inside in impenetrable field; and then you found that the whole planet had been moved; and *Baddest* suddenly appeared; and your heavy-duty torpedos didn't even make a dent, you'd assume that the ship was alien and hostile, wouldn't you?"

"Hmm, Sun, you're saying that a little more carrot might be called for before the stick?"

"In fairness to the garrison, yes."

"OK, good point," Billy concurred. "Mohammed, when you've finished playing Captain Shoot'em'up, back to tight-streaming that precis. We'll sit tight and give the garrison ample opportunity to verify who we are and that we ain't hostile. If they still won't play then it's the stick."

***

"You'll bring us in at six' fifty knots and two hundred feet. The soldiers will drop here, and we'll drop here." Fully suited, Erick was leaning over Billy's shoulder rechecking the drop points with Billy and Mohammed.

Focussed on the plot screen, Mohammed said, "Any fire or lock-on and we'll cry-off primary drop site and take you in here, then you'll all drop together"

"Check."

"Make sure everybody stays strapped-in until we've given the 'green'. If anything kicks off, we'll be executing extreme evasive manoeuvres. Those boys are bound to have plasma batteries. Unstrapped, you'll bounce around like an electron in an ion field," Billy cautioned.

This was Erick's main concern. Drops were something that both the Army and Marines practised and practised. It was something he'd done hundreds of times. However, *Katrina* wasn't fitted with ejection ports, so they had to unstrap; get out of their seats; get to the rear hatch and step out backwards. Not something he was looking forward to doing at six' fifty knots and two hundred feet. Then, they'd have less than a second to kick-in their anti-gravity. Any cockup and you'd be just a long dark smudge on the ground.

Battening down the visor on his helmet - which sealed him in the self-repairing, life-sustaining world of his PADE suit - that would protect him on a planet even as inhospitable as Venus, Erick went back to his seat and strapped himself in and double checked the connections. He'd hoped that this operation wouldn't be necessary, but Major General Guillebaud appeared to be a pretty inflexible, unimaginative and suspicious woman. After

Pilot

they had established comms, Billy had provided everything that the General had asked for in verification. It even turned out that Marandolina had been at the Naval Academy with a pilot on one of the ships in orbit around Celice and could still remember his birthday. But the General wasn't having any of it. Billy and Eva offered to meet her face to face. Still, the Guillebaud wouldn't play.

Then Grim figured out that the General was stalling. With ships already in orbit, she was all set to go looking for Earth. But Celice had been placed in an uncharted part of the galaxy, so the General was probably using her navigators to get a fix on 'here' by plotting the relative positions of recognised galaxies - not a very accurate fix but accurate enough. So, now, Erick and his team were going in to take out their Command and Control before the garrison calculated their approximate position...

"*Eva, we're sitting tight and ready to roll,*" Billy transmitted.

"*Roger*, Katrina. *Jump and auto-launch in fifteen seconds,*" came Eva's crisp response.

"*OK boys and girls, sit tight. Here we go,*" Billy informed them.

Erick knew that after dropping them, Billy and Mohamed would stay low and fly *Katrina* west, out over the sea. There they would hold station until the retrieval, or, if the mission was blown, come to find them with Sun's Darts providing top cover... Fifteen seconds can seem like an incredibly long time... Just as his vision was beginning to clear after the super-light hop, he felt a thump in the back as *Katrina* auto launched. Then they were tumbling in free-fall. Erick assumed that, with the stealth screen up, Billy and Mohammed were allowing the shuttle to drop like an unguided object. The nauseating, chaotic, toppling descent continued for over a minute...

"*Thirty thousand feet. So far so good...*" Mohammed started.

"*Don't say things like that, you jinks!*" Billy rebuked.

"*OK, I Won't... Twenty-five thousand feet, all is well. No lock-on, tracking or things such to our peril... Twenty thousand feet, still atumble. Check shields, check drives, check map, we're looking indomitable... Fifteen thousand feet, still on track. Changing to glided flight, and yet no flack... Ten thousand feet, drives enabled. Banking left, weapon platform stable... Five thousand feet, steady at six' fifty knots. Soldiers, Marines, standby for your drop... Two hundred feet, our path is clear. Approaching first target, from the rear... 'Tis time to get, moody and mean. Team one, standby for your green.*"

Erick gave the thumbs up to David and his team as they unstrapped and unsteadily made their way to the rear hatch. Flying at two hundred feet *Katrina* was being buffeted by ground effect turbulence. Only an Air Force jockey could be this blase, Erick could almost picture Mohammed as the Offices Mess lounge lizard wearing a smoking jacket and cravat...

The hatch opened and a swirling hurricane erupted in the cockpit. "*Green. Go!*"

One, two, three - the soldiers were gone. With the hatch closing *Katrina* banked hard to the right.

"*Fifty seconds to drop two. Next team, stand by for your cue.*"

Taking a series of deep breaths to try and slow his racing pulse, Erick unstrapped and led his team to the hatch. Standing closely, so closely that they continuously bumped into each other as the ship lurched, one behind the other, they turned around to face into the cockpit. "*Green.*" With the hatch opening he was about to take the backward step but was sucked out of the craft as he heard, "*Go!*"

Anti-gravity on! Check HUD (Head Up Display). Check height: two hundred; one fifty; one hundred; fifty; thirty' twenty; ten; maintain! Check drop area: no incoming, no lock-on, all greens, enemy not seen. Check weapons. Check position. Check direction; maintain!

Check speed: six' fifty knots, maintain! Check team: two blue dots on the HUD showed Guido and Peach at the same height, speed and heading about three hundred metres either side of him. Check terrain: passive horizon to horizon scan, nothing seen. Drop drill complete.

Hurtling along in the pitch dark at six hundred and fifty knots, no more than ten metres above treetops wasn't something he'd do for fun. But it *was* something he was trained to do. His reactions weren't fast enough to fly at that height or at that speed, however, he didn't need to; his PADE suit, like all intelligent weapons systems, was semi-thought activated. No need for tactile or verbal instructions, the suit's secondary computer was able to discern a range of specific thoughts, desiring definite outcomes. Once he'd told the suit's C2 his preferred height, speed and direction, its primary computer would fly that profile until he told the C2 otherwise. Having that major task automated meant that he could devote his attention to other matters, such as the enemy terrain.

With both light-intensifier and infrared images superimposed on the HUD, he had a better view of the terrain than the naked eye in full daylight. What he saw told him that the undulating alien landscape didn't have trees. He was flying above a dense mat of fern-like plants that were about thirty feet tall. On foot the plant cover would have proved impenetrable, even in a PADE suit... Suddenly he saw a series of flashes, just over the horizon to the west. Mortars? No, too bright and too lingering. That must be plasma batteries, presumably shooting up at *Baddest*. Wisplike glowing fingers of orange, reaching up to the sky, confirmed his speculation. The plasma jets were burning the atmosphere... There was another rapid series of shorter, more intense flashes. This time further over to the west, almost due west.

Erick stared agog at the eerie violet afterglow that dominated the entire crescent of the horizon. The HUD registered gravitational disturbance caused by the annihilation of matter. The garrison wasn't pulling any punches, they'd actually launched missiles from the planet's surface directly into the super-light. The fleeting violet radiance was the result of a 'minor' spacetime implosion. Major General Guillebaud had obviously used the time that she'd spent in discussion with Billy to prepare her grand reception. Erick couldn't see it, but the suit's instruments were tracking the rapidly approaching shockwave caused by matter collapsing in on itself and then exploding outwards. He calculated that by the time the shockwave reached his position most of its energy would have dissipated and that the suit's gyroscopes could easily cope with the turbulence. It made sense; the garrison wouldn't start ripping up the spacetime fabric in the neighbourhood of their HQ, they must have launched the missiles by remote.

Good girl! Clearly Eva was keeping *Baddest* over to the west, drawing the garrison's fire and attention away from his team's line of approach. 'Take risks early', Erick told himself, and was about to accelerate to Mach 1.2...

"Mayday! Mayday! This is Katrina. *We were clipped by an energy vortex. We're losing lateral control and height. We'll have to put her down. All stations, stay on it."*

Billy sounded ludicrously calm and unconcerned considering that *Katrina* was probably caught in the wake of the missile launch and was about to crash. Still, Billy had said to continue with the mission and not start a search and rescue mission for them... Accelerate Mach 1.2, attain! The suit accelerated and he checked that Guido and Peach had matched his speed. Two minutes to target. The HUD showed a squadron of aircraft streaking down from the north, heading over to the west that were certainly searching for *Katrina*. The map changed to show a schematic of the subterranean C-n-C and its immediate area, which had been cleared of foliage. Then the schematic was superimposed on the real-time visual. What he saw was a ring of eighteen UV laser gun emplacements, eight mortar turrets, and four iron rocket batteries - a standard air/ground defence dispersal. Still no lock-on and no tracking. Was it possible that those defences weren't manned? Decelerate eighty knots, attain!

As the suit rapidly but smoothly decelerated, he used eye tracking to pre-target two of the gun emplacements and a mortar turret. This was simply a precaution; if anything kicked off, he could just point and shoot the grenade launcher. Still no lock-on. At maximum magnification there appeared to be no activity around the defences but he did see a couple of suited sentries at the entrance to the C-n-C. Thirty seconds to target; they were inside the gun perimeter, passing the mortar turrets, his heart was pounding so hard he could hardly breathe. On his HUD the crosshairs changed from orange to red confirming he'd locked-on to both sentries. Without pausing to think about it he pressed the trigger and they both fell. Ground! Run! Speed, maintain!

He was about four hundred metres from the entrance and running towards it at a frightening eighty kilometres per hour. He stayed focussed on the entrance, Guido and Peach would be covering the flanks. The proximity detectors automatically slowed the suit as he approached the solid wall of the C-n-C. At the entrance he bent over one of the dead sentries and stuck a connector from his suit into theirs.

No sentry, or their suit, would have the codes to open the door, but they would be connected to the C-n-C's defence net which would be connected to the main InfoSys. *And*, his Marine Green Beret PADE suit's code breaking algorithms would make a hacker wet their pants. Hopefully, the sentry's suit wasn't damaged in any critical areas...

In the second or so that his C1 took to download the door codes Erick noticed the neat, still smoldering hole his laser had burnt in the sentry's armour. Through the visor he saw that it was a woman, well, more a girl, no older than perhaps twenty; rookies always drew the shit details.

He fed the uploaded codes into the optical interface and the door started sliding open. Blue laser fire danced out of the ever-widening gap. Lobbing a grenade in he waited for it to detonate, then opening up with his laser he leapt into the corridor. Through the clearing smoke all he could see was blood stained walls and mangled bits of bodies, none of the defenders had been suited. Checking the schematic, he headed for the control centre at a run with Guido and Peach immediately behind. On audible he could hear the C-n-C's intruder alert blaring out. That was unfortunate, he'd have preferred to make it to the command centre without encountering any more opposition. The garrison weren't expecting a ground assault, had been caught with their trousers down, and were ill-prepared for hand-to-hand combat with PADE suited individuals. If the situation allowed it, he'd try limiting his laser fire...

More blue laser fire erupted from a side corridor. In that instant Erick could tell that his team wasn't facing trained infantry; the defenders were standing in the middle of the corridor, all bunched together like sheep. If he'd had a non-lethal option, he'd have taken it, but lasers and grenades were designed with only one purpose in mind - to kill. Diving across the entrance to the corridor, he fired a grenade down it, then rolled back to his feet. Before his grenade could detonate, Guido fired another. As the double concussion hit, a cluster of about ten unsuited people appeared ahead of them and stood there, like skittles, loosing-off more laser bursts. For the first time *ever* in his career, Erick hesitated. Bad! This was bad, like shooting fish in a barrel. If only the defenders weren't armed with lasers, then he'd have some alternatives...

A grenade whizzed past his left shoulder to obliterate the human obstacle, fired by Peach he figured. Moving swiftly on, ignoring the entrails dripping from walls and ceiling, following the schematic they went down a few corridors, blew off the doors to an elevator, used anti-gravity to descend hundreds of levels, dived out of the elevator shaft, met no resistance, made a couple more turns and found themselves at the entrance to the command centre...

This was silly!

There was a precarious barricade made of bits of furniture, storage equipment and any other junk that had come to hand. Behind it stood about fifty terrified looking individuals. One grenade would blow the whole lot sky-high.

"Cease fire. Watch and shoot," he transmitted to Guido and Peach, then switched to the suit's external communicator. "I am Captain Bolt, Marine Green Beret. Lay down your weapons."

Laser fire blazed out from holes in the barricade.

Erick jumped back around the corner, forcing Guido and Peach to jump back as well. Were they all insane? Couldn't they see that the people confronting them were wearing PADE suits? These fuckwits couldn't even shoot straight. With intense laser fire blasting the floor, walls and ceiling, a cascade of grey snow laced by dancing blue light formed in the T-junction ahead of them. Stupid people! Lasers couldn't fire around corners. Perhaps he could...?

"*We're wasting time.*" Grenade launcher at the ready, Peach stepped past him to the lip of the corridor.

Reluctantly, Erick fed a H-TAP (Hyper-Torque Armour Piercing) grenade into the chamber of his launcher, checked to see that Guido was ready, and nodded. "OK."

Without looking or exposing any of her body Peach fired around the corner, then stepped back. Stepping in front of her, Erick waited for the blast debris to whistle past, took a quick look around the corner, aimed at the C-n-C's reenforced door, fired, then stepped back. Moving up smartly Guido did the same and stepped back, then Peach moved back to the front and fired again. Finally, Erick went to the front and peeked around the corner. After three hits from H-TAP grenades the C-n-C's doors looked as if a giant, mischievous hand had simply prised them apart, folded them like drapes, and squashed them against the wall.

Stepping out, Erick sprinted down the corridor and burst into the command centre. There had been a barricade inside the doors as well, but the H-TAP's had taken care of that. Chunks of still quivering flesh, bits of bone, slithers of cartilage, and pieces of blood-soaked electrical equipment were scattered all around the entrance. That's what H-TAP's did, rip things apart. In a darkened corner, over to the right, a head popped up to take aim with a laser rifle and simply disappeared in an abrupt flash of violet as Peach blew it off.

"Cease fire! Garrison, stand and surrender!"

Hesitantly about thirty people stood up, slowly put their hands in the air, and began to move from behind their various hides... There she is! Like a caged wild animal. Erick could see it in her eyes, Major General Guillebaud was quite mad. However, her insanity was clearly rooted in a fanatical dedication to the primacy of the human race, and Earth. Glancing back at some of his team's handiwork, Erick was hit by the sickening realisation that they'd faced a skeleton force of *administrators;* most of the infantry must be up in orbit, on the transports. Assaulted by a sudden fit of involuntary twitching, he stove to get a grip of himself and was about to order the General to stand down all her forces when he

Pilot

noticed that Lieutenant Guido Monacelli, the hard man of the 23rd Squadron Marine Green Beret, had puked up inside his PADE suit.

***

"That's an armoured car, what do we do?" Mohamed asked.

"Finish shutting down the bird, then go and say hello."

"They're pointing their gun at us, shouldn't we go and say hello now?"

"Naw, let 'em wait."

"You know best," Mohammed didn't sound totally convinced.

The hatch flew open and a twin barrelled laser stuck itself into the cockpit about six inches from the side of Billy's head. "*Hands off the controls! Stand up! Out!*"

Billy kept his hands on the controls, turned, and said disdainfully over the barrel of the laser, "Solider, stop pointing that gun at me."

"*Out!*"

"Mr Grunt, please tell your commander that we'll be out *after* we've shut the ship down."

"*Final warning!*"

Mohammed leant across, behind Billy, to direct additional verbal abuse at the twin barrels. "Or else what? This is a super-light ship. It's suffered some minor damage to its engines. If we don't shut them down it might explode. Do you know what happens when a super-light ship explodes?"

The barrels wavered uncertainly between Billy and Mohammed.

"You don't? Well let me enlighten you," Mohammed continued with this haranguing. "Matter/anti-matter annihilation, that's what. We're not talking one of your 'anaemic' little missiles here. We're talking a crater a hundred miles..."

"More like a hundred and fifty," Billy interrupted.

"...a hundred and fifty miles across. And that's just the crater, never mind the ejecta. The blast area must be, what, a thousand?"

"Yeah, about that," Billy mused. "But that isn't the problem. A blast like that would rupture the planet's crust. Gargantuan earthquakes - might just cleave Celice apart. Even if it doesn't, it would definitely strip the atmosphere."

The barrels wavered even more uncertainly.

Turning back to the controls Billy lobbed a final sally over his shoulder, "Now Soldier Boy, get that fucking gun out of my face, we'll be out when we're done."

***

Mohammed was in a steaming rage about being handcuffed. As they bounced around, each sandwiched between two suited soldiers in the back of the armoured car, Billy tried to not let it get to him. Instead, he focussed his mental energies on the logistical problems of getting *Katrina* repaired. They had replacement engines on *Baddest,* but *Baddest* could never make it downside. So, they'd just have to commandeer something after they'd sorted out the garrison. Speaking of which, he couldn't help feeling that he and Mohammed were dealing with a bunch of hand-picked zealots who weren't entirely right in the head. For instance, they had been told that they were being taken to Alien Interrogation. Did they look like aliens?

The armoured car lurched to a sudden halt. The rear door was flung open and he and Mohammed were none-too-gently 'assisted' out. He ended up face down in some foul-smelling mud before being yanked back to his feet. All he could see, thanks to the flashes

170

from the distant plasma batteries, was that they were being frogmarched, like wayward children, towards what appeared to be a huge, squat, bunker-like building. His guards seemed intent on dishing out some hurt without appearing to be doing anything of the sort, the soldiers' grip on his arms was fierce. Trying not to be too distressed by this, Billy consoled himself with the thought that if either guard had a mind to they could, with the suit's strength augmentation, squash his head like a soft-boiled egg, or rip his arms off as easily as pulling the wings off a fly.

Just as they entered the enormous subterranean depot-cum-forward attack base both guards rapid surefooted strides, which he'd been almost running to keep up with, faltered. It was as if they'd just seen or heard something quite unexpected. Billy's suspicions were confirmed when, on some unheard signal, the activity level of the small number of seriously tooled-up personnel inside the base redoubled and they started running around like headless chickens. Any feelings of satisfaction he felt because Erick's team was probably in, were easily countered - the guards were trying to mangle his bloody arms.

He'd expect to be dragged off to alien interrogation, wherever that was, but, instead, the guards appeared to be taking them towards the OpsCen. As they approached OpsCen a uniformed officer flanked by two heavily armed and suited soldiers, stepped out and started over to them. Their guards pulled them to a jolting halt and, as the officer approached, he exchanged a questioning look with Mohammed. Turning to the officer, Mohammed beamed his most charming smile. "My dear Provost Colonel. Well, congratulations on your promotion." Still smiling warmly, he turned back to Billy. "At last. Someone who knows that we're human."

With a twisted smile the Lieutenant Colonel came to a halt in front of them. Casually drawing her neuron whip from its holster, she absentmindedly started twirling it. Still smiling, one hand still twirling, the other slowly fingering a jagged purple scar on the left side of her face - which would have taken less than five minutes of surgery to rectify - the Lieutenant Colonel slowly paced around them. Smiling, twirling, fingering, looking them up and down, the Lieutenant Colonel did a couple of gleeful, leisurely laps. That scar made her look rather, well, menacing...

"Gentlemen," she intoned at last, stopping and facing them. Then, looking up to the ceiling as if on a tight-stream to God, she added happily, "And it's not even my birthday."

The twirling stopped. The whip was pointed directly at him.

"The military's *primary* function is to protect Earth and her colonies from any and all alien threats," the Lieutenant Colonel mentioned as if in passing.

With all the background hubbub Billy was surprised at how clearly he heard the 'click, click, click' as she cranked-up the whip's setting.

"Apparently," she continued, and licked her lips, "An Air Force crew has aided unknown aliens in attacking and destroying Earth. Not only that, this crew had declared themselves allies of said unknown aliens," she spoke as if in wonderment.

There was a distinct and final click. He could see from the look in the Lieutenant Colonel's eyes that explaining that Earth hadn't been destroyed wasn't going to cut any ice. Guillebaud hadn't listened to a fucking word he'd said, and this woman had also jumped into the gene pool when the lifeguard wasn't looking.

"The charge, trial, judgement and sentence of this Judas Air Force crew has been carried out in absentia," she added, just for information.

The grip on his arms tightened, as if it wasn't tight enough already. To stop him from running? Like there was anyway that he could escape... Detachable arms, now there's a thought.

Pilot

"High treason is punishable by death," she cited, as she gave the scar on her cheek one final, loving caress.

If you wanted to simply execute someone, you'd give them one in the head from a laser; quick, clean, no pain. A neuron whip was a different affair all together: much higher up in the dastardly stakes. *Every* muscle in the body contracts and goes into violent spasm; atriums and ventricles collapse; veins and arteries rupture; the spine snap; rip cage punctures lungs; tibias, fibulas, femurs, ulnas, radiuses and humeri crack; ligaments and cartilage rip; tongue bitten off, etc., etc. Groovy! And, of course, you're fully conscious throughout.

He decided he'd keep his eyes open - just to let her know that he wasn't afraid of her, or of dying.

One moment he's giving the Lieutenant Colonel the eye, the next he's staring at Hontay's naked back. From the corner of his eyes he saw that his guards were no longer suited or armed, and noted, incidentally, that his arms were no longer hurting. He heard a roar... Well, that wasn't strictly accurate because, first of all, he didn't hear it - the sound was in his head. And second, 'roar' doesn't do justice to the noise in his head - a galaxy-load of vituperative banshees was more like it.

The next moment he was back eyeballing the Lieutenant Colonel except now her expression was several magnitudes beyond terrified astonishment. He noted that her escorts were now also bereft of suits and weapons, but, funnily enough, the neuron whip was still in her hand. He figured that this was a 'Go on, if you dare!' from Hontay.

Now, despite having to follow three elder siblings up through school, he'd always made a point of sorting out his own difficulties/disputes/altercations. Having said that, he was suddenly beginning to see the virtue of always having top cover.

With all the background hubbub Billy was surprised at how clearly he heard the 'phruuuu' sound as the Lieutenant Colonel shat herself.

21

THEORY

Dropping from super-light they launched the Darts, flew an attack search pattern with Darts fanned out on either side - nothing seen except *The Beast.* Eva recalled the Darts and headed for the RV with *The Beast.* Billy called for a SitRep.

"Nothing, zilch, zip, zero. We're glad to have some company," Nice reported. *"How was your mission?"*

"The garrison is locked down," Billy reported back.

Mohammed wondered if this was what it took to be a Captain; the ability to give precise and factually accurate information that didn't say anything. Like, the garrison commander was barking mad. Like, how Eva had, had to threaten to blow their flotilla to smithereens before the Captains would obey the captive General's orders to surrender and hit downside. Like, instead of just repairing *Katrina,* the garrison engineers had attempted to hide a fusion bomb in her. Like, Billy and Eva spending over six hours with the infantry to get them down from a serious guilt-trip high. Yeah, the garrison had been locked down, eventually.

Eva gradually brought *Baddest* to within 150 kilometres of *The Beast.* Mohammed sat up and paid particular attention to the manoeuvre Eva and Wendy were attempting. *The Beast* wasn't stationary, it was tumbling quite slowly about its centre of gravity through a spiral that, over a period of about six minutes, enabled it to scan the entire sphere of operations. Eva and Wendy synchronised with this motion but had *Baddest* facing in the opposite direction. In unison, the ships commenced a subtle space ballet.

"It pains me to say this, but that was real heads-up flying Truckie," was Nice's compliment.

"Yes, not too shabby Navy. But it's going to make delivering over our recreation interesting," Ventrice added.

"Say something Eva, that was praise from the Captain of the Air Force's Ace Crew I," Billy ribbed.

Eva perked up. "Roger, thanks for that *The Beast.* By the way, did I hear you mention 'recreation'? We're at full alert. What recreation?"

"She had to go and spoil it, didn't she."

Pilot

Mohammed figured that to be Riet, *The Beast's* N° 1 compassman, a most insatiable woman. Sun came on the net, *"Sorry to interrupt, but business calls. I suggest we have two Darts permanently manned as a quick reaction flight."*

"What duration?" Billy asked.

"Four hours on."

Billy pondered for a moment. "OK."

"Gill, we'll take the first. Then Kaye and Varsha. Last, Vimla and Sabine."

There was a chorus of, *"Roger, Dart leader."*

"Fine. Stand down, changeover to waiting rota," Billy ordered.

"Roger Baddest, changing to waiting rota," Nice confirmed. *"Billy, after you're thoroughly rested, please get your brain round how to pass a little happiness our way without the ships being connected. The Beast, out."*

***

Stripped of his bloodstained PADE suit and transported back to the cockpit, Erick was slightly surprised to find Billy sitting on the back of his womb facing the remainder of the crew. Billy rubbed his eyes, then looked over to him. "Right. Now that the infantry are back with us, I want to throw open to discussion something Alfred has just put to me. You in on this, *The Beast*?"

"Roger Baddest." Holograms of *The Beast's* crew appeared.

"OK Alfred, you want to explain your theory or whatever it is?"

"Well, it's hardly a theory," Alfred started self-consciously. "It's just that I can't help thinking that Billy and Hontay's 'wedlock' is statistically improbable. The chances of such biological similarity occurring must be staggering. Over and above that, it also means that a being from one of the most advanced civilisations in the galaxy was careless enough to allow herself be contaminated." Alfred looked apologetically at Billy.

"We've already had an explanation of how..." Sam pounced.

"I know." Nodding, Alfred cut him off. "That *explanation* also concerns me. I mean, is it coincidence that this unlikely 'match' was made with our mission commander, no less?"

"What are you getting at?" Cynthia asked impatiently.

"We're aren't even supposed to be sapient, but our quarantine procedures are such that we could never be infected by, say, a laboratory rat."

"So, what's your point?" Kazuhiko was also getting impatient.

"If we encountered a lesser civilisation, one strategy we'd probably employ to reduce their culture shock would be to invent a commonality, if one didn't already exist, of course." Alfred was warming to the task.

"What you're saying is that the Ig'tams have fabricated this wedding business, to... well, insulate us?" Nice seemed interested.

"Precisely..."

"You're only saying that because she didn't threaten you," Sabine complained.

"Obviously, the ruse would have to be convincing, striking at the very heart of our psyche. What is more human than being possessive about one's mate?" Alfred continued smoothly.

Erick could see that Alfred's notions were gathering momentum with some of the crew, who were looking at Billy, waiting for his comments. But Billy simply sat on the back of his womb rubbing his eyes. No one seemed inclined to speak, so Alfred continued, "Now, this attempted linking or whatever it was with the Flushi. Wasn't that just another way of letting us down gently?"

Billy was still rubbing his eyes, so Erick simply said, "That's rather an elaborate theory, isn't it?"

"No more elaborate than what we've been told," Alfred replied, now totally sure of himself.

"*Well Billy?*" Riet asked.

Billy stopped rubbing his eyes to slowly look over his audience. "Being sceptical and not taking things at face value must be a prerequisite to being a scientist I suppose. That's why I opened this up for debate. But I suspect that if you ask me specific questions, I'll know the answers."

"OK then, Alfred has a point. If they're that advanced how were you able to... contaminate her?" Eva asked, rather aggressively.

Billy pondered for a while. "The Ig'tam immune system is very sophisticated, they're unlikely to be *contaminated* by a foreign body. So, it's probably erroneous to think of our union as an 'infection'. If you wanted to accuse the Ig'tam of anything, it wouldn't be carelessness. It's more a case of arrogance. About as arrogant as *knowing* you'd never find a chimpanzee sexually attractive."

"That's a fair point Billy but think about it for a second: Earth has been isolated; we are isolated. It's exactly what we would do with an inferior species: flatter them and then keep them occupied but out of the way until it was all over. It's too much of a coincidence." Kazuhiko appeared to have moved over to Alfred's camp.

"There's also Hontay's threat to Sabine and Eva to consider. How is it possible for so intelligent a species to be driven by such primitive instincts?" Cynthia had moved from being opposed to sitting on the fence.

"*The perceived threat was real. On* The Beast*, we got our share of hostility from our Hontay.*" Nice informed them.

"Who got the hostility?" Grim quickly dived in.

"*Krishna.*" Nice raised her eyebrows to Billy.

"Oh, a bit of history there then, Chief?" Pipsqueak asked cheerily.

Billy stared questioningly at Krishna.

"*Flight school, Cadet Officer Zarcroft.*" Krishna reminded him, looking genuinely hurt.

"Wait a minute. That implies that Hontay knows something Billy has forgotten. Is that possible?" Sam seemed perplexed.

"Of course, it is possible!" Cynthia snapped, then calmed down. "How often have you forgotten something then later retrieved the memory? But we're getting away from my point: why would an intelligent race be so savage, and specifically towards members of the same sex of their own species?"

Again, everyone waited for Billy's answer, but he just sat there looking thoughtful.

"*It was the night of our graduation.*" Krishna was still smouldering.

Billy eventually looked up and said, "Sorry Cynthia, I was just trying to figure out how come I didn't know about the incident on *The Beast*. I did know about it, I just didn't realise that I did. Now, to answer your question, Ig'tams didn't evolve into being top predator in the same way we did - by developing intelligence and using..."

"*I was a virgin you bastard!*"

Billy's eyes snapped to Krishna. "It took me two hours to lose my parents. You'd changed into a sari, a garment I'd never seen. You looked captivating... Don't you have some things that you just file away and never think about because they're so special?"

Krishna blushed, Eva looked really annoyed, Erick hid a smile, Billy continued, "We weren't the biggest, the fastest, or the strongest, but we had intelligence. The Ig'tams got to be top predator by being the most ferocious, intelligence was incidental. This ferocity has evolved primarily through the Redits and it starts with other Redits..."

"Are Redits significantly larger than Gemarchs?" Sam interrupted.

"No, they're the same size. Why do you ask?"

"In terrestrial species where males physically compete for females, natural selection obviously favours the larger and stronger males. So, in time, larger males evolve," Sam explained.

"I see... Only Redits have pseudolimbs. They're the same size as the males but much, much, *much* deadlier."

"Comparable to, say, some species of deer where only the stags have antlers," Cynthia added, and then continued. "Surely once intelligence emerged their aggressive tendencies began to wane?"

"Would you estimate that we're less aggressive than cavemen Cynthia?" Billy asked back tiredly.

Erick felt that, that didn't answer Cynthia's question. "But Billy, the Ig'tams aren't just intelligent, are they? They're super-intelligent. I'm no biologist, but that order of intelligence, ought to overwhelm their natural instinct towards violence."

Billy scratched his chin. "This could get confusing, so let's keep it simple. Intelligence is only one of many evolutionary strategies. It's no more than a tool to aid a species survive. What I'm saying is that just because it was our route to 'top predatorship', we don't want to overplay its importance. Now, sapiency, that's another matter altogether. Sapience is what stops Redits killing other Redits. But it doesn't stop them going through the motions, at the emotional level."

"*Are you saying that Redits don't actually harm each other?*" Riet queried.

"Rarely since sapiency, and only when one mess with another's Gemarchs. Look, as I understand it, one aspect of sapiency is the ability to use not just intelligence but any other evolutionary attributes, for a purpose other than its reason for being there in the first place."

"Then why were you so stressed out when I was telling her where to get off?" Eva demanded.

Billy looked exasperated. "Eva, get this through your head. Hontay is a fourth stage sapient. She doesn't have to *do* anything. Her thoughts, by themselves, can have pretty serious consequences. The fact that you're still here giving me grief proves that she's sapient - her every instinct is to kill you!"

"*We have Art, music...*" Shirlie started.

"I know that," Billy said with measured restraint. "These serve a wholly evolutionary purpose. Artistic creativity keeps us sane."

"How do you know that?" Sun asked doubtfully.

"I just do... Look folks, as the Flushi would say, 'it's important for us to believe'. But from a mission point of view, it's important for you to believe what you've been told." Billy smiled patiently. "Hence this debate."

Erick suddenly understood what Billy was doing and where he was going with this. Sooner or later what had gone down on Celice was going to become common knowledge. Billy wanted this argument out in the open, done and dusted, before the rights or wrongs of killing other humans on the sapients' say-so became an issue.

"I was simply exploring a hypothesis," Alfred said defensively.

"One worth exploring," Billy replied soothingly. "Now, where have we got to?"

"Standard operating procedures cover this: 'In the absence of additional data, continue operation with what is known'," Nice announce in a tone of finality.

"Yes," Billy agreed, his patience visibly waning. "This is to try to define 'what is known'."

"Let's not forget that we had orders from Marshal..." Grim was in the middle of saying when Billy pulled a face. A fraction of a second later Flet appeared. Erick had no idea how he knew that this was Flet. She and Hontay were, as far as he could tell, identical but he *knew* that this was definitely Flet.

"Greetings. Apologies for interrupting your discussion. Billy, we need you."

"Why?"

"You know why Billy. Change in command; Flight Lieutenant Schove, mission commander. 2ic, Lieutenant Commander Gümann."

"Wait a minute. Mind telling the humans what's going down?" Nice's hologram jumped up, obviously addressing someone on *The Beast*.

"Hontay is, again, dysfunctional. Think of her as being in season, but without the possibility of becoming pregnant."

"Yes, and?" Eva asked.

"A simple solution would be for her to select another husband. Humans, however, are not a polyandrous race. Billy would undoubtably become dysfunctional, so we need to send him to her. And, Eva, he is also correct in his assessment that you are developing Redit-like characteristics."

Billy stared at Flet. "There's something I don't understand here. You're going to *send* me, not *take* me?"

Erick got the sensation of 'impatience'.

"Yes. You have now been exposed to me. So, I must eschew contact with Hontay until she is assured that, as you humans would say, 'there has been nothing between us'."

"This is absurd!" Cynthia announced.

The sensation of impatience increased appreciably.

"I understand your puzzlement Cynthia. Hontay sees Billy as a Gemarch, I see him as a man. This situation would be impossible if he were a true Gemarch."

"But occasions must arise where Redits are away from their Gemarchs," Cynthia persisted.

"Yes, and another Gemarch would act as her emissary if she could not attend in any of her persons. Now we must go."

Without further explanation, Billy and Flet disappeared.

22

DISTRACTION

Absurd!

He knew exactly where he was. But for the life of him, couldn't figure out why. As his eyes swept the darkened room, he spotted her peering at him from behind some very expensive furniture - she'd dived for cover when he'd appeared. He waited for understanding to permeate into his consciousness. It didn't, so he said, "I'm sorry if I'd startled you."

Slowly and hesitantly she got to her feet, the look of utter disbelief still on her face. "William?"

She had something in her hand. In the dim light he thought it looked like a laser. Thankfully, she wasn't pointing it at him. "Yes, it's William."

"How you... you get here?" Rooted to the spot, she continued to stare at him as if she were seeing a ghost.

Because of all the things going on in his head it took him a little while to note her attire - something like a skin-tight black rubber suit with holes that exposed her breasts and crotch. Again, he looked at the thing in her hand. No, not a laser, a vibrator, a very large vibrator. He suppressed a smile. "I was transported here by Matter Transfer, it's a military secret. I'm sorry if I... interrupted you."

Her eyes followed his to the vibrator. Instead of being embarrassed, she smiled then said, "Matter transfer? Military trying to put me out of job." Her smile was adorable. "I thinking about you."

Casually she dropped the vibrator and started slinking over to him. She stopped, less than a foot away from him, and stared up expectantly into his eyes. He stared back, somewhat surprised. She must have remarkable resilience. He'd appeared, literally out of nowhere, scaring her silly. Yet she had readily accepted the improbability of all this and was now back on her original agenda. Wasn't she in the least bit curious about how he'd got here, or where he'd come from?

Somewhere in the back of his mind it suddenly dawned on him that him being here was all to do with what passed for Ig'tam humour. Flet was trying to antagonise Hontay; the sort of thing that Redits did to each other as a matter of course. "I can't Coraliè."

"I think of you. Then you come to me in Love Room. You must!"

Did Flet get this from him? And/or, was she able to read God knows how many billions of human minds and then single out the one individual thinking specifically about him...?

178

This close and he was finding her outfit... Her gaze was disturbing; so honest and unashamed, but at the same time so demanding... The fact that he was having these thoughts meant that Hontay hadn't...

Coraliè took the final, small step closer. Now, her breasts were pressed firmly against his chest. "A girl in every port William." Looking into his eyes, she gave him a wanting smile. "You screw them, then leave them with long memory of you. Not right, Air Force pilot?"

How was he going to get out of this? He could hardly just stroll out of the door. Hontay would... It didn't bear thinking about. He wasn't sure of exactly what Hontay *would* do, but whatever it was he was fairly sure it would be unpleasant. "Coraliè, I can't."

Determinedly nudging him towards the bed, she didn't appear to be listening. The fact that he had a monster of an erection wasn't helping the situation. Not only was Coraliè ridiculously beautiful, he knew, from personal experience, that she was libidinous in the nymphomaniacal sense of the word.

"I no let you leave without fucking me." Impatiently she shoved him onto the bed.

Lying there, he looked up at her... Something had to give. On the one hand, he wanted Coraliè like he'd never wanted any other woman - was Flet messing with his mind? On the other hand, there was Hontay, his lethal, extemely possessive, telepathic Ig'tam wife.

"I miss you William. I no think I do, but I do."

As he started expertly unclipping the umbilical of his flight suit, he marvelled at his own behaviour. Gemarchs didn't have the capacity to be unfaithful, not unless their brains had been filched by another Redit. His brains hadn't been filched it was just in the wrong part of his anatomy. Coraliè lost any sense of decorum at the sight of his bared chest, her impatience rose several notches and she started pulling at the suit in an attempt to hurry things along. As soon as he was out of it, she was on top of him, hungrily pinning him to the bed. He'd been ravaged by women like this before, usually when some female crew hit downside - it was a novel experience getting 'the treatment' from a civilian.

There followed at least two hours of incredible sex, which only served to reenforce the phenomenal differences between a woman and a Redit. Not really surprising, men and women had evolved for mutual compatibility, leading to maximum physical satisfaction. Mentally, however, there was no way round it, Redits won hands down. Mind you, although he'd escaped the bruised midriff, Coraliè had inflicted some serious scratches, they felt more like deep gouges, on his shoulders and back. Maybe it was universal for females to...

"That was good. We do again?"

Though it was phrased as a question there was an underlying statement about it. Well... He felt Flet's subtle presence. "I just wanted to see you. I missed you too. Now I have to go."

"Is dangerous what you do?" Reluctantly, she seemed to accept the need for him to leave.

He'd guess that what they had just done wasn't merely exceedingly dangerous, it was probably suicidal. "No. Kiss Reuben for me." As he got into his flight suit, he hoped that Flet would allow him to get out the door before he vanished into thin air.

"Reuben, I send him Air Force Academy Japan when he is ten, OK... You come again, quick. OK?"

"OK." Scrambling, he just made it through the door.

***

He arrived, if 'arrived' was the correct term, naked, and floating in zero G. She was already there, naked, floating, tentacles dancing. Interesting. He knew that she'd already checked him for clues of possible molestation by Flet and he had been given the all-clear. Hontay also knew all about the incident with Coraliè but, surprisingly, had exonerated him of *all* responsibility - he wasn't even going to bother trying to figure out why. If, however, Hontay ever bumped into Coraliè... she'd kill her on sight.

He knew he was on board a 'proper' Ig'tam ship. Somewhere in his head was 'all' its technical details. His non-sapient brain had distilled this info down to a simple to understand 'much bigger than *Baddest*'. It was pretty amazing just how much information could be imparted 'in an instant'. But his mind couldn't really grasp any of it, so it went walkabout. Puzzling over concepts that it could readily comprehend; like, where did their clothes go when she made them vanish? They had to be somewhere...?

Hontay then did something he'd only half suspected she was capable of, she made him think about what she wanted him to think about - her predicament: she had liberated probity, she should be pregnant. There wasn't an intermediate stage, the one should automatically follow the other. Normally, she'd just keep having intercourse with her bevy of Gemarchs until she was pregnant. All perfectly reasonable really because as soon as her eggs had been secondarily fertilised - no more sexual activity for a couple of years. But that wasn't the problem. She knew he didn't have his gonads and that therefore she couldn't become pregnant.

The problems were: one, as long as she wasn't pregnant, she would crave sex. Which led to problem two. Problem two; he wasn't a Gemarch. Physically, he couldn't handle it. Out of consideration for his sensibilities (the human traits of jealousy, envy, and of course, inferiority), she'd decided to be monogamous. Because he couldn't cope with a Redit's sexual demands, she was having to keep herself away from him both physically and mentally. From this, problem three - which none of the very clever Ig'tams seemed to have anticipated - dropped into their laps. Problem three; Hontay, with increasing severity, was being debilitated by their separation. Now, after being away from him for more than a couple of hours and she started to lose it.

Fascinatingly, she was also a pilot, her job was to 'guide' this ship. A task that took up a sizable chunk of her processing power. He didn't understand why, but it did. Dealing with the humans was only supposed to have taken a tiny fraction of her intellect and even less of her time. But now, because she was married to him and not pregnant, she couldn't give her job the attention it demanded. So, the entire crew of this enormous ship was busily waiting for her to get her act together. In a sense, he found it sort of flattering, being responsible for locking-up a super-mind. Of course, none of this would have happened if he were a Gemarch.

Still, he was beginning to feel a little uneasy about the ease with which Hontay was able to control his mind. Well, OK, 'control' wasn't strictly the correct term; she wasn't able to control his mind in the 'slave to her will' sense - she couldn't make him do anything he didn't want to. But she could certainly 'influence' what he wanted to do. This would have been a two-way street if he were a Gemarch...

His unease suddenly ballooned into alarm which then exploded into hopeless panic when he realised why she had 'tickled' and then deposited this bit of information at the fore of his consciousness... It was an apology.

As her tentacles seized him, he understood; an apology for what was about to happen. The incredibly intelligent Ig'tams had come up with a simple solution to a complex problem. Even fourth stage sapients got into situations where they abandoned finesse - she had to become pregnant, it was as simple as that.

The detour via Earth had simply been to reunite him with his balls. He was now a fully functioning male. The 'incident' with Coraliè was no more than a test run to ensure that semen production was functioning and adequate. Flet's logic and doing *but* with Hontay's acquiescence. This endeavour had, in a sense, sacrificed Coraliè's life. Because from now on, Hontay wouldn't view Coraliè like just another run of the mill 'other Redit'. Hontay wouldn't even react like she had to Eva and Sabine's 'unconscious desires for her mate'. No, her reaction was going to be somewhere well in excess of excessive. Hontay now regarded Coraliè as a *Bitch! That sperm belonged to 'me'!* repository and semen thief. And the chances were that at some point in the future both females would meet.

Hontay intended to keep him awake until she was both primarily and secondarily fertilised. Yes, it was going to be both physically and mentally really hard on him. She was very sorry about that, but this was how it had to be.

***

"I'm not hearing things, am I? Flet did say, 'Could not attend in any of her persons', didn't she?" Wendy said to no one in particular.

"You sure did," Pipsqueak replied cheerily.

"*Come now, we've settled this. It's blatantly obvious that they can make simultaneous appearances,*" Nice said firmly.

"We've settled that an Ig'tam can be in two places at once," Wendy continued undaunted. "But there's something I've got to ask. Surely two of the *same* Ig'tam can't be in the *same* place at the *same* time?"

"That would violate the known laws of physics," Sam chipped in authoritatively.

"*So does being in two places at the same time,*" Nice said thoughtfully then pondered for a while. "*Look, we could keep at this forever, so let's just drop it and go with what we know. Now, back to the waiting rota.*" That was an order.

Nice was right, but Eva thought she'd give *The Beast's* crew something to think about before they closed comms. "Still haven't come up with a solution to your recreational problem," she informed them in mock sadness.

"*Funnily enough we've been giving some thought to just that,*" the hologram of Riet appeared, and with dripping sarcasm interrupted. "The Beast *may not have launch bays for Darts, but it does have a docking bay for service crew ships.*"

"So?" Eva asked suspiciously.

"*A Dart could just about...*"

"*Forget it! We're not a bloody taxi service,*" Sun's suited head and shoulders hologram jumped on that.

"I know this banter is a military thing, however, may I suggest that we have more pressing priorities," Cynthia interjected with strained patience.

"*Like what?*" Nice asked.

Cynthia looked up from her screen to stare intently at Nice's hologram. "Flet has confirmed that Eva is becoming Redit-like. I see exploring this phenomenon as a priority."

Before she could staunch the direction of the discussion, John jumped in. "Absolutely right Cynthia. We also need to get to grips with the 2ic falling in love with our Captain."

"*We haven't any other pressing matters, so we might as well. This is the xenobiologist's area of expertise Cynthia, would you like to lead the discussion?*" Nice's hologram turned to her. "*Eva, we would like candid answers.*"

She didn't know Nice well enough to tell whether she was taking the piss or not. She decided to play safe with the new mission commander. "Of course."

Pilot

"Within yourself, do you feel in any way different Eva?" Cynthia posed the first question while working away at her consul.

"No, I think this is nonsense. Have any of you noticed any change in my behaviour?" she responded rather more defensively than she'd intended.

There was no immediate answer, so Cynthia continued. "Eva, perhaps we should start by asking when it was that you first began feeling affection for Billy."

She felt her ire rise appreciably. "As I've said, this is nonsense. I don't feel any affection for Billy. I..."

"But you've already admitted that you're attracted to him," Sam joined the cross-examination.

"*Eva, before you answer, the aim of this isn't to humiliate or embarrass you. We need to gain a greater understanding of the 'Ig'tam effect' on humans.*" Nice was conciliatory but firm.

She was now convinced that Nice was being serious, making this legitimate business. In which case, she'd be businesslike. "Cath Awunda is Billy's mother, she is the yardstick that all naval pilots are measured against. When her fourth son entered the academy there was a pervasive expectation that, like his three elder siblings, he'd find living up to his mother's reputation an unbearable burden.

"But *this* midshipman Zarcroft seemed to thrive on it, he strutted about like he was the best thing since sliced bread. I was two intakes ahead. We gave him such a hard time because of his attitude, but he took it all on the chin and strutted even more. I'd have called it arrogance, except that his sim-sorties were the best thing since his mother's. His live sorties were even better, first solo age eleven. Even then, one could see that he was special..."

"*Are you saying that this goes as far back as then?*" Nice was incredulous.

"How old were you when you did your first solo?"

"*Fifteen, and that was considered pretty exceptional. I get your drift. Carry on.*"

"That's it." She felt that this was more than ample explanation for why she felt the way she did.

"So, you admired Billy's flying. When did that change to affection?" Cynthia was still head down at her screen.

"There is no affection! I said I was attracted to him, that's all."

Cynthia looked up in puzzlement, so Eva set her straight. "What do you look for in a partner?"

"A keen mind and a sense of humour," Cynthia answered without hesitation. "I don't see the relevance."

"Military value systems are different. I guess we look for compatible proficiencies," she explained.

"I presume that Nice is as proficient as Billy. Are you attracted to her?" Alfred enquired, with just a hint of sarcasm.

"I admire her flying skills."

"Yes, but does that mean you find her... alluring?" Alfred pressed.

"Are you asking if I'm bisexual Alfred?"

He stared calmly into her eyes. "Yes, but only indirectly. Now, to answer my question, do you find Nice sexually attractive?"

"Yes." She folded her arms and waited for the avalanche of sarcastic comments.

"*Please continue Cynthia,*" Nice said dispassionately.

"OK. Eva, when did this antagonism towards Hontay start."

"Oh, I don't know, she just pisses me off."

"Does Sabine also piss you off?" Kazuhiko was at pains to sound clinical.

"No." She was getting fed up with this.

"OK then, we all know that Hontay can zap you, *if* you piss her off. How come that doesn't stop you having a dig?" Mohammed seemed genuinely puzzled.

Before she could think of a credible answer Cynthia abruptly remarked, "Yes Eva, that's contrary to every human survival instinct. What is your explanation for that?"

Eva had vaulted out of her womb and covered the distance before she realised what she was about to do - sock Cynthia right between the eyes. Fists still clenched, hovering over Cynthia's womb, she struggled to get a grip of herself. What the hell was happening to her? It was as if her only passion in life was to see Cynthia die agonisingly. Sensing all eyes on her, she still had the irrational desire to inflict pain on Cynthia. It was an undiluted vehement animosity, as if an unguessed at and darker side to her character had abruptly surfaced.

Looking up from her screen, Cynthia seemed surprised to see her towering over her. More perplexed than alarmed she asked, "Yes Eva?"

"Nothing." As she turned to go back to her womb, Sam caught her eye.

"Eva, I see no connection between Billy and Cynthia. So, what was that about?"

Nonplussed, Cynthia looked from one to the other.

"This has nothing to do with Billy. She shouldn't have spoken to me like that."

"You mean me? Spoken to you like what?" Cynthia appeared to be totally confused.

Aware that she was looking at the only person in either cockpit who didn't understand what had just happened, she supplied a neutral answer, "Your tone annoyed me."

"*It was a perfectly reasonable question. And I didn't hear anything in her 'tone'.*" Nice's hologram walked over to stand next to her. This meant that Nice was now strutting around her cockpit.

Her internal deliberation lasted for less than a second before she turned to face Nice. "I would like a 'your ears only' conference."

"*This 'my ears only' business got anything to do with what just went down?*"

Standing there like that Eva started to feel very exposed and extremely vulnerable. "Yes, it has."

"*Request denied. Say your piece.*" Nice was now the hard-nosed mission commander.

Even Nice was becoming irksome. Taking a quick breath, she said, "Mission success and crew safety demand that I be relieved as mission 2ic and Captain pro tem of *Baddest*."

"*Why?*" Nice demanded.

Her feeling of vulnerability increased. "I believe my ability to interface with the female members of the mission is being impaired."

"*What?*" The mission commander seemed vexed.

She felt rather than saw the crew exchanging puzzled looks. It was becoming difficult to concentrate. What was happening to her? "I think it may have something to do with me becoming Redit-like."

"Go on," Cynthia coaxed.

A sudden dampness on her hand caused her to look down. Mystified by the source, she was astonished to discover that her tears were flowing profusely. In the very depths of her being she felt a profound sadness. A sadness caused by a dawning awareness of the true cause of her sense of dread. Behind her were four women whom she couldn't see. Four women with whom she'd spent thousands of hours, on countless missions. Four women, each of whom who she used to trust with her life. Four women who, because she had her back to them, posed a threat.

"I... I..." She faltered.

"Despite what we've been told, I think we're seeing the advanced stages of a cross-species viral infection. That's the only explanation," Sam suggested.

No one seemed prepared to speak. Nice sank into contemplation. Eventually she stared her in the eye and said, "*An infection? Perhaps. Eva, relieving you of your command is the soft option.*"

Eva couldn't help thinking that this was the sort of thing Billy would have said. Her sexual desire for Nice took a fillip. With that came the gut-wrenching appreciation that there was no such thing as a bisexual or homosexual Redit. Redits felt nothing but aggression towards other Redits. How could she feel this way about Nice and the opposite about her crew? "I'm sorry Nice, but I see no other alternative."

Nice pondered some more. "*Let's try another tack, shall we? Why not go eyeball-to-eyeball with this thing?*"

"Whether this is a cross-species infection or not, we need to understand what's happening to you and why it is happening," Cynthia added encouragingly.

"Eva, Nice," Pipsqueak interrupted, bouncing out of his seat to stroll over, "I think I might have an angle on this."

"*Shoot.*"

"Remember when we were trying to tune into the Flushi pilots?" he continued enthusiastically.

"*Yes, so?*"

"Well, as soon as they connected our brains locked onto theirs."

"*Yes, but Eva's isn't 'connected' to Hontay's.*"

"I know, but Flushi are only first stage sapients. What if there was some sort of 'leakage' from Hontay. Couldn't that be as strong as a deliberate connection by a Flushi?"

"I think there's some mileage in this, Pipsqueak." Sam also got out of his womb to come over to her. "Not a viral infection but a... what would one call it...?"

"A noometrical infection?" Kazuhiko suggested halfheartedly.

"*Whatever.*" Nice seemed to tire of the scientists' hypothesising. "*You weren't able to break the connection were you, Pipsqueak?*"

"Well, actually, we could. But we would only think to do that if we were consciously aware of the situation. When they first locked-on, we didn't even know where we were."

Nice opened her mouth to respond to Pipsqueak but suddenly turned to stare quizzically at her. Eva realised that her weeping was now accompanied by a fit of uncontrollable sniggering. As she strove to get a grip of herself, Pipsqueak and Sam moved to comfort her. Which, of course, it didn't; seeing as how they were the cause of the sniggering in the first place. With the last of her rapidly disappearing self-control she managed to ask Kazuhiko, "What is noometrical?"

"From Noology; the science of intelligence."

She collapsed laughing hysterically and Sam and Pipsqueak bent to help her back to her feet. This made her laugh even more. Between them, they then half carried, half dragged her back to her womb. Nice's hologram trailed them. "*Anne, scan Eva.*"

'All Eva's physiological functions are normal. The chemical balances within her brain are also normal.'

"Gemarchs... Sam, Pipsqueak..." she spluttered, still laughing. "Noology..." She stopped because she was choking. Burying her face in her hands she laughed and cried unashamedly.

Eventually, she looked up to find Wendy leaning over her. "Eva, you OK?"

"Yes," Standing behind Wendy, looking on, full of concern, were Sam and Pipsqueak. She composed herself and addressed her next words to them. "I'm not the only one that's *infected*. You're my Gemarchs."

They simply exchanged a look that said 'demented!'

"*Explain!*" Nice had run out of patience.

"How can I explain something I don't understand? I just know that they are... That bitch!"

"*What?*"

"Hontay! This is all happening because Billy isn't here."

"*Make sense Eva.*"

Taking a couple of deep breaths, she launched into her explanation. "You don't understand them, they're so conniving. It wasn't accidental. I'm beginning to understand how a fourth stage sapient can cause multiple outcomes..."

"*Well you've lost me.*"

"I'm going to kill her!"

"*A little less Redit and a little more woman, please.*" That was Krishna.

Yes, she felt that this was definitely the way to control it. "It's exactly what Kazuhiko suggested, an 'intelligence infection'. It wasn't an accident that Sam and Pipsqueak came up with the idea. Nor was it an accident they were the two who came over to me. She programmed it."

"*Pipsqueak, Sam?*" Nice demanded confirmation.

"Sounds like bollocks to me," Pipsqueak ventured.

"Sit down!"

Both Sam and Pipsqueak immediately sat on the floor. Having done so, they stared at each other. With their mouths making a big 'O' of surprise they, looked around the cockpit. Finally, their gaze came to rest on her.

"Call that bollocks, do you?" Calmly, she stared back at them as they got to their feet.

"*Eva, help us to get a handle on this. Are you saying that Hontay has turned you into a Redit?*"

"No, she can't... or, at least, I don't think she can do that. But she can make me react like a Redit. Figuring of course, that if I had my own Gemarchs, I'd leave hers alone. But it wasn't enough to just do it. Oh no, she had to let me know she'd done it. I'm definitely going to kill her!"

"But you said..." Cynthia started protesting.

"Don't you get it?! Redits never pass up a chance to aggravate another Redit."

"But you're not a Redit," Cynthia persisted.

It was so difficult to explain something that she now saw as clear as day. "I don't know *how*; I just know *why*."

"*Where and how does Billy fit into this?*" Nice's hologram had moved to stand directly in front of her.

It was so bloody obvious, why couldn't they see it? "Redits try to steal Gemarchs, but their number one priority is to keep their own Gemarchs. Connecting Sam and Pipsqueak to me is supposed to occupy me. Because they're being 'shared', I'm supposed to be fixated on that."

"*You said that it all had something to do with Billy not being here?*" Sun asked over the net.

"Hontay did it so I'd be less focussed on Billy. It's kicked in because he isn't here. If he were here, we wouldn't be aware of it."

"So, to summarise." Cynthia was head down, working away at her console again. "Hontay is, by methods unknown, making you behave Redit-like. Pipsqueak and Sam are part of the... package. All of this was done to distract you from her Gemarch, Billy. As long as he was present her 'scheme' worked. But now that he isn't here you've become aware of your connection to Pipsqueak and Sam. Is that correct?"

"Sam and Pipsqueak's connection to me," she corrected.

"You're doing it again," Erick protested. "You keep leaving Billy out of the equation. He wouldn't consent to a liaison with you Eva."

She sighed. "Redits aren't motivated by what Gemarchs would or wouldn't do - just other Redits' intentions."

"This is incredible," Mohammed muttered.

"So, what's going to happen when, and if, Billy returns?" Alfred asked.

Good question. "I don't know. All I know is that Hontay sees me as more Redit than woman."

"That's the one thing that doesn't add up. Why should Hontay create such a precarious situation?" Alfred pondered aloud.

"I think it was either that or kill me outright."

Nobody spoke for a couple of heartbeats, then Wendy said. "That's too extreme. I mean, we know that Billy wouldn't play."

"As I've said, it's not really about Billy, it's about me. If I made any moves towards him, I'd be fair game for her."

"Are you saying that Hontay did this to stop you from putting her in the position where she would have to kill you?" Cynthia asked incredulously.

"That's one way of looking at it."

Nice folded her hands and grinned. "*How do you feel about us?*" she said, implying *The Beast's* crew.

Eva shrugged.

"*Is that why you were less than helpful in finding a solution to our lack of men problem?*" Krishna gently teased.

"I suppose so. But lest we forget, I'm not really a Redit."

Looking serious Nice asked, "*Do you still want to be relieved of command?*"

"No."

"*Good. Now 2ic, get five men over here, soonest.*" Nice wasn't joking. Pausing she then grinned. "*We're not fussed if Pipsqueak or Sam isn't among them.*"

23

AGGRESSORS

"Alfred, Cynthia, Kazuhiko?" Sam's quiet entreaty came over the net.

Stirring from her light but anxious slumber, Cynthia opened her eyes. It was the sleeping period the lights had been dimmed. Hearing Alfred and Kazuhiko's prompt response surprised her. They should have been in a deep slumber after their excursion to *The Beast,* which meant that all the xenobiologists were too troubled to sleep properly. "Yes Sam," she answered.

"Sorry for the lateness of this but I think it's essential that I share my feelings about Eva." There was an embarrassed tone to Sam's voice. "I'd rather do it now, when..." he didn't seem able to explain further.

"We understand Sam," she reassured.

"I... I'd assumed that I was becoming fond of Eva..."

"Would you go as far as to say, 'In love with'?" Kazuhiko asked.

"No, nothing like that. I felt, just... a concern for her general well-being. It's only now, when I'm dozing off that the full strength of this *feeling* is becoming apparent."

"Didn't you feel this way, say, last night?" Hands dancing, she brought the hologram screen to life and noted Kazuhiko and Alfred doing likewise.

"No, but Billy was here then."

"OK, explain this *feeling*."

"Well, it's as I said; a concern for her well-being, not what I'd call romantic love. It's more a sense of 'if she's happy, then I'm happy'. However, it's quite intense."

Sensing understatement, she asked, "What do you mean by 'intense'?"

"Well, now I'm aware of it, it's almost impossible to ignore. It seems to permeate all levels of my consciousness. Even now, as I'm speaking, I can feel the pressure of it." He sounded like a man who was struggling to remain calm and logical.

"Can you describe the feeling?" Keeping the conversation analytical might help Sam to remain rational, she supposed.

"It's not that strange, actually. I'd say a pervasive desire to protect; it's almost paternal... No, not paternal, more avuncular, or perhaps sibship."

"Avuncular?" Kazuhiko voiced their collective confusion.

"Well, that's how I feel," Sam answered rather defensively.

"Granted you're not a Gemarch, but surely they don't feel avuncular or brotherly towards their Redits?" Kazuhiko gently pressed.

"I know this sounds strange, OK, but I've been giving it some thought. I suspect that sexual desire can only be initiated by Redits."

Pilot

Her data matrix on the Ig'tams tallied to 73 percent with Sam's assessment. High enough to be used as a basis for a working hypothesis. That still left another ticklish question unanswered. No way around it, she just had to bite the bullet. "If we assume that this is correct for Gemarchs, and that it also applies to you, what about Eva's ability to control you?"

Before Sam could answer, Alfred made a diplomatically weighted suggestion. "To get the maximum from this, perhaps we ought to include Pipsqueak, what do you think Sam?"

"Why not," he sounded relieved.

She connected Pipsqueak to their conference net. "Pipsqueak, you asleep?"

"Uh. What do you want Gabi?"

"It's Cynthia. You're on our conference net. We'd like your views on a number of issues."

"Couldn't this keep till my stint on the waiting rota?" came his very tired response.

"Sorry to wake you, but this is important." It was, but not so important that it couldn't wait - they were being inconsiderate and overzealous. With Billy away and Grim entertaining Nice and her crew, Pipsqueak had just done a double shift, or whatever they called it. "It won't take long."

"OK, what do you want?"

"We are exploring what I thought of as just a fondness for Eva. Now we realise that it's something deeper. How did...do you feel?" It was Sam who responded.

"Oh, I see what you mean. I'd put it down to her being a seriously good fuck. Now I'm just confused."

"What do you mean by 'confused'?" Alfred probed.

"Confused means confused. If we're her Gemarchs, how come I ain't lusting after her body?"

"So, what exactly are your feelings towards Eva?" Alfred continued.

"You sure this can't keep? Ah, what the hell, I'm awake now. If it's not an oxymoron, I feel I want that Truckie to be happy."

"That's it?"

"Yeah, that's it."

That seemed to tie-in with Sam's explanation. "What's your opinion about her ability to dominate you?"

"Lady, you're talking to a Flyboy from the Air Force's Ace Crew II, not somebody's lap dog. She can't dominate me!"

Obviously, she'd hit a nerve. But, just then, she wasn't inclined towards massaging inflated egos. "You used the term 'lap dog' - when she said sit, you sat. So, what's your explanation?"

Pipsqueak didn't immediately respond, instead, it was Sam who offered a tentative answer. "I don't think it's a case of domination. We did as she asked without thinking. I suspect that it will always be our instinctive reaction, but I'm sure that we haven't lost our volition."

"Yeah," Pipsqueak agreed. "That's the first and last time she does that."

As Cynthia took a few moments to collate this information, Alfred asked, "How do you foresee your future relationship with her?"

She stopped what she was doing to listen attentively.

"Which one of us are you asking," Pipsqueak asked.

"Both of you?"

"OK. I for one don't see any change. There's no reason for anything to change," Pipsqueak said flippantly.

"Alfred, to get a true picture perhaps we should ask Eva. She, at least, seems more aware on a conscious level," Kazuhiko was equally flippant.

That seemed like a capital idea. However, they must learn to temper their enthusiasm to unravel the puzzle. Waking Pipsqueak, as they had, might explain his impertinence. "When is she on watch...?"

"I'm on now. And yes, I've been listening; something I learned from Billy. So, what do you want to know?" Eva's amused voice came over the conference net.

She shouldn't have been surprised, but she was. "Eavesdropping seems to be a military pastime. You could start by giving us an assessment of our conclusions thus far."

"Sure. First, let's remember that I'm not a Redit and they're not Gemarchs. Second, their bond to me, and vice versa, is nothing like Billy and Hontay's. The bitch only engineered it to be strong enough to deflect my attention from Billy."

Was Eva aware of the venom in her pronunciation of the word 'bitch'? "Engineered?"

"Absolutely, a deliberate act of malice. Look, she's given me some insight into this. Not through any thought of kindness, I might add, it's just to rub salt in the wound. I think she can see that in 'some other universe' I get it together with Billy..."

"But I thought she said our theories of a multiverse are wrong?" Kazuhiko interrupted.

"They probably are," Eva snapped. "But she saw with her multiple outcomes eyes, or whatever sapiency does, that Billy and me were a possibility. So, she cut that route off, then let me know about it. Bitch!"

"Are you that hung-up on Billy?" Sam asked, sounding a little hurt.

"I'm less hung-up on Billy than I am on you and Pipsqueak," Eva replied tenderly.

Was either of them aware that they were speaking to each other like children? "Right. But Eva, does this *insight* help to explain how she managed it?"

"No, not really, but there's nothing to stop me making a wild guess. The bond between her and Billy is instinctive, she can't control it. I think what she did with us was to play around with our psyche."

"How?"

"I don't know how. Perhaps she did it by interfering with our perceptions."

"OK. What will happen to the three of you now?" Alfred seemed excited.

"Lots of sex, I hope. In fact, my stint finishes at 03:59, want to pay a visit then Sam?"

This was too much. "I meant..."

"I know what you meant Cynthia. It's a little while since I've had a portion, OK?" Eva paused, taking the heat out of the situation. "There's a sort of 'connection' between the three of us, but I don't think much will change. Except perhaps me feeling a little jealous when they match up with someone else."

"Eva, I don't want to appear rude, but that does not stack-up with your earlier emotional outburst," Alfred cut to the quick.

"Oh, come on. I didn't have an emotional outburst, it was shock. The sudden impact of Hontay giving me a taste of what it really feels like to be a Redit - just so I'd know the score. It's past."

"What did it feel like?" Now this was something worth knowing.

"Believe it or not, you already have a pretty good idea what it feels like Cynthia."

She didn't believe that. "How so?"

"Well, you know how you get that prickling sensation in the nape of the neck an instant before Flet or Hontay appears? That's part of it, they sort of broadcast their intentions."

"What prickling sensation? I'm sorry, but I don't see it that way," Kazuhiko disagreed.

"Being a mere man, you wouldn't," Eva laughed.

"I see what you mean Eva." She'd noticed that the men didn't seem to have the same reactions to the appearance of the Ig'tams, perhaps not Ig'tams but Redits. "I also get a sense of... What would you call it...? The appropriate forms. Do you think that this is the Ig'tam equivalent to body language?"

"Absolutely. But there's more to it than that. From the little I understand I can see that it's quite complex, I think of it as Redit to Redit etiquette. An interesting aspect of it is that one Redit never passes up the opportunity to pique another. Which means that Redits are constantly watching their... Shit!"

"Eva! What's the matter?"

"It's Billy, he's back."

Looking up through the dim light, she saw Eva standing in her womb. There seemed to be a flurry of activity amongst the flight crew. She considered going over but changed her mind. "Anne, report on what's happening on the flight deck."

'Billy has reappeared in his womb. He is semiconscious and suffering from: exhaustion, dehydration, calcium, zinc and iron deficiency, and internal bleeding. Eva has instructed me to rectify the deficiencies and repair his injuries.'

"How serious are these injuries?"

'They are not very serious. However, it will take about eighteen hours for the nano engines to help his body to repair the damaged tissues causing the internal bleeding. He also needs to rest.'

"What caused the injuries?" She was almost afraid to ask.

'The injuries are consistent with those caused by intercourse with Hontay, only more severe.'

This she simply had to see, for professional reasons of course. Easing herself out of the womb, she had a quick look around. Most of the crew were asleep, but Billy's womb was surrounded by the entire flight crew. As she strolled over, she heard Mohammed quietly baiting Billy, "...handle it, you should have called in the reserves."

'Billy needs to rest.'

"Keep this up and I'll get her to let loose a Redit on *your* arse," was Billy's weak response.

"If that would reunite me will my balls, I'm sure I could endure."

"Yeah! Too right," Grim agreed. "How did they manage it?"

"You're asking me that question like you expect me to have a possible explanation." Billy seemed drained of energy.

"But you definitely have them?" Grim persisted.

"Yes. Now leave me alone."

Trying to be unobtrusive she stopped on the outside of the crowd and attempted to get a look at Billy. All she could see was the backs of flying suits.

'Billy needs to rest.'

"Sure thing Anne. Now, Chief," John was making a bad job of whispering, "I can't get my head round this dehydration thing. I mean, there's only so much liquid a female can 'milk'. Or have Redits got some innovative moves?"

This, she thought, was an interesting question.

"Fuck off and die John."

"Captain, I should like to know the answer to that question."

Faces turned to look at her, then a path was made for her to walk up to the womb. Moving forward she saw in the light reflected from the instruments that Billy's face looked drawn, as if he'd lost several kilos in weight.

'Billy needs to rest.'

"Not you as well Cynthia."

"I thought it pertinent to assess the physical effects before your recovery."

"Really? What was it you wanted to know?"

"Why are you dehydrated?" she managed to ask without laughing.

"Redits are hot. Forty-seven degrees hot. So, you sweat buckets."

'Billy, you must rest.'

"Hear that? I must rest. Go away all of you, I'll tell you about it tomorrow."

"No, you won't," Mohammed protested.

"You're right, I won't, but go away just the same."

Disappointed, they all drifted back to their wombs. She settled down to compile her report.

***

Peeeeuuuuuuuuuuwwwwwwwwwwwwwww!

He bolted upright, wide awake in his womb.

Peeeeuuuuuuuuuuwwwwwwwwwwwwwwww!

'Alert! Alert! Energy discharges, half a parsec, 1075/0148/2251, coming this way, fast.'

"Baddest, *launch quick reaction Darts and stand by to boogie,* The Beast *will lead,*" Nice ordered.

Donning helmet and gloves, he was checking the screens when Anne added, 'All weapons systems online. Preecha, your PADE suit is not sealed. Get your helmet on Kazuhiko!'

"Nice, I'm home, but you take it," Billy transmitted.

"*Roger Billy, get those Darts out!*"

"Navs ready, got the energy discharges on screen... Bloody hell! That's impossible!" Grim exclaimed.

"*Darts gone,*" Sun confirmed.

"Roger Sun, stay close," Eva ordered.

Mohammed gaped at his screen; it was telling him that something approximating to a Blue Giant star, some 150 times the size of the sun, had appeared out of nowhere and was closing on them at just below the speed of light. As his brain tried to make sense of this Nice barked, "*It's coming straight at us!* Baddest, *break and boogie!*"

The Beast broke right and climbed, he and Billy took *Baddest* left and down. The instruments showed the Blue Giant splitting into two. Inexplicably, each new star had the same circumference and mass as the original and, disturbingly, each star seemed locked onto a ship.

"Oh shit!" That was Wendy.

While they accelerated hard, the two Blue Giants continued to close.

'Nineteen seconds to impact.'

"Sun, stand by for programmed super-light jump."

"*Roger Billy, please get us out of here!*" was Sun's hurried supplication.

'Twelve seconds to impact.'

"Come on Navs... Navs?!" Eva screamed.

"Coordinates in!"

"Super-light, go!"

'The super-light drives have activated, but we are still in normal spacetime. Five seconds to impact.'

"Baddest *we can't jump, our drives...*" Nice's voice was swamped out by static.

'Impa...'

Mohammed expected his last conscious thought to be of *Baddest* vaporised. But as the Blue Giant engulfed the ship, all that happened was that the lights and instruments went down. The cockpit should have been as dark as the darkest night, but he could see as clear as day. In fact, he could see better than that; everything had taken on a dazzling blue-white luminescence. It took him several moments to realise that, actually, he could see *right through* his consul, the bulkheads, the walls of the ship, into the Blue Giant, and out to the stars beyond. It was as if *Baddest* and its contents consisted of the same insubstantial material as the star.

He sensed that time wasn't running as it should. He wasn't sure if it had slowed or speeded up. It was like hearing a discordant note but not knowing if it was pitched too low or too high, just that it was out of tune. He turned around to look back at Wendy. Through her helmet he saw her staring at him, her face was a ghostly transparent mask of fear; mouth opening and closing, but no sound coming out. Hesitantly, her hand reached for his shoulder. It wavered, then continued on to touch him. Horrified, he watched as her hand passed unimpeded thought his flying suit, and then his flesh. Every bone, muscle, vein, and capillary in her arm was visible. Even her blood, pulsating along the arteries could be seen.

Wendy's eyes suddenly flashed to the left and he turned to follow her gaze. Billy's flying suit and helmet were as indistinct as everything else but, inside, Billy himself had faded to almost nonexistence. Also seeing this, Eva tried to stand but her feet simply passed through the bottom of her womb. Startled, she tried to counterbalance and fell, through her womb, through her console, through Billy. She tumbled, ever so slowly, towards the front of the cockpit. Drifting helplessly, with nothing to halt her motion, she was heading towards the insubstantial shell of the ship. Mohammed's brain struggled to comprehend what his eyes were telling him: Eva had inertia, but like the rest of the ship, no mass. That was absurd!

Billy's flying suit (it was no longer obvious whether he was still inside) started making downward waving gestures, signalling to the rest of the crew: stay put! Keep still! Mohammed's speculation about Billy's presence, or otherwise, was confirmed as the waving motion stopped. There was an empty phantom flying suit in the Captain's womb. Much too long after-the-fact, it occurred to him that this must be what death was like. Not a sudden nothingness, but a slow and gradual dissipation into entropy. Of course, it all made perfect sense. In a few moments there would be nothing left of any of them.

With the realisation that these thoughts were nothing more than the residue of a past consciousness came a calmness. He felt it appropriate to use these few last moments to reflect on the question of whether or not there was a God. He didn't believe there was, *but* if there was, He/She/It ought to be making an appearance around, well, now really. He could see so clearly, out beyond the ship, past the Blue Giant, almost to infinity. There was one of the Darts. He wasn't sure where the other Darts or *The Beast* was, nor could he see anything that could pass for The Supreme Being.

Something at the periphery of his vision caught his attention. He guessed it was towards the centre of the Blue Giant. It was difficult to gauge scale or distance but, here, the blue-white light was considerably brighter. Somehow it was bluer and at the same time whiter, like an almost unimaginably intense cold heat. It was so bright that he should have shielded his eyes (if he could). The source of the brightness didn't seem to be moving relative to *Baddest*. What was it? What generated it? If this was God, then He/She/It was a spectacular disappointment.

He changed his focus back to the immediate surroundings. Eva had drifted almost to the edge of the cockpit. She was thrashing about wildly, trying to stop herself from wafting out into the... whatever it was. He could see that she was screaming but, of course, he couldn't hear. He wanted to tell her to relax, after all, they were already dead. That sparked a thought, possibly his last. Could he talk? He attempted to say, 'My name is Mohammed

Amma Ashad.' His mouth opened and closed. His lips formed the words. But his ears didn't hear, nor did he feel his diaphragm contracting or vibrations in his larynx - there was no air in his lungs. Why should there be? He was dead.

At that moment everything seemed to become noticeably less substantial. Turning to have one last look around the cockpit, by way of a final goodbye to his crewmates, he spotted Sam who was out of his womb and thrashing about as wildly as Eva. He figured Sam was trying to get to her, but the xenobiologist was drifting in the opposite direction. Turning to look at the Navs, as he expected, there was Pipsqueak, also out of his womb, doing a crazy breaststroke in midair and getting nowhere fast. Well, if you're going to fade out of existence, why not go out laughing your head off?

***

'Eva, please remain calm. Think of yourself, as being a disembodied intelligence.'

It was Hontay's voice... no, not voice... thought. She had been deprived of all senses, but she could still think. Interesting. 'Where am I?'

'You can think of yourself as being in N-space although, in reality, there is no such thing. Suffice it to say, you are everywhere and nowhere.'

That almost made sense. 'What's happening? What has happened?'

'You are being held here by the aggressors. They are now aware that humans are not sapient but have discovered that you have made contact with us, so they've put you on ice, so to speak.'

She wondered if Hontay was deliberately pissing her about, then she remembered Billy saying something along the lines of "if humans saw any action it meant that the sapinents had been thumped by the aggressors". 'Have we lost? '

'The battles have not yet started.'

She was about to demand more information, when it hit; why the hell was Hontay talking to her, why not Billy...?!

'I need your help. I need Billy.'

A Redit was asking for help from another, albeit honorary, Redit - this must be serious. 'How can I help you and why do you need Billy?'

'We now have some understanding of the aggressors. They operate on female/male parings. To combat them, so must we. They've removed the mechanism from Billy's belt. I need you to tell him to find it and replace it.'

'I don't underst...? ' She was suddenly overwhelmed with information about opposites: yin and yang, light and dark, hot and cold. Apparently, that was what fifth stage sapiency was all about - making opposites coexist. The fifth stagers were, and used, opposing forces. The Milky Way sapients could generate multiple outcomes, the aggressors could go far beyond that. As she grappled with the idea of positive and negative charges coexisting, she got a sense that Hontay's explanation was a gross oversimplification. Even so, she could appreciate the significance of matter and anti-matter without mutual annihilation.

'I don't know where he is, or how to...'

'He is with you, think of him.'

'Can you get us out... of here?'

'Yes, but not now.'

She got the impression that rescuing a handful of humans was an exceedingly low priority. 'When?'

'Time has no meaning where you are. Give Billy my message.'

She felt Hontay's abrupt departure. There was so much she wanted to know. So, she was a disembodied intelligence, was she? Really? If that were so, why could she smell cinnamon? 'Billy?'

Pilot

'Yeah.'

It was so weird, feeling his thoughts. 'Hontay has told me we've been placed in some kind of stasis by the aggressors. She wants you to find your belt. Can you tell where it is?'

There was a longish pause before he answered. 'I'm not sure... maybe. Are they trying to get us out?'

'No.' She'd let him mull that over.

'Didn't think they would. OK, she wants me to find the belt and then what?' He seemed ridiculously calm.

'What she actually said was that they have removed the "mechanism" from the belt. That's what she wants you to find and put back. Does that make any sense to you?'

'Yes, what else did she say?'

If they were communicating telepathically, why did it feel as if they were speaking? With Hontay it hadn't been like that. And why was there such a strong smell of cinnamon? 'That was it. Why didn't you think they'd get us out?'

'Bait.'

'Bait?'

'Yeah, if they wanted the new players to show their hand, what better way than to leave out a small offering.'

'You mean, Hontay knew and...?'

'No. If she knew about the game plan then, at some point, I'd know. But think about it, when we got to the sphere of operation we should've gone to electronic silence, shouldn't we?'

That made sense. Their orders shouldn't have specified super-light silence or even radio silence, but no radiation of any kind - electronic silence. 'Was that how they found us?'

'Yep.'

'How? Our radio transmissions couldn't have travelled more than a couple of light hours.' Not seeing or being able to move was becoming maddening.

'Still thinking non-sapiently, aren't you? These boys have got keen eyesight.'

'How can you be sure, and why are you so... relaxed?'

'Say you were checking out a civilisation at the Stone Age level of development. Then you came across a native with a knife made of tungsten carbide. You'd give that native some extra attention, wouldn't you? Well, I was the native and the belt was the knife. From the kinds of questions I was being asked, I was able to figure out what was going down.'

'You were interrogated?'

'I'd hardly call it that, it was more like tinkering around in my head. These guys aren't menacing, well, not to us at any rate.'

'Are you saying you've "communicated" with a couple of giant suns?'

'They're heavyweights, but I don't think those suns are a manifestation of them or their life force. I'm pretty sure that at some point, way back, they were a carbon-based life form.'

'You mean that wasn't them?'

'Yes and no. I mean that literally; it was, but it wasn't. I suppose they showed us something we could recognise. Eva, we've tasted the fourth stage, haven't we? Believe me, this is something well past that. And I think I've got a handle on this suppression business.'

He sounded like he'd gone well past awe. 'Yes, and?'

'Well, I don't think they're really after the sapients. But just by being in the neighbourhood they upset the locals. My best guess is that they take over the *states* where the sapients normally hangout.'

'But wasn't the sapients' original plan, to hide?"

"Yes, but I don't think it was to hide physically. Probably more a case of hiding their sapiency. How? Dunno.'

'What now?'

'The belt, I can tell it's around here some place.'

'Can you see?'

'No. You're not going to believe this, but that belt's "mechanism" is almost a living thing. I can feel its life force just like I can feel yours.'

'You can *feel* my life force?!'

'Sure. Can't you feel mine?'

Now that she thought about it, she could. 'Billy, I was too scared to ask, but why didn't Hontay come to you direct?'

'Smart move that. She must have figured that I wouldn't be wearing it, without it she'd just fry my brain.'

She hadn't thought of that. 'But she didn't fry mine.'

'That's because you're not her husband; you ain't *connected* to her.'

'Oh...! Can you smell cinnamon?'

'Cinnamon?'

'Yes, there's a strong smell of cinnamon.'

'I can't smell anything. I think your mind is playing tricks on you... Here it is. What's going to happen when I connect with it?'

'I don't know. Can you feel the presence of the rest of the crew?'

'Yes of course, can't you?'

As soon as she thought about it, there they were. 'I can now.'

But Billy was no longer there.

24

THE SHIP

This was definitely alien, but exactly 1 G? That seemed improbable. From horizon to horizon there was nothing to see except purple grassland. The grass shimmered and was a uniform height, coming up to just under his armpits. A pervasive smell of polished wood, tinged with burnt rubber, wafted on the gentle breeze. The cloudless sky was a strange colour: yellowish green. Despite the dazzling brightness bathing the landscape, the local star providing this odd-looking daylight wasn't in the sky. Turning slowly, he scanned the surroundings; none of the planets he'd ever hit downside was anything like this. Apart from the eerie colours the uniformity of the terrain said 'artificial'. He suddenly understood that this was the outside of the Ig'tam ship. A ship the size of a respectable planet. Interesting.

He wasn't the least bit surprised when Hontay appeared before him. Like him, she was dressed in a one-piece suit. But her all-important belt was missing and her pseudolimbs were coiled around her waist. He got the sensation that she was hungry, and uncomfortable. Hunger, that was pretty straightforward. Uncomfortable? It had something to do with the gruelling burden of her body striving to accommodate a semi-alien foetus. He also got the sensation that she was only partially secondarily fertilised and sorting this was one of her priorities. After all the bonking they'd done, how come she was only partially fertilised? Because his millions and millions of sperms could only survive in her body for minutes, as opposed to the days they could stay alive inside a woman.

While he busily locked inside his head struggling to think of a tactful way of crying off, she suddenly turned away from him. The hairs on the nape of his neck prickled with tension. Without warning, she sprinted off. Inexplicably he found himself running, flat-out, on a parallel but slightly divergent course. Head down; leaning forward; arms outstretched; her gait was smooth, powerful, and consisted of great leaping strides. Cutting a swathe through the grass, she covered the ground with mind numbing speed; no doubt about it, her distant ancestors had walked on all fours. Why the hell was he running?!

Four hundred yards ahead of her about a dozen odd looking animals, the same colour as the grass, suddenly erupted from their camouflage and scattered. They moved like kangaroos, but each hop they took was in excess of 100 yards as they glided, bobbing, just above the grass. Too far away and moving too fast to make out details, he guessed that each animal was about the size of a cow. Subconsciously, he named them grasshoppers.

Abruptly, Hontay, who was now over a mile away, changed direction and accelerated. Leaping she seemed to collide with a grasshopper, as it reached the top of its hop. They fell into the grass and disappeared.

Still at an all-out dash, he changed course; although he couldn't see her, he knew exactly where she was. Suddenly the grasshopper, with Hontay clinging to its back, suddenly shot 50 feet into the air. Twisting violently, and obviously trying to shake her off, it crashed back to the ground. With Hontay's body to add scale, he reappraised; the grasshopper was actually about twice the size of a cow. Then the sound of the animal reached him; as alien as it was, there was no mistaking its dying bellow. With Hontay still hanging on to its back, again, it burst into the air but this time not so high. And again, it crashed back to the ground.

He was now close enough to see a huge area of flattened grass, and rising dust, where the grasshopper was rolling about brutishly, trying to crush Hontay - she stayed put. It wasn't lost on him that she was clamped to the beast in the same way that she'd clung to him; arms, pseudolimbs and legs.

Still a couple of hundred yards away from the battle, he stopped. Or, more accurately, Hontay told him to stop; the grasshopper wasn't yet subdued. He looked on as the animal slowly went through its last dying rights, the shrieking and wailing reducing to a hoarse pathetic braying. Rolling with steadily decreasing fervour, it eventually came to rest on its side, its six legs shuddering spasmodically.

After several minutes he knew it was safe to approach. Hontay was hunched over the grasshopper's body, which was segmented like a worm's. Its front and rear limbs were long and powerful, whilst the limbs in the middle were more delicate. Though still longer and thicker than his arms and tapered at the ends, it was clear that the mid-limbs were used for manipulation. As he moved towards the beast it occurred to him that the planet on which the Ig'tams had evolved... he searched for a name, but nothing came... seem to produce animals with a propensity for six limbs. Getting nearer still, he saw long claws on the fore and hind legs which were jointed, much the same as a hedgehog's. Evidently so that the animal could stay low in the grass - he was looking at a predator.

This was confirmed when he trotted over to them. Fangs showed in the animal's partly open mouth. Looking over the bulky carcass, he was eventually able to discern how the huge grasshopper had managed to move as fast and gracefully as it had; by compressing its segmented body like a spring. Staring down at the grasshopper he couldn't think of a terrestrial animal that would have stood a chance against it. Now he understood Hontay's tactics; the only way to avoid its teeth and claws was to be on its back. Somehow, he knew, without getting anything from Hontay, that this creature wouldn't run from anything other than an Ig'tam, a female Ig'tam.

So intent was he on the grasshopper that when Hontay bared and sank her teeth into the animal's hide he jumped back in astonishment. Her teeth were smaller than the grasshopper but had that same terrifying terrible canine pattern - Ig'tams and grasshoppers were distant relatives. Appalled, he watched as she used those teeth to tear off a long strip of skin, exposing, rich purple, still quivering flesh. His nostrils were assailed by a pungent stench, like rotting garbage mixed with sulphur.

Spitting out the skin from her blood-splattered mouth, she tore off more strips. He gagged with nausea. Ignoring him, she straightened her fingers and stabbed both hands into the flesh. Belatedly he noted her pseudolimbs also buried deep into the beast. Straining to force her hands further into the carcass, she ripped off a piece of fibrous looking meat and chewed at it voraciously. Just as he reached the point where he thought he was definitely going to be sick a sudden calmness overtook him. This was how Ig'tams ate - only fresh meat. Nutrition was absorbed directly through hands and pseudolimbs, as well as the more human digestive tract via the mouth. All well and good, but she was slowly being covered with the strange looking blood. This info about Ig'tam eating habits was stuff he already had filed somewhere in his brain. And with this he realised that even if he were to be overcome by some sudden madness and wanted to join her in her feast, he couldn't; it would be difficult for a human to digest this meat. Plus, his metabolism wouldn't be able to cope with either the venom or anti-venom she'd injected from her pseudolimbs, the faintest trace of either would kill him in a matter of seconds.

Fine, but why slaughter a living breathing creature? Surely Ig'tams could manufacture their food... Wasn't Hontay injured? As soon as he thought about it, he knew that she wasn't. More than that, she hadn't even sustained a graze from the grasshopper's furious endeavours... Redits were killing machines. Much after the fact, this was now obvious. Was it obvious? Hontay was feeding him information. Or, more accurately, she was activating selected bits of information in his brain; bringing them to the fore, so to speak. Redits were the hunters; they brought down prey for their Gemarchs and their... Oids... They also went to great lengths to avoid other Redit-led hunting parties. What if the Gemarchs didn't...? The answer surfaced as the question formed: Gemarchs hunted without their Redits but they'd never dream of tackling anything like a grasshopper.

Mouth stuffed full of meat, Hontay nodded in a pretty human-like gesture, indicating that she wanted him to squat opposite her. This was Redit instinct; concern that her Gemarch shouldn't end up as a titbit for some other predator. Complying, he sat cross-legged. This close and the stench was almost overpowering. Finely balance between utter disgust and calm understanding, he stared at her over the bulk of the butchered animal. He really ought to be utterly terrified of her.

"How much are you going to eat?" He'd know the answer by simply thinking about it, but the scene was taking on an almost hypnotically surreal and macabre quality. Talking helped to break the spell.

She obviously understood because after she finished chewing, she said, "I am almost finished. I've absorbed the equivalent of about 3700 calories."

God! He'd never get used to *that* voice. Along with her answer he got that this would only last her a couple of days. "Do you always hunt...? You're pregnant!" He shot to his feet and immediately felt lightheaded.

Although she couldn't laugh, she conveyed her hilarity - it could only take this long to register in a non-sapient brain. "Yes Daddy, mother and baby are doing fine. Now, sit please."

As he slumped to the ground, he realised that she was definitely pandering to a man. A Gemarch wouldn't react like this, he'd be aware of it the instant she became pregnant. As the shock of being an expectant father finally registered, he sensed an undefined tension beginning to build between them. It was almost as if the air around them was rapidly becoming electrically charged - he could feel the hairs on his arms and on the back of his neck bristling. She sat there, calmly regarding him through dark unblinking eyes. He got a sense that if she wanted to, she could explain what was happening, but this time she was going to leave him to figure it out for himself. The tension continued to grow to an intense level and, as it did, apparently, so did her feeling of impatience.

Eventually it all started making sense, she was a primarily fertilised Redit, who wanted to be administered to as a primarily fertilised Redit. Slowly untangling herself from the grasshopper, she stepped over the carcass and stood in front of him. He sat there looking up at her knowing that there was no way he could stand for a couple of hours with her wrapped around him - he wasn't a Gemarch. But that was exactly what she wanted. No zero-G, no messing about, she wanted to be secondarily fertilised, and she wanted to be secondarily fertilised now!

Slowly getting to his feet, he stared up into those unreadable eyes; there was something almost predatory in the way she looked at him. OK, this was a challenge, and he was going to do it if it killed him. He sensed that he should stand with his feet further apart. As he started shifting his weight, she made their clothes vanish. He had an erection yet at the same time he was trembling with trepidation, how much did she weigh?

In zero-G she'd seized him with her pseudolimbs first, and then enveloped him with her arms and legs. This time, as she stepped up to him, it was arms around his neck; pseudolimbs around his waist; then she placed all her weight on his shoulders and lifted her legs to clamp them around his thighs. She moved slightly to facilitate penetration; he knew that she was being particularly gentle, if he'd been a real Gemarch she'd have been a damn-sight more businesslike.

God, she was heavy. No way. No fucking way was he going to be able to do this. As she tightened her grip with the pseudolimbs he could tell that she was laughing. Here he was, a fine specimen of the human male, surely, he ought to be able to stand like this for a mere hour or two. Slowly it dawned on him what she was finding so amusing and why; she was already primarily fertilised, she didn't need hours of sex to bring her to oestrous. All she needed was for him to ejaculate, and she could make him do that whenever she wanted to.

Was it just her, or did all Redits like taking the piss...?

Searing pain shot through his midriff as she suddenly tightened the grip of her pseudolimbs. Wincing he would've doubled-up in agony if he wasn't already embraced in a Redit's bear-hug. The pain was so intense that he didn't notice that he was about to come/was coming/had come.

"All right, all right. Get off!" he whimpered as his knees almost sagged.

She didn't get off, but the pressure of the pseudolimbs slackened, a bit - she was definitely taking the piss.

"Darling," she said, in what he supposed was her attempt at a soothing tone, "I'm going to give you something akin to an Ig'tam kiss."

With the same suddenness the pseudolimbs tightened, but this time all he felt was intense euphoria washing over him. Incredibly, he ejaculated again. Lights danced in front of his eyes; he was floating on ecstasy while drowning in pleasure. It felt as if he was having a genuine out-of-body experience. Feeling himself going limp, he keeled over.

Whatever she was doing to him eventually eased off. Somewhat dazed, he found himself crumpled on the ground, drooling profusely, with Hontay still wrapped around him. Despite this he was rather disappointed that she'd stopped. Panting heavily, it took him some time to focus on his wife and the surroundings.

She released him and in an ungainly sort of way stood up. It took him a ridiculous length of time to simply sit up. After that, all he could manage was to stare at her open mouthed. She couldn't laugh, but she was definitely laughing at him. Under the laughter he sensed a mild frustration. Frustration? Of course, playing around with each other's pleasure centres was the Ig'tam's more direct approach to petting. Unfortunately, he couldn't get into her head, well, not *directly*. Moreover, she had to be sparing about how frequently she 'kissed' him. This was exceedingly addictive - to a human.

Summoning up the remainder of his dignity he said, "I'm afraid you'll have to settle for a good old-fashioned human kiss."

As he shakily got to his feet, he realised that kissing her when she'd been in feeding mode might not be a smart move - her lips would simply absorb nutrition from his. He continued to rise. There was only so much humiliation that the masculine ego could take. Sticking out his chest, he nonchalantly stepped up to her. Her face wasn't as expressive as a human's, but she was giving him a look of curious amusement. Even if he went up on tiptoes, he couldn't reach far enough to kiss her. Effortlessly taking him under the armpits, she raised him until their heads were level. Then she snarled, showing her full set of fangs. Ignoring this, he leant forward and kissed her.

She didn't sink her fangs into his flesh, nor did he suddenly feel drained of energy. In fact, the only thing that happened was she returned his kiss with a closed mouth. How come he didn't taste the grasshopper's blood on her lips? Because, although apparently naked, he was sealed in an Ig'tam space suit. He was surrounded by a body-hugging semipermeable field, tuned to him. Any harmful matter or energy that came into contact with it was either repelled or converted to something harmless. Not only that, when wearing it he would always be subjected to gravity at 1 G. Interesting. An invisible space suit, with its own gravity regulator, that you didn't have to take off to have a shag. How was that possi...? Apparently, it was possible; he could piss, shit, even spit, whilst wearing it. Was she also wearing a suit? Was that why she wasn't hurt? No. That was incred...!

"Was that a demonstration of the 'male ego'?" she asked as she put him down.

"What?"

"A man displaying absence of fear, especially fear of his mate?"

She was toying with him. He stuck out his chest even more.

"And I suppose a certain degree of passivity and compliance is expected of his mate?"

She was definitely toying with him. "Only if she's that way inclined."

An image of a pair of lion cubs, playing rather boisterously, came into his mind. What was she trying to tell him? That Redits and their Gemarchs relaxed by wrestling each other. No, more than that: good food and great sex, now, how about a romp. A Redit - relentless, remorseless slaughterer - could also be frolicsome, but *only* with her Gemarchs. She would normally be outnumbered by them by at least eight to one, and yet she would usually win. So, here he was, wearing an Ig'tam space suit, which made him almost invulnerable, what was he waiting for? Give it his best shot.

Facing her as he was, the most obvious route of attack was the direct one. He lunged with the intention of knocking her back and pinning her to the ground. As his shoulder impacted against dense muscle, she did move back. In fact, she rolled all the way back and over, pulling him with her. With a consummate ease and a certain grace, she was now sitting on him, pseudolimbs around his wrists, pinning them to the ground. Pleasure centres in both their brains were enjoying this.

Just how strong were those pseudolimbs? Reaching up, with one hand, he grabbed her arm and yanked to his right. Again, she offered no resistance and rolled in the direction of his pull. But keeping her pseudolimbs locked around his wrists, she neatly pulled him on top of her and continued the roll. They ended up just where they had started, with Hontay on top. How the hell are you supposed to wrestle someone when they know every move you're going to make before you make it...? He got the feeling that he shouldn't stop trying...

This time he began to move to his left, like he was going for another roll. Suddenly, he arched his back and threw her off. Rolling away, he scrambled to his feet in time to see her already upright, coming low and fast, and about to hit him at waist-height. Dropping, he took her legs out from under her and dived on her back. Arms around her neck, legs around her waist, he clung to her like she had to the grasshopper. Just like the grasshopper, she leapt into the air, twisting and trying to shake him off, before crashing back down. She landed right on top of him with a heavy 'thud'. He was pretty sure that if he hadn't been wearing the suit, he would now have several broken ribs.

It was abundantly clear that she could easily prise his arms and legs off her. But that was far too easy. Instead, she continued to snap, snarl, leap, twist, land, and roll. All he had to do was hang on until she tired - easier said than done. At one point, she went up, twisted viciously through God knows how many degrees and he found himself, arms and legs flailing, flying through the air. He landed on his head and couldn't believe he hadn't broken his neck. Dizzily he got back to his feet.

She hit him from behind with such force that he cut a neat swathe as he sailed through the long grass. Landing some twenty feet away, he found himself staring up at the strange looking sky. Then he saw her, a maroon shadow, a good thirty, or maybe forty feet up in the air, falling like a stone - falling on him. Slamming into him she had him spreadeagled, pinning his hands with hers, pseudolimbs tight around his neck. So, this was what passed for Ig'tam cavorting. Great! He knew he wasn't hurt, she wouldn't deliberately hurt him, but it was also pretty obvious that if she wanted to, she could snap his spine without too much effort.

"Have you ever considered taking up the pole vault? I mean, without a pole."

"I could leap higher if I wasn't 'with child'. It's funny, don't you think, you finding this behaviour primitive?"

Primitive? Oh, of course, she even knew his subconscious thoughts. Now, here was something else that had been bothering him. Why were Ig'tams so damn physical when they had such phenomenal mental power? Surely, she could have zapped, or whatever, the grasshopper?

"Billy, we only eat when we are hungry. Our digestive system is only stimulated by hunting. If I were hungry and you gave me a steak, I couldn't eat it. A cow in a field, now, that's a different proposition."

He considered the evolutionary implications of this. Did it mean that Ig'tam genes were sure that their carriers would always be able to catch food on the hoof? This might go some way to explaining why Redits were so deadly. That didn't explain everything, he supposed that was because of the human expectation that if you were intelligent, you didn't need to be so physical.

She got off him and pulled him to his feet. "My non-sapient husband, it is far more complicated and, at the same time, much simpler than you think. You equate being human with being intelligent. Humans were human long before they became intelligent. Intelligence was only an accident. What you perceive and pursue as 'intelligence' is only an attempt to stop being yourselves."

He opened his mouth to ask a question, but she continued, "Your physical bodies aren't just vehicles to transport your intellect. The purpose of your intellect is to aid your physical body in the task of survival. Your physical and mental *states* are part and parcel of the greater whole - one is useless without the other."

He pondered this. "OK, but surely that doesn't apply to you, a fourth stage sapient, does it?"

"No, it doesn't. Think of it as a different set of rules applying." Then she did something that took him completely by surprise. She put her arm around his shoulders, and gently pulled him to her, very much in the way a man would to a woman: a very tall man, with a very short woman. "Because we sapients occupy many *states,* we need to give particular attention to our physical selves."

He didn't understand, and he knew he never would. "OK, if you say so."

"I do say so." Playfully making a point of bending down to do it, she kissed him lightly on the lips.

"That's not bad for a nonhuman. I suppose French is out of the question?"

"These are razor sharp." She gave a shocking grin, displaying a mouthful of fangs. "It's not just French kisses that are out of the question."

Did she have a genuine sense of humour, or was it just that she was super intelligent? "I hear that!"

Pilot

Reaching down to take his hand she said, "Let's go for a stroll."

A pretty human thing to do. Except that, he wasn't used to having to almost run to keep up. This was silly, he felt like a child going for a walk with its mother. "Nouns and telepathy are generally incompatible. Nouns are a function of language. Language is a function of intelligence. Telepathy is a function of sapiency and has nothing to do with language or intelligence."

What the hell was she trying to tell him? "Do you mean that sapiency can exist without intelligence?"

"No, but in the sense you mean it, yes. However, what I mean is this: there are many things that sapient races don't have names for. We use something akin to mental symbols. You can only think of them as mental nouns, but they aren't. Because with sapiency, there is mutual understanding without language - our home planet, doesn't have a name. This ship doesn't have a name."

"Do you mean that two sapients from different races would instantly understand each other the first time they met?"

"Yes."

"Well, in that case, surely part of telepathy and/or sapiency is only a universal language?"

They strolled along in silence for a while. It occurred to him that for the first time he might have said something that she needed to consider. Just before she spoke he sensed that she was going to attempt to supply an answer because she knew that his human ego didn't respond well to being told, 'You aren't sapient, you won't understand.'

"Sapiency is a state of *being*. When sapients communicate we're *being* the same thing. Language plays no part."

She'd lost him. He'd just have to accept that he couldn't understand. Why had she started this in the first place?

"We are about to go inside the ship. There, you will see and experience many things that you won't be able to put a label to, like 'grasshopper.' I won't be able to supply a label because there are no labels - we do not use nouns."

"But you're an *Ig'tam*, your name is *Hontay*, so you *do* use nouns."

"Relics of a distant past. We have them, but we don't *use* them."

Fine, so he'd just have to invent...

"Billy, in order to understand, humans label. You won't be able to label. Try not to become confused or disorientated."

The next instant, still arm in arm, still strolling along but now dressed in their flying suits, they were inside a... a what? Inside a space. A cubical space. A space surrounded by hazy pink walls, hazy pink ceiling and hazy pink floor. There were lots of other Ig'tams in this space. Some were near, others far away, but, even so, he found it difficult to judge distance or scale. His eyes began to hurt as he strained to bring an image, any image, into sharp focus. Giving up, he focussed on Hontay. Her suit was now devoid of blood. Instant dry cleaning? He wasn't going to ask.

Hontay stopped. There didn't seem to be anything significant about the place where she'd halted. He stood beside her, trying to make sense of what his eyes were telling him. The other Ig'tams were also just standing around. There were fewer Redits than Gemarchs. The Germarchs were easily identifiable by their lime green skin. How come he hadn't known that Gemarchs were green? Somewhere in his brain he had known, but his assumption that they were the same colour as adult Redits had overridden this.

"Is this real? I mean, this feels a bit like being inside the Blue Giants."

"This is real. We are in the cockpit - a cockpit operated by sapients."

As far as he could see there were no instruments, no controls and no flashing lights. Where were the gadgets? How can you have a cockpit without gadgets? Pretty damn disappointing. In fact, there was nothing to see except pink space occupied by Ig'tams. "How large is the cockpit?"

"It has no defined size. This cockpit is being shared by other ships. It is both here and also several other places."

He let that wash over him like a cool shower. "Let me see if I've got this right, I'm here, in the cockpit on *this* ship, but you're here as well as on the other ships?"

"Yes."

He got the impression that, that wasn't the complete answer, but it had to do. "How can I see inside the cockpits of the other ships?"

"You can't, but I can. You're seeing and experiencing part of what I see and experience."

She didn't need to add, 'the non-sapient parts.' "What do you want me to do?"

"Just be here with me Husband."

Her voice couldn't produce the sort of tonal inflection a mother used when her child was becoming bothersome. But she wanted him to be a good boy, and to stand still and not ask any more questions. Good. She might be super-smart, but he could still distract her. He toyed with the idea for a while then concluded that it was perhaps best if he didn't. Who knows how she'd react when she was annoyed? He knew, that's who. She couldn't stop him from thinking or speaking. She couldn't disconnect her mind from his, but she *could* dump enough information to totally overwhelm his thought processes. OK, he'd behave.

Part of what his brain was seeing was what Hontay was seeing. What about what his own eyes were seeing? He closed his eyes. The images of the other cockpits remained. Opening his eyes, he saw little difference. What was the *little* difference? It took him about fifteen minutes to work it out. There was one other Redit, in *this* cockpit, over to the left. His eyes didn't hurt when he looked at her. She didn't seem to be doing anything either... He felt it as Hontay left. He turned. She was still standing there. He knew that if he asked a question, she'd answer it. He also knew that a significant chunk of her intellect/being/person was now somewhere else... no, other places. She was busy flying the ship...

Hontay doing whatever it was she was doing, must somehow have locked up his brain. He'd been in some type of trance for over an hour when a number of things suddenly occurred to him. First, he was a human being, not an Ig'tam; he wasn't used to standing indefinitely. His legs were beginning to ache. Second, all this time she hadn't released his hand. By rights it should have been hot and sweaty, but it wasn't. Probably due to the Ig'tam space suit. Third, he knew where their clothes went when she made them vanish - nowhere. She unmade and remade them. Fourth, now he understood the lack of instrumentation in the cockpit; Ig'tams went from swinging in the trees, or whatever, straight to manipulation by thought. They'd missed out the tool making bit. Although they had four fingers and a thumb their hands were nowhere near as dextrous as a human's. Very interesting to be sure, but he badly needed to sit.

Out of nowhere a largish stool appeared in front of him. Climbing on, he was pretty sure that it hadn't materialised at his instigation. He was also pretty sure that it was oversized so that Hontay could keep hold of his hand without having to reach down. Her physical self wanted... needed, to be in touch with his. Why? For some unfathomable reason she needed this contact with him to fly the ship. How did he know that...?

Several minutes passed before the answer materialised. It seemed that he literally knew *everything* Hontay did. But the sapient bits were beyond him. The expression 'object permanence' reverberated in his mind until he finally understood its meaning and relevance: object permanence was knowing that objects didn't 'cease to exist' when they move out of view; sapiency was 'out of sight' to non-sapients, and because they were non-sapients they couldn't make the, mental, object permanence leap.

As for the non-sapient parts, unless she emphasised some particular aspect they simply didn't register. He suspected that she didn't emphasise this type of thing because, to her, it was irrelevant detail. So, why did she need this physical contact? She'd already told him the answer; sapients needed to take special care of their physical selves. He would never *understand* why, although he *knew* why, they needed to do this.

25

RELEASE

"You are about to be released from the aggressor's effect and returned to normal spacetime. You will experience some discomfort. Once back in normal spacetime, and recovered, you are to jump to a preprogrammed coordinates. There, you will receive further orders."

"What...?"

He heard Eva begin to ask, but he could tell that Flet was no longer in the vicinity.

"...OK, everybody standby, I have no idea what's going to happen," Eva continued.

Suddenly he could see. Well, that wasn't strictly true, the veil of total darkness was lifting to reveal a dim light, but there was nothing to see. Then, he could feel. First, internal feelings, like his heart beating and lungs breathing - the sort of things one only noticed after they had been absent. Then, he felt the flight suit fabric and fittings against his skin. He was in his womb; he began to feel the pressure of the lymph duct connectors on his back - God, did it feel reassuring.

Just at that moment, when he was beginning to feel happy, a sickening dizziness came over him. He was going to puke, then he wasn't. He had a pounding headache, then it was gone. He had motor control, then none at all. For a second, he could see vague patterns in the dim light, then he couldn't. Christ. It felt like he was fading in and out of existence. Suddenly, very suddenly, *Baddest* and everything was solid, reality had arrived. He sat up and bent double as both ends of his alimentary canal spouted.

'Erick... Erick... Erick... Erick. I know that you are conscious. Erick, can you hear me?'

"Yes Anne." He knew that he'd responded, but the voice belonged to a remote and enfeebled octogenarian. He assumed that he'd passed out. It took an unimaginable amount of effort to simply open his eyes; even then he couldn't focus on anything. He felt far too weak to move.

'I cannot detect any physical damage to you or any of the crew, but you are all registering symptoms of severe trauma. You are the first to regain consciousness. Please advise on the condition and the appropriate medication'. Anne sounded like a troubled mother.

He tried to answer but only managed a feeble croak.

'Erick, some of the crew are in catatonic shock, but all their bodies are functioning normally. I need to know how to treat them.'

"Nothing," he mumbled. His head was spinning, so he closed his eyes, took a deep breath, and tried again, "You don't need to do anything, Anne."

'Are you sure? They are...'

'...no time has elapsed. Erick is awake.'

Pilot

"Welcome back Erick, I won't ask how you're feeling. Listen, we need to do something with the flight crew, they're still out cold."

That was David's voice, sounding almost as strained as his had. Trying to sit up, so that he could take a look around, he raised himself a few centimetres, then slumped back. He wasn't sure if it was because he didn't have the strength or because he'd slipped on the vomit in his womb.

'I would advise you keep still Erick.'

"How long was I out Anne?" That sounded more like his voice.

'Paradoxically, all chronometers show that no time has elapsed or is passing.'

"Funny that," David started, "That's exactly what I asked. How can time *not* be passing?"

This time he managed to sit up. Looking over at David, who was also slumped in his womb, he gave the age-old sign - nose inside a circle made of index finger and thumb - 'fuck knows'. "Anne, do you mean to say that you can't tell how long we've been out?"

'I can estimate time from the oscillation of molecules Erick. However, the chronometers show that time remains fixed.'

"What is your estimation of elapsed time Anne?"

'Seventy-nine hours, three minutes, plus or minus twenty hours, eight minutes. There has been sizable and indeterminable temperature variations.'

Three days! "What's the state of play with the flight crew Anne?"

'Grim, Marandolina and Ruth are slowly coming to. The others remain unconscious.'

"Ideas David?"

"If there's no immediate danger, I vote we pull some R&R."

David had a point; everybody was going to feel like shit. "Anne, scan to maximum range and report."

'With the crew unconscious I automatically shifted to an autonomous defence mode Erick. I have not detected any potential threat to the ship, but we are not completely in normal spacetime.'

"What do you mean by 'not completely' Anne?"

'Sensors detect phenomena that I do not recognise. I have computed that the most probable explanation is that we are gradually reentering normal spacetime.'

"Do you mean that it's like a very slow drop from super-light Anne?" David asked astutely.

'The phenomena could be loosely compared to a slow drop from super-light David. Although I cannot be certain, I do not think that is what is happening.'

Since their Supercomputer was baffled, he'd have to go with his instincts. "Anne, any idea on how long before we're back in normal spacetime?"

'No Erick, time is static. If, however, you mean as compared to the 'rate' of drop, then it seems to be linked to the rate of recovery of the crew. Unfortunately, I cannot be more specific than that.'

"So, Anne, you mean when everybody is conscious, we'll be back?"

'I estimate that it will be so, but I am not sure Erick.'

***

It was maddening. Like finding something, after an exhaustive and unsuccessful search, when you no longer needed it. He'd been sitting here for hours like a bloody lemon. It was now obvious that he could still talk to her. Only discussions which distracted her sapient mind were off limits. He knew this. He'd known it all along. He just didn't realise that he did. Dammit! In that case... "Do you know how the sexual suppression on *Baddest* worked?"

"Yes. Hypnotism, conditioning, belief and telepathy."

What? That was a very matter-of-fact answer. He'd always suspected subliminal suggestion, but 'belief, conditioning and telepathy'? He opened his mouth to ask another question...

"The process is simple. Space Service personnel have sex suppressant suggestion planted early in their training; this is particularly effective with the military because your training for space starts pre-puberty. You are then told that, when in space, you will be subjected to an unspecified sex suppressant. All your early experience of being in space confirms what you have been told because the hypnotic suggestion is still effective. Over time, you condition yourself to completely disregard your sexual desires although no suppressant exists."

Super-intelligent being or not, he could pick a dozen holes in that explanation. "But..."

"There is no mechanism on *Baddest* to suppress your sexual desires."

"But..."

"Billy, you *believed* in the sex suppressant, so your sexual drives were suppressed."

"But how about when we hit downside?" After spluttering it out, he remembered it was an Ig'tam wife he was having this discussion with.

"A result of the same conditioning."

She didn't seem to be having a Redit's reaction to the thought of him having sex with other females - sometimes, lots of other females. Good, but he still didn't believe what she'd said. "Are you saying that Supreme Command and the government is that smart?"

"No, despite the patent evidence to the contrary they *believe* that the hypnotic suggestion worked by itself."

"What 'patent' evidence?"

"Sex is a primary motivator in both humans and Ig'tams. Aggression is one manifestation of this. In humans, aggression is explicit in the male and latent in the female. With us, aggression is invested exclusively in the female."

"So?"

"You are a military pilot. Aggression and violence are part and parcel of your job. Earth's military would be beyond nonaggressive - they'd be totally passive - if its personnel's sex drive was really suppressed."

She had a point, but even so... "What about the civilians. They haven't been trained for space, so they couldn't have..."

"Telepathy and belief. You are semi-telepathic. Because all the military on *Baddest* 'believed' that their sex drive was being suppressed, and it is widely 'known' that sex drives *would* be suppressed, the civilians also believed..."

"And because they *believed* in the sex suppression their sex drives were also suppressed. Is that what you're saying?"

"Yes Husband."

This was starting to sound plausible, but he still didn't believe it. "All right then, how was it lifted?"

"Again, subliminal suggestion - the General Recall. When setting the General Recall principle, the authorities assumed that if Earth was threatened any human capable of reproduction should be released to do so."

Naw, he wasn't ready to buy this. "How do you know that?"

"Deduction from what you know."

"So, you haven't tapped into some InfoSys to get this?"

"No, I haven't."

He was about to tell her that he didn't believe her theory when some inner awareness cautioned against it. It was already too late - she knew he didn't believe her. He tensed himself for whatever it was that she was going to do. Nothing happened. Patience was what he felt emanating from her, a strained patience, but patience nonetheless. "Sorry Hontay, but this is hard to get to grips with."

"Your semi-telepathic abilities have sometimes been described as 'morphic resonance' by some of your scientists." By addressing the part that he found most difficult to believe, she accepted his apology. "Billy, please take this as fact: you and Mohammed could not fly *Baddest* as well as you do if you were not 'aware' of each other's thoughts."

Pilot

He mulled that over.

"The degree of coordinated effort required to fly an Air Force spaceship is far beyond the ability of the individual members of the crew. Despite what you believe, most of the training and drills you do hone your semi-telepathic abilities not your physical coordination."

"I don't want to argue or contradict, but we can fly *Baddest* because the C2 senses our individual thought impulses and passes them to Anne who does the coordinating for us."

"Your reliance on technology also masks your latent sapient potential."

He'd heard the 'humans are semi-telepathic' bit before. 'Latent sapient potential', however, was new...

"Billy, although I did not wish for this union, I'm happy that you are my husband. However, if you did not have at least *some* sapient potential, I would have severed the mental bond between us."

But Flet had said that Hontay couldn't break the bond... Sometimes he felt really dumb. Their mental attachment could only be 'severed' in death - his death. "OK, but *you* rely on technology as well, don't you?"

"We 'use' technology, humans 'rely' on technology. Unfortunately, this reliance hinders your sapient potential."

He got the impression that this talk about 'sapient potential' was beginning to distract her from flying, or whatever it was she was doing to, the ship(s). How to pursue this without getting further into sapiency? "Technology is only the cumulative application of our intellect on the physical world."

"Precisely. And if you had similarly applied your intellect to, what you would call, 'the metaphysical world', you would be aware of having fulfilled some of your sapient potential."

They were still in the realms of sapiency. "What we have done is develop advanced science and mathematics. Surely that takes high mental functions?"

"Yes, it does. However, mathematics is not an absolute, it is just another of your languages. Nor does your sapient potential necessarily reside with your higher mental functions. Billy, I know you place great faith in the human ability to change and control your environment but, from a sapient standpoint, there is little difference between your engineers building *Baddest* and termites building mounds."

Rather than get annoyed, he opted to attack her argument about mathematics. "Mathematics *is* an absolute. It predicts and describes known phenomena..."

"It describes to humans what other humans believe to be known phenomena - just another language."

"Look, one and one is two - that's an absolute. Or do you sapients want to argue about that?" There was no disguising his annoyance.

She didn't say or do anything. Out of nowhere more Hontays appeared; one in front, one on his other side and he didn't need to look around to know that he was surrounded by four of her.

"Are you *absolutely* sure about that?" the one behind him said, with more than a hint of sarcasm.

Sarcasm? Good, she was taking it like a woman. On the other hand, he *knew* that each of them was his wife. Not facsimiles of her, nor projections of her, each one was the real living and breathing Hontay. He also *knew* that she could have produced several more, but that would have distracted her from her flying. This was all too much to take in, so he stuck to his guns. "But if we understood..."

"I know you find it difficult Billy, but please accept that this is beyond the ability of any mathematics you have now, or will develop in the future, to describe."

No! He wasn't going to accept that. The Flushi had said something about influencing probabilities. This must have something to do with Quantum Mecha ...

"Billy," the Hontay to his right started patiently, "Indeterminism; Heisenberg's Uncertainty Relation; superstring theory, and parallel universes could only be conceived by non-sapient minds. I am here."

From the one behind, "And here."

And the one in front, "And here."

"Measurably so and all at the same time, because I am a sapient being," the original Hontay finished off, then added, "Mathematics is simply a non-sapient language."

He sulked about this as the alter-Hontays vanished. OK, so she might have a point, but he wasn't going to accept it.

"That's right, oh husband of the disjointed intellects. You know I'm right, but you aren't going to *believe* it." He felt the warmth of her smile. "You know what? The human mind is quite interesting. It holds so many contradictory and conflicting ideas, it's a wonder that you aren't all clinically insane."

He didn't want to laugh. After all, he was supposed to be sulking. Despite himself, he did.

"You are distracting me. But I would like to give you a definitive explanation. So, here is another example: human intelligence is a patterning process - your higher mental functions produce vertical thinking. Let's use your mathematics to demonstrate this. A random number generator produces the numbers 371, 1156, 88976 and 188897346. What is the next number?"

To work this out he needed a quantum comp...

"You do not require a calculating device."

He tried. After all, maths was his forte... And got nowhere fast.

"You tried to discover the pattern. You checked to see if they were all prime numbers. Then, if they were all divisible by a specific number. Next, you simplified your approach, perhaps it was much more obvious? You looked for common digits. After trying several other approaches, you finally decided that you could not work it out without a computer. But you continued to believe that the pattern could be derived if you had one."

So?

"I did say that the numbers were produced by a random number generator."

"But you asked what the next number was. How can anyone guess what the next number will be?"

"I could, but neither you nor your greatest mathematicians, assisted by their most sophisticated computers would be able to. There is no pattern, but there is an answer."

This was almost giving him a headache. "How could you?"

"Mine is not a patterning intellect and I am also sapient. I am able to *conceptualise* the next number, but that's not the point. This demonstrates your disjointed and patterning thinking. A random numbers generator - no pattern. Despite knowing that, you were unable to look at the problem in any but a pattering way."

Conceptualise the next number?! "OK, what's the answer?"

"If I told you that I would only have half of your attention because your brain would then go into overdrive trying to calculate how it was derived. You know there is no pattern, therefore, the answer cannot be *calculated* - but you won't be able to help yourself," she said teasingly.

We'll see about that. "If we discuss your non-pattern thinking would that distract you?"

"Not in the least."

"OK. How can you plan, organise, or problem solve without thinking vertically?"

"One of the many forms of thinking can be considered to be 'conceptualisation': picture the solution or desired result, then bring all available knowledge to bear."

In considering this he tried an experiment. He wanted to understand what the hell she was talking about. Trying to bring all knowledge to bear wasn't producing any results...

"Visualise thinking as being a vast plane; this plane has packets of knowledge on it. Intelligence is the maximum potential density of the knowledge packets. With sapiency however, each knowledge packet can grow, and their maximum potential size is the level of sapiency. Now, problem solving using vertical thinking is taking the knowledge packets and stacking them, just like building a skyscraper. With conceptual thinking, however, a depression is created in the plane itself, like a gravity well and all the knowledge packets within the circumference fall towards the focus of the cone."

He got the sensation she was finding this conversation stimulating and he could certainly picture her analogy. "OK, but how does conceptual thinking help you plan? I mean, I can see that it would be good for problem solving, producing a sort of melting pot of all the variables."

"Your question is a result of vertical thinking. You cannot help but make a comparison - find a link - form a pattern. Both types of thinking are *different*, but one isn't *superior* to the other."

She hadn't answered his question; vertical thinking seemed more appropriate for planning and conceptual thinking better for problem solving...

"As I've said, vertical thinkers cannot help but make comparisons. It has its advantages and its disadvantages. In order to build your skyscraper a knowledge packet either fits on top or it doesn't, which gives you only yes/no, true/false alternatives. It's no coincidence that your computers work on the binary - on/off - principle."

"But that's logical and eff..."

"As logical and effective as on/off/neither? How can something be neither on nor off? A circuit has to either have a current flowing through it or it hasn't, right? Wrong Mr. Vertical thinker. There are an infinite number of states between the two, think of it as yes/no/maybe. In other words, is binary the most efficient? How about the computing possibilities of something like this: on/off/changing from on to off/changing from off to on? You're struggling with this, aren't you? This right/wrong aspect of your higher mental functions inhibits your sapient development. In a sense, sapiency can be considered to be the gap between *on* and *off*."

Slowly, he chewed on that.

"I *can* think vertically, which is part of the reason why I understand you. However, it's not how I normally think. For instance, if I thought vertically, we would not be married because I would have *anticipated* 'the human male effect'. As it was, I was aware of the possibility, but my focus was on minimising streamshifting damage to you and your crew and also on establishing comms with Earth."

"You've just admitted that conceptual thinking led to a mistake."

Squeezing his hand lightly he felt her mental chuckle. "If I'd made a mistake, you would be dead. Let's just say that I didn't get the ideal solution. Not a simple right or wrong, but somewhere in the middle."

***

They were all conscious now. He'd even made it out of his womb, just. He'd never thought that he would find death an attractive proposition but, just then, it was very appealing - compared to enduring this living hell. Mind you, he was in good company - every single member of the crew wanted to die. Twenty-five individuals who all felt as if they were being turned inside out. According to Anne they were back in normal spacetime, the chronometers were ticking. Big deal! Normal spacetime felt like shit! Nobody was doing anything except lying about and moaning. It hadn't felt like this when the aggressors took them in...

"Anne, is *The Beast* anywhere around?" He heard Eva asked feebly.

'No Eva.'

"How about Sun or Gill, Anne?"

'There is nothing within sensor range Eva.'

"How about the Blue Giants?"

'Nothing Eva.'

Despite his pounding head, a nasty thought occurred to him. "Anne, when you say 'nothing', do you mean literally nothing?"

'That is correct Mohammed. We are surrounded by an absolute vacuum all the way to maximum scanner range.'

"But that's impossible," Pipsqueak muttered.

"We can see stars, so obviously there is something out there," Eva started thoughtfully. "Anne, check all sensor systems."

'All sensors are functioning at their optimum and I cannot detect anything external to the ship. Where are the stars Eva?'

"All around Anne, can't you pick them out on visual?"

'No Eva.'

"Then how do you know we're in normal spacetime Anne?"

'Because my detectors show that the spacetime continuum fabric is normal. Are you sure you can see stars Eva?'

"Yes. Everything looks, well, normal."

"*My systems are all online but showing a blank as well.*"

That was Kaye, Sun's 2ic. He'd forgotten that the four remaining Darts had crewed up but hadn't launched by the time the Blue Giants struck.

"*Same here,*" came the replies of the other Dart pilots.

"I hate to say this, but I see only two options," Wendy started hesitantly. "One, we're all hallucinating. Or, two, all sensor systems are malfunctioning in a big way."

"Navs, I know we are in an unknown part of the galaxy, but can you check our pre-Blue Giant star plots and get a fix on our current position?" Eva asked.

"Do you know how long that will take manually?" John weakly protested.

"You have something better to do or somewhere to go?"

"OK, let's get busy guys," Marandolina interceded, "Grim, why don't you project the last plot on Billy's screen and I'll go sit in his womb and compare it to the star field?"

Grim took a while to answer and when he did, he sounded like death warmed-up. "No, that'll take too long. Anne, punch up our last attitude grid and if you pilots can stick the ship in exactly the same orientation, we can compare star field."

The attitude grid came up on his screen. "Take it Mohammed," Eva instructed and he started to manoeuver the ship.

"If only we had a sextant or theodolite," Gabi complained.

"A what?" Wendy asked.

"A sextant is an ancient navigation instrument, and a theodolite measures vertical and horizontal angles - just what we need right now," Gabi explained.

"Are they complicated? I mean to make," he asked.

"I don't know. I've only ever seen a sextant in the Academy's museum. Why did you ask?"

"I'm with you on this one Mohammed," Grim said more brightly. "Anne, does your databank have the technical information to manufacture a sextant and a theodolite, and can you estimate how long it would take?"

'Yes Grim, and I can machine both in seventeen point four seconds.'

"Then do it Babe."

"I'll get them," John volunteered, then unsteadily got out of his womb, and tottered towards the fitness room.

"This sextant, what exactly is it?" Eva asked.

"That's strictly a Nav's instrument, far too delicate for ham-fisted pilots to handle," Pipsqueak made a rather flimsy joke.

Mohamed was pretty sure he vaguely knew what a sextant was, so he decided to put these uppity Nav's in their place. "Wasn't a sextant used by *pilots* on sailing ships?"

"Right," Eva started businesslike, "Erick, let's occupy the non-flight crew, get them cleaning. Gabi, when you get the sextant and theodolite what are you going to do with them?"

Gabi made her way to Billy's womb, got in and started to adjust it. "Measure angles. Anne, show instructions for using both instruments."

Pilot

'On screen Gabi. Eva, I believe I may have a possible explanation for why the sensors are blank.'

"Yes Anne, what is it?"

'I suspect that the battle has started.'

"What? Explain Anne," Eva demanded.

Anne had everyone's undivided attention. 'The Flushi data hints that a battle between sapient races would deactivate some types of technology.'

"How can... I mean, why... why do you think that, Anne?" Grim spluttered.

'This is a best guess, with a probability of less than 50 percent accuracy. My interpretation of some of the data indicates that a prerequisite of conflict between sapients is the neutralisation of certain mechanical enhancements.'

"But you said that all sensors were functioning."

'That is correct Eva, this is what led me to search the Flushi data banks. Internal checks show that all sensor systems are functioning. But if you can see stars which I cannot detect, then all sensor systems must be malfunctioning. This situation presents a logic bomb. However, Flushi data suggests circumstances where this would not be the case. In sapient conflict situations machines are not deactivated, merely inhibited from carrying out certain specific functions.'

"But Anne, you're functioning, the ship is functioning."

'Yes Eva, we are.'

It took a while before Eva seemed to realise that Anne had finished speaking. "Anne, continue explaining your deductions."

'I have concluded my explanation Eva.'

Returning with sextant and theodolite, John handed them to Gabi, and said to Eva, "Sounds weird to me."

"Any idea on how we could test this?" Eva asked the flight crew.

"Perhaps you pilots might tackle this one while us Navs manually fix our position," Grim suggested.

"Fair enough," Eva agreed. "Pilots and Darts' any ideas?"

What he really wanted was to see how a sextant worked, but... "If sensors are down, logically, weapons should also be down."

"*Agreed,*" Kaye said.

"But all weapons show 'on-line'", Wendy countered.

"Precisely, we need to see if they actually are on-line," he explained.

"You think we should loose off a round or two?" Eva asked.

"Yeah, why not?"

"*Our instruments won't pick up an energy discharge, so how will we know that the weapons are working?*" Vimla asked from her Dart.

After sitting back to ponder for a while, Eva said, "How about this? We launch a low speed dummy torpedo; visually track it; take it out with lasers; wide beam; half a millisecond burst."

"A torpedo is too small to track and target visually," Wendy stated.

"*We could pre-programme its route and fire at where it should be... Best make it a live one so that we can see the detonation,*" Sabine suggested.

"That checks," Wendy agreed.

"Mohammed, can you programme the torpedo?"

"Sure, but C1 said that there's an absolute vacuum out there. Most of the torpedos have matter/anti-matter warheads."

"Weapons inventory shows some good old-fashioned fusion tipped, fire one of those," Eva ordered.

"I'm on it." He got busy... "Track on your screen... now. Note the fire solution puts the target dead ahead centre when it's hit. Should be quite a show."

Both Wendy and Eva scrutinised his plot, then Eva gave the nod, "Launch torpedo. Fire when solution criteria's matched."

Tracking the torpedo's plotted path, he waited for the fire solution... As he pressed the fire button, his brain seemed to explode in a crescendo of wildly extreme emotions and sensations. Even so, or perhaps because it was so, he understood what was happening: his intellect was literally being ripped apart; a sapient being was holding his mind in... in... in *places*!

26

EXACTION

Before he could ask her why, the pinkness of the cockpit suddenly changed to a whiteness. Hontay collapsed... no, not collapsed, she dropped. Instinctively he grabbed at her, just managing to retard her fall so that she didn't hit the deck. In the process he was yanked off his stool. Straddling her prone figure, with his hands around her torso, one thing was certain, she wasn't being influenced by 1G.

What's going on?! Keep her upright? Now he understood. Hontay was unconscious - a rear occurrence for an Ig'tam. Their physiology wasn't geared-up to them being prone. Left like that for more than about five minutes and their internal organs would begin to arrest. What the hell was he going to do? Looking around the cockpit for some inspiration, it dawned on him why the eerie pinkness had suddenly changed to whiteness. An Ig'tam's visual range included the infrared, and now their minds were 'disconnected' only his vision was at play. So, all the weirdness of the other cockpits had vanished. Apart from a prolapsed Redit over to his left, with a Gemarch lying either side of her, all there was to see was the whitish, not-quite-real, not-quite-here, walls, floor, and ceiling.

Then inspiration came. Gently lowering Hontay, he ran over to the other Redit. Grabbing her and one of her Gemarchs by their arms, he tried dragging them. It was like they were both stuck to the floor. The Gemarch looked a tad lighter, so he released her and pulled him over to Hontay. He was panting by the time he'd accomplished that. Why the fuck didn't these super intelligent beings build strength augmentation into their space suits? Because they were super intelligent beings who didn't 'rely' on technology, that's why. He moved the Redit next. Then, almost on the point of exhaustion, the other Gemarch.

Time was of the essence. He turned the stool upside down. In opposing pairs, he struggled lifting them and hooking the backs of their collarless flight suits over the ends of the stool's legs. Collapsing on the floor and gasping for breath, he pondered the situation. Now the four Ig'tams were sitting, bums just off the floor, being held up by the four-legged stool. That would just have to do, there was no way he could stand with even one of them. How long had he taken? Maybe too long. Instead of their normal deep mauve colouration, both Redits had turned a reddish orange. The Gemarchs were yellowish instead of lime green. All this he took to be a bad sign. Perhaps he should....

Sensing a presence behind him he turned and saw, a few feet away, the biggest fucking slug one could possibly imagine! No, it wasn't a slug. It didn't even look like a slug. This thing was a jelly-like, opaque, pyramid shaped mass, about six feet tall and just as wide at its base. He was far too exhausted to run, but he got to his feet. Yeah, right! Like he was going to fight this *thing*... Then he remembered he ought to move away from the Ig'tams. What...?

In a hazy sort of way, he remembered that the thing was trying to communicate with him. Taking a couple of unsteady steps to his left, he then remembered that the thing was here to protect the Redits and he was getting in the way. Shuffling further to the side, he looked back at the Ig'tam quartet. For some unknown reason he'd expected to see the shimmering of a quantum force field, or something like that, around them. But there was nothing. Turning back to the thing, he staggered and almost fell over as a substantial block of knowledge slammed into his consciousness - it was like the full-on resurrection of a lifetime of half-dreamt memories:

His brain was so primitive that there was no way the thing could directly connect to it without causing permanent damage. Mind you, it wasn't the least bit fussed about damaging his brain, but it was afraid. Not afraid of him, but of what Hontay would do to it if it harmed him. It was contemptuous of this non-sapient moron for being worried about the Gemarchs instead of prioritising the two Redit pilots. His presence was inhibiting it in its sentry duties.

He took a little comfort from this. If the thing was afraid of what Hontay might do then, presumably, she would recover. It also occurred to him that if the thing was responsible for the wellbeing of the pilots, then it had been damn tardy and should thank him for his prompt action - he hope it understood that thought...

More memories: the thing was another fourth level sapient, a crew member of this extraordinary ship and, although it functioned as a Moderator, it wasn't wise for him to piss it off.

While he tried to get his brain around what a Moderator did, he remembered about the Ig'tams relationships with other sapients...

Ig'tams were the embodiment of a pure hunter-killer species. That, in itself, wasn't unusual, there were loads of hunter-killer species around. Sapient hunter-killers were, however, extremely rare. And a fourth stage hunter-killer species was almost an oxymoron. Any species that butchered its kin with amoral disregard should, in theory, self-destruct long before attaining intelligence, let alone sapiency. The Ig'tam seemed to have niftily got round this by having only the Redits geared-up for killing out-of-hand. That and Gemarchs being the highest ticket item for a Redit. So, even though Redits used to kill other Redits, including daughters and mothers, Gemarchs were never harmed directly or indirectly.

Short of xenocide, which was considered and rejected on grounds of self-preservation, the other fourth stage sapients couldn't alter the Redits' propensity for wholesale slaughter. The strategy they settled on was to 'contain' them. Wherever there were concentrations of Ig'tams, there were also Moderators. The Moderators did not get involved in Ig'tam affairs; their job was to restrain/delay/curb the Redits' instinctive reaction to dispatch anything that crossed their paths.

Also, the other fourth level sapients considered humans to be a non-sapient nascent hunter-killer species; so mindlessly barbarous that they were unlikely to evolve much beyond reliance on technology. This was the reason why the Ig'tams, Flet and Hontay, were given the task of being human liaison officers.

Digesting this, Billy concluded that no matter what these sapients could do, they still couldn't design a decent space suit which protected its occupant from muscle strain.

Pilot

However, rather than get shirty with the Blob, he figured that it might be more productive to try and find out what was occurring.

The aggressors had launched their first strike (along with this memory came the ancillary information that the aggressors had done no such thing, but that was how his brain would interpret it). Now, whole *states of consciousness* were closed/denied/unattainable to the galactic sapients. Those caught in the *exaction,* such as Hontay, were mentally desiccated. The alliance was attempting counteraction to nullify the aggressors' psychic bulwark. Incidentally, they were also trying to protect his ship and its stupid crew.

Indeed? This didn't make a lot of sense to him but, what the heck, he was only a non-sapient after all. Wondering what was going to happen next, he got the feeling that all that was going to happen was them having to wait for perhaps several hours. With his inverted stool carrying out the vital task of keeping the Ig'tams upright he thought about another one appearing. As he'd expected another stool didn't make a showing. So, he hunkered down to sit cross-legged on the floor - he was going to show this thing just how patient humans could be.

***

After about a minute the pain and dizziness passed, in fact, she was amazed at just how clearheaded she felt.

"What happened to the torped...?" Mohammed started to ask.

'We are the Ermoor. Disarm weapons.'

"What do you mean by that Anne? "

'The ship and I are functioning normally Eva.'

What? "I mean what do you mean by that business about the ear moor Anne?"

'Ear moor Eva?'

"Yes Anne, you said something that sounded like, 'We are the ear moor'," Wendy confirmed.

'Apart from my answer to Eva's last question, I have not communicated with any member of the crew since confirming we are the Ermoor that self-tests had corroborated that the ship and disarm weapons I are functioning normally Wendy.'

"Wait. Fine Anne; inadvertent activation." John jumped in. "Nobody say anything to C1 for a sec. What are you ear moor?"

'Disarm weapons.'

"I think we should Eva," John said.

While she considered this Wendy added, "I can't see any immediate danger."

"Anne, disarm weapons."

'Weapons disarmed Eva.'

"What are you ear moor?" John asked again.

'Recall Darts on EM frequency.'

"What are you ear moor?" John persisted.

'Recall Darts on EM frequency.'

Enough was enough. "John, what's going on?"

"Nothing much, just a wild idea. I think something is trying to communicate with us through C1."

There might be something to this. "The ear moor?"

"Maybe. Could be what the aggressors are called."

"Hmm. The two Darts aren't showing on any instruments..."

'Recall Darts on EM frequency.'

"Ear moor, we will not recall Darts until you explain who you are and what you waaaah!"

'Recall Darts on EM frequency.'

"Oh Christ! Do what it says Eva, my head feels like it's going to explode," Wendy begged.

Although that's exactly how her head felt as well, girding her loins she said, "No. Not till we know more."

'Eva, I have deduced that you are communicating recall Darts on EM frequency with an unknown third party. I would strongly suggest that you comply recall Darts on EM frequency with their request, whatever it is. All crew are showing signs of extreme discomfort. Although I do not know the cause, if this condition recall Darts on EM frequency remains unchecked, it may lead to permanent brain damage.'

"No!"

'Recall Darts on EM frequency.'

"Come on Eva, do it!" Sabrina whimpered.

"No! Don't. Tell them to fuck off," Pipsqueak countered even though he sounded like he was in excruciating agony.

'Kazuhiko, Kaye, Marandolina recall Darts on EM frequency Grim and Mona are now unconscious, Eva.'

Although one, she felt humiliated and two, she couldn't see how the Darts could find *Baddest* if they couldn't detect them, she had to remind herself that these were fifth stage sapients they were messing with. "Sun, Gill, come to mummy. Comms EM only."

"*Roger* Baddest. *EM comms, docking in three.*"

The pain immediately subsided. "Sun, do you have a fix on us?"

"*Affirmative* Baddest. *Instruments are down but we have you eyeball.*"

"Where are you, and can you see *The Beast?*"

'All crew are again conscious Eva. None are showing signs of permanent damage.'

"*We're in your seven o'clock. It's a negative on* The Beast *but those two giant stars are still around.*"

"Where?!"

"*Your four thirty, level. Difficult to judge distance but about five hundred million kilometres.*"

'Transit sub-light to coordinates on screen. Keep weapons offline and await further instructions.'

She saw the coordinates come up but chose to ignore them. "What are they doing Sun?"

"*Not much. But if I were forced to, I'd say they were executing some type of search pattern.*"

'Transit sub-light to coordinates on screen. Keep weapons offline and await further instructions.'

"Maybe they're looking for *The Beast*," Wendy suggested.

"You mean..." Desperately trying not to think about it, she hoped that the rest of the flight crew understood. "Right Sun, let us know when you're in the cradle."

"*Docking now. Hanger doors closing.*"

'Transit sub-light to coordinates on screen. Keep weapons offline and await further instructions.'

Good, the ear moors weren't on to it. She saw Mohamed and Wendy slowly reaching for the flight controls. Excellent!

'Do not attempt to enter the super-light!'

If they could just keep them occupied for long enough then, maybe, *The Beast* could escape. "Boogie!"

'Super-light drives are humans do not try our patience carry out our instructions offline Eva.'

Shit!

"I've got a fix." Gabi turned to her sextant still in her hand. "We've moved less than seven hundred thousand kilometres from our original position."

"If that's even vaguely accurate, it will only take us about a couple of centuries to get to these coordinates sub-light," Pipsqueak muttered.

Pilot

'Transit sub-light to coordinates on screen. Keep weapons offline and await further instructions.'

She'd go through the motions, an opportunity to breakout was bound to present itself. "Navs?"

"Flight profile on your screen, now" John answered.

"Mohammed, Wendy, you take this, OK?"

"Sure. We have control. Transit, sub-light," was Mohammed's prompt answer.

"What's at these coordinates Eva?" Erick came through on the command net.

Good question. "Navs, any idea what's there?"

"It's uncharted," Ruth answered. "All we can say in that it takes us into the centre of the galaxy. We've got C1 searching the Flushi data. Will let you know if anything turns up."

Punching into the command net, she thought she'd play a hunch. "Sun, were you privy to the comms with our unexpected guests?"

"*Yes.*"

"How?"

"*C1's voice over the RT. I believe we have no alternative but to treat them as hostile.*"

"I concur, and would further suggest we consider ourselves POW's," Erick added.

Her hunch was probably a longshot, but the outline of a plan was beginning to form. She needed to flesh it out with her senior officers. "Agreed. Darts, stand down. Sun, come to the fitness room."

"*Standing down. Fitness room. Roger.*"

"Erick, you too. Anne, disable all comms in the fitness room."

'I cannot disable *all* comms Eva. If I disable main comms, backup comms automatically come on-line. If I disable those, emergency comms will be activated. The emergency systems cannot be overridden.'

An artificial intelligence knows it's not supposed to have a personality. It wouldn't willingly allow itself to be programmed with one. This was another longshot. "John where did you write C1's personality?"

"At home..." He paused for a while and she hoped he understood the real question. "Monorail tunnel, between sections twelve and seventeen." He paused again. "We'll have to walk. The cars are, see?"

"We?"

"You won't be able to find the relays."

"How far?"

"Roughly fifteen miles."

"Metric please."

"About twenty-five klicks."

"OK. Flight crew, Erick, Sun, John ,and I are taking a stroll. We'll be out of comms for a while. Grim, you have the bridge." She eased herself out of her womb.

"Fine," Grim answered. "By the way Eva, this is an Air Force ship, there isn't a bridge," he joked halfheartedly.

As Sun joined them by the fitness room, John suggested. "Best jog it out, it'll take forever otherwise. We'll go down tunnel three. Won't have secure comms till section twelve."

There wasn't much to say. They'd find out soon enough just how effective their fitness regimes had been. "Lead on."

***

"Where have they gone?"

"Shut it Alfred," came Grim's stern order.

"I must say Grim! That was a perfectly..."

"You shut it as well Cynthia. David, find something to occupy them."

Mohammed had a pretty good idea of where they'd gone, what to do, and why Grim didn't want it discussed; he was having enough difficulty trying not to think about it himself.

"There!" Wendy suddenly exclaimed. "Eleven O'clock, low. It's *The Beast*."

"How far?" Grim asked.

Spotting the other ship, he answered, "About three hundred and fifty miles, I'd guess."

'You may communicate with the other humans but only on EM frequencies.'

"Hello *The Beast*, this is *Baddest*. We're in your five o'clock, high. About three, five, zero miles. Answer on EM frequency only. Over," Grim transmitted.

"*Hi* Baddest, *this is* The Beast. *Instruments are down. Hostiles have infected our C1 and instructed us to fly towards the centre of the galaxy. Are complying. Over.*"

That sounded a bit like Krishna, *The Beast's* 1st pilot.

"Same here Krishna," Grim answered. "What coordinates?"

She read them out.

"We have the same coordinates. I need Nice on."

"*She and Ventrice are in the MedCen. We have a medical emergency with Riet.*"

"What happened?"

"*Not sure. When we tried to turn and burn, the Ermoors - that's what they call themselves - did something. We lost consciousness; Riet didn't recover.*"

"There's some divergence with our experience," Grim commented over the flight crew's net, then transmitted, "How long ago was that Krishna?"

"*Ten, perhaps, twelve minutes,* Baddest."

"*I'd say it's more like fifteen minutes. This is Shirlie by the way, I've got the second stick while Nice is away.*"

"Fifteen minutes? Sounds like they worked *The Beast* over then came after us," Wendy suggested.

"That doesn't stack," he pointed out. "If that was so, it would make them a lot dumber than the Ig'tams, who can do things simultaneously on both ships."

"Easy with the speculation," Grim interrupted. "How serious is Riet? And what precisely happened when you tried to turn and burn?"

"*Not sure on the Riet situation, but I'd say it was pretty serious...*"

"*Last we heard, Nice, Ventrice and C1 were fashioning nanno's to repair severe synaptic damage.*"

"*As for the turn and burn: don't know about you, but we had a really painful release from those two blue stars. Then, just as we were getting our act together, these Ermoors turned up and started bossing us around through C1. At first, we thought they were the blue stars so Nice boogied and tried to make a run for it. Don't know what they did but when we came to, we were back in normal spacetime, Riet was out cold, and weapons and instruments were down.*"

"So, you saying you actually made it to super-light?"

"*Maybe not to super-light, but certainly trans-light.*"

"Grim, sorry to interrupt but I've been monitoring this," David came through on the internal net. "While Erick and I were waiting for you to recover, C1 speculated that the rate of release from the Blue Giants was related to the rate of recovery of the crew."

"Yes, so?"

"There's a smaller crew on *The Beast*, they could have been back long before us."

"Fair enough." Grim seemed to consider this. "Krishna, what do you mean by, 'At first you thought the Ermoor were the blue stars'? Aren't they?"

"*No. Definitely not. We don't know exactly who they are, but they aren't those suns*"

"Don't see why," Wendy interrupted.

"*From what we can gather the blue suns are still looking for us. Apparently, providing we don't mess with the super-light they can't pinpoint us. That's why the Ermoor were so pissed off when we boogied. We think they are here to guide us away from the suns.*"

"What do you mean, 'they can't pinpoint us'? How the hell did they find us in the first place?"

"*Don't know, but that's the impression we got. It ain't easy communicating with them'er Ermoors.*"

"Billy's belt," Pipsqueak suggested. "And because he and his belt aren't around, they can't find us, what do you think?"

"Who knows?" Grim sounded resigned to the imponderables. "OK Krishna, we'll drop level and close up. Keep us posted on Riet, and when Nice is free ask her to give us a shout."

"*Roger. The Beast out.*"

"Who or what are you Ermoor," Grim suddenly demanded.

'Temporary human liaison officers. Do not interrogate us further.'

"Us? What do you mean by 'us', Ermoor?" Marandolina asked.

'We are a collective. Do not interrogate us further.'

"Why can't we ask questions?"

'Providing answers is taxing. It may also expose us and is harmful to you. Do not interrogate us further.'

"Grim, do you get the feeling they are getting pissed off?" Wendy enquired cautiously.

"I sure do. Was just about to knock the conversation on the head. Don't see why it should..."

"*Hello* Baddest, *this is* The Beast." Nice's head and shoulders hologram appeared in front of the pilots' wombs. "*Where are Billy and Eva?*"

"Billy is with Hontay, we think. Eva is taking a stroll with John down the monorail tunnel." Grim paused at that to pull one of his sombre stares before asking, "How is Riet?"

"*Still out. The nanno's are doin' their stuff but her chances don't look better than 50:50. We really won't know for another twenty-four hours or so. When John gets back ask him to pop over will you, could do with taking a stroll myself. Plus, we're a Nav down.*"

"Sure. We've assumed POW status."

"*Not necessary. The Ermoors are part of the alliance - just poor communicators. And we're not sure if they are here in person. Our best guess is that what we could be dealing with is a self-organising, self-writing programme, sent directly into our C1's, which thinks it's alive. It can also make direct telepathic contact.*"

"Nice, do you have any idea how farfetched that sounds?"

"*Compassman Chang, if you have a better alternative then let's hear it.*"

"I don't. But if what you've said bears any relationship to the real universe, why do you want to go for a stroll?"

"*Insurance. They don't like questions, but from what I've inferred I'm not convinced that they're up to fulfilling their mission.*"

"Their mission? What mission?"

"*They've implied that some other sapients, probably the Ig'tams, got us out of the blue suns. These guy's job is to get us safely away from the aggressors, but I think that what we have here is a hive mentality which is finding it impossible to adjust to and deal with a race of individuals, hence the Riet fuck-up."*

"You saying it was accidental?"

"Exactly. When the aggressors intercepted us it was weird, but we weren't harmed. When the sapients 'rescued' us, it hurt like hell and we puked for hours. Think about it. It's got to mean that the sapients' powers are greatly diminished in the presence of the aggressors and/or it is they who need to hide from the aggressors. Moreover, the Ermoors went apeshit when we boogied. Now, I'd call that a serious sense of self-preservation."

"I thought you said they were just a bunch of programmes?"

"I said that was our best guess. If we hit some serious problems, I don't intend to rely on something I can't have a proper conversation with."

"It's going take forever to reach these coordinates sub-light."

"I know, which I've taken to mean that they expect something to break anytime now. Another reason why I'd like to take that stroll with John, soonest."

"OK. Will pass this on to John as soon as he returns."

"That wasn't a request Grim."

27

SPACETIME

It was beginning to occur to him, after an hour or so, that the flow of time must be a pretty subjective thing. Not only that, but sapients must be able, in some undefined way, to mess with time. In other words, it was unlikely that a human would be able to outlast the Blob in terms of patience.

"Mind telling me when something is going to start happening and how long I'm going to have to sit here?"

He got the sensation that a great deal was happening but being a mere semi-civilised non-sapient, he was too unenlightened to appreciate it.

Taking his time in scanning the cockpit, he concluded that exactly fuck-all was happening. Perhaps, if the Blob wasn't being so damn patronising it would be polite enough to explain. As soon as that thought formed, he realised that no such thing was going to happen. Him being here was proving to be the mother-of-all-monstrously-large-pain-in-the-arse distractions. While he was telling himself that there would be little point in getting upset the pinkness of the cockpit returned. Hontay was back! Getting to his feet, he turned to look at the four Ig'tams expecting to see some change in their disposition. As far as he could tell, there had been no such change. So, what *was* happening?

Hontay's dislocated mind was desperately trying, across the continuum, to connect to his. The Blob was actively trying, and conspicuously failing, to stop this. He stood there feeling confused. If she managed to make a full connection, she would pull him to wherever she was. And if that happened, they would both be immediately exposed to whatever the aggressors wanted to throw at them. He was still confused. Wounded Ig'tams instinctively locked onto their mates; this aided their rate of recovery or, in a worst-case scenario - death, the mate would act as a repository for their spirit/essence. However, because he wasn't an Ig'tam or sapient, if Hontay locked onto him, *his* spirit/essence would be transported to wherever the hell she was, and neither of them would be able to stop it. And if that happened then the aggressors would act. Still confused.

Incorporeally speaking, the aggressors operated on something akin to male/female pairings and if confronted by any male/female pairings from the galactic alliance they would instantly act to neutralise them. He got a feeling that the term 'neutralise' didn't really do justice to what the aggressors would do to the galactic sapients. Concentrating on 'neutralise', he pondered, and got a sense that what happened to them was simple - they stopped being sapient and lost the ability to do the wonderful little tricks that sapients could. Having got his brain partially round this, he concluded that if *he* was threatened with an involuntary lobotomy, he'd not only be somewhat miffed, he'd also have a major sense-of-humour failure. But he still didn't really understand what the issues were. After all, symbolism and metaphors could only take you so far. What he really wanted to know was how, and why, would the aggressors do this...?

Laser rifle with grenade launcher in hand and wearing a marine PADE suit, he found himself standing in the middle of a dense humid jungle, with visibility only a couple of feet. Next to him was Hontay, naked. Presumably, this meant that Mr. Blob had finally thrown in the towel. Why was he in a PADE suit? Surely his Ig'tam space suit would be more appropriate. Yes, he knew it was a jungle, but it was like no jungle he'd ever seen. For a start, all the foliage was a luminous pinky yellow. Then there was the not quite real, not quite here feel of the place; similar to, but not exactly the same as the feel of the Ig'tam cockpit and the Flushi room - this was more real...

"Billy, you know everything you need to know, just act instinctively."

He could tell that she was feeling well below par. Conversely, he felt more alive and alert than he'd ever felt. It was as if pure adrenalin was flowing through his veins. Suddenly, head down, arms outstretched, she stampeded off into the bush. Although he couldn't see her, he knew she'd only moved about thirty feet to his right. Cautiously, he started forward; there was serious danger up ahead which they had to confront and then destroy. He didn't even bother speculating about how he knew that because like she'd said, he was going on instinct. And though he wasn't a Grunt, everyone did section battle drills during officer training.

The rifle felt comfortable and familiar in his hands. With feline poise, stepping lightly, he edged stealthily through the tangled outlandish thicket. He knew he shouldn't be feeling anything like the way he was because it was years since he'd played soldier. Hontay was moving in parallel to him.

In another situation he would have stopped to examine this fascinating plant life, but he was focussed: focussed on destroying. Despite this, somewhere in the dark recesses of his mind a recurring thought was slowly ticking away; if it was the aggressors up ahead, and aggressors were rogue fifth stage sapients, and this place was a construct of their minds, then a laser rifle wasn't going to be much fucking use, was it?

"Can you sense their presence?" Hontay shouted.

Why the hell was he creeping about while she was moving with all the hush of a bull in a china shop? Maybe the aggressors were deaf? Cranking up the volume on the suit's external communicator, he answered, "Yes, I think it's..." It was as if a radar was working in his head. "...about 200 yards, dead ahead."

"As soon as they are visible, attack," she bellowed.

They? It was an 'it': there was definitely only a single entity. "OK." He didn't need to shout.

Why was she talking to him? Obviously, he was feeding off her telepathically, she should know whether or not he could sense the enemy. As soon as these thoughts formed, they were immediately replaced by even weirder ones: it was all down to the human him - he wasn't feeding off Hontay at all. What she'd done, as he was projected/transported to her, was tickle part of his sapient potential; senses that were normally dormant in humans were now active in him. She'd also dumped a sizable block of her persona into his brain - the bristling, sharp-as-a-knife, always ready to strike, hyper-alertness he was feeling was how Ig'tams normally felt. She wasn't connected to him in the here-and-now, but she *was* connected to him.

There was already a monumental multi-dimensional/parallel universe/sapient-type altercation going down. His conscious mind was actually registering, considering and responding after-the-fact. So when Hontay asked a question she - or rather, some other part of her which was not in the here-and-now - would already know his answer and be acting on it by the time his inner-ear detected the sound waves. She was not anticipating his answer, she was 'conceptualising' what his answer would be in the future. All this was almost too much to take in; surely, if she could manage this then she didn't need to ask the question in the first place? Apparently, she did. The nearest he could come to understanding this was that she was, possibly/probably/only fuck knows how, taking his answer from the present and projecting it into the not too distant future. So, he had to give an answer, otherwise she had nothing to project. Mentally, all this was too much to handle, so he thought he'd just go with the flow.

Thrusting through the dense undergrowth, he stepped into an unexpected small clearing. Simultaneous with his brain registering what it took to be an upright dark green bat, about half again as tall as Hontay, on the other side of the clearing, his finger pressed the trigger. The beam burned a swathe through a clump of innocent-looking yellow plants because where there had been one bat there were now two, standing a couple of feet apart; he'd fired between them.

If he hadn't come across this 'splitting in two' business before with the Blue Giants, he'd have doubted his vision. There was a slight movement in left-green-bat's wings - not a flapping exactly, more a ripple - and, effortlessly, it started rising into the air. With an awesome burst of speed, Hontay suddenly crashed into the clearing and leapt up to yank the creature out of the air. Together, they crashed down somewhere not too far out of sight. Now he understood why he was in a PADE suit - with it, he could fly. He realised that he was wearing his Ig'tam spacesuit underneath it.

A similar ripple in right-green-bat's wings and it started to rise. He fired a percussion grenade. Not at where it was, but at where it was going to be. The grenade hit as the bat reached treetop high; the explosion should've ripped the thing apart. Instead, as far as he could tell, the concussion simply knocked the bat backwards, out of the sky and out of sight. But unfortunately, right-green-bat still seemed very much intact. Arming another grenade and pulling the rifle firmly into his shoulder, he kicked in the anti-gravity. Rising and then skimming above the treetops, which extended as far as he could see in all directions, he went looking for Mr. Huge-Bat. Come to think of it, it wasn't really like a bat at all, he'd figure out what it was like *after* he'd killed it.

Mr. Huge-Bat was considerate enough to identify where he'd spiralled down by making a conspicuous hole in the uniform, yellowish, carpet-like canopy. Rather than follow the thing down, he simply lobbed a HE grenade in after it. There was a searing flash and fragments of vegetation were ejected hundreds of feet into the air. He noted that the grenade had cleared a neat area about twenty feet across. Slap dead centre of the area was a prolapsed Mr. Huge-Bat. Obviously, the blast had knocked it off its feet, or whatever it was it stood on. Descending warily, he set about it with the laser.

The thing didn't move, it didn't point anything, nor were there any projectiles or beams emanating from it, but in a couple of seconds the left side of his PADE suit gradually vanished and he plummeted the fifty, or so, feet into the clearing. Landing heavily on his back, he mused that one of the toughest materials known to human science was simply been boiled off of him. As the remains of the PADE just vaporised like dry ice at room temperature, he figured that he'd be more gracious about Ig'tam space suits in future. Springing to his feet, he doused Mr. Hugh-Bat with more laser fire. Instead of doing the decent thing and dying, the thing sort of flipped up and had the temerity to charge. It took two H-TAP grenades for its trouble.

After a hit from just *one* H-TAP, by rights, there ought to have been only minutely shredded bits of bat flying about the place. After *two* H-TAP's Mr. Huge-Bat had been knocked over - which was good, but not entirely satisfactory because it was still inconsiderately not playing the game by refusing to cease-to-be!

Now here was an interesting thing: each time a grenade detonated, or he opened up with the laser, his vision blurred momentarily. Preoccupied with taking out the thing, he'd assumed that the blurring had something to do with explosive shockwaves or the ignition of the atmosphere. Now he wasn't so sure; he had a funny feeling that his vision was fine and that it was the world around him that was blurring.

He felt the rifle evaporate in his hand. At this point he knew he should have been frightened, very frightened, but he wasn't: Ig'tams had no equivalent emotion to fear. *Oh! Didn't they?!* This was something to consider at another time...

Mr. Huge-Bat made as if to fly but didn't make it off the ground. Clearly grenades and laser had taken some toll. As he stood there, without even a toothpick for a weapon, trying to decide what to do about this thing that was twice his size, it sort of lazily flapped over and knocked him head over heels. Getting back to his feet he felt heat; he felt pain in his back, so maybe Ig'tam space suits weren't all they were cracked up to be. Still, something told him that, despite its size and apparent imperviousness to percussion, HE and H-TAP grenades and laser fire, Mr. Huge-Bat wasn't anywhere near as heavy or as strong as a Redit.

It was charging at him again, this time he let it come. At the last moment he lunged, putting all his weight and momentum behind his shoulder. He slammed into it like he was breaking down a door. Irresistible force meets immovable object? They ended up in a heap. He'd actually felt his collarbone go 'snap' long before he felt the pain. Untangling himself and getting to his feet, he realised that he was the least concussed of the two, so he started stamping on the thing. Beneath his feet he could feel, with each stomp, what he hoped were bones fracturing and gristle smashing. The pain in his neck, shoulder and back he converted to fury and bounced up and down on the thing like a pneumatic hammer. The world around him became increasingly ephemeral, like a hologram slowly forming, but in reverse.

He started to laugh hysterically; here he was, a pretty intelligent human being, kicking the shit out of a hyper-intelligent sentient creature. Where's a wooden club or a stone axe? Because if he had one, he'd certainly be using it - this made him laugh even more...

Some time later, he wasn't sure just how much later, he figured that he must have been on the edge of madness. He must have been because he was dripping with sweat; on the point of exhaustion; in excruciating agony; laughing his head off; trampling on a creature that was positively, absolutely, 100 percent dead. Supporting his damaged shoulder, he stepped off the creature, tottered for a while, steadied himself, and for the first time looked closely at the only thing that was still sharply defined - the enemy.

Although it was a bit of a mess, it definitely wasn't bat-like; rectangular in shape, its green colouring came from what he could now clearly see were iridescent palm-sized scales. There were no obvious signs of sensory organs; no depression or protrusions, only an uninterrupted scaly surface - not even laser burns. Just a green 12' x 6' rectangle that was thicker in the centre than at the edges, like... like a very large dark green pillow. So, what was its method of locomotion? There weren't any signs to help him make an educated guess.

It was pretty unsatisfactory thinking of the thing as a pillow. If he was forced to name an animal that it bore even a passing resemblance to, he'd say a manta ray. Yes, he could get some mileage out of that. And he had a sense that this was a creature that was equally happy in the air, on land, or in water - a serious top predator. It was also a male of the species. He wasn't sure how he knew that, but it was...

Pilot

He'd always figured that when you fainted you passed out. So, he hadn't fainted, exactly; he just became light headed and fell over. Getting up was a bit of a trial but he managed it just in time to witness Mrs. Manta-Ray nee Huge-Bat gently fluttering down into the clearing. Although she hovered only a couple of feet from him and could see - or however they perceived the world around them - that he'd killed her partner he knew that she wouldn't attack, this was a male/male female/female conflict. He didn't know how he knew any of this, but he did. She sank to the ground, small ripples running up and down her body creating a scintillating luminous display of greens. This he supposed was a sign of distress but didn't dwell too much on it because if she was here, where was Hontay? He knew where she was. She was only about half a mile away, and he also knew he needed to be there, soonest. In a PADE suit it would have taken a couple of seconds. On foot, through the jungle, with a broken shoulder? Staggering out of the clearing he didn't bother to look back.

Now, you'd imagine that moving through the Enchanted Ephemeral Forest would be easy, wouldn't you? After all, every leaf, branch, and sapling seemed fuzzy, indistinct, and insubstantial. Without his PADE suit, movement was slow, strenuous and painful, because every leaf, branch and sapling was very real and very solid. *Except* occasionally he came across smallish geometrically precise clearings; no doubt the result of Mrs. Manta-Ray and Hontay's scrap. Although he didn't stop to examine any of the areas in detail, it was pretty obvious that they hadn't been created by detonations, beams or anything of the sort - considerably neater than an HE grenade. Well, what do you expect from super-smart sapients? These clearings looked like someone had more than vanished a chunk of the forest, it was as if they had removed an actual piece of reality.

Absolute nothingness just hanging in space! He always considered the total absence of anything to be black - no light, no anything - this seemed a logical conclusion. Counter-intuitively, nothingness appeared to be white. Not white as in 'reflective', but a white he'd never seen before; impenetrably opaque. As he hastened to Hontay, his non-sapient mind couldn't help trying to figure this out: spacetime defined everythingness. Therefore, logically, there ought to be nothing outside everything. Light was a product of the spacetime continuum; if it existed, then in outside spacetime there could be no light - beyond spacetime should be dark. So, how can there be something external to the universe and why should it be whitish?! Fuck! He was in agony and this was doing his brain in!

Trying to ignore the pain he moved as fast as he could, he had to get to Hontay. While making his way, he realised that the Ig'tam space suit was self-repairing, it was also trying to repair him. It would take a couple of hours to self-repair but, unfortunately, it would take several days to fix him. Eventually he found Hontay. She lay, like a broken doll, high up in the canopy. Even from the ground he could see, through the eerie semi-transparent foliage, that a pseudolimb had been torn off; grasshopper coloured blood was slowly trickling down her side and dripping to the ground. He feared he'd taken too long to reach her; she was obviously unconscious. How the hell do you climb a 30-foot tree with a broken shoulder?

It was probably the most excruciating twenty minutes of his life, but he did it. As he got close to her, he felt fondness washing over him...

"Good job, my non-sapient husband. You got them," she said weakly.

"I did?" He put his curiosity aside, there were more pressing matters. "I can see that you're hurt. What do you want me to do?"

"Nothing. We wait... Billy can you try to think of nothing, please."

What he was thinking about was trying not falling as he crawled the last couple of feet to her...

"Silly me. You are human, you can't control your thoughts, hey?"

She looked so uncomfortable all tangled-up in the branches. "I don't think I can move you."

"No need to, just stay here and maintain my physical self."

Maintain?

"Yes, maintain. Now, I have to leave." She closed her eyes.

***

"We have something on instruments!" Pipsqueak suddenly said in alarm. "Five o'clock; level; one hundred and ten thousand miles; closing fast!"

'Arm weapons; evade pursuit; do not enter the super-light.'

"Anne, arm weapons!"

'Weapons armed Grim.'

"*Dogfight formation; launch positions Darts;* Baddest, *stick to us like glue.*" Nice's hologram flashed on and then off.

"Roger Nice," Grim acknowledged. "Heads up everyone. I have two ships, size unknown, still five o'clock level, now at sixty thousand miles, closing at point six light speed."

"All instruments online, I have them," he confirmed.

"*Stand by to split S... Roll!... Targets illuminated. Locked on... Firing... Take your shot* Baddest."

"Locked on... Torpedos away," Wendy confirmed.

"*Breaking right, stay tight* Baddest."

"Confirm hits Anne."

'I cannot give tracking information Grim; my higher functions have been deactivated.'

"Shit! John, switch her back on!"

'Eva, Erick, Sun and John are out of comms, Grim.'

"Oh fuck! We have six torpedos, or something, incoming," Marandolina said with laboured calmness, "Do your pilot stuff... Still closing, you haven't shaken them."

'Do not enter the super-light.'

"Decoys gone," Wendy said, as she hit the controls.

"The six torpedos are now showing up as twelve. Haven't bitten on the decoys, still clo... Break! Break! Mohammed, break! You're turning into them!"

"Correct," was his unconcerned response. "Can't shake them, so we'll take them out... Firing nukes, wide-spread. Sit tight, short range detonation."

There was a moment of silence then *Baddest* began to be tossed about like a feather caught in a tornado.

"Looks like we took a couple of hits. Those torpedos stripped our tri-lattice shields, and if I'm reading my screens correctly, they did it by separating ship from fields," Pipsqueak said breathlessly.

"Come again?" David asked.

"I mean; the instruments say that the shields are still there, but they're in a different spacetime continuum to the ship, or something like that. In short, we're as naked as the day we were born People."

With Wendy, he was too busy trying to bring the ship under control to begin to worry about this.

"*Launch Darts,* Baddest."

"We have a stable platform!" Wendy advised, as *Baddest* finally stopped spiralling.

"Darts, launch!" Grim ordered.

Pilot

"*Darts gone,*" Kaye confirmed.

"Nice, can you confirm our hits?"

"*Hits confirmed but bandits still closing. Let's go head to head, get up close and personal. Darts, cover our backs.*"

"*Roger, Nice.*" Kaye sounded as if she was actually enjoying herself.

"Our shields are down Nice," Grim advised.

"*Same here Compassman Chang, but we can't run, and we can't hide so let's get down and get really dirty.*"

"Too right!" Grim agreed. "Let's give them one in the eye for the human race and see how many of them we can take with us."

Totally focussed on bringing *Baddest* around to being parallel with *The Beast,* he was surprised to hear Cynthia's incredulous exclamation, "Kazuhiko! Is that the Lord's prayer you're reciting?" Smiling to himself, he figured that this was as good a time as any to 'get religion'.

"*Firing.*"

"Firing... Can see the detonation hits but haven't eyeballed any ships. How about you Nice?" Wendy asked.

"*Same here, no eyeball... wait... registering some kind of plasma cloud.*"

"Yeah, I have it on screen," Gabi started, "How the hell do we kill that?!"

'The aggressors have come down to fight. They have taken the form of energetic molecules.'

"Make sense Ermoor," Grim snapped.

'The aggressors have left the infinite sapient states. They are now solely in normal spacetime. They cannot be destroyed but they may do immense damage to the spacetime fabric in this region. You must force them back to the sapient states.'

"That didn't make any sense to me," Marandolina protested.

"Fight fire with fire?" he suggested.

"Go for it," Grim ordered.

"Switching to plasma cannons... Firing."

"Collision, nine seconds," Pipsqueak warned.

'We are trapped. We are about to be desiccated.'

"Keep firing..." Grim started, then the cockpit was suddenly plunged into total darkness. "...What's happening?!"

"All systems, repeat, all systems down," Ruth needlessly warned.

"Everybody stay in your wombs, otherwise you'll start floating all over the place," Grim shouted into the pitch blackness. "OK, let's go for a restart."

"I'm doing that by feel, but everything is dead," Wendy answered.

"We're sitting ducks," Gabi complained. "Hit the backups."

"Been there. All dead," he replied, then added, "We need C1 with her higher functions for that."

"Anything to say on the subject Ermoor?" Marandolina asked sarcastically.

"Quiet!" Grim voice echoed in the inky gloom. The crew fell silent. "Can you feel that? Vibrations, like mini detonations."

"Yes, but it doesn't feel like hits," Pipsqueak ventured.

"It doesn't *feel* like anything. This is spooky," Ruth whispered

"We're deaf, blind and dumb. Do we abandon ship?" Gabi whispered back.

"We can't bang out, we need emergency power for that," Grim pointed out.

"Emergency life support?" Wendy asked.

"Same again. I reckon we have about eight hours air supply."

"Kazuhiko, will you stop that mumbo jumbo hallelujah shit!" hissed across the darkness of the cockpit. He guessed that that was Guido's hushed admonition.

'We are no more. Our mission is accomplished.'

"What...?" Grim started to ask but all systems suddenly came back online.

"My God! Will you look at that!" Wendy hollered, leaping up from her womb.

"*Holy shit!* Baddest, *do you see what we're seeing?!*" Nice screamed across the airwaves.

All the non-flight crew rushed up to the flight deck to stare out of the cockpit.

***

One second he's up the strange looking tree cuddling Hontay; keeping her upright, attempting to staunch the blood flow and, at the same time, desperately trying not to fall. The next, he's back on the floor of the Ig'tam cockpit still cuddling her. The blob and the other Ig'tams were nowhere to be seen. Then he gleaned that, in one sense, he and Hontay had never left the cockpit. Really? If that was so, why was his shoulder pulsating agonisingly. Obviously, Mr. & Mrs. Manta-Ray were just figments of his imagi...

Opening her eyes, Hontay looked up at him. "We have no equivalent to the Medal of Valour or the Military Cross."

She was alive, recovering, and the bleeding had somehow stopped on its own, so he wasn't going to give her the satisfaction of asking what the hell she was talking about. He just raised an eyebrow.

"Mind you, those titles would be somewhat of an understatement, don't you think? 'Saviour of the Galaxy and all its Sapient Races' might be more appropriate."

He sensed that lying in his arms was becoming increasingly uncomfortable for her, but she intended to remain where she was until she'd finished teasing him.

"There'll also have to be an enormous parade in your honour, of course."

She wasn't just uncomfortable, lying like that wasn't helping her recovery. He thought he'd give in. "I take it that we've won."

"No, not won, but the danger is passing/has passed." She remained where she was.

"Hontay, wouldn't you like to stand?"

"Stand? Leave the protective arms of my husband?"

"Com'on, get up and stop taking the piss." He released her from his to grasp. "Want to share with me what happened?"

Ungainly getting to her feet, because Ig'tams are unaccustomed to having to stand up, she pulled him up after her. "What happened? You saved us. Oh, my Hero!" She threw her arms around him.

She certainly didn't have the vocal equipment to play a dizzy blonde, but he got the gist. "Really. How?"

"Billy, you will never truly understand 'how', in the precise sense of the word. And I don't suppose an explanation of 'you just did' would be acceptable, would it?"

Looking up and down her naked body, he answered, "You're damn right."

The largish stool reappeared next to him and he climbed on. "In all the galaxy, you were the only non-sapient married/bonded/linked to a sapient."

"Yes, and?"

"And I conceptualised that the aggressors would come down to fight."

"You can tell when I'm getting frustrated, can't you?"

"OK, impatient human. We now know what the aggressors are; a super-predator species, with limited sapient potential, that have been assimilated by a fifth-stage sapient species..."

"Run that past me again."

Pilot

"It's not a symbiotic relationship. It's more akin to bacteria and viruses that can only survive in the human body and the human body wouldn't function properly without them - they are a single organism. Now, because you and I are the alliance's nearest and only approximation to that arrangement. When we, you and I, engaged them, they were locked into what you'd call normal spacetime."

"Whoosh."

"Over your head? Any sapient that came into contact with them was frozen out of the picture. That was what happened earlier..."

"The exaction?"

"Yes. When I extracted you to where I was, although in reality I was literally 'nowhere', because you didn't belong and could not survived there, they created a portion of normal spacetime, placed us in it and followed us down."

"That was a serious whoosh, but carry on."

"They had to engage us in your non-sapient normal spacetime instead of the infinite sapient streams."

"And when we got them on a level playing field, normal spacetime, we kicked arse?"

"Not really. Mr. Manta-Ray isn't dead. They don't 'die' in your sense of the word, but in order to 'renovate' him Mrs. Manta-Ray had to return them both to the sapient states, thus leaving us behind."

"How... how did that fix anything."

"We'd conceptualised that if we forced them to come down, in any sapient/non-sapient pairing it is the sapient component that is most vulnerable..."

"Why?"

"Firstly, instinct. Our instincts aren't optimised for engaging sapients non-sapiently. Nor are theirs. So, providing that the non-sapient component is heavily protected; Ig'tam spacesuit. Aggressive enough; Ig'tam predatory diathesis. And destructive enough; PADE suited human with a penchant for wanton destruction..."

"Steady! Are you saying this happened because we... I was fighting in my own back yard, so to speak?"

"Yes. You were able to chase them out by creating a situation that left them no option but to return to the sapient states. And for sapient beings having either a limited or no choice at all is almost akin to a mortal injury. The higher the stage of sapiency, the more severe the damage. Secondly, as I've said, sapients have to give special care to their physical selves. It is probably several millennia since these fifth stage sapients have had to produce physical manifestations of themselves so, when they did, they were less 'ministering'."

He pondered this. "You're telling me this even though you know I won't understand because if you don't my brain will go doolally trying to puzzle it out, right?"

"Right."

He pondered some more. "This super-predator, I figured it was a bit of a badarse in the air, sea or on land."

"Not only that, but they can also generate tremendous heat."

"Hot enough to vaporise a PADE suit?"

"Certainly."

"Oh, I thought that was caused by some sapient moves... When I was looking for you, I came across some weird clearings, was that the same thing?"

"No. Billy, I cannot explain the clearings in any terms that you would understand."

"But it was a kind of 'total void', right?"

"Kind of."

Despite ego, he accepted this. "So, what you're saying is that these creatures can naturally generate thousands of degrees of heat, is that right?"

"Yes, tens of thousands."

"Hmm, barbecue merchants. Is that why they first appeared as Blue Giant stars?"

"They're fifth-stage sapients Billy. The Blue Giants weren't them. If they were, we wouldn't have been able to retrieve you or your crew. Think of those suns as their window into normal spacetime."

Wow! "So, how *exactly* did we... beat them?"

"They have not been defeated. Thanks to you, we were able to link with other non-sapients. We forced the aggressors to come down, then compelled them to go back. This, we believe, has persuaded them to leave the galaxy."

"You haven't called a truce or anything like that?"

"They are fifth-stage sapients, we cannot communicate with them."

More pondering. "But they are leaving the galaxy?"

"We believe so... Aren't you interested in who the other non-sapients were?"

It hadn't occurred to him to ask. "Who were they?"

"The crews of *Baddest* and *The Beast*."

"If I ask 'how', will your explanation make any more sense?"

"Probably not," she teased.

"In that case, all I'll ask is, is everybody OK?"

"Riet suffered some permanent brain damage. Although she will recover and live a normal fulfilling life, medically, she'll lose her aircrew status."

"Where are they? And has *Baddest* sustained any damage?"

"Both ships are undamaged and in orbit around Earth. Earth is back in orbit around the Sun."

"Really?!"

"Yes. We lost thirty sapients who were linked with the two crews."

He could tell that his killing-machine of a wife felt no sense of loss, but he felt it necessary to make some comment. "I suppose, in the great scheme of things, thirty casualties aren't a bad result."

"Along with the thirty Ermoors, seventy-four billion individual sapients and some two-hundred and twelve entire races were lost."

He couldn't really believe what he'd just heard; the numbers were staggering. He was now utterly shocked by her lack of emotion. "When you say lost, you don't mean... dead, do you?"

"No, they are not physically dead but they are no longer sapient, so they might as well be." She turned to face him, a gesture he recognised as unnecessary. "Billy, you are aware that one of my pseudolimbs is damaged."

He was, so? Why the abrupt change of tack? "Yeah."

"You are concerned for my well-being."

"Yeah."

"Somewhere in your unconscious mind you know it will regrow and that I'll make a full recovery."

He got the feeling that she was still toying with him. "If you say so."

"You humans, the saviours of the galaxy, are an interesting species."

He'd play along with her. "How so?"

"For a start, your genders have conflicting reproductive strategies."

"We do?"

"Yes. The males' sperm production means that they are biologically geared to impregnating a female every two to three days. On the other hand, your females are biologically geared to being impregnated once every twenty-eight days. This difference means that your males devote a lot of thought, time, and effort to bridging the gap - ambushing your females. And your females devote an equal amount of thought, time and effort attempting to counter this."

"Are you saying that men want to have sex every two days and women only once a month?"

"Yes."

"I'm finding this harder to accept than that business about the aggressors and normal spacetime."

"You know it's true."

"No, I don't. And I don't know any woman who would agree that they would be satisfied with sex only once a month."

"That is because men have been partially successful at closing the gap and women have been coerced into modifying their reproductive strategy."

"Hontay, you know I bow to your greater knowledge on most things. However, on this one I have to say I disagree. We're talking human beings here. And who's the human being? Me! Now, there is a theory that says; because men can impregnate lots of women and then contribute nothing to the rearing of their offspring *whilst* women make a large investment in their offspring, women have devised a strategy to ensure that their mate stays with them. That's why the human male is probably the only male mammal that cannot tell when his mate is in season. So he has to remain with her and have sex regularly if he wants to impregnate her."

He felt her do something akin to laughing in his face. "Wrong. Firstly, there are significant changes in women when they are in season. Men are aware of these changes but not consciously so. And, secondly, a woman's biological focus is her offspring, having the male around is a distraction. She is, however, prepared to compromise if the male aids her in her investment."

This was ludicrous. "Why are you telling me this?"

"It's entirely different for us Ig'tams. As you would say, 'it ain't even the same sport'. You know the sexual process cannot, repeat, *cannot* be initiated by a Gemarch. But you aren't a Gemarch, you're a man and, quite naturally, think about sex a lot."

"So?"

"If you think about sex, I'm not only compelled to think about sex, I also have to give consideration to my physical self."

"Yeah, and?"

"I'm secondarily fertilised and, biologically, am not capable of having sex for at least two standard years after our child is born."

With that he got that the foetus, his child to be, was doing fine, but he still felt he was missing something. "OK."

"Billy, if you think about sex, I think about sex. This sets up within me conflicts between intellect and biology and, as I've said, we sapients need to give extra attention to our physical selves."

"You want me to stop thinking about sex?"

"You're a man. You can't. You even dream about it." He felt her laughing. "I have an alternative. It's not ideal but, as I hope you now understand, my intellect isn't focussed on ideal solutions."

"OK, what is it?"

"I can't tell you."

She was definitely toying with him. "Why not?"

"That would cause you to actively start thinking about sex and if you start thinking about sex, etc., etc."

"Wait a minute, I thought that if you knew something then I'd know it too?"

"You do, but do you understand it?"

This was getting a bit much. "Whatever you say. Anyway, what's brought all this on?"

"When you were thinking about the injury to my pseudolimb you *were* concerned for my health, but you were also unconsciously considering whether or not we could still have sex if only one pseudolimb was functioning." She took both his hands in hers.

He just smiled, then felt her suddenly becoming *deadly* earnest. Fearful for his life, he sat there petrified.

"Billy, humans say 'I love you' a great deal to their mates." She paused, as if to emphasise her dreadful intent. "You know there is no need for protestations of love with a telepathic race. Because you aren't fully telepathic it is impossible for you to feel *all* my love for you." Again, she paused. "What I am about to do is exceedingly difficult for a Redit to do, it sets up another conflict between intellect and biology. I do it because I *do* love you."

Perceiving the full efficaciousness of a Redit's death-dealing bloodlust boiling over, he thought he was going to lose control of his bowels. Now that Hontay was pregnant and secondarily fertilised with a semi-alien inside her, she had to pay even more attention to her physical self. In that state, her human husband was simply a hazard to her and the foetus - no more than a virus demanding exigent eradication. He was all prepared to face down Provost Lieutenant Colonel Jansen and die with aplomb, but he wasn't prepared for this. To kill without hesitation and having killed feel no remorse is an Ig'tam atavism. He found that he was shaking uncontrollably, and tears were trickling down his cheeks. Though it took more courage than he realised he possessed, he forced himself to ask, "Do what...?"

Leaping from the bed, she pinned herself against the wall and gaped at him.

Blinking the tears away, he shook his head in disbelief. Standing there for a moment, he let it all wash over him. Then he gave her a wry smile. "Sorry about this, but this time I think I'm going to be here for a while."

Hungrily she grinned and started moving purposefully towards him.

God! This woman must have unbelievable recuperative powers.

"Easy. I've got a busted shoulder, Coraliè."

THE END

INTERDICTOR

ISBN 978 0 9506087 8 1

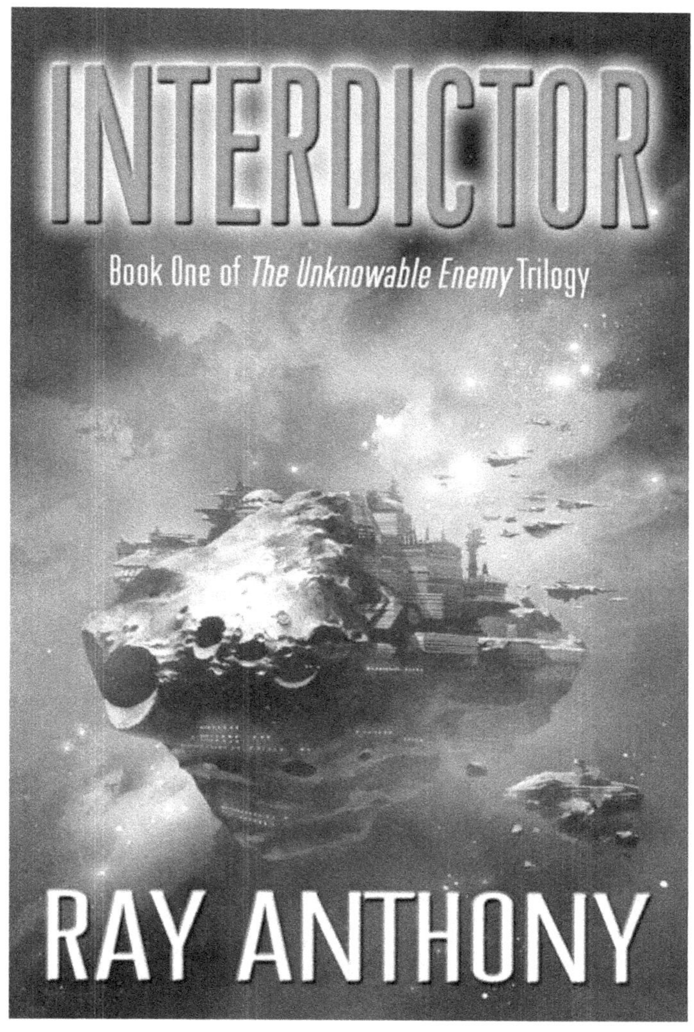

For decades, Earth's Attack Cruisers have taken a pounding from an undefeatable enemy. An enemy so alien and so incomprehensible Earth's armies are close to utter devastation; clueless as to how to challenge the impending annihilation of the human race.

For the first time in the twenty-seven year war the enemy has placed a base of operation on a planet and Admiral Ezocaagbo Akobundu-Tan is willing to risk the destruction of her fleet in order to get one man on to that planet, Lume, a highly trained special forces operative. He is also a Stinger, a human adapted for a single purpose - to kill…

ARMOUR

ISBN 978 0 9526287 9 8

In a war to end all wars the ultimate armour is not what you think...

The war against their unknowable enemy – 'The Bulges' - rages on, for many of the soldiers battle is the only life they have known or will ever know. As a new wave of attacks devastates their fleets and destroy planets in humanity's battle for survival the best of the very best soldiers are enlisted into a secret carder.

The Guardsman is an exceptional soldier not just for his skill but something more…

CAPTAIN

ISBN 978 1 8382975 3 4

In the endless war against the Bulges, Captain Magambál Talberg has steadfastly focussed her career on a single goal; to captain one of the fleet's 'big sticks'. At last, and now vastly experienced, she is given command of the brand-new, fresh from the shipyards, heavy cruiser *Kumasi*. In time *Kumasi* would be at the sharp end providing close support for planetary assaults. But for now, its first mission was is to transit to Earth and show-off, to the civilian population, the fruits of their tax-credits. During the three-week, undemanding voyage, Magambál also has to shakedown the ship, getting systems and crew combat ready.

That was the plan...

EMPRESS

ISBN 978 0 9506087 4 3

She was the only one who could reunite the Empire and restore to its citizens the security that this brought. Without any doubt she was, singularly, the most important being alive. She and her cousin were the last of an Imperial bloodline. But her cousin could not easily supplant her. For Hial to sit on the Imperial throne she would need to be victorious in a bitter and bloody war. Such a war was to be avoided if at all possible. Therefore the primary task for Empress Morturina I, and those who served her, was to ensure her survival - at least until she had borne an heir to the Imperial throne.

A bitter and bloody war was inevitable...

All Woman

ISBN 978 0 9506087 2 9

There you are getting on with your life. When up pops THE blast from the past... The dim distant past - not seen, not heard of in eight years - but there he is. He's telling you the story: 'Sorry I dumped you but having trashed all my subsequent relationships, I've finally come to realise that you are the one for me, we should be together.' It just so happens that he was the love of your life and it also happens that things are more than complicated...

What would you do?

INTERFACE

ISBN 978 0 9506087 7 4

It's the 80's. Clare is white, Patrick is black. They are from entirely different worlds, *but* when they met, they fell madly in love - perhaps opposites do attract. Now they plan to get married.

A straightforward proposition, right?

Well, maybe not. Set against them and their wishes are a host of 'interested parties': Clare's sister, Emma. Patrick's best friends, Harry and Nathan, and his ex-girlfriend, Otis. And of course, their parents want to have a say as well.

All the ingredients for a delightfully outrageous exploration of the *Interface* between: black men and white women; black men and black women; the maturity (or immaturity of men); strong personalities domination of weaker personalities.

Will love conquer all?

"There are many books written for women about the pregnancy and childbirth phenomenon. There doesn't seem to be much in this plethora of literature for men. It's about time there was!"- Ray A.

Thinking Man's Guide to Pregnancy, Childbirth & Fatherhood (ISBN 978 0 9526287 3 6) provides a male's tongue-in-cheek perspective of said phenomenon - a humorous slant on all things an expectant father needs to know but is too afraid to ask.

Disclaimer
Ray Anthony makes no claims to having any special qualifications for writing such a book, apart from having been there, seen it, and done it!